TWO MORE DAYS AT NETHERFIELD

HEATHER MOLL

Quills & Quartos
PUBLISHING

Copyright © 2020 by Heather Moll

All rights reserved.

This is a work of fiction. Names, characters, businesses, places, events, locales, and incidents are either the products of the author's imagination or used in a fictitious manner. Any resemblance to actual persons, living or dead, or actual events, is purely coincidental.

No part of this book may be reproduced in any form or by any electronic or mechanical means, including information storage and retrieval systems, without written permission from the author, except for the use of brief quotations in a book review.

Edited by Sarah Pesce and Regina Silvia
Proofread by Linda D'Orazio

Cover Design by CloudCat Designs
Lady in a Garden by Edmund Blair Leighton

ISBN: 978-1-951033-27-9 (ebook) and 978-1-951033-28-6 (paperback)

For Peter, who has still never read Pride and Prejudice, but supports me all the same

Chapter 1

Friday, November 15

Elizabeth was gazing over Netherfield's lawn, watching a flock of birds peck at the ground while she waited for Mrs Hurst to join her on a walk. She stood alone by the hedge when she heard voices coming from the adjacent walk on the other side of the shrubs.

"Have you anything else to propose for my domestic felicity?"

There was no mistaking Mr Darcy's voice, and Elizabeth was surprised to discern dry amusement in his tone. Elizabeth had presumed the man's sense of pride and self-importance forbade him from having a sense of humour. She pitied the woman unfortunate enough to become Mrs Darcy.

"Oh yes." Miss Bingley was laughing. "Do let the portraits of your uncle and aunt Philips be placed in the gallery at Pemberley."

Your uncle and aunt Philips? What reason does she have for teasing Mr Darcy about marrying one of my sisters?

As Elizabeth considered this, Miss Bingley continued. "As for your Elizabeth's picture, you must not attempt to have it taken, for what painter could do justice to those beautiful eyes?"

"It would not be easy, indeed, to catch their expression, but their colour and shape, and the eyelashes, so remarkably fine, might be copied." Mr Darcy answered with what in any other man would sound akin to sincerity.

Elizabeth felt a sudden constriction in her chest. *Your Elizabeth? Mr Darcy admires my eyes? Your Elizabeth?*

At that moment Mrs Hurst finally joined her, and they were met from the other walk by Miss Bingley and Mr Darcy. Miss Bingley blushed and avoided looking at Elizabeth, likely knowing they had been overheard. Mr Darcy stood as far apart from Miss Bingley as was possible while still supporting her arm, his features as composed as they were ever known to be.

"I did not know that you intended to walk," said Miss Bingley, in some confusion.

"You used us abominably ill," answered Mrs Hurst, "running away without telling us that you were coming out." Then taking the disengaged arm of Mr Darcy, she left Elizabeth to walk by herself. The path just admitted three.

Mr Darcy, while holding Elizabeth's gaze, said, "This walk is not wide enough for our party. We had better go into the avenue."

"No, no, stay where you are. I should check on Jane."

Elizabeth's feelings as she walked back to the house were scarcely to be defined. *Mr Darcy thinks I have beautiful eyes? It cannot be true!* She suppressed the flattered feeling in her heart.

She went to her sister's room where Jane rested in bed. Elizabeth's impatience to acquaint Jane with her unintended eavesdropping could not be overcome, and she related it all with increasing furore.

"She was taunting him about a statement Mr Darcy expressed about me. Did he tell Miss Bingley that to incite her into disapproving of me? Or did he say it to mock me?"

"Our acquaintance with Mr Darcy has not been long, but we have no reason to believe him to be deceitful or spiteful. He must have spoken so about you because he thinks it is true." Jane swallowed roughly and brought a hand to her throat.

"Are we to believe that I have gone from being not handsome enough to dance with to having eyes so beautiful that he feels compelled to share his high estimation of me with Miss Bingley? I could hardly credit such a notion. And was Miss Bingley attempting to provoke Mr Darcy into further disliking me by talking of our supposed marriage?"

"Mr Darcy must admire you and said so to her. She was merely speaking of her hopes for his happiness should his admiration develop into a stronger emotion."

"You never see a fault in anybody. All the world is good and agreeable in your eyes."

"I would not wish to be hasty in censuring anyone."

"He is a teasing, teasing man!" Elizabeth was tempted to criticise her for taking the good of everybody's character and saying nothing of the bad, but she thought better of it. There was no reason to distress Jane when she was ill.

Jane tugged on her pillows, turned on her side, and settled into bed. "It must gratify your own self-respect, to be admired by such a man."

Elizabeth was struck. Had she been too hasty in censuring Mr Darcy? He was agreeable enough among his intimate acquaintance, and although Mr Darcy had proud manners, she had not seen anything that betrayed him to be dishonest. It was unlikely he would praise her for the purpose of allowing Miss Bingley to laugh at her and taunt *him*.

He was too proud to do it, she knew, but if Mr Darcy *were* the sort of man to apologise for his rude comment at the assembly, Elizabeth would forgive him. *But had I not overheard Mr Darcy's compliment, I would never consider revising my impressions of him.*

As Elizabeth dressed for dinner, she resolved to act no differently towards Mr Darcy in spite of what she overheard. She had little expectation of pleasure during any evening at Netherfield, but she now was disquieted by the idea of encountering Mr Darcy. Facing such an unpleasant man after hearing such a compliment was sure to be an awkward business.

Elizabeth found herself approached by Mr Darcy. He gave a tight-lipped smile. "May I escort you to dinner?"

She took his arm and, as they entered the hall, she sensed Mr Darcy's attention. Their eyes met. Elizabeth felt something pass between them and, for a moment, she thought he might be holding some fervent emotion in check. Then he turned away, his expression once again inscrutable, and she found herself looking only at the clear-cut lines of his profile.

Elizabeth remained unsettled as he seated her with his usual grave propriety. He was a proper dinner partner, offering her the dish nearest to him when her plate was empty. Mr Darcy did not speak often, although he spoke intelligently when he did. He presented himself as an honest man who was agreeable among his friends. Elizabeth acknowledged that if Mr Darcy said she had pretty eyes, then that was the truth as he saw it.

Elizabeth admonished herself. How vain and conceited had she become? Was she so flattered by his admiration that she was willing to reconsider his character?

When the ladies removed after dinner, Elizabeth attended Jane into the drawing room where she was welcomed by her two friends. Miss Bingley's powers of conversation, so restrained in the dining room, were greater in the absence of the gentlemen.

When the gentlemen entered a short time later, Mr Darcy addressed himself to Jane with a polite congratulation.

"Miss Bennet, allow me to express my compliments on seeing you well enough to join us. You have my best wishes for continued good health."

Mr Hurst had been walking towards the sweetmeats, but after watching Mr Darcy, he made Jane a slight bow, and added that he too was "very glad."

Mr Darcy could not be so uncharitable if he offered Jane his congratulations, but Elizabeth was still unwilling to think too well of him. She did, however, think highly of Mr Bingley, for he was full of joy and attention to Jane. The first half hour he spent attending to her comfort, and he then sat by her and talked scarcely to anyone else. Elizabeth, seated in the opposite corner, saw it all with quiet delight.

Elizabeth sometimes looked up from her book to see how her sister was faring, but she was disengaged from the group. She was happy to allow Jane the opportunity to speak a little apart with Mr Bingley. She was, therefore, taken unawares when she was addressed some time later by Miss Bingley.

"Miss Eliza Bennet, let me persuade you to follow my example and take a turn about the room. I assure you it is very refreshing after sitting so long in one attitude."

She wanted to roll her eyes, but thanked her instead. When Elizabeth joined her, she noticed the real reason for Miss Bingley's civility: Mr Darcy looked up from his book and closed it.

"Would you care to join us?" Miss Bingley asked him.

"No, I can imagine but two motives for your choosing to walk up and down the room together. And with either of which motives, my joining you would certainly interfere."

Elizabeth noticed a gleam in his eye and suspected he was waiting for an invitation to elucidate. *He shall receive no such encouragement from me!*

"I am dying to know your meaning! Miss Eliza Bennet, can you understand him?"

Elizabeth suggested the surest way to disappoint him would be to ask nothing about it, but Miss Bingley was incapable of disappointing Mr Darcy in anything.

"Mr Darcy, I must know what is on your mind! I shall not rest until you have explained your reasons to my satisfaction."

"I have not the smallest objection to explaining them. You either choose this method of passing the evening because you are in each other's confidence and have secret affairs to discuss, or because you are conscious of the fact that your figures appear to the greatest advantage in walking. If the first, I should be completely in your way, and if the second, I can admire you much better as I sit by the fire," he concluded with a self-satisfied smile.

Elizabeth did not hear Miss Bingley's reply. She hoped the semi-darkness hid the flush she felt across her cheeks. *First my eyes, and now my figure!* Her heart pounded and she felt warm. It would not do to allow Mr Darcy to discompose her. Did he have any design of alarming or embarrassing her? *No, it was unconsciously done. He seems smug as he ever was.*

Miss Bingley said something about punishing Mr Darcy for his speech. For once, Elizabeth and Miss Bingley were in accord. *I will not allow that arrogant man to drive me to distraction!* Elizabeth felt her courage rising and decided her opportunity had come to set down the proud Mr Darcy.

"The surest way to punish Mr Darcy for his speech is to insist he join us. We shall force him to listen to us debate the merits of spotted or tamboured muslin. I am certain that while our figures are tolerable"—she paused and met his eye—"they are not handsome enough to tempt him to remain where he is."

Mr Darcy was not a man whose features displayed a wide variety of emotions, but Elizabeth saw he was affected when she used his words against him. His eyes went wide in comprehension. Mr Darcy set his jaw, turned his gaze to the floor, then sat back in his chair.

Elizabeth turned away to hide a triumphant smile. She had let Mr Darcy know his cruel remarks were known to her, and she had the gratification of knowing he was embarrassed by them. A trivial success, but a victory nonetheless.

"Do let us have a little music," cried Miss Bingley, tired of having failed in securing Mr Darcy's attention. "Louisa, you will not mind my waking Mr Hurst." Her sister made not the smallest objection, and the pianoforte was opened. Elizabeth returned to her chair and fought to keep from laughing.

Mr Bingley and Jane were oblivious to these goings-on, and Elizabeth had no wish to interrupt their tête-à-tête. She resumed her needlework, but soon became conscious to the fact that, although he gave every appearance of attending to his book, Mr Darcy continued to glimpse at her.

She hardly knew why she would be an object of interest after her taunting remarks. Elizabeth could not explain his behaviour, and so she resolved to think on it no longer. She liked him too little to care for his approbation and would delight in her small private conquest over Mr Darcy's self-satisfaction.

He will think no further on the matter, so why should I?

Chapter 2

Saturday, November 16

Darcy's horse was full of spirit, but its master was out of sorts. He rode to distract himself from the reflections that had plagued him since last night.

...tolerable, but not handsome enough to tempt me...

It had taken Darcy a moment to make sense of Miss Elizabeth's words and piercing look, and they remained in his mind. It was a strange sensation to have his own words used against him. He was not accustomed to being confronted, and to be done so by a flippant turn of a phrase, by such a woman, left him hesitant on how best to proceed.

Someone at that miserable assembly must have told her that I refused to seek an introduction to dance with her.

He ought to have suspected that eavesdropping and gossip would occur in such objectionable company. There was no reason for him to feel guilty for Miss Elizabeth's wounded spirits, no reason to show her any particular civility and apologise. After all, it had not been he who committed the rude act of listening to the conversations of others.

Then why did he suffer from this unfamiliar pang of guilt? Perhaps he *had* been inconsiderate. Yet why should he take upon himself the trouble to apologise when he had spoken the truth?

Because not long after that occasion, I realised she was superior to my initial judgment.

Miss Elizabeth deserved an apology, yet there was a danger in paying her much attention. An apology might be perceived to be a sign of admiration. He ought to do nothing that might raise her expectations. The proper course of action was to treat her with distant civility.

ELIZABETH WROTE TO HER MOTHER TO BEG THAT THE CARRIAGE BE sent for them today. Jane was still asleep, and she was therefore at her leisure until she received her mother's reply. She hurried down the stairs to take a solitary ramble around the park.

Her expectation for an invigorating and private walk was dashed, however, when she met Mr Darcy as she descended the stairs. He looked up at her approach, but instead of bowing in silence while she curtseyed and attempted to sidle past, he addressed her and asked how her sister fared.

"She is still asleep. I believe she exhausted herself last night."

Since the formal courtesies were complete and an awkward pause had ensued, she expected him to leave. He surprised her by asking, in an agitated tone, "Might I persuade you to take a turn in the garden with me?"

Elizabeth had no polite way to refuse. It was a cool November morning, and Elizabeth was prepared for similar coldness from her companion. Mr Darcy said little, and she did not give herself the trouble of talking to him.

They passed along the avenue when he finally spoke. "Miss Bennet, I must speak candidly."

She blinked at him in surprise and allowed him to lead her to a bench along the gravel path.

"Miss Bennet, last night you made it apparent that an opinion I expressed in confidence became known to you. I do not know who was eavesdropping on my private conversation with Bingley, but I nonetheless feel it is my duty to apologise for any remarks regarding yourself that you may have mistakenly interpreted to be discourteous."

Elizabeth's astonishment was beyond expression. *Was that speech intended to be an apology?* She tried to contain the grin that pulled on her lips, but it became a soft giggle. Mr Darcy fixed his eyes on her face in surprise. This further amused her, and her laugh grew hearty as she considered it likely Mr Darcy had never been laughed at in his entire life.

"Madam, is this the manner in which you typically reply to those who humble themselves before you?"

Her high spirits fell at this absurd speech. "Humble? I might as well enquire if that is the manner in which you typically beg for forgiveness. I heard your words myself, as I was seated right by you. 'She is tolerable; but not handsome enough to tempt *me;* and I am in no humour at present to give consequence to young ladies who are slighted by other men.'"

He looked stricken, but the emotion was short-lived and was replaced by the hauteur she had come to expect from him. "You were not meant to hear that comment."

"You looked me in the eye, and then you coldly withdrew your own before you spoke; you knew I could hear you. I will have you know that I have never been so offended or insulted in all of my life!"

Mr Darcy stood still, but the disturbance of his mind was visible in every feature.

Elizabeth continued. "I can assure you that I lose nothing by not suiting your fancy, for you have been disagreeable and conceited from the moment of your arrival in Hertfordshire!" She rose and marched towards the house. This roused him, and Mr Darcy called after her.

"Wait, please. I have nothing to say in my defence. I rarely…" Mr Darcy broke off. "It is not often that I find myself in the position of wishing to retract my words or defend my conduct. I was mistaken in discounting your beau—"

He sighed. "I made a hasty judgment of you, and I spoke wrongly. It was neither true nor well-mannered. My cruel remark cannot be defended, and all I can do is beg you to forgive me."

Elizabeth had believed Mr Darcy was in possession of overbearing pride and disdain for the feelings of those he perceived to be beneath him. But she was struck by his earnest expression, and there was no mistaking the remorse in his voice.

He has apologised. Do I still have reason to cling to my initial dislike? His posture was still reserved and commanding as it ever was, but in his expression, Elizabeth thought she discerned a sincere wish to be forgiven. Knowing Mr Darcy admired her eyes softened her opinion of him enough to consider his feelings. How ought she behave towards anyone who had, ultimately, admitted his fault and asked for her pardon?

"I do forgive you." Part of her longed to add that her mercy was easier to grant after hearing his high opinion on her eyes. "I am sorry for my outburst. I was offended by your words, but that does not grant me leave to speak to you that way."

He bowed. "All is forgiven."

They remained five feet apart, neither looking away. Elizabeth felt a curious pull from inside her stomach. Mr Darcy had a captivating presence, and seeing his earnest desire to be forgiven had softened her opinion of him. It was sad that one with so much in his favour was conceited—though perhaps not as selfish as she had thought.

WHEN THEY RETURNED TO THE HOUSE, MISS BINGLEY WAS PASSING through the hall. She turned on her heel and came towards him before he could take off his hat.

"I had almost despaired of seeing you this morning!"

"I had pressing business that could no longer be put off." Elizabeth doubted Mr Darcy's first business of the day had been to offer his apology, but his gaze returned to Elizabeth. It was only then that Miss Bingley acknowledged Elizabeth. "Your sister is awake and has had a note from your mother."

Elizabeth went to her sister's room where she learned that Mrs

Bennet, having calculated on her daughters remaining at Netherfield till the following Tuesday, which would exactly finish Jane's week, could not receive them with pleasure before then.

Elizabeth, in a fit of pique, tore the paper in half and tossed it into the fire. It spoke to Miss Bingley and Mrs Hurst's overt dislike for her to make even this small holiday from Longbourn a tedious burden. She often preferred whatever means that could temporarily give her a respite from the fracas of her family life at Longbourn. Other than Jane's company, it was often lonely for her amid that set of people who little understood her.

Jane was lying abed and looked at her sister from under heavily lidded eyes. "I am sufficiently recovered for the carriage ride home. Are you resolved against staying longer? I could ask to borrow Mr Bingley's carriage."

While Mrs Bennet's answer was not propitious, at least not to Elizabeth's wishes, she thought of Jane's wishes. Perhaps another day or two of rest would be to her sister's benefit. She might also prefer to spend more time with her friends, such as they were, as well as learn a bit more of Mr Bingley. Although Miss Bingley and Mrs Hurst would still be a trial, now that Mr Darcy had offered an acceptable apology, she could tolerate his company a little better.

"We might as well wait until our mother can send the carriage. It will grant you two full days to enjoy the attentions of Mr Bingley."

"Lizzy!" Jane's cheeks flushed, and Elizabeth was certain fever had nothing to do with it.

"It is evident he does admire you, and you ought to yield to the preference that you entertained for him from the first of your meeting him. You are in the way to being in love, and since our mother is not here, it shall be up to me to ensure that he falls ever so much in love with you!"

"You shall make me anxious!"

"Forgive me for being too lively when you are not well. I blame it all on Mr Darcy. I walked with him in the garden, and it took every bit of my restraint not to tease him as much as he deserved, so now I am expending that energy on you."

"You spoke with Mr Darcy? Do you still condemn him to be the worst of men?"

Elizabeth was a little ashamed that her dislike of Mr Darcy had been so strong. "He is not as ungentlemanly as I thought, but he is unfamiliar with having his sharp judgments disproven. I suppose we have that in common, as I assumed he would be above offering an apology. He apologised for his remarks, and we can meet agreeably from this point forward. However, I cannot think highly of a man who takes a disinterest in dancing."

"I never thought Mr Darcy so deficient in the appearance of goodness as you used to."

"I meant to be uncommonly clever in taking so decided a dislike to him. I am ashamed of it now. I am not as astute as I thought I was."

"You can meet as friends now that you have no further reason to dislike him."

"You have the most generous heart in all the world! Mr Darcy has no interest in maintaining a friendship with one so decidedly beneath him. The only thing he has to recommend him is his excellent taste in the style of ladies' eyes he admires. But you need not fear—I shall be all ease and courtesy with Mr Darcy, if only for the sake of you furthering your acquaintance with his friend."

Jane blushed again, and Elizabeth left to tell Miss Bingley of their intention to stay until the carriage could be sent for them on Tuesday. Thoughts of Miss Bingley brought to Elizabeth's mind the object of that lady's attentions. Mr Darcy would not have been concerned with being forgiven if he loathed her. His general character elicited respect, but she could not feel the slightest inclination to continue the acquaintance after Mr Darcy left the neighbourhood.

Chapter 3

Darcy was relieved to escape his hostess's interminable attentions and join Bingley and Hurst in the gunroom. The necessity of taking care of their shooting equipment could not be minimised, and neither could the necessity of remaining occupied in a way that was of no interest to the women. Bingley was seated at one of the tables, having already finished cleaning the weapon that lay before him, and Hurst was sprawled out on a sofa.

"No, we went shooting on Wednesday."

"All I know is we have been confined to the house for days." Hurst groaned. "I have hardly taken out a gun since we arrived."

"We had tolerable sport over the first three days we were in the country," Darcy said.

"But there has been hardly any attempting anything since then. If it does not rain, I say we go out at first light."

"No, tomorrow is Sunday," Darcy said.

"Blast it all! Not enough shooting and too many women in our party."

"I for one am thankful that the Miss Bennets decided to

remain," Bingley replied. "I could not in good conscience send the elder home before she is well."

Hurst made a grumbling sound and rolled over on the sofa.

"You do not believe Miss Bennet is suffering from a mere cold?" Darcy was surprised. "I am certain that a few good nights' rest would cure her."

"I understand from my sisters that she was feverish those first days. What if Miss Bennet was moved too soon and developed a putrid fever? Or whooping cough?"

Darcy looked unblinking for a long moment. Bingley's earnest countenance faltered. "Well, that is unlikely, but one ought not to trifle with one's health. Miss Elizabeth is generous to tend to her sister. She is a most willing and active nurse, do you not agree?"

"Who else but a beloved sister would be so willing to take the greatest share in the fatigue of nursing one who is ill?" Darcy conceded that the genuine affection she showed towards her sister was admirable. Miss Elizabeth had an excellent heart and a caring disposition; it was a shame she came from such a regrettable situation.

"You are right. Miss Bennet's spirits must be languid and low from the nature of her malady. Her speedy recovery must be in no small part due to her sister's solicitous attendance."

Darcy nodded. Miss Elizabeth had a sweetness of temper and a playful manner that made her a commendable sister, whereas Miss Bingley quarrelled with Mrs Hurst whenever her sister did not agree with her. If his own sister were ill, Georgiana would be better served by Miss Elizabeth's lively disposition and selfless care than that of a woman like Miss Bingley. Regardless of her persistent attentions, Darcy would never pay his addresses to her. Caroline Bingley only wanted to aggrandise and enrich herself by him.

A proper distraction was in order to push Miss Elizabeth from his mind. Darcy asked Bingley to join him in a game of piquet and pulled a deck of cards from a side table drawer, setting aside the twos through sixes. Bingley drew the high card and dealt first, and for several turns, Darcy enjoyed the game's absorbing strategic nature.

His companion resumed their conversation, but Darcy was

preoccupied with trying to decide whether or not to discard his nines and eights.

"... fortuitous they will remain. I shall make the most of the time with her."

Darcy looked up from his cards. "What did you say?"

"Miss Bennet. My sisters expressed their wish of being better acquainted with her, and I aim to do the same. I quite admire her."

"What has she done to deserve attention from you? How has she indicated any preference for you?"

"Why, she is a lovely creature! Such uniform cheerfulness and sweetness."

"She has done nothing to help you on. I still say she smiles too much. Point of five."

This declaration brought Bingley's eyes back to his cards, but the game did not reclaim his attention. "Miss Bennet has hardly moved from her sickroom until now, so she has had little chance to help me on. As she improves over the next few days, I intend to learn more of her."

"You have known Jane Bennet less than a month. You danced at Meryton and have dined in company with her four times. I do not imagine much of her character has unfolded. Run of four." Darcy was determined to pay attention to the game.

"You forget that we spoke at length last evening. How high?"

"King."

"Equal." Bingley considered his cards, then looked at Darcy. "If she were leaving tomorrow, I may not have considered it, but since they are to remain until Tuesday, I believe an opportunity has befallen me. I admire Miss Bennet, but I have seen her only in large, mixed parties. I ought to make the most of every half hour in which I can command her attention to know her better."

Darcy fixed his friend with a severe gaze. "Her family, her connexions, and her entire situation in life are utterly unsuitable."

"Be that as it may, she is a sweet-tempered girl, the daughter of a gentleman, who may have a preference for me."

"A slight, thin sort of inclination at best."

"Will you cease your chattering?" interjected Hurst from his sofa. "You gossip like a group of women!"

Bingley threw down his cards and suggested Darcy join him in the library as he had letters to write. Although Darcy was inclined to voice his opinions further, in this instance he knew enough of his friend's temperament to remain silent. The affection of such a man as Bingley would be too great a distinction for a woman in Miss Bennet's position. Thankfully, Bingley was often in and out of love, and this interest in Miss Bennet could not be long-lasting.

Darcy held fast to similar hopes in his own case. After Elizabeth Bennet's outburst divulged she thought him conceited and disagreeable, Darcy was surprised she had even accepted his apology and treated him with civility. She was a gracious woman. *Miss Elizabeth Bennet is a woman I esteem—nothing more.* He could withstand her charms for two more days and then part as acquaintances.

By the time the two men arrived in the library, Darcy was comfortable with the knowledge that simply because he admired a woman, there was no reason to suppose that admiration would develop into a stronger, more matrimony-inducing emotion.

THE GENTLEMEN WERE OCCUPIED FOR THE DAY, PASSING THE TIME however men did while confined to a house where women outnumbered the men. As a result, Miss Bingley and Mrs Hurst were not often absent from Jane's room, as there was nothing for them to do elsewhere. Elizabeth tolerated their company for the sake of her sister, who still felt Miss Bingley was her unequalled friend.

Jane was nearest the fire and covered by blankets to protect from taking a chill, but she chatted with Miss Bingley and Mrs Hurst while they sat at their work. Elizabeth had spent too long at her own needlework and felt weary with both it and the ladies' conversation. She turned her attention towards whatever ugly thing Miss Bingley was embroidering. *What is the purpose in doing some long piece of needlework of little use and no beauty?*

"Miss Eliza, you cannot be idling away upon a sofa. Why not employ yourself as we do?"

If not for the opportunity for Jane to enjoy Mr Bingley's company, she might regret her decision to remain at Netherfield. Elizabeth checked her temper for the sake of Jane's tranquillity. One inappropriate and self-indulgent outburst was more than enough for the day.

"I have passed many hours on my own work while nursing Jane. I delight in taking a holiday from the task to take up a book." She made a great show of turning her attention to her well-worn poetry volume.

"You ought to remain at work with us. Needlework is the one accomplishment considered necessary for women of all social classes. I could teach you some elegant stitches."

It was at her tongue's end to suggest what her hostess might do with her work, but it was a poor-enough reflection upon Elizabeth that she had lost her temper in front of Mr Darcy. Elizabeth tried to follow the example of her eldest sister's serenity before she answered through clenched teeth.

"If Jane can spare me, I will go to the library and select another book."

Elizabeth ignored the critical smiles between Miss Bingley and Mrs Hurst and left. It was only after she came farther into the library that she realised she was not alone. Mr Bingley was at a writing table with quill and ink, twirling his pen knife. Mr Darcy was seated in one of the leather chairs several feet away, perusing the *Morning Chronicle*.

She was about to leave, but her movement caught Mr Bingley's attention. Mr Darcy had yet to lower his newspaper.

"Miss Elizabeth! How are you this fine Saturday? I am pleased you and your sister will remain at Netherfield. How is your sister? Is there anything I can do?"

Elizabeth could not help but laugh at his charming high spirits. "Everyone is well, I assure you. My sister is resting in the company of yours, and I have taken the opportunity to retrieve a book. I have been reading poetry; have you anything to recommend?"

She regretted her request when Mr Bingley offered a nervous laugh. "Ah, I wish I had more books for your benefit and my credit, but I would not be surprised to learn that your interests were a bit above my touch. You enjoy poetry? Have you read *Marmion*? I might have a copy..." He began to search his shelves.

Elizabeth was not in the mood to read that epic poem again, but before she could speak, Mr Bingley heaved a sigh. "I cannot find it, in any event. There must be something..." He seemed perplexed, and Elizabeth sought to dissuade him from an impossible task.

"Do not trouble yourself on my account."

"No, I insist on being of service to you..." He paced the sparsely filled shelves until he suddenly turned to his friend. "I say, Darcy!"

The newspaper was lowered to reveal Mr Darcy's questioning gaze.

"You buy more books than you do anything else. I wager you knew of the negligent state of my library and brought your own provisions. I need to speak with Caroline before we leave to dine with the officers, so if I may, I charge you with finding Miss Elizabeth Bennet something to read."

Mr Bingley bowed with a smile and departed before either Elizabeth or Mr Darcy could speak.

Mr Darcy set aside the newspaper and rose. They had parted amicably after their walk this morning, but she was not pleased with the idea of spending much time in his company.

"You are a great reader after all." He did not ask, but stated as a matter of fact.

Elizabeth gave him a saucy smile. "I am sure you think that whatever I may read, it will not be extensive enough to warrant me accomplished. I am a hopeless case, so you had best return to your newspaper."

"Are you consulting your own feelings in the present case, or do you imagine you are gratifying mine?"

He seemed to want to be of use to her, and Elizabeth had no reason to remain critical. She remembered his earnest desire to be forgiven and start anew. She could at least be polite while they remained in the same house until Tuesday.

"I spoke harshly; I am sorry. I have nothing in the world to say for myself. If you have a recommendation, I would be obliged."

Mr Darcy smiled and walked past her towards the sparse bookcases. "What think you of books?"

"I doubt we ever read the same, or with the same feeling," she answered, not unkindly.

"I am sorry you think so, but if that be the case, there can at least be no want of subject between us. We may compare our different opinions. What were you last reading, and do you seek the like?"

"I was reading *Lyrical Ballads* and would not be opposed to reading something comparable. I prefer Wordsworth to Coleridge. I enjoy his themes extolling the virtues of nature."

He looked at her over his shoulder and smiled. "*Tintern Abbey* is a favourite of mine." He then turned back to the shelves. "I find his Lucy poems to be genuine and yet irresistibly tragic."

"You enjoy an examination of unrequited love?" She had never credited Mr Darcy with being a romantic. "Perhaps she was not a real woman, but only a poet's muse?"

He turned to face her, crossing his arms across his chest with a small smile. "The poems illustrate more than that. Lucy represents an ideal, admired from afar, and she is mourned for her early death. The narrator's private grief illuminates the common fear of losing one's beloved."

Why is he eager to pursue a conversation where I challenge his opinion? "Beloved? If she were real, I doubt the poet declared his love, and I also doubt Lucy was cognisant she had been an object of affection. I imagine that they did not mean as much to one another as you suppose."

He seemed unnaturally still for one who was supposed to be perusing book titles. It was a long time before she heard his quiet reply. "Regardless, the narrator's feelings were unreciprocated, and whether muse or lover, Lucy was unattainable."

She had a strange sensation his words were meant for her, and she blushed at the unbidden idea. An unsettled feeling developed between them, and Elizabeth was anxious to dispel it. She said in a playful tone, "Let us imagine our poem's narrator to be the darling of the season. He need only wait for the procession of accomplished women to parade before him to select another muse."

"And might I expect she also has a substantial dowry to add to her inspirational capabilities?"

"At the very least! She also ought to have eligible connexions to a titled family. Can you advise our poet on what is necessary, since you likely seek the same?"

"But of course; I require a woman of at least fifty thousand pounds and would settle for no fewer than five titled connexions from the woman who becomes Mrs Darcy. In fact, a connexion to royalty would suit both me and our poet well." Mr Darcy spoke in a dry tone and, instead of his usual reserve, he appeared amused.

"Then I doubt your ever finding a woman to suit you." She smiled widely.

He only looked at her, and to interrupt the silence, she said, "I am still awaiting a recommendation. *I* would hate to be confined to reading the second volume of whatever *you* chose to read."

The words mocking Miss Bingley tumbled unthinking from her mouth. With Charlotte or Jane she could be teasing, but not with Mr Darcy. *I am not on familiar terms with him to make such a remark—and about our hostess no less.* Mortified, she became engrossed in the fringed and looping fabric of the window draperies and considered hiding behind them.

"Miss Bennet?"

She found the courage to face her companion with an expression of contrition. Mr Darcy had a grin tugging at his lips. *He is entirely amused!* He offered smiles now and then, but Elizabeth was certain she had not heard Mr Darcy laugh. She wondered what a hearty laugh from him might sound like.

By now, his features were relaxed, and she understood her remark would be overlooked. Mr Darcy changed the subject, for which she was grateful. "I think Bingley's library has little that would hold your interest. May I suggest a volume of my own? Are you familiar with William Cowper?"

"Not in the least."

"I find him to be one who celebrates the beauty of nature. His poems are not dissimilar to Coleridge and Wordsworth. I have his formative work, *The Task*, although perhaps his shorter comic ballads might be more to your liking?"

She would certainly meet any challenge that Mr Darcy might set before. "You think me frivolous? I assure you I can give Cowper's work its due attention." A sudden desire to be thought well of by Mr Darcy darted through Elizabeth's mind.

"And I assure *you* that I do not doubt your ability to comprehend anything. Bingley, Hurst, and I are dining out with the officers this evening, but shall I have the first volume brought to you before we depart?"

"Yes, thank you."

"I look forward to comparing our differing opinions on Cowper."

She smiled warmly and agreed. There was a silence between them for a little while, but it did not last because he suddenly asked, with a searching look, "Do you truly find me disagreeable and conceited?"

His question surprised her. "I admit my initial appraisal of your character may not have been correct. When one is called not tolerably handsome, one's opinion is unfavourably skewed."

Elizabeth watched Mr Darcy clench his jaw, but he said nothing. "Nonetheless, your behaviour has given rise to the general impression that you believe yourself superior to all you encounter."

"You ought not to hold my reserve against me. Bingley and my other friends would say I am remarkably agreeable."

"But Mr Darcy, those who are not your friends only see that you never speak much. Whether you *truly* think meanly of all the rest of the world, I cannot determine."

His lips parted, and he leaned forward as if he were about to take a step towards her. Elizabeth watched his tight expression relax, and she instinctively found herself smiling in response. But then his countenance changed, and Mr Darcy once again appeared as grave as he was ever known to be.

"Is it not very late? I must go and dress." Mr Darcy bowed and left.

Elizabeth checked on Jane before she returned to her room to learn that Mr Darcy's volume had been delivered. She opened it and took notice of the book plate. Its circular design, with what was presumably the Darcy coat of arms at its centre and 'Ex Libris Darcy' around its outside, was unpretentious and elegant. She traced the image with her fingertips.

Its style ought not to surprise me. It is not as if Mr Darcy makes an ostentatious show of himself.

This brought to mind the owner of the book. She had misjudged him, she knew that now, just as he admitted doing so to her. He generously offered his own book for her amusement, but more than that, this afternoon she actually had a genuine conversation with Fitzwilliam Darcy without him showing the superiority that she had often associated with him. He even betrayed that he had a sense of humour. Over the course of the day, she had gone from not having the smallest interest in him to being intrigued by him.

Chapter 4

Sunday, November 17

Darcy repressed the urge to shift his weight in the pew. Though he was disinterested in the dull sermon, it would not do to give the impression that he would rather be trapped at his aunt's home and forced to listen Lady Catherine's impertinent advice than be sitting in church this morning. For him, attendance was a moral and social obligation. Proper behaviour was a tenet he lived by, and Darcy was resolved on living a virtuous and respectable life.

He felt guilty for his distraction until he looked across the aisle and saw Hurst was sleeping. Bingley leaned in his seat to look across Hurst's shoulder and caught Darcy's gaze with a smirk.

I owe Bingley a guinea. Darcy had failed to appreciate the extent of Hurst's indolence and had taken Bingley's bet that his brother-in-law would be snoring before the sermon was over.

While they were settling this bet before they left for church, Miss Bingley pointedly said to Miss Elizabeth that the elder Miss Bennet, who Darcy had understood to have been feeling better, needed someone to remain by her side, and Elizabeth volunteered to stay.

Elizabeth.

He had caught the droll expression in her dark, laughing eyes when Miss Bingley insisted someone remain behind the moment he had offered to hand Elizabeth into the carriage. He discerned her resigned expression as she made a show of slowly removing her bonnet and pulling off her pelisse.

"Very well. Do tell me this Sunday's message when you return, Miss Bingley."

He wondered if she had the opportunity to read Cowper and whether she would discuss the poem with him. He had enjoyed their repartee in the library yesterday. She was lively and unreserved, and although her manners were hardly fashionable, they drew him in. Darcy hoped she had not changed clothes so he might see her wear the lilac gown. The light purple colour complemented her pale complexion, soft pink cheeks, and rosy lips.

Stop it!

It would not do to think of how charming he found Elizabeth to be whilst sitting in church. It would not do to think of her at all. She was as he had described Miss Bennet to Bingley: unsuitable. But her personality exuded laughter and intelligence, and she attracted him more than he liked. Yesterday when she had asked whether he truly thought meanly of all the rest of the world, he nearly stepped forward to grasp her hand and pledge that he thought highly of *her.*

Darcy was jolted to attention when the congregation rose. He had been too engrossed in his thoughts to perceive that the service had continued, and he scrambled to his feet. Even Hurst had managed to get himself upright. Darcy returned his attention to his prayer book and did not raise his eyes until the service was over.

Bingley's party lingered near the church door, and Sir William Lucas approached them with his characteristic grin. "I have it on the finest intelligence, Mr Bingley, that you intend to give a ball. What a charming amusement!"

Bingley bowed and promised that an invitation would be forthcoming as soon as the particulars were arranged. Sir William managed to smile even wider before turning his attention to Darcy.

"I presume that you shall be prevailed upon to dance. I say, it would be cruel to deny me the pleasure of seeing you dance."

"I believe by this time you comprehend my feelings on dancing, sir." Darcy withdrew his eye to indicate he had no desire to continue the conversation. Sir William, however, was either too gregarious or too obtuse to oblige him.

"I hope that you might pay the compliment to your friend's establishment and petition some of our fine Hertfordshire jewels to dance. The ladies of the neighbourhood will be delighted."

Darcy stared at Sir William for a moment before bowing and walking away. He mounted his horse, keeping his gaze from all who passed him. Hurst returned to the carriage and fell asleep, but Bingley and his sisters tarried longer as they spoke to their neighbours. He sighed with relief that he had escaped before Mrs Bennet captured Bingley's attention. Darcy had no interest in being sociable with those who did not warrant his consideration.

Bingley finally mounted and rode alongside him. It was another cold morning, but it was unlikely to snow. Darcy was enjoying the quiet stillness when he felt Bingley's gaze. He turned to his companion to realise that his friend was looking on him with disapproval.

"What troubles you?"

"I must speak my mind. You were unfeeling, almost rude, and you placed me in the uncomfortable position of having to apologise for your behaviour."

"When have you ever known me to be impolite?"

"You were rude to Sir William Lucas, an obliging gentleman who is my neighbour."

"How do you mean?" he answered sharply.

"Although you maintain every mark of propriety, you made no effort to disguise your intention to shun all company in the churchyard."

Darcy was taken aback. "You know my character well; how can you mistake my dignity and reserve for ill manners?"

"Forgive me." Bingley's tone softened. "Imagine we were attending services while I was your guest at Pemberley. How might you react if I refused to speak with your neighbours? It would be a poor reflection on you if I stood to the side and spoke to no one."

"I would not force you to submit to the company of lower orders."

"*Sir* William is an amiable man who has risen to the honour of knighthood, *Mr* Darcy," Bingley offered with a wink.

"He may be a good-natured man, but he is all affectation. He feels his distinction too strongly."

"Yet he is all attention to *everybody*. We all know you are the greater man in consequence, but I hate to see you acting in that silent manner. You might take a page from Sir William's book, else you become in the habit of making yourself agreeable nowhere." Bingley raised an eyebrow in emphasis and drove his horse ahead.

To think that anyone believed Fitzwilliam Darcy's behaviour merited reproof! He had been in no way rude to Sir William Lucas, and there was no point in engaging in mindless conversation with anyone in Meryton, in whom there was little beauty and no fashion, no one in whom he felt the smallest interest.

No one except Elizabeth Bennet.

Bingley's criticism was easy to deflect as his friend was guided by his desire to avoid conflict and ensure everyone was at ease. However, Elizabeth had said his conduct offended her beyond what she had overheard him say at the assembly. Her words wounded his feelings more than Bingley's scolding.

No one had reprimanded his behaviour since he was a child, and in the course of four-and-twenty hours, both his closest friend and the most enticing woman he had ever met challenged his conduct. But neither Bingley, in his desire for everyone to meet agreeably, nor Elizabeth, who, by her own admission, had been prejudiced against him, could be a trustworthy arbiter of his manners. He could not acknowledge the justness of their remarks.

When he and Bingley entered the library after church, they were greeted by the ring of feminine laughter. Miss Bennet sat by the fire, and Elizabeth was in the middle of relaying an amusing story. Darcy was drawn in by her earnest merriment.

She is still wearing the lilac gown. He admired the way the fabric glided along her slight curves. Her hair was arranged in dishevelled curls with purple ribbons throughout. He smiled softly at the thought of pulling them out and watching her hair tumble down her shoulders.

The ladies looked surprised by their sudden appearance. They rose to their feet and reined in their laughter, to Darcy's dismay.

Bingley immediately enquired after Miss Bennet. She answered him with the sweetness of address that always attended her. "I am tolerably well again. You have my thanks for your kind concern for my health."

Bingley heard her with earnest attention, and he spoke of his pleasure at seeing her recovered and of the ball he intended to host. Darcy had little interest in speaking of a ball, and Elizabeth asked him if he did not enjoy his evening out with the officers.

"It was as every other party with the officers has been. I would rather have remained behind and enjoyed the honour of y—the honour of the ladies' company." He had nearly declared himself right then and there. Something about Elizabeth's presence made him incapable of rational thought.

"I can little imagine Mr Bingley to be the sort of man to prefer staying at home," she replied to him, but with her gaze on the gentleman who was in earnest conversation with her sister. "I suspect he is always glad of company."

"Bingley cannot refuse an invitation, you know. He must dine out wherever he is asked." His smile was met with a laugh. Darcy's heart skipped a beat.

"Darcy, I was speaking to Miss Bennet about the ball," Bingley called to him. "It is a settled thing. Shall you attend, or will you go to bed before it begins?" Darcy gave his friend a long, hard look, and knew his behaviour was again being challenged.

"Little had I imagined, when I first came to Hertfordshire, that so many engagements would occupy us. However, I have every intention of attending; I would not dishonour you by keeping to my rooms. I make no promises as to whether I shall dance, however, and you must be content with that."

"I am more than satisfied."

"I am glad we shall have the favour of your company, Mr Darcy," Miss Bennet offered.

She is as pleasing and obliging to me as to my friend. I can discern no mark of interest for Bingley.

"It is no sacrifice to join occasionally in evening engagements?" Elizabeth asked him playfully.

"I suppose intervals of recreation and amusement will do me no bodily harm."

It was not until she saw the smile he was trying to hide that she laughed, and Darcy thought the sound so lovely that he ought to try to make her laugh again. His attention was pulled from her by Bingley and Miss Bennet's conversation.

"It has been some time since anyone in the neighbourhood hosted a ball."

"Well, mine is to be a real thing. Less than a fortnight exists between the young people of Meryton and happiness."

"My greatest happiness will derive from spending a cheerful evening with your sisters and wearing a new gown."

Miss Bennet is as animated about Bingley as she is about passing an evening with Miss Bingley and Mrs Hurst.

"You always dress handsomely," said their host, and she blushed. Likely to preserve her from embarrassment, he then addressed her sister. "Miss Elizabeth, shall you also have a new gown for the occasion?"

"You ought not to include me in your conversation. You take upon yourself the chance that my sister and I will speak of dresses and balls. Stockings, lace, and shoe roses will be next."

"Do be kind enough to spare me! What gown or headdress you wear on the occasion may be *your* chief concern, but I know little about such things."

"You mean to say that a gentleman is not affected by what is costly or new in a lady's attire?"

"I could not guess the price of one yard of muslin."

"The cost might depend on whether it is spotted or tamboured," Miss Bennet supplied.

"Alas, I cannot take notice of such things."

"Not even after having two sisters at home?" Elizabeth asked.

"My sisters would never trust me for their choice of gown!"

"And you, Mr Darcy?" She fixed on him with her fine eyes.

"Are you an excellent judge of selecting muslins for your sister's gowns?"

"Never."

After a pause, she continued the conversation. "Mr Bingley, I assume, therefore, that you are unaware that muslin can be delicate, that it easily frays, and does not wash well? What a lapse in your world knowledge."

"It is, indeed! I do not even buy my own cravats. And you, Darcy? Have you a great deal to say about how ladies dress for a ball? Is your heart biased by the texture of muslin?"

"Neatness and fashion are enough for me."

With this closed-ended reply, their chat was abruptly finished, and for a moment, the foursome looked at one another in silence. Bingley then addressed Miss Bennet. "Now that you are feeling better, I wonder if you might walk with me. No doubt you know something of the striking portraits in the gallery, being a lifelong resident of the neighbourhood."

After assuring her sister that she was well enough for a short walk, Miss Bennet left with Bingley. Darcy's eyes followed them with a serious expression. *Bingley ought to be careful, or he will find himself entangled with an unsuitable woman who does not care for him.*

"Does our bantering about muslin and gowns trouble you? You hardly spoke."

"I see no purpose in speaking when I have nothing to contribute that would further the conversation."

"Perhaps you are shy."

"Shyness is the result of a sense of inferiority. I cannot define my temperament as anything of the sort. My sister Georgiana is exceedingly shy because she fears doing or saying wrong." He sighed at the memory of her lately more profound reticence. "I see her follow a conversation, but she lacks courage enough to join it. I never fail to join a conversation that is of interest to me."

"I was only teasing you again, Mr Darcy." She sighed. "I do not misconstrue your gravity and silence for shyness. I do wonder, though, at your being so reserved."

"I cannot imagine you assume that the quality of a man's character must be in direct correlation to how talkative he is in company."

Her gaze fell, and Darcy thought her spirits were no longer high. She appeared as though her own thoughts were employing her, and she was not satisfied with the results.

"Well, I do not want people to have too good a character as it saves me the trouble of liking them a great deal."

Darcy doubted this statement was close to the truth. He asked whether she had begun the volume of Cowper, and the shades of melancholy were quickly banished from her countenance.

"I see why you recommended him after I told you I admired Wordsworth. Cowper clearly was an influence on him and others of his ilk. I appreciated the mock-heroic account of the wooden stool becoming a sofa," she said with a laugh.

Darcy smiled. "I thought you would be drawn to his witty and satirical manner. However, he contemplates larger religious and humanitarian concerns."

They spoke at length on Cowper, poets, and the beauties of nature. He admired her insights, although he did not always agree with them. That hardly prevented Elizabeth from sharing her opinions and trying to convince him otherwise. *What a novel experience to spend half an hour with a woman who challenges me!* She leaned towards him in her enthusiasm, her eyes sparkling, and Darcy knew she enjoyed debating with him as much as he did with her. The intense pulling sensation he felt whenever he was near to her seemed heightened.

"If you do not mind parting with it, that is?"

Darcy had been admiring her rather than attending to their conversation. Not willing to ask her to repeat herself, he took a leap of faith. "Of course, I shall have the second volume brought to you." Darcy paused with bated breath and released it when Elizabeth thanked him. "I hope you will discuss it with me. I enjoyed hearing your opinions on the first."

"I think that has less to do with me and more to do with your inability to add anything to a conversation about muslin and balls."

"I assure you, Miss Bennet, my enjoyment of our conversation had everything to do with you."

Elizabeth blushed beautifully and murmured a quiet "Thank you."

He thought of Bingley's ball and considered that an evening of dancing might not be trying after all. Darcy leaned forward in his seat, and Elizabeth met his gaze with bright, eager eyes. He had always thought them to be fine, but in this moment, they were arresting. He was about to speak, but his words were lost when the library door was thrown open and Miss Bingley came into the room.

Chapter 5

Elizabeth gave a start at the sound of Miss Bingley's voice, and Mr Darcy sat back in his chair. She felt the loss of their peaceful companionship as their hostess rushed into the library, out of breath.

"I met Charles and Jane in the gallery, and they said you were left to your lonesome." As an aside to him, but audible to Elizabeth, she said, "I can scarcely imagine how you passed your time." Mr Darcy had been so at ease, but after Miss Bingley's entrance, he was again stern and reserved.

"We were discussing the ball."

This took her by surprise. She wondered if he, like her, preferred to keep private the memory of their pleasant conversation. The thought that Darcy admired her intellect as much as her eyes gave her an unexpected thrill.

Miss Bingley heaved a dramatic sigh. "Charles is enthralled with the idea of hosting a dance. My brother has no idea of the effort I need to put forth. I doubt we have adequate space for everyone he wishes to invite."

"You must not distress yourself," Elizabeth said. "Everyone

enjoys a crowd. If there are more dancers than the room can conveniently hold, that shall be more than enough to constitute a good ball!"

Unsurprisingly, Miss Bingley could not appreciate her humour. "Miss Eliza, I should not wish it said that my dancers passed the evening in a room that was too full of company and insufferably hot. But there are more requirements for hosting such an event, and the preparation is tedious. Do you not agree, Mr Darcy?"

"Indeed. It is unfortunate if such a lot is unacceptable to you."

Miss Bingley began on a different course. "I fear we shall have to dine tonight on food prepared this morning. Charles had it in his mind to permit the kitchen servants the favour of time off for churchgoing. What strange notions he takes! I am certain you would not cause such a disruption at Pemberley while entertaining guests."

"I would not wish to inhibit the morality of my servants by always prohibiting their Sunday observances."

Elizabeth watched this conversation, if it could be so called, with silent amusement. Undaunted, Miss Bingley pulled out a swathe of silk from her box for Mr Darcy to admire. "What think you of my embroidery?" Mr Darcy only nodded.

"I must take advantage of the rest of this afternoon light; I spent too much time with Nicholls. Miss Eliza, there is a time for everything; a time for balls and a time for work. You ought to follow my example and be useful."

Insolent girl! Before she could form a polite reply, Mr Darcy crossed the room to sit at the writing desk by the window. "You ladies will forgive me, but I ought to write to my sister."

Traitor. Elizabeth was more diverted than offended that Mr Darcy made his own escape and left her with Miss Bingley.

Elizabeth pulled out her borrowed Cowper to read it again, determined to wait in the library until Jane and Mr Bingley returned. She knew Miss Bingley wished her gone, but Elizabeth was in no humour to leave her alone with her prey. Their hostess lost her interest in her work now that her object was no longer in a position to admire her skill. She rose to pace and fell into a pattern Elizabeth found amusing, walking along the unfilled shelves under the pretext of searching for a book. When she neared Mr Darcy, she tried to engage him in conversation. He would pull a blank sheet over what he had written and give a short reply. Miss Bingley pouted, then browsed more empty shelves, and Mr Darcy uncovered his paper and resumed writing until she approached him again.

Elizabeth felt compassion for him. He had likely been the subject of all manners of pretence in an attempt to secure him. She supposed he might be sick of civility, of deference, of officious attention, of women who were always eagerly seeking his approval. She decided to offer the poor man a reprieve.

"Mr Darcy, may I interrupt you? I wonder if I could trouble you to send for the second volume to this." She held up the poetry they had been discussing. "I would like something new to read while I wait for Jane."

Some emotion flashed across Mr Darcy's eyes. Gratitude? Relief? She could not be certain, but he hastily gathered his sheets of paper and rose. "Of course. I shall retrieve it myself."

"Let me ring for a servant," Miss Bingley called.

"I thank you, no." Mr Darcy bowed and, after giving Elizabeth a smile, left the room.

Elizabeth turned away to hide her own smile as Miss Bingley shrugged her shoulders. Elizabeth decided to follow Mr Darcy's example and sat at the writing table to begin a letter to her aunt Gardiner.

Elizabeth selected a sheet and dipped her quill into the ink, and then noticed a neatly written missive. It was one of the sheets on which Mr Darcy had been writing; the ink at the bottom was still wet. In his haste to excuse himself from Miss Bingley, he had left one of his pages. Careful not to smudge the ink, she set it aside.

Elizabeth endeavoured to keep her eyes on her own letter, but her natural curiosity would not be moderated. She could not help but raise her eyes to the evenly written words inches away from her own lines.

> *... His engaging manners hid vicious propensities that could not be known by you. How were you to know that such depravity and vengefulness existed in this world, let alone in one man? I know of no other way to express to you that you*

have not lost my good opinion. Your fears are undoubtedly based upon what you saw of my temper when you first told me of Mr W's intentions. It was not your actions that offended me, but his. I will not deny your imprudence, but I am gratified and proud that you acknowledged the whole to me. Please forgive my initial response to your confession, and know I was not angry with you, but only fearful of losing what is most dear to me. I saw little reason to enlighten you of Mr W's character, as never in all my considerations did I believe that he would follow you to R. My resentment of the entire circumstance…

Elizabeth's heart was pounding. To unavoidably overhear a conversation is one thing, but to read a gentleman's letter was quite another. She regretted her unintended invasion of Mr Darcy's privacy, but truly, how could it be avoided? Between the lamp, inkwell, sander, and the writing box, there was no other place for a page with wet ink to lie but right next to hers. Elizabeth's hand, still holding the quill, hovered over the inkwell. *What had happened to Miss Darcy?*

"There you are, Mr Darcy!" Miss Bingley's voice shattered Elizabeth's reflections. She was so surprised her quill tumbled from her fingers and splattered ink across her letter.

"Miss Bennet." He held out the volume. His endearing smile made him appear strikingly handsome. She met his eye and took the offered book. Once again, she felt something pass between them. Then the moment and its emotions, whatever they were, slipped away. She could not leave his letter out in the open and she called for him to remain.

"I spilt ink over my letter. How careless of me. Tell me, do you think I could trim the page and save the paper?" She picked up his letter, covered it with her own, and handed him both pages. The effect was immediate. A deep shade of hauteur overspread his features, but he said not a word. He glanced between the page and her. His eyes were stony. *He knows. He knows I have read it.*

"Mr Darcy, will you not return Miss Eliza's letter and join me?"

This roused him, and Mr Darcy handed Elizabeth her sheet. He folded his letter into quarters and placed it in his pocket without looking at her. She ventured to return them to their former equanimity.

"I hope you will speak with me about this volume of Cowper. I enjoyed our earlier discussion." She looked at him hopefully, but his expression remained cold and critical. Mr Darcy bowed towards both ladies and left.

Elizabeth soon returned to her own room. She preferred to be alone with her thoughts, for she was feeling uneasy, and sitting across from an irritated Miss Bingley was not conducive to inner reflection. She lay across the sofa, her legs sprawled over the arm in an unladylike fashion, staring at the ceiling.

Why should I feel guilty and unhappy?

Because Mr Darcy was displeased with her. She had disappointed him at the moment she had begun to value his friendship. She was remorseful, but he ought to be grateful she returned his letter without anyone else reading its distressing contents. Elizabeth was angered by the manner in which he took his letter and stalked out of the room. *He is the one who left his private correspondence out for all to see! How dare he look at me with contempt? I could hardly help seeing his letter.*

His letter had been right before her eyes, and she could not deny that the subject of Mr Darcy was of great interest to her, and she wanted to learn more of him. He was reserved, but amiable among his friends. He had said something ungentlemanly about her, but earnestly wished to earn her pardon. Mr Darcy was clever, and although reticent, he was not as critical as she had previously thought him to be. They had passed a pleasing half an hour together in the library today, and she delighted in his near-open admiration of her. Not two days ago she cared too little to desire his approbation, and now Elizabeth wanted to be thought well of by him.

She had erred in reading the letter and regretted it, but he ought not to have left it behind. Mr Darcy would never own that he had been in error. He did not even thank her for returning it. *I ought not to be surprised by the way that proud man acts!*

"It may do you good to speak of your distress, whatever it may be."

Elizabeth looked up and saw Jane standing inside the door. She swung her legs down and made room for her sister to join her.

"I did not hear you come in. Did you enjoy your walk with Mr Bingley?"

Jane gave a little blush. "Yes, we spent an agreeable hour together. I had no idea of the time, it passed so quickly. We returned to the library, but only Caroline remained."

Elizabeth's mind wandered back to Mr Darcy's letter. Under her eldest sister's entreaty to speak, she related the chief of the scene in the library between Mr Darcy and herself.

"And how could he look on me with disdain? He left his letter on the desk."

"Was the letter confidential? I ask because perhaps Mr Darcy fears you will betray his confidence if you learned something he would not wish the world to know."

Jane's delicate sense of honour forbade her from asking about what she had read, and Elizabeth would not elaborate. She would never earn Mr Darcy's confidence again if she discussed the letter. "He was writing to his sister, and although I learned no specifics, I can assume he fears his privacy has been invaded. And what of it? Does Mr Darcy think I would start a rumour about a girl I have never met? That I would gossip about him?" The fact that until their stay at Netherfield she had been willing to speak against him at any opportunity added to Elizabeth's guilty feelings.

"Perhaps he is embarrassed. He is a private man. You might give him the benefit of the doubt."

"Do you not think he ought to do the same by me?"

"You could apologise for reading the letter, and then Mr Darcy will apologise for putting you in a position to see it, and that will be the end of the matter."

"He is the one who placed me in this position! If anyone ought to make a conciliatory gesture, it is to be Mr Darcy!"

"That is not the manner in which to view a friendship. Both parties must be willing to concede."

"Our lessening of tensions is *not* a friendship, but whatever acquaintance had been growing has now waned." Her anger was now a smouldering ember in her chest.

"Lizzy, you are so quick to criticise! Have you not learned that things are not always as they seem?"

Had she not recently learnt she and Mr Darcy shared a mutual appreciation for poetry? He had been less fervent in his enthusiasm than she, but she saw a kindred spirit in him. It made his dismissal of her all the more distressing and rekindled her resentment.

"Concession is out of the question! I was not in the wrong, and *he* will never own that he was. He is too proud."

She then changed their discourse to one more gratifying to each, and on which there could be no difference of sentiment. Elizabeth listened to the happy, though modest, hopes which Jane entertained of Mr Bingley's regard, and said all in her power to heighten her confidence in it.

When she and Jane went to dinner, Miss Bingley said Mr Darcy expressed his regrets that he was unequal to dining in company. *What else could demonstrate that he could not forgive me for reading his letter?*

DID SHE READ IT? THE BRIEF LOWERING OF HER EYES, THE SLIGHT crack in her voice. *She must have.*

Darcy paced in his dressing room, with nothing to do and too much on his mind. He could not tolerate another one of Miss Bingley's dinners, the inane conversation and her insincere fawning. But more than that, Darcy had no interest in seeing Elizabeth. He had paid her too much attention, and now he would suffer for it. He had been so impatient to show thoughtfulness towards her that he had left a private letter out in the open.

When he first returned to his room, he analysed every word, carefully considering what an impartial third party might assume. His irrational response was that it was clear that Georgiana Darcy had been compromised in the most reputation-damaging way. When his breathing slowed, he read it again; the second reading was marginally better. No specifics were mentioned, no full names were used, but the hint of a scandal was enough to pique the interest of any gossipmonger. A rumour alone could ruin Georgiana forever.

Elizabeth had thus far conducted herself with decency and

compassion, but who was to say she would not pass along a hint of Miss Darcy's misconduct to her mother? Mrs Bennet and her younger daughters displayed a total want of propriety. There was no way of knowing what they might say.

He threw himself into his chair, his arm hanging over the armrest, the letter dangling from his fingertips.

Should I exact a promise of her silence? Darcy could not see how to introduce such a topic. Besides, it would attract more attention to a situation that still brought pain to Darcy's heart.

He was angry at his own mistake, at his own thoughtlessness, as well as angry with her. *A sincere smile and fine eyes, and what do I do? I leave damning evidence of my sister's near ruin for anyone to see!* The fear of anyone learning what had happened to Georgiana brought a flood of memories of what had passed in August. His sister's endless tears and lost self-respect, his regret at failing his most beloved relation.

He would go mad with restlessness. Darcy's natural reticence notwithstanding, he was inclined for good company and had the power of appreciating what was elegant and clever. *Why should I hide in my room when there are five other people in this house I might converse with?* He need not speak to Elizabeth Bennet.

He must be resolved against further conversation with her, but he wondered at his ability to carry forth his own resolution. *She fascinates me.* She was a clever young woman who was arch and lively, yet compassionate. He admired her strength of understanding, and Elizabeth's conversation had yet to disappoint him. He could now admit he was bewitched by her. It was Sunday night; could he truly not speak to her again while they resided in the same house? *Yes. Think of Georgiana.* He would not associate with one who might spread enough gossip to ruin his sister's reputation.

It was already late; an hour downstairs would suffice before the party broke up for the evening. If he was a fortunate man, the party would be lively and Elizabeth already retired for the evening.

Chapter 6

All of Darcy's hopes were in vain. Hurst was on the sofa staring at the ceiling; Miss Bennet, Bingley, and Mrs Hurst were playing vingt-un and speaking only as far as the game required; Miss Bingley sat with her embroidery abandoned on her lap; and Elizabeth was reading his volume of Cowper.

What a torpid gathering. The *one* person who interested him was an unsuitable acquaintance. She may be unsuitable as a wife, but if she could not be trusted not to invade another's privacy, Elizabeth could not even be considered a friend.

Miss Bingley leapt up to express her pleasure in his joining them. He made some civil reply, but what Darcy really observed was that Elizabeth refused to look at him. He expected she would seek him out to apologise. Thankfully, Bingley also had something to say to him and drew Darcy's attention away from his sister.

"I have decided to remain behind tomorrow. My sisters will take the chaise to make calls, and my guests may feel neglected if I go shooting." He spoke of his guests, but Darcy saw his friend's attention on the eldest Miss Bennet, who smiled as she always did.

Hurst had managed to pull himself upright, his face flushed and his eyes aqueous. *There is no way I can spend a day shooting with only Hurst.* The dogs would offer better and more lucid conversation. With a composure of voice under which was concealed his annoyance, Darcy agreed to postpone their shooting.

The dull headache that had begun while he was in his rooms was escalating into a painful throb. A Sunday evening, with nothing to do and no one to speak with. Darcy stared at the clock on the mantle while the room remained in silence. The minute hand ticked towards the six once, then twice, its slow descent a mocking reminder of the tedium that awaited him.

"What a languid group we are!" cried Bingley. "We must all play a game. Why not Speculation?"

Various protestations came from all sides, save Elizabeth and himself, who remained silent.

"None care for cards?" Bingley asked. "Shall we play Consequence?"

Miss Bennet agreed, and she then appealed to Mrs Hurst, who prompted her husband to join. Darcy knew Miss Bingley was waiting to hear his answer before expressing her opinion. *A word game would be better than sitting in silence or listening to their inane conversation.* Darcy consented and, of course, so did Miss Bingley.

"Shall you join us, Miss Elizabeth?" asked Bingley.

Elizabeth briefly turned to him to give him a cold look, as if to say, "I would rather not if *Mr Darcy* is." Aloud, she said to Bingley that if he reminded her of the rules, she would go along with the rest of the party.

"Splendid!" Bingley retrieved a pencil and several sheets of paper. "We must sit in a circle; the paper will be passed to the person to your right. The first shall write an adjective that describes a gentleman. He will fold the paper to cover what he wrote and hand the paper to the next."

"We are not to see what the previous person has written?" asked Elizabeth. "What do we write for each turn?"

"I shall write it for you. The game shall be more amusing if we confine our answers to people of note or our mutual acquaintance."

"Charles, you have a very bad hand," Miss Bingley cried. "Miss

Eliza will not be able to decipher one word." She took the sheet to the table and wrote:

       1. Adjective for gentleman
       2. Gentleman's name
       3. Adjective for lady
       4. Lady's name
       5. Where they met
       6. What he wore
       7. What she wore
       8. He said to her
       9. She said to him
      10. The consequence was
      11. What the world said

"There are eleven words or phrases to complete, but only seven of us," Elizabeth said.

"We can pass the sheet again until the phrase is complete," Mr Bingley answered. "For each round, a different person might begin, since you know I shall not be able to think of many examples of what a lady might wear."

The gentlemen arranged the chairs in a circle, and Darcy had the misfortune to find the last open place in a chair between Hurst and Elizabeth.

Bingley offered the sheet to Darcy, and he scribbled an adjective before thrusting it towards Elizabeth without looking at her. She snatched the paper and angled her body as far away from him as her chair would allow.

His turn came again, and he now had to write a phrase that answered 'what he might say to her.' If only he could release the frustration against Elizabeth that had been building in his chest. With a cold glance towards her, Darcy recalled a line from Plato's *Phaedrus* and decided on a fitting quote. He brusquely handed the sheet and pencil to her.

She glared before she wrote her answer to 'what she said to him.' The sheet made its way back to Bingley, and he read the phrase aloud:

"Clever Sir William Lucas met virtuous Jane at the altar. He wore a powdered wig and she wore a wide-hooped petticoat. He said, 'to be curious about that which is not my concern, while I am still in ignorance of my own self, would be ridiculous.' She said, 'What the weak head with strongest bias rules is pride, the never-failing vice of fools.' The consequence was they drank much more than they ought. And the world said, 'saints protect us from such an evil!'"

The drawing room exploded with laughter.

"I wish you joy with Sir William, Jane," snickered Miss Bingley.

"I would drink more than I ought if I found myself at the altar with him!" laughed Hurst.

"You need less reason than that to drink more than you ought!" called his brother.

Miss Bennet tried to rein in her amusement. "You are being uncharitable to Sir William."

"Miss Bennet, you are too good. Your virtuous description is very apt," said Bingley.

It took Darcy and Elizabeth a moment to realise what the other had written. Darcy scowled at her while she turned red in anger. Amid the others' amusement, they had a hushed and tense conversation.

"You *still* contend that pride is my greatest vice?"

"I am *not* curious about your affairs!" she hissed.

"Did you read my letter?"

"You ought to be grateful I returned it to you."

"I might have been grateful had you not read it!" Darcy struggled to maintain a whisper.

They had no opportunity to speak further, as the game resumed. Bingley turned the sheet over and was about to hand it to his brother when Elizabeth called, "May I begin?" Darcy was suspicious. She wrote an adjective to describe a gentleman and passed the paper to Mrs Hurst.

If I were to wager, I would bet ten to one she writes something to insult me!

When Darcy's turn came, he had to answer 'what she wore.' He felt Elizabeth's eyes on him. He considered an appropriate reply and handed Elizabeth the folded-down paper with a bow. She frowned, but became aware of the others' expectant gazes and wrote her reply to 'what he said to her.'

Miss Bingley completed the final line and read the phrase aloud:

"Resentful and disagreeable King George met tittle-tattling Elizabeth on Drury Lane. He wore a bicorn hat and she wore a spinster's cap. He said to her, 'Our own self-love draws a thick veil between us and our faults.' She said, 'I must trim my new bonnet!' The consequence was Napoleon Bonaparte surrendered. And the world said, 'we shall not be in charity with you ever again.'"

Self-love? And I am neither resentful nor disagreeable! Bingley's comments regarding his conduct towards Sir William Lucas edged close to his mind, and Darcy pushed them away.

"For shame, Miss Eliza, a gossiping spinster on Drury Lane?" Mrs Hurst shook her head in mock disparagement while the room chuckled.

"What is the greater shock, that Miss Eliza is a spinster or that she meets the King on Drury Lane?" asked Miss Bingley.

"What does that matter if it meant we defeated Napoleon?" Bingley asked.

"Then we must suppose it to have been a fine bonnet!"

"But not fine enough to entice a gentleman to marry Miss Eliza, the spinster gossip," called Hurst.

The party turned their amused eyes towards Elizabeth. Darcy was about to utter an aside to her about the harm of a gossiping nature when he took notice of her expression. Her downcast eyes, the quick inhalation of breath and its shaky exhalation, the way her fingers clenched the chair arm.

Good God, what has become of me?

To be intentionally disrespectful was beneath him. He may not have written Elizabeth's name, but he *had* been intent on sending her a cruel message, that she would be a spinster with no status. Darcy was utterly ashamed of himself. Had he learned nothing as a result of his callous remark at the assembly? She had simply noticed a letter he was foolish enough to leave out in the open and returned it to him.

"You looked me in the eye, and then you coldly withdrew your own before you spoke those words. I will have you know that I have never been so offended or insulted in all of my life!"

Darcy knew his initial judgment had been incorrect, but he never carefully considered Elizabeth's words. How disgracefully he had acted. It showed an appalling lack of both gentlemanly manners and common benevolence; his own father would be ashamed of him.

"Lizzy, are you well?"

"Oh, yes. I relish my role as your Napoleon-defeating, gossiping spinster sister." Darcy wondered if her voice sounded hollow to anyone else's ears.

"Let us play again!" Bingley gave a new sheet to Hurst to start another round.

"Miss Elizabeth, I—" Darcy began, but Elizabeth threw him a look that silenced him.

Darcy needed the name of a penitent man when his turn came. His mind raced through Bible passages and Shakespeare, but he could not recall one. He knew his turn was taking too long. Darcy wrote Bingley's name for lack of any other and passed the sheet to Elizabeth; she refused to look at him.

I shall have to wear sackcloth and ashes until I leave Hertfordshire.

When his turn came again, Darcy wrote his answer for 'she said to him': "Whatever is begun in anger ends in shame." He *was* ashamed that he had been ruled by his uncompromising temper.

A SPINSTER'S CAP! WHAT AN INSUFFERABLE MAN. ANY SINGLE WOMAN of sense, with a narrow income, knew that her fate was to be thought a ridiculous old maid who could only tire everyone to death. Elizabeth could not tolerate the humiliation of remaining dependent on the charity of her family. For Mr Darcy—an intriguing, eligible man—to imply she lacked honour, that she was a gossip who would never marry, made Elizabeth feel a furious anger. She would send him a message that she was respectable, and not a gossiping spinster!

Elizabeth wrote 'honourable' for an adjective describing a lady and did not raise her eyes again until her turn came again. She was busy trying to remember Shakespeare: *'The purest treasure mortal times afford is a spotless reputation; take that away, men are but gilded loam or painted clay.'* Mr Darcy thought so well of his reputation, but *she* knew how ungentlemanly he was! Mr Darcy could despise her all he wished, but she would not allow him to believe that she was a disreputable gossip. She had her pride, after all.

Mrs Hurst completed the phrase and read the consequences aloud:

"Drunk Mr Bingley met honourable Miss Darcy in Gretna Green. He wore a blue coat with gilt buttons and she wore a second mourning evening dress. He said to her, 'Your gown ought to be let out.' She said, 'whatever is begun in anger ends in shame.' The consequence was that the purest treasure mortal times can afford is a spotless reputation. And the world said, 'such persons must be cut from our acquaintance!'"

Elizabeth turned her attention to Mr Darcy. She had expected to see the full extent of his arrogance and indignation at having his conduct challenged. *Mr Darcy could benefit from some criticism!*

"Miss Darcy is not known to the Miss Bennets, and we agreed to confine our answers to those of our mutual acquaintance," complained Bingley. Mrs Hurst shrugged while the others laughed.

Mr Darcy's face was the familiar mask of hauteur, but his eyes were all anxiety rather than the anger she suspected.

Then she thought of the hint of an indiscretion in Mr Darcy's letter to his sister. She felt a sudden wave of sickness overtake her as she realised she had contributed to his current distress. *Is he thinking of his sister's reputation?*

"Is the quote about the importance of reputation from *Othello*?" Bingley asked.

"*Richard the Second.*" She had not intended to send a message about *Miss Darcy's* reputation. Her adjective 'honourable' and the line from Shakespeare was an attempt to express her anger at Mr Darcy for assuming she was a gossip with no honour. She meant to imply she had done nothing inappropriate, that *his* conduct merited reproof, but with the addition of his sister's name, it had gone horribly wrong.

How despicably have I acted! Tears pricked her eyes. *Is this the way a respectable woman behaves?*

"I cannot imagine Charles or Miss Darcy acting in a manner that would lead to the loss of their reputations," said Miss Bingley.

"And I cannot imagine Bingley being so foolish as to suggest that Miss Darcy is too large for her gown," guffawed Mr Hurst.

"And why might Miss Darcy wear a mourning gown that needs to be let out?"

"She is mourning the loss of her figure and her reputation!" The rest of the party, save for Elizabeth, laughed.

"I will thank you not to speak of my sister in coarse terms!" Mr Darcy brought a sudden end to their party's frivolity.

When had she become so hateful and resentful? Mr Darcy could not know that she would never betray a confidence. *I do not even know the particulars to which the letter referred.*

Miss Bingley rang for supper, and the group chatted again. Mr Darcy pinched his fingers at the bridge of his nose and exhaled, as though his head was pounding. He looked fatigued, agitated, and morose. It made her feel like comforting him. All of the spleen and vitriol she felt against him slipped away and was replaced by the desire to return to their former burgeoning acquaintance.

Perhaps his formal manner conceals that he feels a great deal. He feared for his sister's spirits and reputation, and devotion to a sister was a sentiment that Elizabeth could not help but admire.

"Why do we not play another round while we wait for supper?" Elizabeth asked. She picked up a sheet of paper and pencil and handed them both to Mr Bingley.

"Would you be so kind as to begin? And do pass it in the other direction this round."

Mr Bingley was too courteous to deny a lady. Elizabeth printed 'apologetic' to answer an adjective for a lady and handed it to Mr Darcy without folding the sheet over. He reached for the page, but she held it fast, forcing him to pay attention. He resignedly looked at the sheet, and she saw his eyes widen as he read her word. Mr Darcy looked at her, but his expression was inscrutable.

When Elizabeth's turn came a second time to answer what the consequence was, she left the sheet unfolded. Elizabeth thought that when he closed his eyes after he read her reply, it might have been in relief. *Or it might be in impatience.* He then wrote what the world said. Mr Darcy held the sheet in his hands for a long moment before he read aloud.

"Chivalrous Mr Hurst met apologetic Queen Charlotte at White's. He wore an ankle-length great coat and she wore a hat with ostrich plumes. He said to her 'You are so altered I should not have known you again.' She said, 'I am forever plagued by nervous headaches.' The consequence was that all their trespasses were forgiven. And the world said, 'to err is human, to forgive divine.'"

He forgives me!

The party's laughter and conversation were interrupted as the servants entered carrying trays. Miss Bingley directed them, and her brother put the chairs back to rights. The group moved to the table, but Mr Darcy walked to the fireplace. Elizabeth weighed the desire to apologise against the likelihood of distressing him further, then resolved to speak with him.

"Mr Darcy," she said softly, and his eyes looked her way. "I beg you to forgive me. I should have never tried to antagonise you, nor did I intend to discredit your sister. I am certain, absolutely certain, that none of us has any reason to think any harm of her."

The disturbance of his mind was clear to her, and Elizabeth suspected his keeping his back to the room was by design. "You are mistaken, Miss Elizabeth, if you believe I am distressed only on my sister's account."

"I do not understand."

Mr Darcy fixed his eyes on her face. "I am exceedingly sorry for my behaviour. I was uncivil, and there is no excuse for it. I ought not to have treated you, or anyone—but particularly one whose acquaintance I have come to value—in an unfeeling manner. I think it for the best if we suspend all conversation between us."

Elizabeth was astonished. She had no idea he regretted his conduct or their lost amity. Elizabeth raised her hand to rest it on his arm, a gentle, reassuring gesture that felt perfectly natural. As her hand moved, Bingley called him and he stepped away without noticing. Elizabeth made her excuses and retired for the evening, but she could not sleep.

Did he mean to suspend conversation between us for this evening, or forever?

She tossed and turned and wondered if she had once and for all lost his good opinion. He, too, had acted badly, but she was ready to forgive him. *He appeared so contrite and pensive.* The only source from whence anything like consolation could be drawn was in the resolution of her own better conduct. She would never again be so hasty to censure another person.

Chapter 7

Monday, November 18

Since the incident at Ramsgate, Georgiana had been wallowing in guilt and shame. Darcy knew from his own observations and from his correspondence with Mrs Annesley, his sister's new companion, that her fragile self-confidence was shattered. Georgiana was reluctant to leave her home and recoiled from meetings in public.

His cousin, who shared guardianship with Georgiana, was certain that time and maturity would heal her wounds. But how would Georgiana survive Christmas with Lady Catherine? He could only shield her so much from their aunt's demands for Georgiana to speak up, to assert herself, to exhibit her accomplishments, to prepare her for coming out in society.

November 17, 1811

My dear Sister,
Your letter made me happier than anything in the world

could in your absence. It is a comfort to know that you are settled in town. I have deferred Lady Catherine's visit until Christmas. Your Fitzwilliam cousins will, therefore, also be in attendance, and you shall not have to endure the burden of her attentions alone.

I can discern you are not as content as you would have me believe. I wish that you would not cast the blame upon yourself and instead lay it at the feet of he who is truly at fault. You are but fifteen and must not allow what happened at R to plague you. Your youth must be your excuse. His engaging manners hid vicious propensities that could not be known by you. How were you to know that such depravity and vengefulness existed in this world, let alone in one man? I know of no other way to express to you that you have not lost my good opinion. Your fears are undoubtedly based upon what you saw of my temper when you first told me of Mr W's intentions. It was not your actions that offended me, but his. I will not deny your imprudence, but I am gratified and proud that you acknowledged the whole to me. Please forgive my initial response to your confession and know I was not angry with you, but only fearful of losing what is most dear to me. I saw little reason to enlighten you of Mr W's character, as never in all my considerations did I believe that he would follow you to R. My resentment of the entire circumstance must not be misconstrued as implacable resentment of you.

Since writing the above, I have made a grievous error. You will recall my last in which I wrote of my acquaintance with Miss E.B. and since then I have, with design, offended and insulted her. I suspect that I have been selfish, prideful, and prejudiced. Your generous heart will attempt to absolve me, but I know that I have judged hastily and harshly, and acted with indefensible spiteful-ness. My purpose in writing this is to, I hope, save you from making the same errors in judgment. I shall reserve the particulars until we meet. I shall return the week before Christmas in order for us to return to Pemberley together.

My compliments to Mrs A. All our friends in Hertfordshire are well.

I remain, your affectionate brother,
Fitzwilliam Darcy

AFTER DARCY SEALED THE LETTER, HE RUBBED HIS HAND ACROSS his face. *Another restless night since making the acquaintance of Elizabeth Bennet.* Instead of expressive eyes and a pleasing figure haunting his dreams, Darcy was plagued by thoughts of the cruelty he demonstrated during last night's game.

"*A little pride, son, which reminds you what is due to yourself, and a little good nature, which suggests what is due to others, are the prerequisites for the moral constitution of a true gentleman,*" was a tenet Darcy had heard often from his father.

Where did I go so wrong in my life?

Darcy thought of the principles his parents had instilled in him and of the disappointment they would feel, had they been alive, to see the arrogant man he had become. Darcy could still recollect his father's frown and his mother's saddened sigh when he had been found wanting.

His thoughts were interrupted by the breakfast bell. The idea of sitting across from Elizabeth made him feel wretched. He could not shrug off the knowledge that his general behaviour could be so repulsive. Darcy suspected Bingley was right about him, and his recent conduct towards Elizabeth correlated to the manner in which he treated everyone outside his circle.

Darcy was the last to enter, and although the food was faultless, the thought of eating turned his stomach. He drank only coffee and was grateful for the newspaper. Hurst consumed his food with a fervour not seen elsewhere; Miss Bingley and Mrs Hurst tittered amongst themselves; Miss Bennet and Bingley spoke animatedly; and Elizabeth was perusing a letter.

"Charles, I hate to interrupt your tête-à-tête"—Miss Bingley's tone betrayed that she felt no regret—"but Louisa and I must be off. We have been remiss in returning calls; as you know, we have been kept at home these last few days. You shall not see us again before dinner."

"I have not called for the horses yet because I will not have them standing in the wind waiting on you to primp."

Miss Bingley refuted any suggestion that she took long with her toilette. She then persuaded Hurst to finish his breakfast, as he was to take the chaise to join the officers and then leave it with the ladies to make their calls.

"Mr Darcy, do you not think my brother purchased a darling chaise? Louisa and I insisted he needed one."

"It is striking."

"You have a stylish curricle at Pemberley; it is an elegant vehicle. You ought to consider one as well, Charles."

"I would tip it over. Darcy is more of a first-rate whip than I shall ever be, though he would never confess to it."

"Yes, Mr Darcy is a talented driver. He also has a barouche landau if I recall, and—"

"I will now put your horses to, if you are ready." Bingley gestured to the servant, who bowed and left. Miss Bingley bristled at being interrupted and stalked from the room with her sister; Hurst grabbed a roll and stuffed it in his pocket as he left. Darcy felt the remaining occupants exhale a collective sigh of relief.

"Your chaise is a recent purchase?" Miss Bennet asked.

"My sisters demanded it as a note of distinction, but it ought to have been done, and I am pleased with it."

"It is a gentleman's responsibility, after all." Darcy kept his newspaper raised, but stopped reading at the sound of Elizabeth's voice. "There are certain items a gentleman is responsible for purchasing—wines, musical instruments, vehicles. Even books." Darcy lowered his newspaper. "Do these abilities indicate the accomplishments of a well-educated gentleman?"

Bingley laughed. "I cannot say my accomplishments include

buying books, but I trust I purchased a sporting chaise. Also, I am skilled at carving a joint at table."

Miss Bennet smiled. "A critical achievement."

"Yes, it would not do to have your guests go hungry for want of a roasted joint of meat," Elizabeth added. "We have spoken of ladies' accomplishments, but the gentlemen have been left unexamined."

"You have an opinion on the subject, no doubt." Bingley's amusement was clear.

"You begin to comprehend me, do you? Since you insist on hearing my opinion, I shall proceed. Dancing and riding, of course, mark an accomplished gentleman. A command of French, naturally, as well as competency in Latin and Greek. Fencing, cricket, or some other sport is also necessary to be esteemed an accomplished gentleman."

"Let us hope there is more, for I fear that other than my carving skills and dancing, I must be the least accomplished gentleman of your acquaintance!"

Elizabeth turned from Bingley and looked directly into Darcy's eyes, and her lips curled into a smile. "Yes, something more substantial must yet be added; perhaps the capacity for polite conversation?"

After the innuendo of last night's Consequence game and his subsequent self-examination, Darcy could not determine her meaning. *Is she playful or is she sending another veiled message regarding the ways I am found wanting?*

When he remained silent, Elizabeth asked him playfully, "Does this topic hold little interest for you, Mr Darcy? You may select one of your own choosing. After all, an accomplished lady is taught to defer the topic of conversation to the gentleman."

"I expect that often leaves you victim to tedious conversations," he replied.

"I have never suffered such with you."

Their silent look was interrupted when Bingley told them that he intended to see to his correspondence after breakfast. "How will you pass the time, Darcy?"

Darcy had given little thought to the day beyond surviving

breakfast with his dignity intact. "I shall ride into Meryton. I have a letter to post." He hoped Bingley would not offer to send a servant on the errand. An escape from the house and its occupants might settle his mind.

"Did you not say you had letters to post, Lizzy? I know you were eager for a walk."

"I had thought to walk to Meryton."

Darcy looked at Bingley and saw the threads of thought weaving together to form an idea in his mind. He tried not to cringe when the words came.

"Darcy, would you escort Miss Elizabeth to Meryton?"

"I am no horsewoman; I am resolved to walk. Nor do I wish to deny Mr Darcy the enjoyment of a ride."

Darcy did what politeness required and requested to be allowed the honour of accompanying her. Elizabeth stared at him for a moment before consenting. "In that case, I promise not to pay my duty to the shops this visit."

Shopping for silk stockings and ribbons would be a fitting punishment to add to what would be an uncomfortable afternoon.

SHE AND MR DARCY APPROACHED THE LANE THAT LED INTO Meryton in silence. He normally never said a great deal, but Elizabeth wondered at their uncomfortable lack of conversation. She had been quick to anger and eager to injure last night. A week ago, she would have left the trouble of finding a subject to him and not given herself the trouble of talking or listening much if he did. But she was ashamed, and now he would not speak to her.

When they reached the lane, she could no longer tolerate the crushing desire in her heart to confess all. To remain next to Mr Darcy and not speak with him now felt peculiar.

"I must tell you what you will not ask." He looked at her in surprise. "I read your letter to your sister, and there is no excuse for it. Let me assure you that her situation is entirely unknown to me, and I would not speculate about her. I am no gossip."

He looked troubled; she had not wished to embarrass him by speaking candidly, but there was no turning back now. "What is more, I am mortified at how callously I treated you. I thought the worst of you, even after I said all was forgiven from the night of the assembly."

Elizabeth waited for him to answer, but she had either shocked him or angered him so much he could not speak. She felt her cheeks redden in shame. "I am sorry for causing you pain while we played that game. Speaking to you in the manner I did, with the intent of being insolent, merely to protect my wounded pride, is the cruellest thing I have ever done."

"You apologised last night; you need not say it again." There was a dreadful pause before he continued. "I did fear what you might presume about my sister and what rumours could be circulated about her, but no motive can excuse the unjust and ungenerous behaviour I exhibited in turn."

"I provoked you," she immediately replied.

"A gentleman does not insult a lady. Nothing can excuse my cruelty."

"If I can forgive you for calling me not tolerable enough to tempt you to dance, then I can certainly draw on my charitable reserves to forgive you for treating me in the same manner I treated you."

"Do not, Miss Bennet, let your kindness defend what I know your judgment must censure."

"I have done too much judging and thought too highly of my own intellect." She again felt all the shame she had experienced last night. "In a way, I am thankful for the consequence game, for it helped me see myself as I never had before. I did not like what I saw."

"I cannot excuse my offensive and insensitive conduct, even if you are so generous as to forgive me. I lacked any delicacy towards the feelings of another person."

"Perhaps we ought not to quarrel for the greater share of blame annexed last evening. The conduct of neither will be irreproachable."

"I cannot so quickly reconcile myself with my behaviour to you, nor to others. I cannot express my own abhorrence of myself."

Elizabeth glanced up at him, keen to hear him speak openly.

However, he seemed surprised by his own words. "Forgive me, I have said too much. Let us agree that last night's conduct was not to our credit and speak of it no longer."

They continued towards Meryton, and Elizabeth's gaze kept returning to him. His jaw was set and his face was a mask of hauteur, but one careful look at his eyes was enough to tell her that he was not as calm and cool as he believed himself to be.

"Mr Darcy." She stopped and turned to him. "I trust that behind your proud manner, and despite your conduct last night, there is a true goodness to your character. I hope that you have a favourable opinion of me, in spite of my incivility. I hold you in esteem, and if you find something admirable about me"—*aside from my 'fine eyes'*—"then we must put this matter behind us and continue forward in friendship."

"I do not suffer trivial, disinterested friendships. Acquaintances, yes, but friendships are a serious matter." His lips formed a small smile. "Despite our bitter words, I do desire your good opinion."

Elizabeth again felt affectionate feelings towards him. Even Mr Darcy's uncivil behaviour had not driven them away. That he sincerely and eagerly welcomed her friendship produced a significant change in her attitude towards him. He was no longer the proud and rude Mr Darcy, but rather her friend Darcy, whose unreserved conversation, similarity of taste and opinion, and willingness to make amends made him all the more dear to her.

"Then we are in agreement to be friends." Elizabeth held out her hand while her heart fluttered. "Come, shake hands with me."

Mr Darcy's gaze never wavered as he raised his hand and pressed hers gently. The touch of their gloved hands, the slight pressure she applied in return of his tender grasp, was the only indication she could appropriately give to express her regard.

For a moment or two, nothing was said, and Elizabeth was unsuspicious of having excited any particular interest until he drew her arm within his to continue their walk. He gave her a warm smile and said, "Come, let us be friends."

DARCY COULD HARDLY COMPREHEND THAT HE HAD BEEN FORGIVEN,

but he was grateful for it. For that reason alone, he ought to take her reproofs to heart.

To delineate their relationship to the confines of friendship was reassuring. He was bewitched by her, but he could not forget the situation of her family, her lack of connexions and fortune. His behaviour *did* need amending, but that did not mean he could fall in love with her.

"Since you and I are on our way to being friends," she interrupted his reverie, "I am within my rights to say something to you." Her expression grew sombre. "I wish to express my hope that your sister is well. I would not speak of Miss Darcy to anyone but you, and if you wish it, I shall never speak of her again, but I cannot in good conscience go forward without offering you my earnest hope for her happiness."

"I do not doubt your intentions, and you are welcome to ask after her. Georgiana's spirits are not as low as they were, and that gives me reason to hope that in time she will be so much improved as to put an unpleasant episode behind her."

"I wish for that very much. And allow me to suggest that you confine your letter writing to those times when you have privacy. Between my inquisitive eyes and Miss Bingley's admiration of your even hand, you will hardly be able to compose a few lines to Miss Darcy while you remain in the country."

"I am amazed by how quickly your disposition can turn from distress to playfulness."

"I am not made for ill humour, particularly since you and I are determined to be in amity. In that vein, since I read what I ought not to, you are entitled to read the note my sister Mary sent this morning."

"I assure you that is unnecessary."

Elizabeth huffed in exasperation. "You do want for a little more liveliness! I was attempting to cheer you by bantering with you. You ought to endeavour to be more agreeable."

"You cannot believe that liveliness is the same as agreeableness. You shall always be animated, and I shall always be reserved. Do you suppose me to be so lacking in address that I cannot make myself agreeable when I wish it?"

"Not at all. But since you raise the question, why do you not take the trouble of being agreeable?"

"By your tone, I infer that you believe that I am a misanthrope. I do have friends, and you would now count yourself among them. How do you justify your claim that I lack affability if I have befriended you, Bingley, and a score of other intimate acquaintances?"

"A whole *score* of intimate acquaintances? You are a fortunate man. For all my liveliness, I have few affectionate friends."

Darcy rolled his eyes but answered with a smile. "Allow me to amend my statement: I have a small circle of intimate associates whose steady friendship I value; those people, who are of good character, would all tell you I am a congenial man."

"Miss Bingley told Jane that you were remarkably agreeable among your intimate acquaintances, but my impression of you, until recently, was that you are scornful of those who are not of that circle."

Conflicting emotions warred within him: anger at her criticism and surprise at being challenged, balanced by recognition of the truth.

"No, it is not scorn. I am not scornful of..." What did he think of those outside his own circle? "I suppose I have somehow come to think meanly of, of simply all the rest of the world—or rather, think meanly of their sense and worth compared with my own." It was a humbling fact to learn about oneself, and not a state in which a self-respecting man could remain. "As much as I am loath to continue on a path of pride and conceit, I am unsure as to how to amend my behaviour."

"You strike me as the sort of man who, once he arrives at a decision, is already in possession of the force of will to carry it out."

"It is not a matter of will, but a matter of the appropriate action. I have no talent with the sort of amiability I ought to present when speaking with those I have never seen before."

"I do not play the piano in the talented manner that I see many women do. I have always supposed it to be my own fault because I would not take the trouble of practising."

Darcy smiled. "You are perfectly right."

"Yes, you shall prove a delightful friend; tell me I am right, and your worth will be invaluable." Darcy resigned himself to being laughed at. "You shall have to practice being engaging and courteous to those who are unfamiliar to you."

"For the sake of argument, let us assume that there are people one suffers to meet who are unpleasant, whose presence is undesirable for no other reason than they are tiresome. It would be deceitful for me to imply I wish to further the conversation or the acquaintance."

She was silent for just long enough for Darcy to mistakenly assume he had won his point. "If you find someone so tiresome such that you cannot hold a brief yet polite conversation, I am of the opinion the fault lies with you."

His own conduct was once again before him. There was much to blame in it, but he had little he could say. They fell into companionable silence as they completed their errand. Darcy proved himself capable of possessing an obliging nature as Elizabeth made a point to look in every shop window they passed. Darcy suspected he was being punished.

"No doubt you are grateful we have not crossed the threshold of any of these shops," she teased. "I am tempted by everything I see, and I am always very long at a purchase."

"I do not believe it, but by all means, let us go inside. Do you desire a new bonnet? There is one in the next window; it is not pretty, but you might as well buy it as not."

Elizabeth turned from the window displaying the dreadful hat, her eyes full of mirth. "I concede! I could never buy an ugly bonnet, even for the gratification of having you carry it. Let us return to Netherfield."

He gratefully led them in the opposite way down the street and observed a man on the other side take notice of Elizabeth.

"Is that gentleman known to you?"

"That is Mr Denny; he is also known to *you*. You have dined with him along with the other officers."

"Their conversation is all the same; I hardly know one from the other."

"Let us greet him. This is a perfect opportunity for you to practice."

Darcy resisted his natural disinclination. They crossed the street, and Mr Denny bowed. "Good day."

Elizabeth remained silent. She adjusted her grip on her reticule and lightly touched his arm, and Darcy knew she expected him to reply. *Behave in a gentlemanlike manner.*

He touched his hat. "Good day, Mr Denny. I trust you are well?"

"Yes, thank you. I was in town; I have just alighted from my carriage at the posting inn."

Darcy silently begged Elizabeth to speak, but he would not be granted a reprieve. *What would I say if this were an influential, titled gentleman from my club?* "I trust your business was conducted to your satisfaction?"

"Indeed it was, how kind of you to enquire. Also, I renewed my acquaintance with a gentleman who, I am happy to say, has accepted a commission in our corps. May I make him known to you?" Elizabeth nodded. "He is there, leaving the inn." Mr Denny looked over Darcy and Elizabeth's shoulders, raising his arm to beckon his friend.

"You need to overcome your reserve to be agreeable, but I applaud your first effort," Elizabeth whispered.

"I shall never share your enjoyment of company, particularly of an unknown person," he murmured.

"You need not fear; we are not meeting a single lady who will set her cap on you. We are meeting a gentleman who is to join the militia; how is there any harm in that?"

Chapter 8

Elizabeth chose not to tease Darcy about his reluctance to make the acquaintance of Mr Denny's friend. She had no wish to inhibit him after a promising beginning. He had said to Mr Denny everything that was correct; behaving within the bounds of propriety was not a challenge. What he lacked was unaffectedness.

The dear, reserved man must now form a new acquaintance. She offered him a smile of reassurance, aware that he was attempting to be more cordial for her sake as much as his own. He would never be a gregarious man, but she liked Darcy, and she admired his intelligence and his honesty.

Mr Denny's friend approached from behind them, and Elizabeth turned to take notice of him. His appearance was in his favour: a fine countenance, a good figure, and a ready smile. The stranger looked at her with a degree of admiration, which she could not be insensible of, and stood next to Mr Denny.

Elizabeth heard a sharp inhalation and saw the sudden astonishment on Darcy's face darken into some severe, forbidding emotion. Although she stood a foot apart from him, she felt his entire body stiffen with tension and saw his face turn red. Elizabeth looked in time to see the cheerful countenance of Mr Denny's friend collapse and all colour drain from his face.

Mr Denny was either ignorant to these goings-on or chose to disregard them, and introduced them.

Mr Wickham flinched as though afraid he was about to be struck. Darcy radiated such ferocity that Elizabeth feared that might happen. Elizabeth curtseyed, and Mr Wickham inclined his head and then raised his eyes to Darcy. He swallowed thickly and, after a moment, touched his hat, a salutation that Darcy just deigned to return.

"We are acquainted," Mr Wickham murmured.

"I was informing Miss Bennet and Mr Darcy of your intention to accept a commission to be a lieutenant in our corps."

There stood Mr Wickham, taking an interest in his own boots; there was Darcy, who looked murderous; and there was Mr Denny, several cognitive steps behind the others, only now furrowing his brows in confusion. Elizabeth felt suddenly protective of Darcy. There was, obviously, a history between them that precluded any civility.

"I am certain we are wanted back at Netherfield. It was a pleasure to make your acquaintance, Mr Wickham. Mr Denny." Both gentlemen bowed, but Darcy stared furiously at Mr Wickham, whose face was still white.

"Darcy," she spoke quietly. The fury in his expression softened when he heard his name and turned from Mr Wickham to look at her. She put one hand on his arm and raised her other to press his hand, but before her smile could widen, his tender expression was gone. He tucked her arm under his and strode down the street, tugging her along as fast as her legs could carry her.

Whilst Elizabeth was not unaccustomed to walking at a brisk pace, Darcy's stride was long, and she went from being escorted to veritably dragged.

"Is there a reason you keep looking at me?" he brusquely asked after they had been marching for a quarter of a mile.

"No, I did not know I was; it was unconsciously done."

They sank into silence and soon approached a stone wall. Elizabeth dropped his arm so he could cross the stile, but instead of pausing after he crossed to hand her down, Darcy continued to stalk towards Netherfield. She hardly needed a gentleman to aid her in stepping over a stile, but they could not go on this way. She could not maintain his pace the entire two miles back to Netherfield.

Elizabeth stood at the base of the stile while Darcy continued through the field. Surely he would notice that the woman he had been charged with chaperoning was no longer on his arm. Ten feet became twenty feet. She was beginning to believe he would continue to walk all the way to Netherfield without her when he whirled around.

"When Mr Bingley asked you to escort me to Meryton, it was implied that you would also escort me back!" she called.

Darcy closed his eyes and stood still, the cool breeze whipping his greatcoat behind him. He looked weary and not at all as proud and noble as he appeared the night of the assembly. She wondered how often Darcy ever laughed, if at all.

He covered the distance between them and remained on the other side of the wall, holding out his hand. Elizabeth took it and crossed the stile.

"I am sorry." Instead of walking on, Darcy leaned back on his elbows against the stone and tilted his head towards the sky. Elizabeth could not ask him about the encounter in Meryton, no matter how much she might have wished it. After reading his private letter, to press him would be inexcusable.

What could be the meaning of it? She put aside her inquisitiveness and did what she would have done for Jane or Charlotte: she stood next to Darcy and offered her silent companionship. After the passage of several minutes, where Elizabeth kept her questioning eyes away from Darcy, the deep timbre of his voice interrupted their silence.

"You are determined, I see, to have no curiosity."

"I am determined to act in the manner that would bring the most consolation to my friend."

He heaved a sigh and crossed his arms over his chest. "There is so little of real friendship in the world." Elizabeth did not know what to say.

Darcy nodded as though coming to a decision. "I believe it is beneath me to lay my private actions open to the world. But if my pride was mistaken before, then I cannot continue in that vein if your acquaintance with Mr Wickham cannot be avoided; you ought to know his worthlessness. At the least, I might hope that you, and your intimates, will be informed enough of his true character as to make it impossible for any woman of character to confide in him. Or," he added quietly, "to love him."

Elizabeth found her interest in the subject increase and listened with all her heart.

"Mr Wickham was a companion of my youth, the godson of my father, and the son of a respectable man who had the management of the Pemberley estates. My father supported him at school and afterwards at Cambridge. My father had the highest opinion of him, and, hoping the church would be his profession, intended to provide for him in it."

Darcy paced. "As for myself, it is many years since I first thought of Mr Wickham in a different manner. The *vicious* propensities, the *want* of principle, which he was careful to guard from the knowledge of my father, could not escape my observation."

Elizabeth listened while Darcy described the legacy his father left for Mr Wickham and the living intended for him, that Mr Wickham was resolved against taking orders and claimed to wish to study the law and sought compensation in lieu of the living. Darcy had known such an immoral man ought not to be a clergyman, and was relieved to have an honourable way of redirecting his father's bequest. Mr Wickham resigned all claim to assistance in the church and accepted in return three thousand pounds.

"I thought too ill of him to invite him to Pemberley or admit his society in town. His studying the law was a mere pretence, and his was a life of idleness and dissipation. For three years, I heard little of him; but on the deccase of the incumbent of the living which had been designed for him, he had the audacity to apply to me again by letter for the presentation."

"Good heavens! You refused, did you not?"

"I refused both it and any repetition of its kind. Mr Wickham's resentment of me was in proportion to the distress of his circumstances, which was of course very bad if he spent three thousand pounds in three years and owed more. He was doubtless as violent in his abuse of me to others as in his reproaches to me."

Elizabeth believed Darcy as a trustworthy man of a month's acquaintance and her new friend. Yet something in his manner made her wonder if there was more to the story. "I am surprised you would go so far as to ask me to turn away from an acquaintance with this man."

Darcy, who had paced as he told his tale, stopped before her.

"I confessed these dealings so you, and your sisters, are not swayed by that man's happy manners." His voice was clipped. "Let me speak candidly. From the moment George Wickham could discern the difference between the sexes and read the numbers on a playing card, there have been ruined women and mounting debts left in his wake."

Elizabeth gasped; her surprise made Darcy remember himself, and when he spoke again, it was with more politeness. "I hope you would rely on my experience to preserve you from a disagreeable acquaintance."

"I shall keep your warnings close to my mind, but I have been too hasty in the past to censure those of whom I have but a slight acquaintance, as you sadly know. I shall decide for myself. Was there more that you ought to tell me?"

"How do you mean?" Darcy's eyes were sharply observing her.

Elizabeth realised the indelicacy of pressing him. "I shall not compel you, but do not expect me to believe that your reaction to meeting Mr Wickham was only because he is a dissolute man."

Darcy crossed the distance between them, caught her hand, and cradled it within his. "I cannot say more. I wish I could, but it is out of my power." His earnestness was unmistakable. "I implore you: be cautious of Mr Wickham."

Elizabeth nodded, and both of them looked at their joined hands. It was an impulsive gesture, and an intimate one at that. Darcy blinked, placed her hand on his arm, and they walked on together.

He is going to dwell in anger as he considers his history with this Mr Wickham. "Must we continue in silence, ruminating on the character flaws of the militia's newest lieutenant?"

"You will forgive me if I am not in a suitable frame of mind for conversation."

"I disagree; you are in need of a distraction. If you do not name a topic, I will be forced to speak about muslin and shoe-roses."

"While we walk, perhaps you will tell me about your sisters." After a pause, he added, with a small smile, "Since you have already read so much of my sister."

"What do you mean?" she replied with mock surprise, enjoying his dry humour. "To be sure, all I know of Miss Darcy is that you say she is shy."

"I should prefer to listen and learn more of you than to speak at present."

She strove to speak lightly and not tease or provoke him. "Our temperaments are by no means alike, but my sisters share a mutual affection. Lydia is the youngest; she is fifteen, with a great deal of natural self-consequence. Her greatest concern is whether or not she has enough partners for dancing. Kitty is the next youngest and follows Lydia in all things. I could not say what Kitty enjoys other than dancing and flirting. Although, if she chose a superior example to follow, Kitty might be less dull."

"Perhaps your youngest sisters ought not to have been brought into public so young?"

Elizabeth laughed. "This is the country, not town. It is a natural progression from dancing at home to attending the monthly assembly. If we had to wait until the elder daughters were married, it would not promote sisterly affection."

"That is a relaxed perspective on what it means to be out, but I shall not argue with you."

Fitzwilliam Darcy chose not to argue his point? He is troubled by this morning's events. She prattled on about her family in the hopes of distracting him.

"Mary prefers to keep her mornings to herself and her attempts at accomplishments. She rarely speaks unless she is quoting from one of her extracts." She shook her head in disappointment. "My mother is desperate to see her daughters settled since Longbourn is entailed and she cannot support us when my father is dead. And my father refuses to restrain the improprieties of his wife or youngest daughters so he can laugh at them. I often cringe at their behaviour."

Such thoughts distressed her. It was easier to overlook her family's conduct since she could not change it. She realised Darcy was looking at her intently and grew embarrassed. "I do not know what comes over me in your presence; I seem to be honest to a fault!"

"If what you say is true, your concern is not unfounded. An individual is judged by the value of one's family, and bad behaviour on the part of one member may tarnish the reputation and position of all its members."

She had never considered that anyone could hold her family's conduct against *her*. The familiar twinges of shame at their behaviour pressed on her mind. "Be that as it may, it was an uncharitable thing to say about one's family. Thank goodness Jane is not here. Her sense of honour does not allow her to speak an unkind word against anyone."

"What can you tell me of the character of your eldest sister?"

She thought this a rather direct question, but Jane was a subject on which she would be happy to elucidate. "Jane has a kindness and a gentleness that I will never have. She loves everybody, is interested in everybody's happiness, and quick-sighted to everybody's merits."

"And is wilfully blind to their faults?"

"No, not deliberately, but she has a pure inability to observe the worthlessness or nonsense of others. I have never heard Jane speak ill of another human being in all my life."

She looked at Darcy, expecting him to say more, but he was silent and distracted. *He is still thinking about Mr Wickham. At least he does not appear as angry as he did in Meryton.*

They reached a fence separating one field from the next, and Darcy crossed the stile and reached back to hand her down. Elizabeth tried her best to appear unmoved when his fingers curled around her own. When she reached the other side, she smiled to show her thanks before they set off again. As he returned her smile, she felt herself flush.

"Your family situation is different, I imagine," Elizabeth said, acting unaffected. "You have one sister whereas I have four, and your titled connexions are greater than mine."

"Connexions to people of rank aside, I agree my situation is dissimilar to yours. An only son, for many years an only child, I was spoiled by my parents. I was provided with whatever I desired as though I was entitled not based on my conduct but by my station. Although it ultimately encouraged me to be selfish, being an only son also made me conscientious, forward-looking, and responsible."

After she accepted the truth of those positive attributes, an amusing idea came to Elizabeth. She tried to remember Darcy's temperament, but a chuckle escaped. He raised an eyebrow as he looked at her.

"It is natural that as a beloved, nearly only child, you were spoiled by your parents. I laugh because you have something in common with Lydia: both of you were spoiled and overindulged!"

"Let us end that distressing conversation now." Darcy spoke with his usual gravity, but Elizabeth knew not to be offended by his manner. At least he allowed her a brief laugh at his expense.

"Very well, sir, I would be delighted to defer to your preference for our next topic." Elizabeth batted her eyelids and offered a submissive, unemotional smile. To her surprise, instead of an amused reaction, her attempt at soliciting his opinion in the manner of the *ton's* marriageable young ladies made Darcy recoil.

"Never look on me that way again. Is that another skill of a lady who is deemed accomplished? Do all mothers instil in their daughters the talent for excessive attention to a gentleman's preferences?"

"I cannot say it is so in my own case. My mother did not insist on her daughters being accomplished in spite of incapacity or distaste, and so I was allowed to leave off both drawing and affected pandering to single gentlemen."

Darcy only smiled; it was genuine and reached his eyes, but she was hoping to hear him laugh.

"I was a trial to my mother, I suspect. I was fond of boys' play and preferred them to dolls."

"You would have me believe you shirked your lessons to play ball with the neighbourhood boys?"

"I never shirked my lessons, but I preferred to be out of doors.

Moreover, my mother said I was noisy, and I hated cleanliness." Elizabeth smiled at the memory. "I preferred games with a ball and running about the country at twelve to curling my hair and attending balls."

"Given that description, I fail to see how the transformation from tomboy to respectable young lady took place."

"I shall tell you precisely how it happened: my mother brought Jane out when I was fourteen, and a curiosity about finery finally overcame my deep affection for dirt."

An unfamiliar sound filled her ears: Darcy was laughing. He laughed in a deep, jovial way. His boyish smile, combined with the warmth of his laugh, sent a shiver down her spine.

"I know what you are doing: you mean to distract and amuse me, and I thank you for it. I confess, however, that I disbelieve part of your narrative, for I observed how you appeared when you arrived in the breakfast room last Wednesday," he said with a knowing smile.

"Darcy, if you had known me when I was younger, you would have been impressed it was *only* my petticoats that were covered in mud."

His smile deepened again into laughter, and Elizabeth joined him with her own delighted burst of amusement.

Chapter 9

*E*lizabeth had called him by his name. *Darcy.* She had touched his hand and gently said his name—only his last name—to reassure him that the distressing encounter with Wickham was over. It felt entirely appropriate to grant her that intimacy. To hear her call him *Darcy* perfectly matched the relationship he felt they shared.

Although this strengthening affinity, this friendship, was heartily welcome, it did not mean he could relate to her the matter of Georgiana and Wickham. *I will conceal that unhappy truth forever.* Nonetheless, the confession of Wickham's more general misdeeds could be made. He could not allow his pride to get in the way of protecting susceptible young ladies, but Georgiana's concern with Wickham was never to be spoken of.

Even if Elizabeth fears being too critical after her past mistakes, with my advice in her mind, I need not fear for her.

Darcy now sat with his letters in the library with Bingley, but his mind wandered back to Elizabeth. She was articulate and opinionated, and though her individuality might not leave some gentlemen with a good impression of her, he found it a great attraction. Her femininity was unique; she was not passive or obligingly attentive, but instead witty and outspoken. She made him laugh. *No other woman has made me laugh out loud*!

"... if you would?" Bingley interrupted his thoughts.

"Forgive me, I did not hear you."

"I asked if you would look over this letter. I need to be in town next Wednesday, and I want to arrange my business before I arrive."

The blots nearly outnumbered the words. *Was that Tattersall or tattered?* If he meant Tattersall's, then those scribbles that looked like 'house' were 'horse'. Either Bingley wanted to see horseflesh on Wednesday in order to buy a new pair of horses when the market was open on Thursday, or he wanted to be hasteful for a wedding in order to buy new poor houses when the mender was open at Tonbridge.

"For those who believe poor handwriting is the mark of a true gentleman, you must be the paradigm."

"How do you mean?"

"Your handwriting is too small, you left out half of your words, and there are more blots than nouns and verbs all together."

"My handwriting may not be large, but it is clear, I thank you. I wanted your opinion on the *content*."

"You misspelt the name of your own house."

"Give it here!" Bingley pulled the sheet from his hand. He read it and then gave a bashful smile. "I could rewrite it."

"Shall I rule your lines for you?"

Bingley's immediate refusal made Darcy smile. The door then opened, and the Miss Bennets entered with workbaskets in hand.

Sooner than Darcy could rise, Bingley sprang up, bowed, and crossed the room to greet them.

"May I say how pleased I am to see you? Miss Bennet, I hope you are feeling well? Miss Elizabeth, if you are in search of another book, may I again offer Darcy's services?"

"Thank you, but we do not wish to disturb you," Miss Bennet replied in her gentle way. "My sister and I had hoped to work here. There is not enough light in the breakfast room this late in the afternoon, and since Miss Bingley is away, I did not wish to ask for a fire to be set in another room."

"It is my fault," Elizabeth interjected. "I have spent most of my mornings in Jane's sitting room and, lovely as it is, I am desperate to spend time inside different walls."

"By all means, I must have you join us. Come sit, please, here, by the fire." Bingley tripped over his words in his enthusiasm.

Darcy returned to his letters. If he intended to remain at Netherfield until going down to Pemberley with Georgiana before Christmas, then there was work to be done.

"I have taken Darcy away from his business with my applications for his assistance with my orthography," Bingley explained.

"Mr Darcy is all goodwill," Elizabeth said. Darcy's heart skipped a beat. "My sister and I are attempting our own mission of generosity; November is half gone, and my charity basket is nearly empty."

"Lizzy and I give blankets, clothes, and baby things to our tenants' families. We intend to deliver them before Christmas."

"I ought to be farther ahead," Elizabeth added, "considering I prefer to engage in useful rather than fine work. It is the only time I use a needle with any eagerness."

Darcy gave a nod of approval. The Bennets were the principal inhabitants of the village of Longbourn, and it was appropriate for the ladies to see to their needs.

For the next half hour, the group worked in companionable silence. Bingley recopied his letter to Tattersall's while Miss Bennet worked on a shawl and Elizabeth sewed what looked to Darcy to be an infant's dress. However, when Bingley was finished, his cheerfulness would not let him remain silent while two pretty ladies were nearby. Darcy attempted to ignore them as he calculated Pemberley's operating expenses.

"Your visits of charity to the village," Bingley said to Miss Bennet, "is further evidence of an accomplished lady."

"It is our duty as Christians to take care of the less fortunate."

"That is not your sole reason," Elizabeth offered. "You are incapable of standing by when another is suffering. Notions of duty aside, you would deliver food and clothes because of your generous nature."

Darcy looked up to see Miss Bennet's blush and Bingley's earnest attention. Soon, their conversation shifted to the upcoming ball: the necessary arrangements, the eagerness the young people would show for dancing, and the invitations to be dispatched. Darcy attended to his own matters until he heard Bingley mention the officers.

He could spend the entire afternoon dwelling on the many reasons why he detested George Wickham, but there was work to be done. He did not look up from his calculations until a shadow crossed over his light. Elizabeth stood by the window nearest to him. She spoke quietly, with her gaze on the grounds. "What say you to the prospect of the officers at the ball?"

She was worried for him. He was surprised by how moved he was by her thoughtfulness. "When there is a ball in view, there is a great deal of insensibility to other things," he replied humorously.

"It appears you have a great deal of sensible things to occupy your attention." Elizabeth gestured to the foolscap with notations next to his pile of correspondence.

"Nothing odious, I assure you. Have you completed your charitable responsibilities?"

"Sadly no. I am better at visiting the villagers to learn what is needed and delivering that to them than sitting long enough at my work to accomplish much." She archly added, "And how does a proper landowner such as yourself compete with the good works of the accomplished, compassionate ladies you see before you?"

"I do what any landowner ought to do to preserve the public good throughout the year. I supply food, medicine, clothing, and funds to those in need at Christmas, but also in times of poor harvest or sickness."

"You are generous."

"That is what they tell me in January and June on rent day."

"Perhaps they tell you that in the hope that you do not raise their rent." Her impertinent smile was replaced by a more thoughtful look. "Your tenants speak to you directly and not to your steward?"

"Of course. They are all invited to the house, and I dine with them. They have an opportunity to represent their concerns. Often there are requests for deductions on their rent, but I also learn what needs to be done—such as land that has not been drained—or I am made aware of difficulties, such as the price of wool being too low. I am too concerned for the good of those who live under my care not to speak with them directly."

"You are a liberal man. Your servants and tenants must give you a good name." She looked as though she approved of him. When Elizabeth was present, nothing and no one else seemed to matter. It both frightened him and delighted him.

The lady responsible for his heart palpitations had no idea of the effect she had. She walked to her sister and said, "I shall go to your sitting room and read until we must dress for dinner."

Miss Bennet said, "I shall join you, Lizzy. I have done all I can in this light."

Bingley parted from them with as much attention as if they were leaving the country altogether. After he allowed them to leave, he threw himself into the chair nearest to Darcy and sighed. "I have never seen so lovely a face as I have on Miss Bennet. She is a beautiful girl."

"That is a rather common cant of phrase."

"I shall explain: her smile is sweet and attractive, and I have seldom seen a face or figure more pleasing to me than hers. She is a charming creature. I cannot conceive of an angel more beautiful."

"Are you attracted more strongly by person than by mind?"

"Miss Bennet has a gentle sense of propriety, that true delicacy that one seldom meets. She is a thoughtful girl. I admire her devotion to the well-being of those of her village. I think, Darcy, that among her other qualities, she would be the one to make this area and all about it a dearer object to me than it could be otherwise."

Darcy's years of proper comportment prevented him from speaking the first thing that came to his mind: *You cannot believe that a pretty face and a generous heart are the sole qualifications for a suitable wife!*

"I did not know you were considering entering the married state."

"It is not as if it is one of those things that one can plan for."

"I disagree. I would not wish for you to be taken in by a woman who feels nothing for you. I admit, Miss Bennet does not appear to be a calculating woman, but I suspect her mother may be."

"You fail to consider that Miss Bennet might return my affections."

"She is so ..." *Placid? Unremarkable?* "Serene. She has an amiable temper, but I can see no indication her heart has been touched. Yet she might accept you despite that in light of the material advantages you can provide."

"You would have me believe that of Miss Bennet?" Bingley laughed. "If you can believe that of her, she of such gentleness and modesty, it explains why you are not married. You are too suspicious."

"I am pragmatic. Marriage is a business in which people expect the most from others and are least honest themselves. It is not every man's fate to marry the woman who loves him best."

"Your argument is irrelevant if Miss Bennet returns my interest. And you have told me nothing to convince me that she does not."

He had been too absorbed by Netherfield's younger resident Miss Bennet to be an acute observer of the elder. "She is a pretty girl, no doubt with modesty, taste, and feeling, but is she not generous to everyone? Does Miss Bennet have a particular affection for you?"

"I have spent a great deal of time in her company these past two days. I had believed that she returned my attentions with sincere regard." Bingley's usual cheerfulness was gone, and he looked pensive.

Darcy considered reminding him of those unrefined relations that an alliance with Miss Bennet would bring, but decided against it. *I shall observe her more closely before speaking.* He had vowed, when he made amends with Elizabeth, to act with more delicacy in regard to the feelings of others. "Your judgment on the matter must, of course, be better than mine. But may I recommend you proceed slowly?"

"I am always willing to consider your opinion. But I will not wait as long as you to marry. You shall be eight-and-twenty not long after the new year?" Darcy nodded. "What are you waiting for?"

"I am of a cautious temper and unwilling to risk my happiness. I have never met a lady to whom I wished to be married." Darcy did his best to keep his voice from wavering as he spoke the last.

Chapter 10

*E*lizabeth finished dressing for their last dinner at Netherfield and was turning the pages of Cowper while Jane gazed at her reflection. Jane was shapely with blue eyes, light hair, beautiful features, and a look of great sweetness. Elizabeth never envied her sister's advantages, for who could hold nature's gifts against such a kind-hearted soul?

"You look handsome—and it is a good thing, since I saw a young man looking at you earnestly in the library today."

"You can never tell her, but I am grateful my mother insisted I ride to Netherfield. The opportunity to have so much conversation with Mr Bingley might not have otherwise presented itself. And I am grateful to you for consenting to stay on. It has been a pleasure to enjoy Mr Bingley's company now that I am well."

"He is a good-humoured host."

"Mr Bingley is so much more than that! He is cheerful in his civilities, unreserved in his manner with so much ease and perfect good breeding. He was genuinely concerned for my health and comfort, and he took great interest in our charity work in the village. I believe Mr Bingley has a true tenderness of disposition."

Elizabeth only gave her sister an expressive smile, and Jane fiddled with a green ribbon, fraying its edges. "You have provoked me to speak too openly."

"Forgive me, please?" Elizabeth took the ribbon from Jane's hands and forced her to meet her eye. "I laugh too much, but do not take it to imply that your feelings are not natural. Mr Bingley has unaffected manners and a pleasant countenance, as I am sure you could not help but notice. I give you leave to like him." She prompted Jane to stand and tied her sash.

"Do you suppose he might…do you suppose Mr Bingley's feelings equal mine?"

"You must suspect he is over head and ears in love with you."

"I am certain of the degree of my own regard, but until I can say for certain of *his*, I shall not speak further on the matter."

"There is not a better kind of girl in the world than you, or one who more deserves a good husband. And I think Mr Bingley would make you a good sort of husband."

They arrived early to the drawing room. Jane admired the watercolours on the wall, but Elizabeth was lost in thought. Mr Bingley was young, handsome, and agreeable, though perhaps not as steady as Jane. Unbidden thoughts came to her mind about the steadiness and character of Mr Bingley's friend. When Elizabeth had stood near Darcy's side in the library, she had seen his notations and calculations. She tried to reassure herself of the accident of seeing them, and Darcy's likely perfect unconcern. What she had observed was that Pemberley's income from rent and dividends from other investments was greater than its expenses.

Recognising that he cared deeply for both his home and its people placed him in an amiable light. He might be proud, but Darcy was not the sort of young man who thought of nothing but himself. Her attention was then attracted by the arrival of Darcy and Mr Bingley. The object of her thoughts asked if she was still reading Cowper.

"I finished *The Time Piece*. It is unfortunate that we leave Netherfield tomorrow without my having the chance to read the succeeding books."

"You are welcome to borrow the next volume and take it to Longbourn."

"Thank you. It is rare that my father allows me time in his library. He is unwilling to share his space of leisure and tranquillity in a house full of women."

"I would be pleased to supply you while I remain in the neighbourhood," he replied, his usual gravity softened by his smile. He was reserved, but behind it all, Darcy was a generous man.

They spent several minutes in pleasant conversation with Jane and their host, with Elizabeth and Mr Bingley carrying most of the weight. She was feeling a comfortable familiarity between the four of them when that ease was shattered by the arrival of Miss Bingley and the Hursts.

Miss Bingley attached herself to Darcy, expressing her regret for not seeing him since breakfast, enquiring after his health, and making it impossible for him to speak to anyone but her. They made their way, with formal procession, to the dining room, where for the first half an hour Miss Bingley and Mrs Hurst regaled their company with commentary on their morning calls. Elizabeth did not speak at all until after the first remove, when Miss Bingley asked, "Miss Eliza, you must be looking forward to returning home. It will be satisfying to return to the bosom of your own family."

"As it happens, I have had a note from Longbourn that says we shall have a houseguest of our own."

"May I ask if this person is your relation?" said Mr Bingley.

"Yes, it is, but it is a person whom I never saw in my life."

Jane added, "Our sister writes that my father's cousin and heir has become ordained and intends on arriving this evening to wait on our family. His father and mine had a longstanding disagreement, but he now wishes to heal the breach."

"What are his connexions?" asked Mrs Hurst.

"All I know of Mr Collins is what my sister Mary wrote in her note. She states his name, but the whole of her commentary was that his idea of offering some sort of amends for being next in the entail was well-expressed."

"What can he mean by apologising for being next in the entail? That is not sensible," said Darcy.

"Though it is difficult," said Jane, "to guess in what way he can mean to make us the atonement he thinks our due, the wish is to his credit."

Mr Bingley agreed with her, and nothing more was said on the matter while they remained at the table. However, when the ladies withdrew, Miss Bingley broached the topic.

"Oh, consider it, Jane," she said with a grin, "perhaps this man who will inherit Longbourn has a particular motive in seeking reconciliation with your family."

"I do not understand."

"Your father's heir must be in want of a wife. And, with apologies to Miss Eliza, you, as the eldest and most handsome, must be his choice."

"Miss Bingley, could not the same to be said of your brother?" Elizabeth was eager to redirect her. "He is an amiable young man who must be ready to exchange his solitary evenings for the society of a lovely wife."

Jane flushed while Miss Bingley and Elizabeth glared at one another. There was no doubt in Elizabeth's mind as to Miss Bingley's intentions to keep Jane from her brother.

"I am certain my brother is in no hurry to enter the matrimonial state. This Mr Collins is a practical option. The Bennet ladies ought to consider his suit since, as I understand it, he might turn you all out of Longbourn when your father is dead."

"I would rather he turn us out of the house as soon as he pleases rather than marry without affection."

"A marriage must bring good connexions, not affection. Marriage to the heir of your home would be to the credit of all of you. I wish to advocate for what would be to the advantage of my newest friend." She gave Jane's hand a little pat.

Elizabeth felt a righteous anger on her sister's behalf. "And what about the importance of the sensibilities and opinions of both parties? To pursue a man for the sake of situation shocks me."

"Then I pity you. You ought not to take a romantic, limited view on the matter, since those from low connexions such as yours already have so little chance of marrying well."

Oh, to be able to say exactly what I think of Caroline Bingley!

To think she had once thought Darcy lacked delicacy towards the feelings of others.

Before Elizabeth could offer a reply more civil than her hostess deserved, the gentlemen returned. Mr Bingley sat across from Jane and his younger sister, but before he spoke more than two words, Miss Bingley called to Mr Darcy.

"We were speaking of the importance of a marriage bringing about good connexions. Do you agree?"

"Certainly."

"You see, Miss Eliza, Mr Darcy and I are of the same opinion," she crowed. "You place too great a value on romantic affection. What is essential is a comfortable tolerance among two people of equal character and position in order to make a marriage an agreeable establishment."

Elizabeth wondered if Miss Bingley had accurately expressed the opinions she had applied to Darcy. "You and Mr Darcy are entitled to your opinion, but I feel that anything is to be preferred or endured rather than marrying without affection."

Miss Bingley and Mrs Hurst snickered. Darcy was watching the proceedings, with arms crossed over his chest. She suspected he was amused by Miss Bingley, but then Elizabeth wondered if this was true or if she *wished* it to be.

"Miss Eliza, as you ought to know, one must make proper allowances for worldly advantage."

"Caroline, wealth or grandeur are not the only means of attaining happiness. What is necessary to one person might be readily sacrificed by another." Mr Bingley was not one to enjoy an argument. "May we not agree that a large income may well be the best recipe for one's happiness while another might desire a spouse with a warm heart and a sweet temper?"

"Yes, but one should not forego the chance of benefiting him or herself and their family by marrying well." Miss Bingley's gaze went to the gentleman standing in front of the fireplace.

"I did not suggest one ought not to consider marrying well should the opportunity present itself." Elizabeth was struggling to keep her tone even. "I propose that mutual love is at least as important a factor as connexions and fortune."

"Mutual *respect* may be important, but the necessity of being advantageously married cannot be understated. Mr Darcy, I must hear your opinion on the matter."

"I would rather be happily married than well married."

"Of course one wishes to be happily married!" replied his faithful assistant. "I feel sorry for Miss Eliza's impractical romantic delicacy. It is idealistic to place too great a value on love, and I am sure as a well-educated man of the world you must agree."

"You have mistaken my meaning. How could you imagine me an advocate for marriage without love?" Elizabeth bit her lip to keep from laughing outright at the sight of Miss Bingley's red face. Darcy's expression was unreadable, and when it became clear that he had shocked their hostess into silence, he bowed, crossed the room to select a book and settled into a chair.

The amiable Mr Bingley leapt into the stillness. "Yes, I cannot imagine marrying a woman I could not like. Miss Bennet, you prefer Vingt-un to Commerce? Does anyone care to join us? Caroline, may I prevail upon you for some music?"

Elizabeth sat at her work while Mr and Mrs Hurst joined the game. Miss Bingley chose a song that required the sort of assertive percussive sound that her feelings likely currently required. As uncharitable as it was, Elizabeth felt satisfaction in observing Darcy subdue Miss Bingley's insolent spirit.

It was clear to Elizabeth that Miss Bingley saw herself as Mrs Darcy, with all the advantages associated with that position, regardless of Darcy's feelings. Elizabeth now was certain Miss Bingley's dislike of her had originated in jealousy. Miss Bingley knew Darcy admired her eyes and had watched their conversations with a possessive, envious glare.

I am not rich or grand enough for him, so Miss Bingley may rest easy. Gentlemen such as Darcy were not likely to offer to a woman beneath him in consequence. In the library on Saturday, Darcy had quipped that he required a dowry of fifty thousand pounds and several titled connexions, but he did not truly aim too high.

I cannot deny that I think highly of him, that I like him. She had no reason to doubt the sincerity of his friendship, but their rank, fortune, and prospects were separated by a chasm of disparity. She grew more affected as she felt all the distance between Darcy and herself.

It is no concern of mine which heiress Darcy chooses as his wife. I wish him happy.

Elizabeth shook off her distraction and rose to refresh herself by taking a turn around the room.

DARCY STARED AT THE VOLUME IN HIS LAP, TURNING A PAGE EVERY few minutes, never reading a word. His eyes hurt from suppressing the desire to raise them to look at Elizabeth. Although he did not know the details of their exchange, Miss Bingley's dislike for Elizabeth must have culminated before the gentlemen returned. And yet she dealt with Miss Bingley's incivility without being uncivil in return. He admired her for it.

He had meant it when he said he preferred to be happily married, but the idea that reciprocated love would bring him *the most* happiness was new. Romantic sentiments that had once sounded idealistic now seemed perfectly rational. It impressed him that a woman from meagre connexions and fortune would not consider those advantages unless she held affection for the suitor. It spoke to Elizabeth's integrity.

A flash of yellow crossed his vision: Elizabeth walking to the window and staring into the night. The drawing room was fully lit, and there were no lights on Netherfield's lawn; there was nothing outside Elizabeth could see. Perhaps Miss Bingley's rudeness affected her more than he realised.

His attention was captivated by how her curls had been piled high on her head, exposing her neck and shoulders. One small brunette curl had escaped its pin and was dangling behind her ear, and Darcy stifled the desire to cross the room and spiral the ringlet between his fingers.

Her face, her voice, her laugh; everything about her is lovely.

He could envision it perfectly: the two of them entirely alone. He could see himself walk up behind Elizabeth and slip one arm around her waist, the other tracing his fingertips across her shoulder and down her arm. Darcy imagined pressing his lips against her skin, moving down the gentle curve of her neck towards her shoulder. The thought that she might lean into him, if he were to wrap his arms around her now, sent his blood coursing through his veins.

Stop it! There are five other people in the room!

She still appeared troubled. Elizabeth had shown him kindness and patience this morning after his encounter with Wickham; he must return the favour. He wanted to be of use to her, and a gesture of friendship would be more appropriate than his futile lusting.

Darcy walked to the window next to the one Elizabeth was looking through. He gave every appearance of looking out into the night and listening to Miss Bingley's Scottish airs. "Are you certain you do not feel a great inclination of dancing a reel?"

This elicited an arched eyebrow. "I fear such a boisterous dance would not be in line with your tastes, Darcy."

"I am not interested in my own preferences, but instead am inquiring after yours." Darcy did not know how to best express his wish of being of comfort to her.

She smiled; it did not reach her eyes. "We need either one more gentleman or lady to dance a reel. If she could, Miss Bingley would split herself in two to both dance with you and exhibit for you on the piano."

Only years of proper behaviour allowed him to contain his laugh at Caroline Bingley's expense. Before he thought of a suitable reply, Elizabeth spoke. "You forget that we are friends now. I would never compel you to dance anything that might be construed as less than genteel."

She was trying to be playful, but her heart was not in it. What could he say to make her smile? "Perhaps a cotillion would be more suitable? However, we are still short on dancers; it is such a shame that gentlemen always seem to be scarce," he said with a raised eyebrow. If it cheered Elizabeth, he could make himself the object of sport, for a short time.

"Yes, as you know, I deplore a ball where ladies are forced to sit down for want of a partner." Some of the sparkle was now returned to her eyes. "It is a situation with which I am all too familiar. Let us hope Mr Bingley's ball will not suffer from a lack of eligible gentlemen who are willing to dance with ladies who are only tolerably pretty."

"Please, you must keep two dances for me," Darcy heard himself say with an eagerness that similar requests had never before elicited. A strange feeling of self-consciousness then crept over him. He tapped his fingers absently on the glass as he kept his gaze out into the night. "If you are not otherwise engaged." Darcy clamped his lips closed.

The brief pressure of her warm fingers on the back of his hand made him look at her. "I shall certainly keep two dances for you." She offered the first genuine smile Darcy had seen all evening. "Thank you."

Darcy bowed his acknowledgement, his pleasure and relief concealed. As much as he preferred to remain in private conversation with Elizabeth, the more gentlemanly thing to do would be to compliment Miss Bingley on her playing. Elizabeth agreed, and after he promised to give her the third volume of Cowper in the morning, they parted.

When he thought on it later that evening, Darcy was only a little astounded that Elizabeth's warm smile, the promise of a dance, and the mere touch of her ungloved hand could give him such happiness.

Chapter 11

Tuesday, November 19

Darcy sat in the library, skimming the volume he intended to give Elizabeth before breakfast and before she and her sister left Netherfield. The idea of giving her attention in front of Miss Bingley was not agreeable to him. He did not want Miss Bingley's behaviour towards him becoming desperate. He would have to have a discreet conversation with his friend to explain there would never be an attachment formed on his side towards Bingley's sister.

"What makes you look so grave?" Elizabeth asked as she entered. "You often look serious, but today even more so."

Darcy overlooked her question, but rose to greet her and asked if she and her sister were prepared for their return home.

"Yes, and Jane's friends are finally willing to send her home now that she is well."

Elizabeth was perfectly polite, but Darcy recognised her irony. Perhaps it was because she was leaving, or because Miss Bingley had insulted Elizabeth, but Darcy threw propriety aside and asked if she was recovered from her quarrel.

"Oh, it is of no consequence," she said with a wave of her hand, "though you are kind to ask. We have a difference of opinion on what best constitutes domestic felicity. I am sure *you* have an opinion; you always do. Did you not, in this very room, tell me that a fifty-thousand-pound fortune and titled connexions were required? I wish you luck," she added archly.

"We were speaking facetiously about Wordsworth's narrator of the Lucy poems and his need for a new muse. You applied opinions to me that I did not earnestly own. I am not so severe or fastidious."

"Then I would not wish for your playful feelings to run away with you again before you properly express your opinion."

They were now sitting close together. "I hope to be married to a gentleman's daughter. I think she should be active and confident. Her manners would be equal to her generous heart and keen understanding. Some sort of elegance and beauty I would not be opposed to."

"Is there such a lady in the world, where loveliness and character are united to worth? Such a creature would be perfection itself. For my part, perhaps I shall take Miss Bingley's advice and sacrifice every better feeling to worldly advantage."

"I think too well of you to suppose you would ever give your hand without your heart."

"You have come to know me well, Darcy."

He was aware of how unreserved and demonstrative their words were. Their eyes came together, and in that moment, some emotion entered the room with them, compounded by their privacy and by the sincerity of their conversation.

Could I marry Elizabeth Bennet? Darcy's mind spun with the possibility, the hope of it, as he gazed at her earnestly.

Elizabeth, as was often the case, spoke first, and her trembling voice led him to believe she was as affected as he. "The problem with being lively is that I fear I do not always know where the teasing ends and the truth begins."

Elizabeth's words broke the spell that had been cast over them. Reality and its requirements of family responsibility and propriety came back into the library. She blinked and looked away while Darcy gave a little shake of his head. What was he thinking, wondering if he could marry Elizabeth? Their union would be impossible, of course. Friendship or not, their conversation was inappropriate. He handed her the slim volume.

"This is *The Garden*. I anticipate that you will enjoy it and that you will soon be equal to discussing it with me." Darcy's voice raised to a question.

"You are always welcome at Longbourn. I ought to take proper leave of you now, for I suspect if I offer you my hand in front of other members of our party, I will not win any friends."

It made sense to him that they should part with a private shake of hands. Not so much as a sign of leave-taking, but more a mark of their newfound amity. He would be a better man, he decided, a less selfish man, for having befriended Elizabeth Bennet. In their short time together in the same house, she had reminded him what it was to be a gentleman with a greater consideration towards the feelings of others.

He held her hand for a long moment, relishing the feel of her soft skin and the way her delicate fingers curled around his. Elizabeth did not immediately relinquish his hand either, and Darcy wondered if she was as unwilling to break the connexion as he was. He tenderly squeezed her hand at parting, and she repaid him with one of her gentle, sincere smiles and a bewitching glance of her eyes.

At breakfast, Darcy saw how Miss Bingley's enthusiasm for her guests had grown overnight. Elizabeth accepted her increased civility with grace. Their hostess expressed concern about her comfort, the packing of their bags, when their carriage would arrive, when would they meet again, and so on. When Miss Bennet entered, *she* became the object of Miss Bingley's greatest affections, though Darcy supposed she was more convinced of their hostess's sincerity than Elizabeth.

Darcy remained behind his newspaper until his attention was called by Bingley. "I understand a new gentleman has joined the regiment. Hurst and I are talking of dining with some of the officers on Thursday. Is that agreeable to you?"

He lowered the newspaper and avoided meeting Elizabeth's eye.

Bingley was familiar with some of his history with Wickham, but he did not wish to discuss the situation in front of everyone.

"No, thank you. I shall remain at home. You and Hurst are, of course, welcome to join them without me."

Bingley looked a little surprised, but was too good-mannered to speak further of it in company. Darcy was about to return to his newspaper when he saw Miss Bingley's attention on him. She had fixed her eyes on his face and a look of delight crossed her countenance.

Good God, she thinks I wish to remain behind to be with her! There was nothing for it now; better to speak about Wickham than allow Miss Bingley to believe he preferred her solitary company.

"I have learnt a man that I have the great misfortune to be acquainted with is the new officer. He is by no means respectable, and I will not place myself in a position where I must give him any attention. I will not dine with a group of officers that might include Mr Wickham." Darcy felt his mouth twist when he was forced to speak that wretched man's name.

Miss Bingley's triumphant look slipped while her brother's countenance took on a contemplative one. "Wickham? I have heard of him from you, but I cannot recollect the circumstances."

"I have not told you the whole of my history with him, but he has offended me and my family. It has been a most unpleasant association."

"He was the son of your father's steward, was he not? Something about a living he refused?"

Darcy nodded. "The living was left to him conditionally, but it has been his imprudent actions all his life that have caused him to lose my regard. He is a man of questionable morals, and I do not wish to associate with him in a small setting."

"We must exclude him from the ball invitation we extend to the officers!" Miss Bingley exclaimed.

"You need not exclude him. There is little likelihood I shall be forced to engage with him at the ball." *I hope he will take himself out of the way.*

Elizabeth quickly asked Miss Bingley about a stitch in a pattern she had seen in a magazine, and Bingley asked the gentlemen if they would like to go shooting first thing in the morning, which roused Hurst's attention away from his breakfast. Darcy saw through their scheme of distraction, but was grateful for it.

The Netherfield party gathered outside to wish the Bennet sisters a good journey. The Hursts made their brief goodbyes and returned to the warmth of the house. Darcy and Bingley remained with their hostess, who was in the process of saying everything polite and insincere. Darcy bowed and wished them a pleasant journey home; nothing more and nothing less. Elizabeth glanced at him with a knowing sparkle in her eyes.

Miss Bingley wrapped Miss Bennet in a tender embrace. "Jane, it will always give me pleasure to see you either at Longbourn or here at Netherfield." Miss Bennet smiled at her friend with the same welcoming countenance she always wore.

Then Bingley stepped forward to hand her into the carriage, and her expression changed. If Darcy had not been watching, he would have missed it. Miss Bennet blushed, looked down, and then brought her eyes back up to meet Bingley's as he assisted her. She held his hand for longer than necessary. Bingley leant into the carriage and said something to her; Darcy was too far away to hear, but her smile opened into a delighted grin. Jane Bennet was a handsome woman, but in that moment, when she held Bingley's hand at the carriage door and smiled, she was radiant.

Whatever the strength of Miss Bennet's feelings towards his friend, he could no longer claim she was indifferent. It was not a look of triumph, but rather of joy. He had never seen the serene Bennet daughter display any such open expression.

Miss Bingley moved to Elizabeth and, to Darcy's surprise, offered her hand.

"Miss Eliza, it has been a pleasure to have you stay. Your sister's rapid return to health was due to your capable and generous nursing."

"Thank you, Miss Bingley. You have made me feel very welcome."

She then thanked Bingley for his hospitality and allowed him to hand her into the carriage. Elizabeth looked out the side glass and gave a little wave to the group assembled on the lawn, and then they were gone.

Miss Bingley turned her back as soon as the horses moved. Bingley watched the carriage for longer, then all but bounced towards the stairs.

"Wait a moment," Darcy called. His curiosity could not be abated. "I must ask, although, of course, you would be right to refuse to answer me. What did you say to Miss Bennet?"

"You may ask questions which I shall not choose to answer." Darcy bowed before Bingley laughed. "Darcy! I tease! She looked happy, did she not? I did not imagine it?"

"Whatever you said caused her to smile in a way I have never before seen."

"I told her I would call on the Bennet ladies tomorrow and that I particularly hoped she would be at home."

"You have expressed a marked interest now."

"I wanted to indicate how much I enjoyed her company. I need to know Miss Bennet better. I say, you ought to come with me tomorrow! Nothing untoward could be construed by both of us calling."

Bingley clapped Darcy's shoulder and then bolted up the stairs. Darcy looked back towards the drive. The edges of his lips turned up with the thought of speaking with Elizabeth tomorrow. Darcy shook his head, reined in his smile, and slowly walked up the stairs in a manner more befitting a gentleman.

"Tell me, what did he say?"

"What do you mean?"

"Keep your secrets; I will not ask you again." Elizabeth looked out the side glass, taking in the scenery she saw every day of her life.

A full minute passed before Jane blurted, "He wishes to call at Longbourn tomorrow!"

Elizabeth gave a shriek of glee and clapped her hands. They laughed gaily, Elizabeth with delight at her sister's unrestrained happiness, and Jane with nervous embarrassment.

"You must not tell Mamma that Mr Bingley specifically hoped I would be at home; I will never hear the end of it. Let us say that he is calling on all of the ladies."

"I will not say a word, although who could doubt he comes to see you? I dare not tell my mother. If I do, she will drive all her daughters out into the next rainstorm in the hope of us catching a husband."

"Am I apt to expect too much?" Jane's countenance showed an eager yearning that her affections would be returned. She had a great fondness for Mr Bingley, and there was no proper way for her to show it. *What an unfortunate truth in which it is improper for a lady to be justified in falling in love before the gentleman's love is declared.*

"No, but if Mr Bingley is not willing to offer his proposals, there is always the cousin wishing to make us amends waiting for us at Longbourn. If you have misunderstood Mr Bingley, you can take Miss Bingley's advice and marry this Mr Collins."

Jane looked away. Keeping silent was Jane's way of avoiding expressing a negative opinion. Elizabeth suffered no such limitation. "From our sister's note, our cousin does not appear to be a sensible man."

"Perhaps Mr Collins does not express himself well on the page and will prove impressive in person. We ought to reserve judgment until such time as we have met him." Jane did not speak in an admonishing tone, but Elizabeth felt the reprimand.

She felt anew her resolution to be less disapproving, less hasty to condemn on little evidence. Her pride in her own discernment had been unsettled in the face of her misconceptions regarding Darcy, a man she was now happy to be on friendly terms with. She should give her cousin the benefit of the doubt.

"I will follow your example, and I am determined not to judge him beforehand." After a pause, Elizabeth added, "But you may depend upon hearing my opinion when I do."

"I could expect no less from you. I do appreciate you staying on at Netherfield, Lizzy. What say you of Mr Darcy now?"

Elizabeth's heart beat quickly when she recalled the self-conscious way he requested she save two dances for him. *It is socially unacceptable for me to admit to admiring Darcy before he publicly demonstrates his admiration first.* "I have seen a great deal of him, have heard his opinion on subjects of literature and taste; he is well-informed, and his observations just and correct. He has no mistaken pride, and I am pleased to know him better."

Longbourn was now within sight. The Bennets had assembled outside to receive them, along with a tall, heavy-looking young man who must be William Collins. They were welcomed home by their mother, who was pleased her scheme had been a success.

"Jane, my dear, did I not say you had better go on horseback, because it seemed likely to rain, then you would stay all night? Was it not just as I predicted?" Mrs Bennet fluttered like an agitated butterfly.

"Did you also predict she would fall ill?" Elizabeth asked.

"A trifling cold! I wish you could have stayed at Netherfield longer. Did you see much of Mr Bingley? Lizzy did not keep you to your rooms the entire week, did she? Jane, would you say you are secure of Mr Bingley?"

Mrs Bennet spoke without pausing to take breath. Jane blushed, and Elizabeth was embarrassed that Mr Collins heard her mother's effusions. Mr Bennet welcomed home his eldest daughters and made them known to their cousin, who had been visibly eager for an introduction.

"Miss Bennet, Miss Elizabeth, I am exceedingly gratified to finally make your acquaintance." He offered a low bow. Although she could not be certain of the habits of a man she had just met, Elizabeth thought Mr Collins looked relieved at the sight of them. "The report of your handsomeness and amiability has not been misrepresented in the least."

Elizabeth expected this to be the end of his speech. She was, however, disappointed. She feared Mr Collins would keep them outside, extolling their physical virtues, but Mrs Bennet interrupted to thank him for his kind attention and begged everyone to return to the house. She and Jane led the way, still chatting about Mr Bingley, and Mr Collins followed, continuing to speak at length of his assurances that such handsome daughters would of course be soon disposed of in marriage.

Elizabeth turned her questioning eyes to meet her father's amused gaze.

"Thank goodness you and Jane are returned, so we might tip the scales in favour of sense and education."

Her sisters had more commentary on the behaviour and manners of Mr Collins and clustered around her as soon as they were alone.

"He never reads novels, Lizzy!" Lydia cried. "And he admired the furnishings as though he owns them already."

"He thought we cooked yesternight's dinner," Kitty whispered.

Even Mary offered a critique before begging off to return to her instrument. "He speaks incessantly about his patroness. It is unseemly that a man of the cloth wastes so much breath extolling the qualities of a great lady rather than on concerns of morality."

"I overheard him talking with my mother," Kitty said. "He intends to marry now that he has a good house and sufficient income, and means to choose one of us. He told her that he hoped to meet the eldest two Miss Bennets before making his choice. He did not want us, thank goodness!"

"And Mamma said that she hoped Jane would soon be engaged to Mr Bingley, so that leaves you, Lizzy!" Lydia was laughing. "I hope you shall be happy with such a man!"

By the end of an hour, Elizabeth learned Mr Collins did not need encouragement to speak. His air was grave, his manners too formal, and he had little common sense; she dearly hoped her sisters were mistaken.

Chapter 12

Lydia intended to walk into Meryton, and their father suggested Mr Collins attend her and her sisters. Elizabeth suspected her father wanted a return to tranquillity, and none was to be had while Mr Collins talked of his noble patroness and of his house and garden at Hunsford.

Every sister except Mary was joined by Mr Collins, who told them repeatedly how pleased he was to walk with them. Elizabeth could not believe him, as he laboured to keep up. His breathless pompous nothings received civil assents, but he was not attentive to their conversation. Elizabeth was grateful Mr Collins was more focused on walking than listening, because Lydia had no turn for discretion.

"Have you had any flirting, Jane? You cannot always have stayed in bed. Oh, what do you care what Mr Collins may think? Jane will be an old maid soon, I declare. She is already two-and-twenty! What did you do at Netherfield, Lizzy? It must have been dull to watch Mr Bingley and Jane and have no flirting of your own."

Lydia continued on in this manner, supported by Kitty, the entire mile-long walk. Before they had been in Meryton fifteen minutes, the younger girls' attention was caught by a man they had never seen before.

"There is Mr Denny, but who is with him?" Kitty asked.

It was Mr Wickham. He still lacked his regimentals, but the younger girls manoeuvred themselves in front of them to garner an introduction. Mr Wickham had gained a confidence and amiability that was lacking the day before. Whether that was because Darcy was absent or because today Mr Wickham was greeted by four attractive ladies who were attended by a fool, Elizabeth was unable to tell.

The ladies were introduced to, and Elizabeth greeted by, Mr Wickham, who acknowledged her with a cautious incline of his head. She was reserved in her civilities, and Mr Wickham made no attempt to speak with her. The two men walked with them to the door of Mr Philips's house and then made their farewells, in spite of Lydia's entreaties that they would come in, and even in spite of Mrs Philips's throwing up the parlour window and loudly seconding her niece's invitation.

Lydia interrupted her cousin's lengthy civilities to ask her aunt about Mr Wickham.

"My intelligence is scarcely greater than yours, and I have sat at the window all morning! Mr Denny brought him from London, and he shall have a lieutenant's commission. I could not even tell you where the gentleman is from."

"Derbyshire," said Elizabeth.

All female eyes turned towards her, and her aunt and sisters spoke at once, begging her for more information. Elizabeth hesitated to add Darcy's explicit warning to her, and spoke primarily of what she and Jane had heard that morning.

"Mr Wickham has lost Mr Darcy's good opinion, and not undeservingly. Mr Wickham is the son of old Mr Darcy's steward, and he refused to take orders in order to secure a family living. Mr Wickham was paid a generous compensation in return for giving up his claim to all aid in the church. That compensation has been spent on a life of idleness and dissipation."

"What do you know of it? Only what Mr Darcy has told you, and he hates everybody," cried Lydia.

"Da—Mr Darcy is perfectly amiable, and Mr Bingley would corroborate their history."

"It is impossible for us to conjecture the circumstances which may have alienated Mr Wickham and Mr Darcy, so we ought not to pass judgment," Jane added.

Her aunt was eager to contribute something to the proceedings. "I will tell your uncle to call on Mr Wickham and invite him to dine with us tomorrow along with some of the officers. Your family must come in the evening and you can find more out for yourselves. We will have a nice, noisy game of lottery tickets."

The prospect of such delights was cheering—except, to Elizabeth, the prospect of Mr Wickham's company—and they parted in mutual good spirits. Her aunt and sisters might not wish to consider the implications of having a man of doubtful character in their midst, but it weighed on Elizabeth's mind. Darcy had all but accused him of being a gamester as well as a rake.

"My fair cousin, you have not had the pleasure of hearing about my patroness, Lady Catherine de Bourgh." Mr Collins appeared at her side. "Do not take that to imply that I am offended by your being away from home upon my arrival. In fact, it is providential, since I am now granted the opportunity to expound upon all I have already said to your sisters and to tell you, in detail, of the affability and condescension of that great lady."

Amid complaisant smiles and no encouragement, Elizabeth endured her cousin's ostentatious formality and protracted descriptions the rest of the walk home.

Wednesday, November 20

DARCY HANDED HIS WEAPON TO THE AWAITING SERVANT AND looked with dismay at the retinue that had accompanied them shooting.

"This method of using men with sticks to drive out the birds is not necessary, and I do not need another man to load for me. Why not use the dogs to flush out a few birds at a time?"

From farther down the line, Hurst interrupted Bingley's reply. "I will not allow Bingley's young dogs to ruin my sport again!"

Darcy rolled his eyes, but Bingley just clapped him on the shoulder. What Darcy had hoped would be a quiet morning's shoot had turned into a contest for Hurst to bag as many winged creatures as possible with as many servants in attendance as possible. Thankfully, near midday, Bingley had had enough. Darcy held Bingley back and let the others outstrip them.

"Bingley, I must speak to you about your sister."

His friend's eyes widened. Darcy had never suspected Bingley entertained a hope he might marry his sister. He must do all he could to soften the blow. Elizabeth had said he ought to be more mindful of the feelings of others, and he did not wish to cause his friend pain.

"I have been acquainted with Miss Bingley for two years, and I am in no doubt of her accomplishments ..." Darcy trailed off as he struggled to find the appropriate words to say he would never marry her. In the meanwhile, Bingley had sunk onto a stone bench near the gravel walk. "I must tell you she is not best suited to make me happy."

Darcy felt guilty that he had dashed his friend's hopes of a closer alliance between them. There was an uncomfortable pause. He was about to apologise for his bluntness when Bingley took off his hat and hung his head. He then bounded to his feet with a grin.

"You nearly frightened me to death!"

"Do you comprehend me? No design has ever been formed on my side towards your sister. I have no intentions in any way towards her, now or ever."

"Well, of course not!"

"If you are not disappointed...why did you look stricken?"

"I thought you were going to tell me you wanted to marry Caroline! I allow she is the best judge of her own happiness, but her happiness centres on connexions and a large income, which is why she is fixed on you. Of course she would not make you happy!"

The friends stared at each other a long moment, then broke out into relieved laughter.

"I thought that you ought to know my mind, in the event she ever ..."

"In the event you smile at her and she orders her wedding clothes? I am pleased you broached the subject because I now have your leave to set her down should she become too vocal in believing it is her duty to marry you. You are a good man, and you deserve to find happiness. Besides, I know you are disinclined to marry."

"I do not intend to profess a disinclination for it. I only set it down that I have not yet seen the right woman."

"I think I have."

Darcy looked away to hide his surprise and held back his request that Bingley repeat his meaning so he could believe it. He had to tread carefully; it would not do to speak against a woman who might become Bingley's wife. "I know many who have married in the confidence of some good quality in the person, but who have found themselves deceived, and been obliged to put up with the reverse. Miss Bennet can bring you neither connexion nor fortune, and her accomplishments are nothing out of the common way. You set your domestic felicity on the good qualities of a pretty woman you have barely spoken with outside of mixed company."

"And how often does a man have the opportunity to speak alone with any young woman? A few dances and a conversation in a crowded room is all one is likely to get. Her stay allowed me a greater opportunity to converse with her in two days than I could have hoped for in as many weeks."

"Miss Bennet may return your affections. But what of her family? Their conduct makes it hard for even you to keep your countenance."

"I intend to learn if Miss Bennet could return my affections and if she does, then a ridiculous mother and a few silly sisters would not deter me. I have sufficient resources to marry a poor woman. I wish as well as everybody else to be perfectly happy, but, like everybody else, it must be in my own way." Bingley paused. "Jane Bennet could make me happy."

"She would be a fortunate woman to accept your offer and, if she returns your regard, I wish you joy."

Bingley's face broke into a grin. "I thank you. And perhaps when we call at Longbourn today, we may learn that the cousin to inherit their estate is both sensible and respectable."

MRS BENNET HAD TAKEN IT INTO HER HEAD TO BRING HER GIRLS TO call on their neighbours, and when she refused to allow Jane to stay behind, Jane was obliged to explain Mr Bingley's impending visit.

"My dear girl! He asked to call on you the day after you left? Jane, he must wish to speak privately with you! A daughter married! Oh gracious me!"

"Mamma! Mr Bingley intends to call on all the ladies. He expects you and my sisters to be at home. I am sure he wishes to know that I am not ill after my removal."

"It is a compliment to you! I must think of a way to get you by yourselves! A daughter married!"

"I don't see why we have to stay while Mr Bingley makes love to Jane!" Lydia complained. When Kitty agreed she too saw no occasion for staying behind, Lydia pulled her sister from her sprawled position, and the younger girls left.

Jane tried to say there was no occasion for her sisters' leaving, but her mother overruled her. "And Mary will be at her instrument, and I am sure there will be some errand I will need Lizzy to help me with." Mrs Bennet offered Elizabeth a vulgar wink.

An hour later, Mrs Bennet saw Mr Bingley enter the paddock and ride towards the house. She shrieked with excitement while she ran down the stairs and called for her daughters to partake of her joy. Elizabeth, to satisfy her mother, went towards the window. Before she moved halfway across the room, her mother cried out, "Oh, he has brought the tall proud man with him!"

Elizabeth turned on her heel and sat next to her sister, her heartbeat thudding in her ears.

"Such a disagreeable man," Mrs Bennet continued. "Lizzy, you need not stay. Not handsome enough to dance with!" she scoffed. "I can keep Mr Darcy out of Mr Bingley's way myself. I know how much you dislike him."

"You know nothing of the matter!" She blushed when she received their surprised looks. "I mean Mr Darcy is not as disagreeable as you may imagine, and we have put aside our differences. He apologised for not dancing with me at the assembly. I will entertain Mr Darcy for Jane's sake."

"We might all have some conversation together," said Jane.

"Can you tolerate walking out with Mr Darcy? You need not speak to him; just keep him out of Mr Bingley's way."

"No one needs to be kept out of anyone's way."

They were interrupted by the servant announcing their visitors. Elizabeth looked at her sister and noticed that her expression of delight was hardly any more subdued than the eager expression on Mr Bingley's face. Darcy looked as serious as he was ever known to be, but he returned her smile when she greeted him. Elizabeth thought the four of them could pass a pleasant half-hour together. Then her mother spoke.

"Mr Bingley, how good of you to call! I can hardly thank you enough for taking such good care of my Jane. You and your sisters have been wonderfully good friends to us." As an afterthought, Mrs Bennet turned to her other guest. "You are also welcome."

Before everyone was seated, Mrs Bennet began again.

"Netherfield is a charming house; I know of none better. I do hope you will remain long in the country."

"I am obliged to return to town for three or four days next week, but I intend to stay through December. I consider myself quite fixed here."

Mrs Bennet then looked meaningfully at Jane, who did not acknowledge her. After a pause, she reluctantly addressed Darcy. "Do you also intend to remain until Christmas?"

Darcy replied that he did, and Mrs Bennet turned back to her more favoured guest.

"I hope that you have had good sport." Mr Bingley opened his mouth, but Mrs Bennet did not pause long enough for him to speak. "When you have killed all your own birds, I beg you will come here, and shoot as many as you please." She then added, in the general direction of where Darcy sat, "You are welcome as well, sir."

Mr Bingley said he was thankful for the offer. He then addressed Jane directly with the hope that she was fully recovered. Jane replied she was, but before their conversation continued, Mrs Bennet spoke again.

"My Jane is in very good health. She has a good constitution; she can bear anything with the fortitude of an angel. She has the sweetest temper I ever met with. I often tell my other girls, Lizzy in particular, they are nothing to *her.*"

Elizabeth's misery increased. Jane was mortified, Darcy offended, and Mr Bingley struggled to keep his expression neutral.

Mrs Bennet was oblivious of her own vulgarity. "Lizzy, come here, I want to speak to you." Before Elizabeth could do more than blush on her mother's behalf, Mrs Bennet went on to address Darcy. "Mr Bennet and his cousin are in the library if you—"

"It is a clear day," Elizabeth interrupted her mother. "Jane and I were hoping for an opportunity to walk out." Elizabeth knew her mother was not in the habit of walking, and she would not allow Darcy to suffer further at the hands of her father's scornful humour and her cousin's ridiculous condescension.

"Yes, my dears, show Mr Bingley and his friend the different walks!" The fact that she had not yet ascertained the wishes of the gentlemen was not lost on Elizabeth.

Mr Bingley announced that he would be glad to take a turn outside, as Elizabeth hoped he would, and Darcy bowed. When they went outside, the gauche encounter in the drawing room still pressed on all their minds, and the first minutes of their walk was spent on stilted discussion of whether it was likely to rain soon. Then Mr Bingley offered Jane his arm, and her sister and her suitor soon outstripped them.

"Shall I?" Darcy drew her arm within his.

"It is a while since we have had a comfortable walk together," she said, struggling to come up with something to say to mask her heart palpitations.

"Yes, it has been over eight-and-forty hours. A veritable age."

The slight tug on her arm that pressed her closer to him let her know he understood her playfulness.

They could not hear what was said, but it was clear Mr Bingley and Jane had a great deal to say to one another. An expressive look then passed between Elizabeth and Darcy before he quietly asked, "Would you tell me how your sister enjoyed her stay at Netherfield? Or do I ask too much?"

"Jane considers she received the kindest welcome from Mr Bingley; his hospitality made a distinct impression on her. Since we are friends, I feel as though I might ask you something: would you say Mr Bingley was attentive because he was at leisure to bestow such attention, or was it because of a *particular* desire to be hospitable towards my sister?"

"He takes his attention to his guests' comforts seriously, but Bingley was gratified to give *her* every attention. And so Miss Bennet was pleased to be the recipient of his *hospitality*?"

Elizabeth smiled.

"I am pleased to hear it," Darcy continued. "I had wondered if Miss Bennet appreciated her host's *politeness* enough to reciprocate the sentiment."

"Upon my word, I never saw a young woman so in love in my life!"

Darcy eyed her in wonder; Elizabeth blushed. "You will, I hope, forgive my outburst. This is not the first time I have spoken too freely to you. My sister is much affected by your friend's *politeness* and looks forward to exhibiting her own *good manners* in turn, should the opportunity present itself."

"We might as well drop all pretences: Bingley's partiality for Miss Bennet is beyond what I have ever witnessed in him. I was uneasy that she did not appear to invite his attention, but your superior knowledge of your sister's feelings must of course indicate she is not as indifferent as I feared."

"Jane's feelings, though fervent, are little displayed. I am betraying a confidence when I say that Jane's heart has been touched; but since you feared her to be complacent, I shall not scruple to tell you the truth."

"Perhaps for Miss Bennet, a blush on her cheek and a warm smile are all the outward signs of a marked preference."

"Jane's natural modesty would not allow her to show further emotion at this time. Anything more might be misconstrued as indecent. No young lady can be permitted to fall in love before the gentleman's love is declared."

"Do you certainly understand the degree of affection between them?"

"Yes, but it is not for me, or for us, to say. Come now, should it not be the role of fathers and guardians rather than friends and sisters to ascertain the suitability of the acquaintances of their charges? Mr Bingley is his own master, and my father—well, there cannot be too little said on his involvement with his daughters."

Elizabeth watched her sister and Mr Bingley as they walked in the afternoon light. She was not disposed to be jealous, and she had no designs on Mr Bingley, but Jane, in all likelihood, would soon be happily married. She would be the mistress of her own home, with status, respect, and a husband who loved her and wished for her happiness, whilst Elizabeth's life would remain unchanged but for the loss of her closest companion.

"I have no doubt of their being happy together," she said after a silence, striving to appear unaffected. "I believe them to be mutually and sincerely attached."

"He is a fortunate man," returned Darcy, with energy. "I can vouch for his honourable intentions, and I must be content with his judgment as well as your own that your sister returns his affections with equal fervency."

"Darcy, there are times when I think you older than Mr Bingley by far more than the few years that lie between you."

"My friend has not had the same responsibilities, or the same trials, as I have had. His sense of duty has not been imbued from an early age, and his obligations do not equal mine, nor do the people and affairs within his care suffer the same level of dependence or significance." Darcy paused. "I daresay you will again call me arrogant; I did not intend to appear that way. I too have become unreserved in your presence."

"I am pleased you are less reserved, at least with me. We ought to say what we like to one another since we are friends. And I do not think there is any improper pride displayed by what you have said. Your history and Mr Bingley's are different, and your obligations are greater."

Jane and Mr Bingley had turned back to meet them; her sister expressed a desire to return, and the four of them fell into conversation. They entered the house, and the gentlemen wished to take leave of Mrs Bennet, who was sitting in the breakfast room. Elizabeth suspected she had been watching for the end of their walk in hopes that her congratulations were needed. Seeing that her eldest daughter had no news to impart made Mrs Bennet eager to give them another opportunity to meet.

"Mr Bingley, you must join us for a family dinner. You need not the ceremony of a formal invitation. Are you available tomorrow?" Elizabeth blushed for her mother.

Mr Bingley looked at Darcy before answering. "I would be delighted, but I am engaged to dine with the officers. It is unfortunate that Darcy, who had intended to join us, now finds he is disengaged for dinner tomorrow." Elizabeth saw Darcy's eyebrow rise, but Mr Bingley continued. "I think Hurst and I will leave the officers early so Darcy will not be left alone for all of the evening."

Mrs Bennet's eyes lit up, and Elizabeth feared what idea her mother had fixed upon. "Mr Bingley, your friend Mr Darcy must join us for a small family dinner, and perhaps Charlotte Lucas will dine with us, also. She will see a finer table here than she would at home. And Mr Collins will be one of the party, so we shall have ten. Mr Bingley, you and your brother *must* come in the evening! We will bring out the card tables. Do say you will join us in the evening!" Mrs Bennet's tone became subdued. "Does that suit you, Mr Darcy?"

"Please, Mrs Bennet, do not allow Bingley to trouble you to give any invitations."

"Oh, it is no trouble at all!" Mrs Bennet returned to her first object. "Then Mr Darcy can return to Netherfield with you after supper. And you must stay for supper, Mr Bingley!" Elizabeth could hardly keep her countenance amid her mother's desperation.

"Of course, ma'am." Mr Bingley then addressed his friend in an expressive way. "Is that agreeable?"

Darcy was looking at her mother as though she had two heads, but he pulled his eyes away to look at his friend. Mr Bingley and her mother had placed him in an untenable position: there was nothing he could do but agree. They soon made their bows and went away. Elizabeth and Jane then ran to their room to talk over the gentlemen's visit and lament their mother's behaviour.

"What in God's name was that?"

"What? I thought you would be grateful." Bingley seemed confused.

"Why did you manoeuvre me into a dinner at Longbourn?"

"I thought it would suit our motives perfectly."

Darcy stared blankly.

"You must know I welcome the opportunity to speak again with Miss Bennet," he spoke as though addressing a simpleton.

"That is all well and good, but why am I to dine with the Bennets tomorrow, *without* you?"

"You have no desire to join the officers and meet Mr Wickham, and if you remain at Netherfield, you will be obliged to spend an evening alone with Caroline. This way you avoid both Mr Wickham and Caroline, and I have the chance to spend more time with Miss Bennet." Bingley rode off and left Darcy staring after him in bewilderment.

Chapter 13

Wednesday, November 20

Jane was dressed for the evening at the Philipses when Elizabeth entered their room. She slammed the door and leant against it, closing her eyes.

"I was about to fetch you!" Jane checked her watch.

Elizabeth undressed frantically. They were expected in Meryton in half an hour. "That man is so strange!" She noticed her sister's admonishing gaze. "I have tried to be less disapproving, you know I have! Mr Collins knew I had to dress, and I had to stop him mid-sentence and quit the room. I have enough evidence to say his absurd humility is counteracted by a strong self-conceit. I cannot tolerate him!"

"Is he still in the breakfast room?"

"When I came up the stairs, he was speaking to my mother and father about his scruples of leaving them for a single evening. My father could hardly contain his enthusiasm for being rid of him for a few hours."

Despite Elizabeth's delay, the coach conveyed the Bennet sisters and Mr Collins at a suitable hour to Meryton.

At her aunt's home, the officers soon joined the ladies in the drawing room, including Mr Wickham. When Elizabeth noticed him, Darcy's warning filled her mind. *I implore you, be cautious of Mr Wickham.*

When the card tables were placed, Mr Wickham chose not to play and sat between Elizabeth and Lydia to observe their game. *He probably looks on a game for lottery tickets with a cold eye, if Darcy's report of his being a gamester is true.* She hoped Lydia would engross Mr Wickham, for she was a determined talker, but Lydia grew too interested in the game to have any attention for him.

Mr Wickham was therefore at leisure to talk to Elizabeth. What could she say to him? *Mr Wickham, why did you refuse to enter the church? What happened to your plan to pursue the law? How did you manage to lose so much money in so little time? What immoral behaviour did you demonstrate to alienate Mr Darcy?*

"How far is Netherfield from Meryton?" he asked after the game was begun.

"Two miles."

After Lydia dealt, Mr Wickham spoke again. "How long ... do you know how long Mr Darcy has been staying there?"

Elizabeth was surprised Mr Wickham began the subject of Darcy. "About a month." She then added archly, "Are you well acquainted with that gentleman?" She expected Mr Wickham would be embarrassed and the matter dropped.

"Yes," replied Mr Wickham. "He is a man of large property, and his estate is a noble one. A clear ten thousand per annum. I have been connected with his family from my infancy."

Darcy has told me all I need to know about your connexion. She bowed to indicate she had heard him.

"You are not surprised by my assertion despite seeing the cold manner of our meeting Monday. From what I saw of your interaction with Mr Darcy, I presume you have more than a passing acquaintance with that gentleman."

"Why might you presume that?"

"I have known Mr Darcy long and well. His manners are high and imposing, but you seemed on intimate terms. Indeed, I noticed that he allowed you to address him by his surname only, a privilege he only grants to his intimates. You must admire him, and he you."

Elizabeth could think of no proper reply, but her companion continued. "Is—is he liked in Hertfordshire? What think you of him? That is, how is Mr Darcy spoken of?"

"I—Some might say he is tall, proper, a clever man. Most would say Mr Darcy appears respectable, but with reserved manners that prevent him from being generally pleasing. He is liked well enough."

"I wonder if he is likely to be in this country much longer."

"When he called at Longbourn this morning, he said he was remaining until he went down to Pemberley for Christmas."

A full round of play passed before Mr Wickham spoke again. "Since you are closely acquainted with Mr Darcy, I feel I might ask if he has spoken to you of me."

Elizabeth stared at her cards. He spoke so softly she was certain none of the others heard him. When she raised her eyes, the polite denial died on her lips. Mr Wickham shook his head knowingly.

"It was the prospect of good society which was my chief inducement to enter the militia. Society, I own, is necessary to me. I would hate to suffer the loss of agreeable companionship," he said with an expressive look.

Elizabeth discarded without replying. *Mr Wickham might be a gamester, a man of no scruples, but his story is not mine to tell.*

Mr Wickham spoke on more general topics. Elizabeth nodded when appropriate, but offered no encouragement. It was not her place to publicly deprecate him, but she could not tolerate him, knowing what sort of a man he was. If anyone, it was Darcy who might speak against him, but then again, it was hardly his responsibility to follow Mr Wickham all his life to warn society about him.

Elizabeth thought it was time to have done with cards if Mr Wickham was to keep talking. She asked Captain Carter to take her place. Elizabeth might have observed the whist game, but she realised the danger in appearing too attentive to Mr Collins, who appeared to have lost every point. Elizabeth warmed her hands before the fire, but her moment of reflection was interrupted by the very officer whose company she wished to avoid.

"Miss Elizabeth Bennet, I fear I have offended you," Mr Wickham said as he stood over the hearth.

"Not at all. I had grown dissatisfied with the game." She made no attempt to mask her true feelings.

Mr Wickham bowed. "I had hoped to pass myself off in this part of the world with some credit." After a pause, he added, "Would you do me the honour of telling me what Mr Darcy spoke of?"

The indelicacy of the subject made her hesitate, but she supposed a man had a right to know what was said about him. "Mr Darcy related the details surrounding the living, your refusal to take orders, and the compensation paid to you. He also alluded towards your wide-ranging vices."

Elizabeth willed him to walk away. Instead, he looked distressed, saying, "Mr Darcy has not spoken falsely. It gives me pain to meet him, for his presence reminds me of what I have lost. I do not speak of the loss of wealth, but my loss of the respect of the Darcys. His father was one of the best men that ever breathed and the truest friend I ever had, and I did not value him until it was too late. I am grieved to the soul at the memory of my own scandalous behaviour."

"For how long have you been regretful? Was it before or after you spent the money Mr Darcy had the good grace to give you?"

"I do not blame you for your disbelief. I was indolent in my youth, and ungrateful. For a long time, I cared little for anything but my own pleasure. My habits of selfish indulgence appear in shameful contrast to the life Mr Darcy has led."

He took her silence as leave to continue, and she listened to him speak of Darcy with all her heart.

"Mr Darcy, as his father before him, gives his money freely, he displays hospitality, he assists his tenants and gives relief to the poor. He may be accused of haughtiness and pride, but only by those who do not know what truly lies in his heart. Indeed, family pride has made him a compassionate and respectable man. Intimate friend with him as you are, you must see that?"

She could not contradict him. There was a lengthy pause before he continued. "He also has brotherly pride, which makes him a kind and careful guardian of his sister. Has—has he at all mentioned Miss Darcy to you?"

"Only a little, but with great affection."

"Indeed!" cried Mr Wickham, with a look of surprise. "Miss Darcy was a pleasing child. I have not seen her in years. You asked when I first regretted my behaviour, and it was long before I applied to Mr Darcy for the living I had once scorned. As my circumstances became desperate, I regretted my foolishness. I threw away the life of a gentleman for game, drink, and low company. It breaks my heart to know Mr Darcy will never forgive me."

Elizabeth felt a pang of compassion for Mr Wickham. He looked forlorn, his voice so full of remorse. *It never occurred to me that he might be humbled and desiring Darcy's forgiveness.*

"If I did not know it would cause him grief, I would beg you to remember me to Mr Darcy. I have often hoped that we might find some means of reconciling. But I treated his family's generosity abominably. I am sorry for burdening you with my disappointed hopes."

Supper was called, putting an end to cards and giving the rest of the ladies their share of Mr Wickham's attentions—which was just as well, since Elizabeth scarcely knew what to say. She had presumed him to be the worst sort of gamester, rake, and spendthrift, a man lacking in morality, but instead she had found Mr Wickham contrite and regretful of the loss of Darcy's friendship.

Elizabeth was obliged to wait until the next day to relate to Jane what had passed between Mr Wickham and herself. The possibility of Mr Wickham having seen the error of his ways was enough to interest all of Jane's tender feelings.

"Forgiveness is an important virtue, Lizzy. If Mr Wickham pleads his earnest remorse, then we must believe him."

"Mr Wickham *was* unworthy of Mr Darcy's regard, and Mr Darcy was right to warn me of him, but he sounded penitent."

Whenever Elizabeth thought about Mr Wickham's confessions, her sense of shame was renewed. She was no good judge of character after all and had formed too many hasty opinions on mistaken grounds. What might she have lost if she had persisted in thinking the worst of Darcy? *When will I rid myself of this penchant for presuming the worst of people?*

"Do you suppose Mr Darcy knows his former companion is repentant?"

"No, he did not keep up an acquaintance with one he felt lacking in decency."

"I think, Lizzy, there is nothing to be done but to think well of them both, to defend the conduct of each. It is to Mr Darcy's credit that he distanced himself from one who behaved abominably. Indolence and gaming, and a questionable reputation, are appropriate reasons to sever an acquaintance. But if Mr Wickham is indeed reformed and remorseful, then we must treat him as his current behaviour merits."

Elizabeth was not so easily reconciled with herself. "I thought Mr Wickham did not play cards because our games were below his notice for an experienced gamester, but I never supposed he might instead wish to remove himself from activities that once led him astray. What does that say of me, Jane? After judging Mr Darcy so wrongly, I had hoped to behave better."

"Your suspicions of Mr Wickham were not unkind. Mr Darcy told you the truth as he understood it. There was no way Mr Darcy could have known that for years now Mr Wickham has seen the error of his ways. Now that they are in residence so closely to one another, they could re-establish their relationship."

"You did not see their meeting in Meryton. Ought I to speak to him about Mr Wickham's reformation? Mr Darcy is not a resentful man; perhaps they might be reconciled."

"If you think that would be to the benefit of them both, then I think you should."

Elizabeth and Jane did not have the opportunity to speak further as they were summoned from the shrubbery by the arrival of Mr Bingley and his sisters. They came to give their personal invitation for the long-expected ball at Netherfield, which was fixed for the following Tuesday. After fifteen minutes passed, the ladies rose with an activity that took their brother by surprise; he had been deep in conversation with Jane.

Miss Bingley and Mrs Hurst paused when Mrs Bennet said to their brother, "We look forward to seeing you this evening."

"What plans does Mrs Bennet refer to, Charles?"

"Hurst and I are to join the Bennets in the evening. I did tell you we would be dining out."

"Yes," his younger sister replied impatiently, "but you are dining with the officers."

"So we are, but since Darcy is dining here, Hurst and I are going to join the Bennets in the evening."

The colour drained from Miss Bingley's face. "I thought Mr Darcy would remain with—why is he dining—I had hoped—" Miss Bingley realised the entire room was staring and closed her mouth. Mr Bingley leapt into the silence by expressing his enthusiasm for seeing them all later that evening, gave a smile to Jane, bowed to the room, and then escorted his stunned sisters from the house.

Chapter 14

Thursday, November 21

If Mrs Bennet's manner yesterday was any indication, tonight will be arduous. There was a marked difference between Mrs Bennet's notice of Bingley, a man she saw as a suitor for her eldest daughter, and Darcy, who, in her eyes, was the proud man who had said her second daughter was not handsome enough for him to dance with.

Never mind that I am now of the opinion that Elizabeth is one of the handsomest women of my acquaintance. In the week they had been inmates of the same house, he had begun to feel a powerful regard for Elizabeth. Could he ask a woman to share his life, but at the same time hope her family would never visit Pemberley?

"Stop worrying." Bingley leaned over from the other side of the chaise. "I see no reason for your melancholy in the face of a family dinner with a small party in the evening."

"I hate tiny parties; they force me into constant exertion."

"The party at Netherfield tonight would be tinier still."

"I am being manipulated to provide you an excuse to arrive in the evening to promote your acquaintance with Miss Bennet."

"Of course you are!" barked Hurst. "You"—he pointed at Darcy—"want to avoid being alone with Caroline, and you"—he then pointed at Bingley—"want to flirt with that pretty Bennet girl. You both ought to be content."

Mr Hurst relapsed into silence, and Bingley and Darcy sat in disbelief of that gentleman's knowledge of what was happening.

Bingley eventually said, "I appreciate your amenability. I am not insensible that this was not your choice."

Darcy remembered Elizabeth and Bingley's criticism regarding his lack of sympathy towards the interests and feelings of others. Knowing Miss Bennet better was important to Bingley, and Bingley's happiness was important to Darcy. As the carriage rattled on, Darcy remembered something his father had often told him.

"Son, a gentleman must act with the wish of giving happiness to others. It is one of the marks of true politeness." He would therefore be courteous and obliging tonight, as much as his reserved nature allowed.

"Despite my misgivings about their behaviour, I will make myself agreeable for your sake." *And for Elizabeth's.*

"Perhaps in their own home, with no officers, and under the influence of their cousin who is to inherit the estate, they might be well-mannered and you will enjoy yourself."

Darcy was long enough arrived to have Mr Collins presented to him before it was time to go in for dinner. Unhappily, he was seated as far from Elizabeth as was possible and on the same side of the table.

"We have ten sitting around the table tonight, Mr Darcy," Mrs Bennet said as the first course was laid. "However, you will see dinner enough on it for twenty. I am sure you will see no finer table kept in the country. Two full courses should satisfy for a gentleman of ten thousand a year!"

I thought this was to be an informal family meal. Darcy wondered what reply was expected to her tactless statement, and he decided on silence. Mr Bennet reasoned differently.

"Mrs Bennet, Mr Darcy is in high luck to meet with such attention and indulgence."

His host's sarcasm was not lost on Darcy, but it was beyond his lady's comprehension; her countenance had a look of triumph. Lydia and Kitty giggled, and Miss Lucas looked into her glass. Miss Bennet stared at her plate while Elizabeth hung her head. It evoked a sense of compassion for Mrs Bennet that Darcy had not known he was capable of. "I have nothing but the highest compliment for the table Mrs Bennet keeps."

"I must echo Mr Darcy's commendation of our elegant hostess," added Mr Collins. Darcy expected Mr Collins would then redirect the table's conversation. Instead, he rambled on the sight of so lovely a dining room and how they would all be overpowered by so splendid a dinner.

Various were the subjects that occupied the diners, but none, Darcy thought, worth attending to. There was no happy flow of conversation, either rational or playful. Darcy had been prepared to speak whenever there was an opening, but it became clear he would not be required to take part.

Darcy was seated next to Miss Mary and would have engaged her in conversation, but her answers were so pedantic that he could not advance it. Elizabeth attempted to enquire of Charlotte Lucas after the welfare of her family, but they were interrupted by Mr Collins. Mrs Bennet was doubly engaged, on the one hand collecting an account of the fashions of the Netherfield ladies from Miss Bennet, who sat some way below her, and on the other, talking about them to Miss Catherine, whilst Miss Lydia, in a voice louder than any other person's, was enumerating the pleasures of the morning to anybody who could hear her.

The worst came after the final dishes were removed. Mrs Bennet spoke, piercingly and excitedly, about ways to entertain her guests that evening.

"I look forward to when Mr Bingley will arrive! Don't you agree, Jane? Oh yes, and Mr Hurst as well. You do not suppose the officers' dinner will be late? I am sure we will have a lively party. Mary can play so the young people can dance."

"That would be such good fun! If only you had invited some of the officers," Miss Lydia cried.

"I do not wish to always be sitting out." Miss Kitty sulked.

"And who is to say *all* of the gentlemen will even be willing to dance?"

"I am certain Mr Bingley will dance," added their mother. "*He* is an agreeable, charming young man."

"I shall have to listen to enough talk in the coming days about dancing, thanks to Mr Bingley's ball," Mr Bennet said. "You will spare me in the meantime and find some other manner by which to amuse yourselves."

Groans of disappointment followed this pronouncement.

"I will oblige the company by reading aloud," intoned Mr Collins. "It would give me the greatest pleasure to entertain, and I flatter myself by saying that, on a second hearing, my cousins will be more inclined to attend to the good words of Mr Fordyce."

Darcy wondered what he had done to be subjected to such a punishment as this.

"I think cards might be preferable," said Mrs Bennet. "Lizzy is an accomplished girl. She can play and sing some pretty Italian songs. You have not yet had the pleasure of hearing her, Mr Collins."

"I have no doubt my fair cousin is an accomplished young lady. Not that I am an advocate for a lady acquiring a perfect knowledge in all the languages, arts, and sciences. It is throwing time away, for it will gain a woman some applause, but it will not make her more likely to attract a suitor. Too improved a mind is not an attractive quality in a gently bred female."

Darcy could hardly stand to hear such ridiculousness but was too stunned to speak. He dared not glance down the table at Elizabeth to see how she bore it. Mr Bennet then addressed Mr Collins with the same sardonic tone he seemed predisposed to use on everyone.

"Thank goodness I allowed those daughters who were disinclined to leave off their studies. Your opinion, sir, has justified my lack of expenditure on governesses and masters for my silly daughters."

"Yes, my dear Mr Bennet! I shall not have it said my girls are too clever and keen," exclaimed Mrs Bennet.

Her seriousness made Darcy cringe.

Mrs Bennet then stood, and the ladies made to leave. Darcy, nearest to the door, rose to open it for them. He wanted to comfort Elizabeth as she passed him, but she kept her eyes downcast in apparent mortification. When the door closed and he was left with only the gentlemen, Darcy was unsure whether or not this would be an improvement.

If he was to practise being amiable, he might as well get on with it. It was uphill work for him to be talking to those of whom he knew so little, but he tried to talk over politics in the hopes of comparing the accounts of their relative newspapers. Mr Bennet was not interested, and Darcy learned Mr Collins had no mind for such matters. He proposed shooting and Luddite uprisings as possible topics, but they too were rebuffed in as short a time as Mr Collins's long speeches would allow.

Darcy's attempts at respectful discourse were lost on Mr Collins, and Mr Bennet was content to observe his failure in amused silence. He decided he would force his host to engage with him. He moved to the seat Elizabeth had vacated, closest to Mr Bennet, and fixed his eyes on him.

"Have you any intention of enjoying London in the winter?"

"I hate London." When Darcy could not hide his affront at this curt reply, Mr Bennet spoke with more courtesy. "I am fond of the country and my books. Mrs Bennet delights in the shops and public places, but I do not care for town. It has been several years since my wife or I have passed any time there."

"The amusements and varieties town has to offer must be an attraction to your daughters. Are they disappointed to always remain at home?"

"It is of little interest to me. My daughters are capable of finding their own amusements. My wife's brother is settled in town in a respectable line of trade." Mr Bennet watched him carefully, as though to judge his reaction to this news, so Darcy kept his expression neutral. "His wife is an elegant, intelligent woman, and my older daughters admire her. Jane or Lizzy often pass part of the year with them."

That explains the elder daughters' comportment. London manners and superior behaviour would not come naturally to a young girl who spent all her time in this household. "Did your daughters go to town for the sake of their education? I ask because my sister had been in school before I formed an establishment for her in town with a woman who superintends her education."

"No. They read what was of interest to them. I have some uncommonly foolish daughters—although Lizzy has some quickness—so I chose not to waste my time on hopeless causes."

To say that remaining at the table with the gentlemen was disagreeable was not strong enough to do justice to Darcy's feelings. Elizabeth's father was a mocking man who had detached himself from his family while Mr Collins looked without seeing and listened without knowing what was said. Darcy moved to a window to glance at his pocket watch. *Twelve minutes. How am I to survive an hour of this?*

There was another three minutes of blessed silence, while Darcy paced the outline of the room, Mr Bennet drank his port, and Mr Collins ate the remains of the nuts and fruit left on the table. It was not long after Darcy returned to his own chair and filled his glass when their host decided to provoke him.

"We have had little conversation. I do not presume Mr Darcy to be interested in banter, so I must introduce a subject in which my cousin will shine. Mr Collins, you have managed to pass an entire meal without speaking about your patroness. I cannot imagine that lady to be far from your thoughts."

"My good sir! I can scarcely credit such a notion, for I am acutely aware of what bounty and beneficence I have been so fortunate as to receive at the hands of that great lady. Why, her manners are beyond anything I can describe!"

Thank goodness.

Regrettably, Mr Collins continued. "I have never in my life witnessed such behaviour in a person of rank, such affability, and such condescension, as I have experienced from Lady Catherine de Bourgh."

Darcy coughed on his wine. Tears welled up in his eyes as he tried not to choke. *Of all the unfortunate coincidences!* That this oddity should be the rector of his aunt's parish was astonishing. He considered acknowledging his connexion to her ladyship, but decided to save himself the obsequious attentions of so irksome a man.

The chatter about his own family brought to mind Darcy's Christmas plans at Pemberley: everyone would pester him about marrying; his cousin Viscount Milton would complain about the expenses of keeping both his mistress and his wife; his other cousin, a colonel, would be enjoyable company when he was not arguing with his brother; Lady Catherine would give unsolicited advice from the moment she crossed his threshold; and his cousin Anne would not make her voice heard the entire time they were occupants of the same house.

"… an intimate connexion to Rosings. It shall by my earnest endeavour to demean myself with grateful respect towards her ladyship."

It took both Darcy and Mr Bennet a long moment to realise that the droning sound of Mr Collins's voice had ended. Thankfully, Mr Bennet had grown tired of provoking his cousin into absurdity and suggested they rejoin the ladies.

The gentlemen entered the drawing room, and when they did, the ladies' voices were silenced; Miss Bennet and Elizabeth's faces were red with embarrassment. Darcy did what he had been wont to do when he entered a room where he knew Elizabeth would be: his eyes sought her out. She raised hers to his with a gladdened expression.

His heart jolted in his chest. He also discerned a note of concern in Elizabeth's look; she understood how he passed his time in the dining room. Something in her manner soothed him. He was transfixed by her eyes. They were dark, intelligent, laughing, and he felt her warmth and earnestness in them. It was an intimate moment in a crowded room, the likes of which he had only seen pass between others. *Not just others*; *other couples.*

Darcy walked towards her, but before he had advanced into the room, Mrs Bennet demanded Elizabeth open the instrument. Mr

Collins seconded this request with more dialogue than was required.

"Mary expressed an interest in exhibiting. She may lead the way," Elizabeth answered. "Besides, I ought to help Jane."

Darcy saw Miss Mary, in a corner alone, toss aside her sewing and rise.

"Oh, hang Mary!" Mrs Bennet shouted. "When you are done pouring coffee, I insist that you play."

Elizabeth turned pink and helped Miss Bennet. All the while, Mr Collins entreated Elizabeth to do him the honour of performing and lamented that his own humble abode lacked an instrument. Mr Bennet read his newspaper, and his wife bemoaned the long wait for Mr Bingley's arrival. Miss Kitty and Miss Lydia trimmed a bonnet while they argued over which of the militia officers were the most becoming in their regimentals.

A gentleman must act with the wish of giving happiness to others. It is one of the marks of true politeness. His father's words echoed in Darcy's head. Behaving with politeness to *everyone*, not only Elizabeth and Bingley, was the mark of true gentlemanly behaviour. It would be a challenge, but he wanted to be a more gracious man, so he would rise to meet it.

Elizabeth saw Darcy was seated by Charlotte. They seemed involved in some engrossing conversation. It was an odd tête-à-tête, but she was glad to see it. As she poured Mr Collins's coffee, she felt proud of Darcy. A man who had every advantage, a dignified and reserved man, he was, in his own way, attempting to be more gentlemanly.

Her mother called her attention. "Open the instrument, Lizzy."

Mr Collins abandoned his cup and offered to turn the pages for her. She tried to decline, but her mother spoke for her.

"Thank you, Mr Collins, Lizzy is much obliged. Why do you not select the piece you would like her to play?"

Elizabeth gritted her teeth and sat at the instrument, where another five minutes passed while Mr Collins pawed through the music books. He selected a piece, at random, and drew a chair close to her.

Mr Collins spoke at her while she played, but at the first opportunity he failed to turn the page. She gestured to get his attention as she neared the last measure, but Elizabeth realised Mr Collins could not read music. She knew the piece, but not from memory. Every time Elizabeth raised her hand to turn the page, Mr Collins threw up his own and insisted on turning it, hitting her hand or knocking the sheet music to the floor. He apologised as he struggled to set the music to rights, apologised for missing his mark, apologised for being in her way.

When the song was complete, Elizabeth refused to play again. Mary eagerly took her seat, but Mr Collins followed Elizabeth to the tea table, saying so the whole room heard, "It gives me the greatest pleasure to hear you play. I admit that it is not a talent for which I have much appreciation, but I am without a doubt convinced that you are very musical."

It had been a terrible performance. Elizabeth wished there was someone in the room to look to for comfort. Her father sat behind his newspaper, but his shaking shoulders told her he was delighted by the absurdity. Jane was too busy curbing Kitty and Lydia's disrespectful laughter to be of any use to her. Mary had already taken her seat at the instrument and was playing a ponderous melody. Her mother was boasting to Charlotte and Darcy on her having such gifted daughters.

Elizabeth's gaze settled on Darcy. He turned from Mrs Bennet and met her eye. She was relieved that he looked on her, not with scathing disapproval, but with sympathy. There was a conscious, expressive look in his striking eyes that showed a warmth, a tenderness of his heart. It was a small kindness, but it meant a great deal to her.

While Mr Collins prattled on, Elizabeth looked at Darcy again, and she offered him a subtle look of amused resignation. He smiled, and his eyes expressed all his feelings of commiseration and empathy. It was a brief interlude, and Darcy then gave every appearance of being a reserved gentleman attending to the conversation of his hostess while Elizabeth attempted to attend to Mr Collins expounding on his situation in Hunsford.

"Do you comprehend how well connected Lady Catherine is? She married into the prestigious house of de Bourgh, but she is the sister of Earl Fitzwilliam, one of the greatest landowners in all of England. So you understand, my dear cousin, there are many reasons why I am fortunate in my patroness as she is of that most distinguished, noble, wealthy family Fitzwilliam."

At the mention of Lady Catherine's maiden name, Elizabeth looked at Darcy. His attention was fixed on Mr Collins. Darcy's look was of disapproval, but when he realised Elizabeth was watching, he composed his features and looked back to her mother.

As she watched the changes flicker across Darcy's countenance, Elizabeth was struck. The coincidence of Darcy's name being the same as Lady Catherine's maiden name was no coincidence after all; Darcy had a relationship to Lady Catherine. Mr Collins's veneration for his patroness was already insufferable; to see him bow and fawn over Darcy once he learnt of the connexion would be excruciating.

Elizabeth suggested her cousin might need more refreshment and directed him farther from Darcy to the tea table, where Mrs Bennet fussed over him and supplied him with coffee and cake. Darcy took the opportunity to stare out the nearest window, and Elizabeth found herself next to Charlotte for the first time since her return from Netherfield.

"Eliza, I have hardly spoken two words to you. I cannot believe this is the first moment we have had to ourselves."

"That was in part because you were in conversation with Mr Darcy for a while." She feared she sounded jealous, then said archly, "I hope his conversation was more than affected civility for you to remain by his side for so long."

"He asked after my family, and he spoke affectionately about his own sister. He was gracious enough to appear interested in all your mother had to share about the importance of bringing out one's daughters as soon as they turned fifteen. I never expected Mr Darcy to be so amiable."

Elizabeth looked to where Darcy remained at the window. She

admired the way his coat fit taut and smooth across his shoulders. There was no mistaking his confidence and commanding air, even though his back was to the room. She could make out his handsome face and compelling dark eyes in his reflection in the glass. Darcy's eyes came back into focus and when his gaze met hers, her heart turned over in response. Elizabeth started and turned back to her friend.

"Yes, we were thrown a good deal together while I was at Netherfield and he improved upon further acquaintance." Elizabeth more felt than saw that Darcy had left the window and was moving to the other side of the room. "I had once thought his general expression was disdainful and full of improper pride, but I was mistaken."

"Yes, his *expression* is notable; he *expressively* looks at you a great deal. I observed since the moment he entered the drawing room that he looks on you with an earnest, steadfast gaze."

"Charlotte, be sensible!"

"I always am. I suspect he is partial to you."

"You have always been my kindest friend; please do not suggest there is more to state on the case than his attentions stemming from anything other than friendship." To wish was to hope, and to hope was to expect, and despite their friendship, she had no reason to expect anything from Darcy.

Their conversation could not continue because Mrs Bennet had heard some noise outside and shrieked, "He is come, he is, indeed! Mr Bingley is here!"

Chapter 15

The impropriety of conduct had been present all evening, between the childish laughter of the youngest daughters, the cruel teasing Mr Bennet tendered when he deigned to speak, and the incessant and foolish words that assaulted Darcy's ears whenever Mr Collins opened his mouth. However, it was Mrs Bennet's frantic shrieks that now caused Darcy to silently beg for deliverance.

"I am certain a carriage is driving up to the door! Mr Bennet, do you not hear it?"

"I could listen with more consideration were I not obliged to hear your exclamations on the subject."

"Never mind, it must be the gentlemen! Jane? Jane, come and sit here. Yes, right here."

The next moment confirmed the idea by the noise of the house-bell, which caused further exclamations from the lady of the house, and more sarcasm from Mr Bennet.

"I shall retire to the library."

"What! You cannot mean it!"

"It is my custom to retire to the library after tea. I shall return for supper."

"You have no compassion for my poor nerves. We have company joining us!"

"I was under the impression this was an informal evening. I do not see why I must remain. Do I not always retire to the library after tea?"

"But Mr *Bingley* and Mr Hurst will be here! It would vex me horridly should you leave now."

"You are mistaken; it would not take my leaving the room to vex you, as you appear to be in that state at the present."

Darcy walked away to avoid hearing more, but even on the other side of the room, he heard the not-so-dulcet tone of Mrs Bennet's fretting and her husband's taunting until the gentlemen were announced.

Salutations were just completed when Mrs Bennet descended upon Bingley, offering him whatever refreshment he liked, complimenting his blue coat, exclaiming her pleasure at having him at Longbourn, and promising that cards would be a lively entertainment, but if he preferred anything else, she would see it done. He replied with an easy civility Darcy marvelled at. Mr Hurst followed in silence, likely hoping to see that the card tables were placed.

The servants came in to take away the tea things and, with this distraction, Darcy had a moment to speak privately with his friend.

"I do hope you had a pleasant time at dinner, Darcy."

"It proved to be an intellectual poverty."

"Perhaps over a round of cards, you might find some chat more to your liking."

"I do not wish to be nailed to a card table for the next two hours." *That was hardly gentlemanly.* "I did have a pleasant conversation with Miss Lucas."

Bingley smiled and went to where Miss Bennet sat and admired her work while the arrangement of the card parties began. What Darcy had presumed to be a simple undertaking was complicated by Mrs Bennet's meddlesome input and Mr Bennet's sardonic humour.

"Mr Bingley, would you like to play whist? Is there a round game you care for? Oh, perhaps you prefer to remain where you are." She gave her daughter a knowing look. Miss Bennet turned pink, and Darcy looked away to spare her further mortification.

Mrs Bennet then claimed Mr Hurst as a whist partner, which suited that gentlemen well when he learned his hostess was an accomplished player. Mr Bennet consented to play and called to Elizabeth to complete their table.

"No, Lizzy, you must sit out! I want you to perform again when we have all had enough of Mary."

Miss Kitty offered to make up their fourth, but her father said, "You know no more of whist than you do of algebra!" Darcy heard the girls mutter something about wishing the officers had been invited to enliven their dreary party. Mr Bennet then instructed Miss Lucas to be his partner as she at least was a "tolerably sensible girl," and she could do nothing but comply.

After making up the whist table, there remained sufficient numbers for a round game, and the younger girls decided on Speculation. When Mr Collins expressed a long-winded interest in observing the whist game, Mr Bennet suggested he join the girls instead. Darcy wondered if anyone else heard Miss Kitty and Miss Lydia's groans.

Darcy suspected that despite Speculation being the easiest game on the cards, Mr Collins would not soon find himself master of its rules. Bingley and Miss Bennet joined them, despite Mrs Bennet's insistence they remain left to themselves on the sofa together. The party wanted to play Speculation, and if Darcy was to be obliging, even to those he found tiresome, he would play the simple, noisy game. Then Elizabeth stood before him.

"If you are no card player, Mr Darcy, would you find it tolerable to talk with me while I await my turn to exhibit?"

"I would never turn down good company and intelligent conversation for the sake of cards." They sat together on a sofa, and he noticed she was still at work on clothes for those living in the village.

"I am determined to complete my share before Christmas. You will, I hope, forgive me for working on something useful before company rather than fine embroidery. But we shall remain superlatively stupid if all we speak of is my work."

"Then tell me what you think of Cowper's *The Garden*. Or, if your hands have been too busy sewing to hold a book, I will read to you while you work."

"The poetry you loaned me is the reason why I am behind at my work. I finished the latest volume; remind me, if you please, to return it to you."

They discussed Cowper and the merits of blank verse for some time before Darcy was brought back into awareness of the others.

"What is it you are talking of over there?" Mrs Bennet called.

"Mr Darcy and I were discussing poetry."

"My dear Lizzy! You can be so tiresome. Does Mr Darcy not wish to play Speculation with the others?"

Darcy eagerly expressed his desire to remain where he was.

"You need not feign to be interested in her, sir. Lizzy does tend to run on. Mary, dear! Finish up that dull concerto, won't you? We have all had enough. Let Lizzy have another turn. Then Mr Darcy can join the others in the next round."

"I see no reason to hurry Mary. I will play when she wishes to relinquish her post."

"No need to be bashful, Lizzy; you have nowhere to go but up after your previous performance," Mr Bennet quipped. "Mary! I beg you not to punish us any longer. Let your sister have time to exhibit."

Miss Mary struggled to finish her song, and Darcy felt pity for her. Her voice was weak and her manner affected, but that did not mean she ought to be made the subject of ridicule. She was eager to display; it appeared to be the only time either of her parents noticed her.

Darcy rose and addressed Elizabeth. "I shall cross the room to attend your sister's performance. Perhaps you might like to turn over some of the music books before you perform again?"

He watched her mouth curve into a soft appreciative smile. They looked at each other in earnestness for a long moment before Elizabeth nodded. Darcy took a seat near to the piano while she looked through the music. It took effort to keep his attention on the Bennet daughter performing instead of gazing on the sparkling eyes, full lips, and soft tendrils of hair of the Bennet daughter nearest to him.

Miss Mary's abilities were by no means improved by having a dedicated audience, but she appeared flattered to have someone attend to her performance. He wished to be considerate to her without encouraging her to play again. "Thank you, Miss Mary. I do not know a more luxurious state than sitting at one's ease being entertained by a young lady." She was so flustered all she managed was a curtsey before she scurried away.

"You have done a gracious thing, Darcy," Elizabeth murmured. "Mary has never known the happiness of being truly listened to."

Elizabeth looked at him with such open admiration that Darcy needed a moment to calm his mind. He would listen to Mary Bennet perform all the movements of a dozen concertos if it meant Elizabeth looked at him with approval.

"Are you able to sing, Mr Darcy? Some of my favourite duets are lying on the instrument."

"I am excessively fond of music, but without the smallest skill of my own."

"Is that the truth, or are you disinclined to exhibit?"

Darcy only smiled. Elizabeth made a great show of rolling her eyes and selecting another piece, adding, "Should I ever learn your talents take a musical bent, I shall be seriously displeased."

"I comprehend enough to be able to turn the pages for you." He spoke with his regular gravity—not a single word had undue inflection nor did he turn in the direction of Mr Collins—but Elizabeth had to bite her lip to refrain from laughing.

"I will signal you when it is time to turn the pages. See that you keep the music off the floor, if you please."

Darcy had never given serious consideration to what sort of married existence he envisioned for his future. Indeed, he had never been confident that he desired to share his private life with anyone. But while she played, effortlessly and unpretentiously, Elizabeth raised her expressive eyes to meet his and gave him a tender smile. It stirred something in Darcy's mind and heart.

In that moment, he was certain no domestic comfort could compare to spending a quiet evening at Pemberley with Elizabeth.

His reticent sister could not but improve under Elizabeth's lively influence, and as Darcy's gaze wandered to the other side of the room, it was not a difficulty to imagine that Bingley and Miss Bennet would often be with them. A small child or two toddling up to the instrument was all that was needed to complete the flawless domestic scene.

"That was enjoyable, Lizzy!" Mrs Bennet's voice assaulted his senses as Darcy realised Elizabeth's performance had ended. "Mr Collins, does not Lizzy play charmingly? She may not be the prettiest or the most good-humoured of my girls, but she does have her accomplishments."

"All of my daughters are silly," added Mr Bennet, "but Lizzy does have a bit of cleverness to prevent her from being uniformly senseless."

Mr Bennet's sardonic wink in Elizabeth's direction did little to spare her any mortification. Misses Mary and Kitty looked offended at their father's words, and Miss Lydia spoke louder about militia officers and their dashing red coats.

While Elizabeth had played, Miss Mary joined the card game whereas Bingley and Miss Bennet seceded from it. The pair sat a little apart and were now engaged in earnest conversation. Miss Bennet worked while Bingley admired every stitch she made. Darcy and Elizabeth joined them, and for a time, the assembled group grew quite comfortable. Sadly, it was not to last. Mrs Bennet, realising her scheme of forwarding a match between Bingley and Miss Bennet would never succeed if Darcy and Elizabeth were in their way, attempted to separate them.

"Lizzy, sit by Mr Collins and play speculation. I fear he might need assistance; he seems to have too many cards. Maybe Mr Darcy would like to play as well."

A blind man could see Elizabeth did not prefer her cousin's company. Elizabeth could not refuse her mother's direct request; instead, she pretended not to hear. However, the foursome could not converse when they were being so loudly spoken of by Mr and Mrs Bennet.

"Leave her be, Mrs Bennet. You would not wish to leave Mr Bingley and Jane all alone, would you?"

She made an indistinct mutter of disapproval. "They are hardly alone with Mr Darcy attending them."

"What possible reason could you have for permitting our neighbour and eldest daughter to speak privately? That is not proper."

"Oh, you are vexing! My poor nerves." Mrs Bennet lowered her voice and leant over to speak to her husband in a whisper.

Mr Bennet's response was loud enough for them all to hear. "If so, they will get to the point without your help. I see no more reason to get them by themselves than for Lizzy and Mr Collins to be granted a tête-à-tête."

By this point, even Bingley was struggling to keep his countenance. Miss Bennet could no longer pretend not to hear and took a great interest in the thread she was twisting between her fingers; Elizabeth was cringing; and Darcy refrained from pulling out his watch to wonder how soon he could leave. *If only I could bring Elizabeth back with me.*

Mr Bennet must have noticed how ill at ease those not playing cards were feeling, because he called out to them, "Please take no notice of Mrs Bennet. Lizzy, why do you not fetch that book you were reading? You wanted to return it to Mr Darcy?"

Before Elizabeth answered, Mrs Bennet shouted to her again. "Why do you not ask Mr Darcy if he would like to walk with you? He has not seen that part of the house."

"Why would Mr Darcy have any reason to see our breakfast room?" Mr Bennet was determined to misunderstand his wife. "'Tis a family space, unless you intend to start spending our evenings there."

Mrs Bennet was now speaking through clenched teeth, and with a determined tilt of her head. "Mr Darcy can admire the porcelain figures or the girls' imitation of china. It would be a fine opportunity to take a turn after sitting for so long."

"Should we invite Mr Bingley to join them? He and Mr Darcy might like a formal tour of the decorative arts adorning our breakfast room."

"No! Mr Bingley and Jane are happy where they are." This might have gone on all evening had not Mr Hurst called them to order with bitter complaints of his partner's inattention.

Elizabeth asked in a monotone voice if Mr Darcy would care to accompany her to the breakfast room to retrieve his poetry. He agreed, and he prayed for patience, for the grace to treat the Bennet household respectfully, and for more than his usual self-control to maintain his composure in the face of further ridiculousness.

Elizabeth retrieved a candle and, as he closed the door behind them, Darcy heard Mrs Bennet say to her husband, "You need not worry on that account! She is not handsome enough for him to dance with, you know."

Elizabeth remained in deep, silent mortification while she lit some candles in the breakfast room. The shock of her family's horrifying behaviour, even more outrageous than normal, had left her almost physically ill. She kept her face from Darcy as she gestured towards the table where his volume lay.

She heard Darcy move around the table and assumed he had taken up his book to be gone. But, instead, as she turned from the wall, she discerned that he was now closer and was watching her in compassionate silence. All she wanted was to indulge in the flow of tears that threatened to burst from her eyes at any instant.

"Do you not wish to rejoin the others?" Her voice shook. "Please, take a candle; I shall not be long."

"Thank you, but I will wait until you are ready."

Elizabeth did not think she could maintain her self-possession for much longer. "You do not need me by your side to return to the party. I had thought you were taking great pains to be amiable to your social inferiors." She hardly knew what she was saying; every moment Darcy remained added to her embarrassment.

She deserved a harsh retort, but was instead surprised by the tremulous tone of his voice. "You mistake me. I do not reject their company because their connexions are lower than mine. More than anything, I want to stay wi—" He paused. "I am reluctant to return because I am appalled by the thoughtless way your parents treat you."

She held the same opinion, yet hearing them voiced by someone she respected and admired was distressing. All her equanimity was lost. Elizabeth faced him and felt the tears start to fall down her cheeks.

"Their behaviour is in every way disgraceful! My father mocks my mother at every opportunity. My younger sisters are either indulged or ignored. You have heard my father say more than once that his daughters are foolish. How ashamed I am to realise that I, too, am capable of cruel judgments. It turns my stomach to think if I did not change my ways that I could become like him, exhibiting unkindness through disparaging humour.

"And all the while I am supposed to act as the dutiful daughter, obey them in all things, and pretend I do not abhor their conduct! I fear the entire world knows how little I respect them. What sort of a daughter does that make me?"

Darcy took a quick step towards her and shook his head. "You have never acted disrespectfully towards them, not in my observation."

"Is it any consolation that they are oblivious to their own vulgarity?" She raised her eyes from the floor and met Darcy's compassionate gaze. The look of gentleness in his eyes destroyed all her composure. "Oh Darcy, it is so hard to respect my parents as I ought!"

Darcy tossed the poetry volume on to the table and came around to stand nearer. "I have never seen you fail to treat your parents with the respect and attention due to them. As for whatever you might *feel*, such opinions are entirely your own, and you need not defend them or feel guilty for them."

Elizabeth managed to nod, but was not yet ready to speak. Something about Darcy induced her confidence, but she would pull herself together. She pressed the heels of her hands against her eyes and took a deep breath.

"Welcome to the domestic hurricane that is life at Longbourn." She tried to smile. Darcy handed her his handkerchief, looking both sympathetic and worried.

She forced a smile, dabbing her eyes and blinking furiously. "Come, we must have some conversation. I am the one in need of a proper distraction now. You could share a memory of your parents behaving badly before company."

"I did not have the opportunity to view their marriage or conduct, or to know them at all as an adult. My memories of my father are clearer, but I have few distinct recollections of my mother and father's interactions."

She placed a hand on his arm. "How thoughtless I have been!"

"I am well." He looked at her expressively. "Truly, I am. They have been gone a long time, my mother in particular."

Elizabeth pulled her hand away but stayed near. "That does not make their loss anything less than deeply heartfelt. Please, forgive me for being insensitive. You have taught me a lesson: I ought not to complain of the poor conduct of my parents when I am fortunate to still have them."

"I think it is natural to want to do right by one's parents. My father urged me, nearly with his dying breath, to be an honourable man, to care for Georgiana, and to transmit Pemberley to my children in as thriving a state as he left it to me." He swallowed thickly. "Hardly a day goes by I do not recollect his words."

"I have not had the privilege of your acquaintance for long, but I have absolute confidence that your parents would be proud of the man you have become."

There was a spark of some indefinable emotion in Darcy's eyes; she dared not call it wistful. His voice wavered when he thanked her for her kind words, but in another moment the grief in his expression was gone. In its place was a smile, and he spoke more to himself when he asked, "What is it about you that invokes my blunt sincerity?"

They were standing much closer now; Darcy moved first, but her own fingers ached to reach over and clasp his hands. Suddenly, her gloveless hands were enclosed within his, and Elizabeth felt a nervous thrill all over her body. The warm feel of his skin against hers was simply wonderful. She stared at their joined hands, watching the shadows from the flickering candles move across them; she felt, for the first time that evening, a sense of contentment.

He slowly pulled her hands and rested them on his chest before covering them with his own. She felt his heart pounding, and realised her own heart was drumming away so loudly she was certain he could hear it. Elizabeth's breath came in short, shallow bursts when he clasped her hands even tighter.

She lifted her chin to encounter his eye and saw an ardent gaze of unabashed admiration. She did not have the pleasure of that adoring look for long, because in the next moment, the whole of Darcy's attention was captivated by her mouth. Elizabeth's lips parted unconsciously, and when he leant closer, she realised what was about to happen. A small smile trembled across her lips. Her anticipation was palpable as she leant forward while Darcy tilted his head to the side.

The sight of Darcy's lips so close to her own nearly overwhelmed her, but it was only when she heard him whisper "Elizabeth" that her eyes fluttered closed. She felt his warm breath against her lips.

There was scarcely half an inch remaining between their lips when she heard the doorknob turn. Elizabeth started, but Darcy let go of her hands and took a quick step backwards. Before the door swung open, he turned and took two long strides towards the wall; all Elizabeth managed to do in this time was fall into a chair before her wobbling legs failed to support her.

Therefore, when Mr Collins lumbered into the room, he observed Darcy, hands clasped behind his back, admiring the china on the sideboard, and Elizabeth sitting at the table with a volume of poetry closed in front of her.

"Cousin Elizabeth, your mother has fixed on me the task of attending you back to the drawing room. The supper table is set out, and I would not wish for you to miss the opportunity to dine on any of the delectable foods that your dear mother has put forth for our enjoyment. The minced chicken and scalloped oysters look particularly tasteful. I daresay it could rival one of the very small, more informal suppers that Lady Catherine offers at Rosings."

The shock of being seconds ago nearly in Darcy's arms to now being accosted by the loathsome Mr Collins made it impossible for her to speak. Thankfully, her cousin was neither observant nor inquisitive and had moved to compliment Mr Darcy's discernment in admiring so fine a breakfast set in the first place.

Darcy stared at Mr Collins in expressive wonder. The desire to

TWO MORE DAYS AT NETHERFIELD

shield him from further ridiculousness forced Elizabeth to rise; she picked up the book and handed it to its owner. For a moment, both of their hands held it, and he looked at her with eyes of glowing entreaty. He stretched out a finger and grazed it against the tip of one of her own. She fixed her eyes on his face, but Mr Collins nudged her to offer his arm to lead her back to the others. Miserably, she had no opportunity during the remainder of the evening to have another private moment with Darcy.

Elizabeth did, however, steal down to the breakfast room after the family and servants had retired for the night to pick up a handkerchief on the floor with the initials F.D. embroidered in the corner.

Chapter 16

Sunday, November 24

It had been raining since Friday without intermission, and Darcy now sat in his dressing room, chilled and weary. He sat before the pitiful fire as the wind roared down the chimney and the rain beat in torrents against the windows. It suited his mood as he reread the letter that had arrived yesterday.

5 Upper Wimpole Street
21 November

Dear Sir,
I regret that I cannot give you an account of your sister's improved happiness. Yesterday we encountered Miss Grantley, and Miss Darcy trembled after her friend enquired how she enjoyed her summer at the seaside. Your sister grew alarmed, and I had to whisk her home before Miss Grantley could see she had reduced her to tears. All the way she

fretted that her throat was closing, and even at home she complained of heart palpitations.

Although I remain in ignorance of how Miss Darcy spent the time from when she was removed from school to the time my services were obtained, it is my respectful opinion that an event upset her to such a degree that I am not certain what I can do to aid her.

I would not otherwise speak freely, sir, but your letter said that you desired an honest accounting of my opinion. Forgive me if I speak out of turn, but since neither you nor my charge has seen it appropriate for me to know such details, I can only hope that time will see Miss Darcy restored to her equanimity.

I remain your loyal servant,
A. Annesley

DARCY COULD NOT BEAR THE THOUGHT OF TELLING ANOTHER person of Georgiana's near ruin. He had hoped that as time passed, she would appear more like herself. Before he left for Hertfordshire, she still did not enjoy leaving the house, but she answered questions with more than "yes" or "no" and had begun to laugh a little. She was never an assertive or loquacious girl, but he had hoped those small steps were a sign that Ramsgate would soon be a distant memory.

"All the girl needs is time, Darcy! Leave her alone, and let her be a young lady about town without her brother constantly asking if she is well," Colonel Fitzwilliam had advised him in September.

Three months since Ramsgate. Darcy dropped the letter to the floor.

Georgiana's unnatural reserve and anxious manner suggested there being something more to conceal about her time at Ramsgate, but he doubted she had the strength to speak of it when she could not even make polite conversation with her friends. Despite Georgiana's imprudence in consenting to an elopement, she was not an unintelligent girl, and she had since realised she had nearly thrown herself away on a vindictive, unscrupulous man who wanted her thirty thousand pounds. But why did she continue to suffer these fits of agitation?

It broke his heart.

He must bolster her courage during the impending Christmas festivities when their Fitzwilliam relations would be at Pemberley for a fortnight. Not even her near relations knew about Ramsgate, but Darcy did not know what he would do if his sister trembled, suffered from heart palpitations, or collapsed in tears when speaking with her own family. Even her extreme cautiousness of word and manner would be remarked upon.

Darcy stretched his legs in front of him and leant back in his chair. The constant drumming of rain was almost in rhythm with the pounding pain in his head.

After falling asleep in the chair and passing a miserable evening, Darcy awoke and dressed before the housemaid lit his fire. The thought of another morning with Hurst ranting about the dullness of the weather and Miss Bingley's desperate attempts to earn his approbation added to his despondency. It was too wet to ride, he had no letters to write, no new books to read. Feeling the effects of being prohibited from any sort of exercise, he decided to walk through the house until breakfast.

After passing along the gallery that crossed the lobby above the hall for a third time, he stopped to gaze out the window. Darcy caught a view of the lane he had walked along with Elizabeth a week ago. Before Darcy had time to consider, again, all that happened on the last occasion he had seen Elizabeth, he heard hushed voices from below.

"I could not help but hear you and Louisa, and I must tell you it is out of his power to return your good opinion."

"How can you speak to your own sister that way? No gentleman who married me could ever have the wish to have bestowed himself elsewhere."

Darcy did not dare make a noise by moving above Bingley and

his sister, and he hoped they would walk on, but the footsteps stopped.

"You are not heeding me. I do not doubt your ability to make *some* man a fine wife, just not Darcy. I say this to show you a kindness, to save yourself and my friend from embarrassment. He does not fancy you."

"What do you know of the matter?" Her voice sounded sneering.

"What I know is that all you want is the status a man *like* Darcy can provide, along with the means of spending as much as you like and mixing with people of rank. Darcy prefers activities that you in fact disdain. You would not make one another happy. You will *never* be Mrs Darcy." This last sentence was uttered with the sympathy appropriate to a mourner.

There was a sharp intake of breath. "You misjudge the situation because he has been particular with Miss El—" At this point, Darcy left the gallery to avoid hearing more. He descended the stairs noisily, stamping on every step as he approached where Bingley and his younger sister were loitering.

Miss Bingley looked away in confusion and left, and Bingley made some polite observation about the ball tomorrow and then followed his sister. Darcy went to the library, assured that there he would be uninterrupted.

Never before had the prospect of a ball brought him anything close to happiness: he would see Elizabeth again. He felt the loss of her company. The full truth was that he also felt an irrepressible passionate desire to take Elizabeth in his arms and finish what that loathsome Mr Collins interrupted.

Their near-kiss had been the culmination of every intimate discussion, every heightened glance, every fleeting touch, every blush and private smile that passed between them in the previous week. As a consequence of their arguments and reconciliations, and their many conversations, their acquaintance had progressed from ambivalence on his part and pointed dislike on hers to a sincere attachment. After seeing her face collapse with shame and covered in tears, Darcy knew *he* wanted to be the one to offer her every comfort for the rest of her life.

Marriage is not something to be entered into lightly.

To the lady, there could be no objection; the barrier before him was the Bennet's general behaviour. Want of connexion and want of fortune did not give him pause. No, his obstacle to marrying Elizabeth was the total want of propriety so frequently betrayed by her nearest relations. Even Bingley could not condone their behaviour.

Elizabeth's father was interested in his family only as far as they provided him amusement. Her mother was insensible to the feelings of others, and the business of her life was to get her daughters married at whatever the cost. Elizabeth's younger sisters were ridiculous, and the youngest two were idle flirts. The eldest two Miss Bennets were on the same level as he as far as refinement and comportment, but the rest of the family was likely to cause embarrassment.

His parents' expectations had inculcated him to the mindset of acquiring affluence and power through marriage. Marrying his cousin Anne, regardless of their lack of compatibility or affection, would allow the Darcy family to unify two dignified and wealthy houses, secure a second estate, increase their fortune, and gain more exalted connexions.

But in the course of Elizabeth's stay at Netherfield, ancestral duty and societal expectations seemed less imperative, yielding their place of prominence to happiness and love.

I love her.

He wanted to make her happy; he wanted to be the person she relied upon. He wanted to share with her all that he had and do all that he could to bring her as much joy to her life as he was certain she would bring to his. Connexions, familial duty, and embarrassing behaviour could all go to the devil if she loved him in return. Darcy's heart raced, and his smile gave way to a brief spell of laughter.

"I love Elizabeth Bennet."

In his rational mind, he could not assume that she would accept him, despite that she had seemed willing to allow him to kiss her. His heart, however, told him she loved him as sincerely as he did her.

She had promised to keep two dances for him, but as pleasurable as they were certain to be, a ball would not be an appropriate place to make his proposals. He would be obliged to wait another day. Darcy was decided: he would call at Longbourn at the earliest possible hour the day after the ball. In the meantime, he would send her the next volume of Cowper to read so she knew that he thought of her. Darcy headed back down the hallway with renewed vigour.

I love her!

Before Darcy walked into breakfast, he stopped smiling and put great effort in appearing like himself before the others. After the ball, he would fulfil his heart's earnest desire and ask Elizabeth to be his wife.

Monday, November 25

ELIZABETH HAD BEEN TRAPPED IN THE HOUSE SINCE FRIDAY, AND not even the hope of the dance on Tuesday had made it bearable. On Friday, the family had been discussing the upcoming ball, and Elizabeth's spirits were so high with the prospect of seeing Darcy again that she asked Mr Collins if he intended to accept Mr Bingley's invitation.

How was I to know that not only was Mr Collins going to attend, but he was going to then solicit me for the first two dances?

Darcy had asked her to save two dances for him, but she had hoped that, upon seeing her, he might claim them sooner rather than later. But what could she do? Mr Collins was accepted with good grace, but without any enthusiasm.

Perhaps it was the days of dreary weather, the inability to take a vigorous walk, or the irksome society of Mr Collins, but Elizabeth missed Darcy. What had she become that she, ever full of good humour, ever self-reliant, fell despondent after four days without the conversation of one man? *A handsome gentleman: strikingly tall, with expressive dark eyes that brighten when he smiles. And his laugh! He is resplendent when he laughs.*

He had other admirable qualities: his knowledge of the world, his strong feelings of family attachment, his quiet dignity. He was generous and clever with a dry wit. Elizabeth was convinced Darcy saw her as his equal; he would be a partner she could respect. Darcy was not only a principled man, but he had the desire to be an even better one.

She felt a hot thrill at the memory of his low voice when he had whispered her name a mere breath away from her lips. How many times had she passed over the memory of what happened in the breakfast parlour? Had Darcy only been caught up in an impassioned moment or did he, like her, wish Mr Collins had dropped dead in the corridor?

The uncertainty of the extent of his feelings, and the certainty that he did feel *something,* drove Elizabeth into the happiness of such misery, or the misery of such happiness. She had not even told Jane the extent to which her feelings towards Darcy now reached. She could not expose herself to the humiliation of such a disappointment in the event she was wrong; her private pain would be bad enough.

A glance at the few wet splatters on the window was enough to convince Elizabeth that the rain had let up, and she readied herself for a walk. Any secret wishes that Darcy might also be eager for a walk after such a succession of rain would be best left unexamined.

She kept to the lane towards Meryton, hopping over every puddle, and was able to keep her mind from wandering towards Darcy for nearly a half of a mile.

Only one thing was wanting to make the prospect of tomorrow's ball satisfactory to Elizabeth: its being assured that she might pass half of the evening with Darcy. She would pass more than just the ball alongside him if he asked. She knew the quality of Darcy's character better for having spent a week in the same house, she knew he held her in high regard, but the lady could never speak first in cases such as these.

Elizabeth was lost in her own reveries and was overtaken by a heavy shower half a mile from Longbourn. She had to sprint before she found shelter under the branches and lingering leaves of an oak. Not long thereafter, when Elizabeth was considering making an unladylike run for home, a gentleman with an umbrella walked past her.

"Miss Elizabeth Bennet! What are you doing under that tree?"

Elizabeth cringed. "As you can see, Mr Wickham, I am waiting for the storm to pass before I make my way home." Rainwater dripped from her bonnet and was sliding in rivulets down her dress; she shivered from the cold.

"You are soaked through! You must allow me to escort you home." He stepped off the road and approached the tree, holding his umbrella high and offering his other arm.

Elizabeth offered modest reluctance at inconveniencing him, but Mr Wickham was not dissuaded. She refused his offer of his greatcoat, but she was obliged to admit she was wetter than she would at first allow.

"May I offer you my handkerchief? Your face must be wet and cold."

"No, I have my own." Elizabeth pulled out Darcy's handkerchief to blot the cold rainwater that covered her face and neck. When she returned it to her reticule, she noticed Mr Wickham watching her intently.

She was not sure what conversation to begin. Mr Wickham was equally reserved, and for a time, nothing was said. She again apologised for putting him at an inconvenience.

"It is no trouble. I was to set off on my way to London; the difference of a quarter of an hour will be no difference at all."

"Then shall you miss Mr Bingley's ball?"

"It is a self-imposed absence. I had better not meet Mr Darcy; to be in the same party with him for many hours together might be more than he could bear. If I can show Mr Darcy any small kindness, I should be glad to do it."

"Are your plans in favour of the militia affected by Mr Darcy being in the neighbourhood?"

"Not at all. A military life is not what I was intended for, but circumstances have now made it eligible."

"Why did you not take orders and secure a guaranteed living? It would have been a prudential path." It was an impertinent question, but given all that he had divulged at her aunt's card party, she felt secure in asking it.

Mr Wickham barked an emotionless laugh. "Nothing amuses me more than the easy manner with which everybody settles the abundance of those who have less than themselves! You would look rather blank if your income were to be limited to four hundred a year."

The cold she felt was no longer only from being soaked through from the rain. But, in a heartbeat, Mr Wickham's countenance was mild and pleasant.

"Forgive me. I had always been expensive, and I once thought four hundred a year would be insufficient for what I deserved. For one who now has the pleasure of taking a gentleman's place in a militia for fifty pounds, it pains me to remember the life I might have had. I threw aside every advantage the Darcy family granted me; forgive me if my regrets made you feel ill at ease."

"Of course. Your regrets must be great indeed."

"At that period of my life, I had one object in view: to make my fortune by as quick a process as I could. I have been a disappointed man, and my spirits suffer because it is all my own doing. Please do not judge me from my past behaviour."

Her misjudgment of Darcy had taught her she ought not to take too much pride in her judgment. Should she not allow for the possibility that Mr Wickham was thoroughly reformed? "I do not judge you harshly."

"It is a pleasure to walk with you for many reasons, but among them is that you allow me to speak about Mr Darcy. It reminds me of happier times to hear his name and to know he is well."

Elizabeth felt empathy for Mr Wickham's feelings in this case. She, too, was eager to hear about and speak of Darcy, and she had only been absent from him for four days.

Mr Wickham then said, "I expect that, friends with him as you are, you might tempt him to dance tomorrow evening."

"Yes, he has already secured my hand for a set." She was unable to answer without a smile.

"Indeed! He is not fond of dancing, you know." He raised his eyebrow. "I remember as a child being called into Pemberley's ballroom to take part in his dancing lessons. But perhaps you do not wish to hear more."

"Not at all. I have a great curiosity to know what Mr Darcy was like as a child."

"He was considerate, serious, and not as practised at concealing his impatience as he is now. Can you believe there was a time when everyone could read his emotions?" He laughed. "I think Mr Darcy loathed dancing even then, but he suffered through it without complaint."

"That does sound like him." If she could not speak with Darcy, it eased her mind to speak *about* him. "I suppose the undue attention and matchmaking mothers puts him at unease more than the exercise itself."

"I agree. It is a compliment to you that he singled you out, and in advance of the ball. My childhood companion admires you."

"I could not say." She suspected she blushed.

"I wonder if Mr Darcy could ever learn to think better of me. May I, or do I ask too much—may I enquire if you have spoken to Mr Darcy of me since we last spoke?"

When Darcy had come to dinner, she had not once considered mentioning that Mr Wickham was repentant and wished to make amends. Her own interests in enjoying Darcy's company and cultivating the relationship of the man she admired took priority over the interests of a man she had just met.

"You need not answer. Your countenance expresses your desire to protect your friend from the scoundrel who squandered the Darcys' generosity, whose life of idleness and vice was an insult to his father's kindness."

After several moments of silence, while they neared the house, Mr Wickham continued, "I am tempted to beg you to remember me to Mr Darcy. I have often hoped I might find some means of reconciling with him. Could he ever forgive me?"

"I have not had the pleasure of his acquaintance for very long, but I feel that Mr Darcy is not a needlessly resentful man."

"I doubt," he said ruefully, "such an opportunity to earn his forgiveness will fall my way. You recall the manner in which we met in Meryton." He sighed.

His sadness touched her heart. Perhaps if Mr Wickham was forgiven by Darcy, he might find some peace.

He caught her concerned gaze. "You might not believe it of me, but I am said to have very happy manners. Even Mr Darcy would admit it. You must give me the opportunity to prove myself. I would like to consider you a friend, Miss Bennet."

Elizabeth was not yet ready to give way to his feelings and only replied, "How kind of you to say so."

He appeared disappointed, but said nothing. Elizabeth considered she ought to say something to acknowledge his penitent feelings. "Do not think me lacking in goodwill. I will remember you to Darcy and mention your longstanding regrets and improved character."

"Your kindness overpowers me! It would go a long way indeed if the wo—if a friend of Mr Darcy's would give a favourable opinion of me. I would be so pleased if you speak well of me to him!"

Her companion's face was all animation, and he showed more spirit for the rest of their walk than she had ever seen from him.

Chapter 17

Tuesday, November 26

Elizabeth dressed for the ball with more of a happy flutter than previous balls had ever produced, and she prepared in the highest spirits with the hope of the conquest of all that remained unsubdued of Darcy's heart.

I should try not to forget to speak on the behalf of Mr Wickham. When she had come home yesterday and related to Jane all that had passed between herself and Mr Wickham, Jane again expressed her desire to think well of a man who was reformed.

"*Only think of what Mr Wickham has undergone, Lizzy! Yes, it was all of his own doing, but you say he regrets his bad behaviour. It seems like Mr Wickham carries great guilt for insulting the Darcy family's generosity.*"

Jane was hesitant to condemn anyone whereas Elizabeth had always been critical. But it was Jane who had been moderated in regard to Darcy from the beginning, while Elizabeth had been blinded by her wounded vanity. And who was it who had turned out to be right about Darcy?

Mrs Bennet shouted up the stairs to say the horses had been put to. After hours of preparation, the family climbed into the carriage. On arriving at Netherfield, Elizabeth wasted a few minutes in saying the proper nothings to her host and hostess, but when she was free to move about, she focused her attention on looking for Darcy.

IN MOST RESPECTS, DARCY THOUGHT HIMSELF TO BE A PATIENT MAN, but once he had set his mind to a course of action, he was keen to see it through to its end. The ball was merely another length of time to be endured before he could solicit a private interview with Elizabeth and ask her to be his wife.

The sight of so many people arriving reminded Darcy that he could not remain aloof; it would not be gentlemanly. He made his way through the noise and bustle of arriving guests to the drawing room. He put forth efforts of civility, bowing to several and speaking to some, and when he was finally able to stand at his leisure, he noticed her. His breath caught; words like 'alluring' and 'lovely' failed to capture what he felt when he looked at Elizabeth Bennet.

She curtseyed to those who passed, but her eyes never stayed in one place. Every moment or so, she stood up on her toes and craned her neck to look through the crowd. Her pinned-up hair gave him a view of her smooth neck, and, not for the first time, he wanted to press his lips against her skin. She turned his way, and he watched the tension in her shoulders fall away and a smile cross her lips. Darcy's heart turned over in his chest.

She was looking for me!

Darcy made his way to her. The crowd continued to press against them, but both were caught up in gazing at one another. Elizabeth must have decided they needed some conversation because she said playfully, "I am pleased to see you were *tempted* to attend this evening."

"If Bingley thinks it worthwhile to go to all this trouble for a few hours of noisy entertainment, I have nothing to say against it."

"I have been trapped in the house these many days due to the rain. Thankfully, a dear friend thought to send me a book. It was one of the few things to make those long, dreary days *tolerable*."

"How did you enjoy the Cowper volume?"

"I liked it very well. We can speak about it later; it is hard to talk about poetry in a ballroom." She then added, "I ought to have brought it with me to return it to you."

"May I call on you tomorrow to provide you with the final volume? Perhaps we can take the opportunity to discuss it?" He added with an expressive smile, "But I do not wish to limit our conversation to only our literary opinions."

Elizabeth turned an enchanting shade of pink. "Yes, you would be welcomed at Longbourn tomorrow. I look forward to speaking on any topic you choose to discuss."

Darcy was so encouraged by her avowal that he considered asking if she would speak privately with him *now* when they were, once again, interrupted by Mr Collins.

"My dear Miss Elizabeth, I have been looking forward to our first two dances. The company is moving into the ballroom! Make haste!" Mr Collins dragged her away before Elizabeth could do more than look over her shoulder at him with a grimace.

Darcy tried not to shrug his shoulders in annoyance. He might already have every earthly happiness if not for the vexatious interruptions of Mr Collins!

ELIZABETH KNEW SHE WOULD NOT ENJOY DANCING WITH HER cousin, but when it was over, she could look forward to dancing with Darcy. The hope that his request to call tomorrow was for more than a poetry discussion made her heart soar, but she could not smile, lest her cousin believe her delight had anything to do with him.

The dances with Mr Collins were pure mortification. His movements were awkward, either standing too close when the dance brought them together, or attempting to circle around the wrong lady, bumping into the other gentleman, and leaving Elizabeth standing alone. His apologies became lengthier as the dancing went on. He often walked, rather than danced, but Elizabeth supposed this effrontery was better in the interest of the safety of the other dancers.

Before Elizabeth could make her way towards anyone who might console her after suffering such a partner, an officer invited her to dance. *At least my toes will not be bruised. Or my dignity.* When those dances were over, she was brought to Charlotte Lucas and was in conversation with her when she found herself addressed by Darcy.

"Miss Bennet, may I have the honour of the next dance?" She readily granted his request. They stood smiling at one another until Charlotte left them, presumably because they had grown inattentive to her.

"Given what I know of a lady's hopes for a ball, I thought your family would be the first to arrive."

"It is no easy feat to prepare five young ladies for a ball. We all have a harmless delight in being fine, which can frustrate timeliness. I hope you do not think me too fine."

"No, nothing but what is perfectly proper."

"Do not look fearful! I shall not force you to make me little compliments," she honestly replied. "Although, you have a young sister who will need someone to tell her how handsome she looks. It had best come first from her brother rather than other gentlemen."

Darcy gave her a pained look she did not understand. Elizabeth briefly traced her fingertips across the back of Darcy's hand before returning her hand to her side. He started at the contact, she hoped more out of surprise than alarm. They were standing close together near the wall, far removed from the dancers, and no one would have seen her small gesture of comfort.

"I know Miss Darcy's health and spirits are not what you might wish them to be. Forgive me for speaking about her."

"I said you need not fear speaking of my sister; and you are correct: I ought to take the trouble to practice praising a lady's appearance." He gave her a thorough look. "Your gown seems pretty." Elizabeth raised an eyebrow in disapproval. Darcy struggled for a moment and added, "I like ... these glossy spots."

Elizabeth could not help but laugh. The poor man looked troubled, but it endeared him to her. "Very well, that will do for the present. But Miss Darcy will deserve better from her brother."

"I could not say more without being rude."

Elizabeth silently cursed the convention that forbade compliments outside of one's family. But then, as he offered his hand to lead her to the set, he added in a low voice, "I feel much more than I can possibly express."

Elizabeth's heart danced in private rapture.

WHEN DARCY LED ELIZABETH TO TAKE THEIR PLACE IN THE SET, HE noticed the looks of amazement her neighbours expressed on beholding them.

"Pay them no mind," Elizabeth murmured. "They believe all single men are the rightful property of one of their daughters. Their notice has little to do with *you*."

He forgot the onlookers and contented himself with the attentions of the woman with whom he wanted to spend the rest of his life. *She possesses an uncommon union of intellect, brilliancy, and grace.* He counted how many hours remained until he could call at Longbourn.

When he had to cross over and turn Elizabeth under his arm, he lingered over her fingers, unwilling to let them go. When she circled around him, moving to join another dancer, she looked over her shoulder at him. The liveliness of her countenance as she danced was enchanting, and when she smiled at him, Darcy was struck by his desire to wrap his arms around her. He noticed how her gown clung to her body and outlined her slim curves; her satisfied smile showed she knew he had been admiring her.

Too soon, a half an hour had passed and the dance was over. The dancers dispersed, and he realised they had passed two dances without any conversation. *It is just as well, as the only words I would have been able to string together would have been 'I love you.'*

When he commented on their silence, she laughed. "It is odd for the two of us to be silent for half an hour together." She then lowered her voice. "I suppose my head was full of something else. I was caught up in dancing with my tolerably handsome partner."

She could tease him about his cruel remark for the rest of his life so long as she passed her life along with his. He had scarcely considered what the rest of her statement implied when Elizabeth spoke again. "That calls to mind something I ought to speak with you about. I have, twice in the last week, been in conversation with Mr Wickham."

Darcy's entire body tensed as Elizabeth spoke that wretched man's name and he remembered his sister's tear-streaked face and the sound of her hitching sobs. He drew in a slow, steady breath. "What possible reason did you have to speak with him?"

"He was at a card party at my Aunt Philips's last week, and I saw him yesterday when he came upon me when I was caught in the rain and escorted me home with his umbrella. He gives me reason to believe he is no longer the dissolute man he was previously known to be."

Darcy felt hot, and his pulse was racing. These were not the tremors of boyish excitement he had been feeling. No, what he was feeling now was escalating to rage. This was not the place for confidential discourse. He grasped Elizabeth by the elbow and all but marched her to where the chaperones gathered. Their chattering and cackling stopped as he drew up before Mrs Bennet.

"Madam," he said in a clipped voice, "Miss Elizabeth Bennet tells me she is unwell and wishes to have a maid attend to her in the cloakroom. Will you permit me to escort her, or would you prefer to do the honours yourself?"

Darcy felt Elizabeth's perplexed gaze, but he continued to peer down at Mrs Bennet.

"Oh no, you may. Unless, Lizzy, do you need me? No? Thank you, sir, for letting me remain by the fire. You may go on with Mr Darcy, and send for me if you feel worse."

With a bow, he took hold of Elizabeth's arm and directed her from the ballroom in silence.

ELIZABETH ALLOWED HIM TO ESCORT HER, BUT AS SOON AS THEY

had privacy, she expected him to explain. He had been, for Darcy, brazenly flirtatious, but now, as he stormed into the morning room that had been turned into a cloakroom for the evening, a deep shade of hauteur overspread his features.

When they were alone, he took a few quick steps towards her. "What has led you to speak approvingly of Mr Wickham?"

"He now regrets the thoughtlessness and selfishness of his younger days. He has suffered, and it has caused him to think on his behaviour."

"He has suffered? *He* has suffered!" Darcy struggled for the appearance of composure. "He squandered the compensation I gave him. He has lived a life of absolute dissipation! He is a man who feels entitled to take that which he did not earn. Do you doubt the veracity of what I laid before you?"

She was affronted by his furious attitude towards her, so distant from what it was moments ago. "No, I took you at your word and went so far as to discourage Mr Wickham's acquaintance. However, in a small party, some conversation was unavoidable, and Mr Wickham volunteered an account of his connexion with your family that exactly matched what you related yourself."

"Then why, madam, do you believe Mr Wickham is *not* a scoundrel?"

It was the 'madam' that made her stomach drop to the floor and tears prick at her eyes. Not 'Miss Bennet,' not 'Miss Elizabeth,' not 'Elizabeth,' not even 'ma'am,' but *madam*. Elizabeth admitted to the hope that Darcy's fit of temper would be short-lived and that he did have affection for her.

She met Darcy's icy stare. "I judged him too soon and too harshly, based solely on your information. Mr Wickham says ever since he petitioned you for the living he rejected, he has seen the error of his extravagant and imprudent ways. I admire his efforts to change; it takes character to acknowledge one's failings and strive to be a better person."

"I laid his true character before you. Every year since he came of age has added to his debts. Mr Wickham is entirely done up, ruined by gambling. He always owes a good deal in town, and the officers here will soon find themselves holding his debts of honour.

It will only be a matter of time before Mr Wickham will have to flee his creditors both in Meryton and in the militia."

"That is all your conjecture!" cried Elizabeth. "Do you not think it possible that he might have seen the error of his ways?"

He seemed to struggle for self-control while he paced. "There is, I believe, in every disposition a tendency to some particular defect which not even the best education can overcome. Mr Wickham has *many*: that horrid vice gaming, a compulsion for spreading falsehoods, a readiness to seduce young women who welcome his attentions." He looked at her closely. "You take an eager interest in that gentleman's concerns."

Her breath came in short, shallow gasps. How could he even consider that her heart had been touched by Mr Wickham when she had been anticipating his own addresses? The fear that she did not mean as much to Darcy as he had come to mean to her closed like a vise around her heart. "I have no fancy for Mr Wickham! I simply believe he has enduring regrets for the disregard with which he treated the advantages your family offered him."

"He is a man careless of others' happiness; he thinks only of his own amusement."

"Is your temper truly so little yielding?" During her week at Netherfield, she had supposed Darcy was more gracious than she had originally thought, that he wanted to treat those outside his own circle with more compassion. *Did I only see what I wanted to see?* "Why must you doubt that there might be truth in Mr Wickham's assertions?"

There was a look of restrained fury that crossed Darcy's features. "I stand by my assessment of that man's deficient character."

"His character as you once knew it!" she cried in a less tranquil tone. "All he needs now are friends who approve of him and the nobler life he wishes to lead."

Darcy was struggling for calm and opened and closed his lips several times before he spoke again. "You may not fancy him, but are you determined to have this man as your friend? If that be the case, then you are a kinder friend than he deserves."

"He knows he has been so unlucky as to lose your friendship, but it does not follow that a repentant man must suffer for the rest of his life."

"I do not associate with Mr Wickham, or his intimates." His eyes were coldly fixed on her face. She had no desire to befriend Mr Wickham, but to be told how to act infuriated her. Her anger at Darcy's resentfulness and his disrespectful manner was easier to give in to than to acknowledge that she had assumed Darcy's admiration for her meant more than it did.

"I hope you are not setting conditions on who might have my acquaintance," cried Elizabeth with an energy that Darcy seemed to catch with surprise.

At length, in a voice of forced calmness, Darcy said, "You would take the word of a stranger, a man who, by your own confession, admits his ill-repute? Even if Mr Wickham was sincere, young men are often hasty in their resolutions, and not more sudden in forming them than unsteady in keeping them."

"Is that an accurate representation in your own case? Did *you* not recently resolve to act in a more gentlemanly manner?" She saw him start, but he said nothing. "I had no idea your nature was so resentful that you cannot consider acknowledging Mr Wickham's regrets. Are you so wounded at the loss of three thousand pounds?"

"And *this*," cried Darcy, as he walked with quick steps across the room, "is your opinion of me!" He stopped in front of her, his face glowered, and his mouth formed itself into an expression of contempt. "You astonish me, madam. I thought you had an abundance of sense and discernment."

He may as well have plunged a knife into her heart. "And you are blinded by your prejudice!" Elizabeth turned on her heel and left the room, rushing back into the ballroom where the noise, chatter, and music could, thankfully, make thinking impossible.

DARCY REMAINED IN THE EMPTY CLOAKROOM FOR HALF AN HOUR. By the time the company moved into the dining room, Darcy was master enough of his own emotions to consider leaving the room. His tormented thoughts crossed through his mind in short disjointed bursts.

George Wickham can go to the devil!
How can I marry a woman whose judgment is so misguided?
She doubts my resolve to act in a more gentlemanly manner?
How could Georgiana recover if my wife had even the slightest sympathy for Wickham?

It would destroy every comfort of his life if the woman he married was an intimate of that scoundrel. His heart became a sinking lead weight in his chest. How could he ride to Longbourn tomorrow and declare himself when his mind was filled with fury and doubt? Darcy caught his reflection in the glass. Aside from a few locks of hair out of place, from raking his hands through it in frustration, he looked every bit the respectable gentleman. If he returned to the others, none among them would suspect he was in turmoil.

No one, except Elizabeth. The thought troubled him more.

He walked the corridor and, after lingering for a moment to wait for the musicians to begin, entered the ballroom. He only advanced a few steps before Miss Bingley accosted him.

"Where can you have been all this time?" She latched on to his arm.

I have been learning the woman I had hoped to marry is an advocate for the lying reprobate who seduced my sister. "Was there something you needed of me?"

"I only wished to ask if you were enjoying yourself among the noise"—here she lowered her voice—"and the nothingness of my brother's guests."

"Are they not your guests as well, madam?"

Miss Bingley spoke on another subject. "Am I correct in remembering you intend to spend Christmas at Pemberley?" He nodded. "Your mother's family will join you?"

Darcy suppressed a sigh at the banality. "Yes, my cousin Miss de Bourgh and her mother Lady Catherine come at Christmas, and this year they will be joined by the two sons of my uncle Lord Fitzwilliam." He ought to make some polite enquiry in return, but she was a tax on his forbearance. Miss Bingley realised he was not equal to conversation and left him.

Darcy attempted to keep his attention on anything other than scanning the room for Elizabeth; however, it was too powerful an inclination to be repressed. He was still gazing in her direction when he saw Mr Collins approach her in great excitement. He could not hear what they were speaking of, but Elizabeth shook her head and then looked directly into Darcy's eyes.

She knows I have been observing her the entire time.

A short time later, he heard a gentleman clearing his throat at his shoulder. Darcy turned and had to then lean back in order to avoid being struck by Mr Collins's head, for that gentleman stood too near and had made him a low bow.

"Mr Darcy, I beg you to forgive my ignorance! When we had the occasion to dine together at Longbourn, I was unaware that you are the nephew of my illustrious patroness, Lady Catherine de Bourgh. I am exceedingly fortunate in the favours and position your esteemed aunt has judged to bestow upon me, and I trust you will accept my apology for not having paid my proper respects to you before."

Darcy eyed him in unrestrained wonder. "I am well convinced of Lady Catherine's discernment as to be certain she could never bestow a favour unworthily."

"A man should not omit an occasion of testifying his respect towards anybody connected with the family of his patroness. I am thankful the discovery of this information, which I have found out by singular accident, has not been any longer put off. It must gratify you to meet with another gentleman of distinction, for I consider the clerical office as equal in point of dignity with the highest rank in the kingdom. It is in my power to assure you that her ladyship was well yesterday se'nnight."

Darcy's contempt increased with the length of this speech and with this idiot's ridiculous self-importance. At the end of the absurd monologue, he made him a slight bow and moved another way.

Mr Collins remained close to Elizabeth's side for the remainder of the evening, and Elizabeth did not dance again. The idea of *that* man—any man—courting her attention made Darcy feel a rush of jealousy, but the extent of his own feelings towards Elizabeth were in such a state of indecision that he dared not assert himself. It made

Darcy wretchedly miserable to be so confused on the matters of his own mind and heart.

When the Bennets rose to leave, Darcy was forced into exertion. Elizabeth showed no contrition, no eagerness to part amicably. She was gone, and without a word to him. When Darcy's heart rate slowed, the fire of burning anger in his chest settled into crushing disappointment.

I can hardly credit that I had been wishing to tie myself forever to such a man! He is indifferent to the feelings of others, and I mean nothing to him.
She was plagued all evening by Mr Collins. She owed her only relief to Charlotte, who good-naturedly engaged Mr Collins's conversation. She was free from Darcy's company, but she could feel his stare crushing into her body. That feeling came over her less often as the evening wore on, and she could not say whether his ebbing notice made her satisfied or wretched.

I had thought that I had begun to help him to soften away his pride. What a fool I have been. The entire carriage ride home, Mrs Bennet boasted of how she should see Jane settled at Netherfield soon. Elizabeth could no longer pretend to be lively, but she hoped, given the lateness of the hour and the general fatigue of everyone, that no one would suspect her of suffering from a broken heart.

Chapter 18

Wednesday, November 27

The morning after the Netherfield ball, Elizabeth was imprisoned in the breakfast room with the last man in the world to whom she wished to grant an audience. She had been hoping a different tall young man would ask for a private interview this morning.

Mr Collins's rambling proposal had been unavoidable, and Elizabeth was sensible to the fact that it was wisest to get it over as quickly as possible. But even that was not to be, for when she declined to accept his offer of marriage, he refused to believe her.

"I thank you for the honour you have done me in your proposals, but to accept them is impossible." She spoke slowly, as though to a child. "My feelings in every respect forbid it." Mr Collins's expression was still blank. "Can I speak plainer?" she cried, failing to keep the exasperation from her voice.

"You are uniformly charming!" he cried, with an air of awkward gallantry, "and I am persuaded that, when sanctioned by the authority of your parents, my proposals will not fail of being acceptable."

Elizabeth lacked the words to reason with such an unreasonable man and withdrew. Her refusal was supported by her father, but lamented by her mother. Mr Bennet returned to the quiet of his library while the rest of the household was left in upheaval. Mrs Bennet could not understand why Lizzy would not have Mr Collins; Mr Collins could not comprehend on what motive she refused him; Elizabeth was aggravated by her mother's alternating threats or coaxing; and all the while, Kitty and Lydia were laughing at the commotion.

While the family was in this confusion, Charlotte came to spend the day with them. She was met by Lydia who cried, "I am glad you are come, for there is such fun here! Mr Collins has made an offer to Lizzy, and she will not have him!"

Charlotte's reply was spared by Mrs Bennet. "Tell us, Lizzy, what do you expect from a husband, because I do not see how you might do any better than Mr Collins!"

Elizabeth had been repelling these attacks all morning with playful gaiety or with a short temper; she now answered in earnestness. "I expect my husband to be good-tempered and intelligent, to consult my happiness in all his actions, and to love me with constancy and sincerity." Darcy came to mind, and it tore at her heart.

"These are odd ideas, young lady! You had better discard them before you marry, or you will be obliged to do it afterwards."

Mr Collins then entered with an air more stately than usual. The girls were shooed from the room by Mrs Bennet, who wished to have a conversation with Mr Collins. As Elizabeth closed the door, she heard Mr Collins say, "No, if she does not accept my hand, I can offer it elsewhere, for I am by no means guided by a preference for her over any other young lady, other than wishing to offer all due consideration to your family."

"Your mother fears you will have no one to maintain you after your father dies," Charlotte told her.

"I could not in good conscience accept him! He suggested the notice of Lady Catherine de Bourgh was the greatest advantage in his power to offer. He promised, after we were married, not to reproach me for my father being unable to offer him a dowry of any significance. My greatest attributes, in his estimation, were that his patroness would approve of my modesty and economy! I cannot respect him, let alone love him."

"You won't have him because he is not handsome!" cried Lydia.

He was a dull-looking man, but Elizabeth knew she ought not to say uncharitable things. "I could never marry a man for the sake of situation. His society is irksome, he is not near to clever, and it would be a disgrace to my self-respect to tie myself to a man whose regard and respect for me is non-existent."

Her heartfelt entreaties had no effect on Lydia and Kitty, who giggled over which militia officer's proposals they would be willing to accept. Jane sat a little apart from the others to write a letter, and Charlotte moved to sit near to Elizabeth.

"I thought you refused Mr Collins because you saw yourself accepting the proposals of another man who has recently arrived in the neighbourhood," she said barely above a whisper.

"You cannot imagine I harbour any designs on Mr Bingley."

"You know I speak of his friend. I would not press the subject if I did not believe he admires you. It was plain last night that he paid you particular attention."

"He did not distinguish me above any other creature."

"Eliza! He danced only with you!"

"I disclaim all right to the compliment. Mr Darcy wished to make amends for announcing to all and sundry that he thought me not handsome enough to tempt him to dance."

Charlotte pursed her lips and raised her eyebrows, but Elizabeth had nothing further to say. Charlotte, instead, talked over the evening, and, with rejoinders from the other girls, the conversation flowed long. Elizabeth had only to nod or smile.

I had such hopes before we spoke of Mr Wickham, before he called me 'madam,' before he demonstrated his unyielding temper.

She ought to have judged better and overlooked Darcy's anger. Mr Wickham had led a self-indulgent life that was the opposite of the moral code by which Darcy chose to live. Of course Darcy would be affronted by her advocating for the dissipated man that had thrown away his family's generosity, and after he had warned her against him.

I need not bring up Mr Wickham's name ever again. If he wants to earn Darcy's approbation, he shall have to demonstrate his own improved behaviour to Darcy.

With the passage of a day or two, with a calmer attitude, she and Darcy could reconcile. Mr Bingley had told her mother that he was to be in London for three or four days, but he would call on Jane when he returned, and by then Darcy's anger would have subsided and Mr Bingley would likely bring his friend with him to Longbourn.

If there be constant attachment on both our sides, our hearts must understand each other soon.

"And that gown worn by Miss King! With all those freckles, it was an unfortunate sight."

"To say nothing of the chaperones. They called those things on their heads turbans?"

"The Miss Longs' gowns were outdated—the year nine at the latest."

Darcy was dying a slow death at the breakfast table. What was it about women and their desire to talk over an evening's events? He was up half the night examining his dreadful interactions with Elizabeth, and he knew that it was only a matter of time before he would have to hear Miss Bingley and Mrs Hurst's strictures on the Bennet family.

"Caroline, while I am in town, I would like you to call at Longbourn," said Mr Bingley.

Miss Bingley looked indignant. "I do not know if I shall have the opportunity to call on the Bennets before you return. In fact, Louisa and I had thought to join—"

"I want you to take an early opportunity of waiting on them, on Miss Bennet in particular."

His hostess huffed in displeasure. "I do not comprehend why you want me to give Jane any notice, other than that she is, of course, my dear friend. Must I call on every lady you danced with?"

"Caroline, Louisa, I am in the hope of creating for myself a nearer connexion with the Bennet family."

The only noise heard at the table was Hurst's silverware clattering against his plate. Bingley's disclosure did not come as a shock to Darcy, but to hear it voiced to his sisters made his intentions indisputable.

How fortunate that Bingley has no doubt as to the affection his Miss Bennet feels for him!

Miss Bingley soon found her voice. "When I consider how few young ladies you have yet seen much of and how full of temptation the next years of your life will be, I cannot wish you to devote yourself in honour to my dear friend Jane."

There were so many falsehoods within that statement that Darcy lowered his newspaper.

"I thank you for your concern, but you need not fear I would be anything less than constant to Miss Bennet."

"But Charles," Miss Bingley's voice hitched, "I know you are capable of being really in love, and I fear your interest in my friend is a passing fancy."

I have never heard the phrase 'in love' spoken in favourable terms by Miss Bingley.

"I have formed the strongest of attachments, and I am certain that she has for me. I ask that you call on Miss Bennet at least once while I am gone. Make a civil message, send my compliments to her mother, and leave my card if that is all your time allows."

Mrs Hurst and Miss Bingley shared a look. "I wish you joy, Charles, naturally. Jane Bennet is a sweet girl, but what of her family?" his elder sister asked.

"Yes!" shrieked Miss Bingley. "You may yet make a brilliant choice through an alliance with a more distinguished family." Miss Bingley's gaze darted towards Darcy. "The Bennets' want of connexion is a great evil."

"I shall endeavour to overlook what I cannot change." Bingley stood. "I depart within the hour, and I intend to return late Saturday. I expect you to call on Miss Bennet before then." The door had not closed behind him before Miss Bingley began her tirade.

"Mr Darcy, are you not as shocked as we? My brother is about to throw himself away! He has no right to make a choice that is disagreeable and inconvenient to the principal part of his family. He will be giving us bad connexions, and we have not been used to them, have we, Louisa? We associate with people of rank! And, pray, who is Jane Bennet?"

"Miss Bennet is the woman your brother intends to make as his wife and therefore your sister."

Darcy heard her grind her teeth. "He might yet marry to his advantage. We ought to shut up the house and—"

"It is to your brother's advantage to marry the woman who loves him best." Darcy left the room with a curt bow, shutting the door behind him.

Darcy leaned against the closed door, heaving a sigh. Miss Bingley and Mrs Hurst spoke with agitated voices. He caught the words "detach him," "artful Bennets," "join him in town," and then "convince Mr Darcy." For the next four days, he would be trapped at Netherfield with Miss Bingley and three miles away from a woman who may or may not admire George Wickham.

He stood in the hall for a moment, then made a decision.

DARCY STRODE ACROSS THE YARD AT A BRISK PACE AND SAW Bingley speaking to the servant who held the reins to his horse.

"Darcy! What is all this?"

"I have decided to join you in town. I have sent a man ahead to open my house so you need not spend your vacant hours in a comfortless hotel. I could not leave you alone at Tattersall's; you might come away with a worse pair than you purchased the last time." He mounted his horse.

"It is a great deal of trouble on your part for only three or four days. You are not quitting Netherfield so soon, I hope?"

"I am impatient to see my sister." He tapped his heels to cue his horse, focusing all of his attention to posting the trot and ignoring his friend.

Bingley mounted his own horse and caught up to Darcy. "You must have no reserves from me! I know you do not care to be left alone with Caroline, but there is no need to flee."

"I wish to be of service to you and visit my sister." *I am too angry and my thoughts too muddled to decide on anything other than removing myself from the source of my agitation.*

"You and Miss Darcy are always welcome at Netherfield."

Georgiana could barely leave her home, let alone possibly see Wickham. "I do not yet know if I will return to Netherfield. I may remain in town with my sister until we return to Pemberley."

"When I am in town, I never wish to leave, but when I am in the country, it is pretty much the same. I have an important reason for returning to Hertfordshire; and when you are in town in January, you must come back to Netherfield to be my groomsman!" Bingley spoke with a boyish grin.

Darcy had expected to be making his own proposals this morning, but Elizabeth's defence of Wickham had shattered his resolve. He doubted her judgment, doubted her affection for him, and, far worse, he doubted his own mind. His sudden change in fortune made him angry.

"Would not you be ashamed to be linked by marriage to such a family?"

"I need not judge Miss Bennet based on her family's behaviour in public, for I have had the opportunity to observe her and her family at home."

Darcy scoffed. "It is not to the Bennet daughters' advantage to be seen at home either!"

"The Bennets are a proper country family."

"Proper! Do you not remember how we decamped as fast as we could last Thursday? Their behaviour was disgraceful."

"Darcy, if *I* do not object to the Bennets, it can be nothing to you!" Bingley urged his horse ahead and left Darcy alone.

Darcy cursed under his breath. He had acted a selfish, petulant fool! He had already decided to overlook the Bennets' mortifying behaviour for Elizabeth's sake. What right had he to say such things to his closest friend? He was ashamed to realise he had acted no better than Caroline Bingley.

He sighed heavily. There were many symptoms of affection on Elizabeth's side that, having justly acknowledged, he could no longer persuade himself to feel void of meaning, even despite her defence of that scoundrel. She had been willing to let him kiss her when they were alone at Longbourn, after all. And now, when he ought to be confessing his love and admiration, every step of his horse took him further away from her.

I do love her. I believe she loves me. What a damned fool I have been! I hope her compassionate heart will forgive me.

Her admirable compassion was at the heart of Elizabeth's charming nature. She sat at work she disliked to make blankets and clothing for village families. She tolerated Miss Bingley's rudeness for the sake of nursing her sister. She eased his worried mind after his shocking encounter with Wickham. How many times had Elizabeth reached out to touch his hand or arm in silent sympathy?

And Wickham is hollow and black and devious enough to mislead an unsuspecting, kind-hearted woman for his own amusement.

It must have been easy work to invent a tale of his supposed newfound decency. If she had spoken ill of him rather than acknowledging their friendship, Wickham might have told her lies to make Darcy appear to be a villain. *Did he hope to have revenge on me by convincing a woman who esteemed me to become his greatest supporter?*

If Mr Wickham had told Elizabeth that he had for many years now seen the error of his dissipated ways, then the truth of what happened three months ago in Ramsgate would be enough to convince her of his wickedness. He, Colonel Fitzwilliam, and Georgiana had sworn not to reveal the truth to another person. He was not master of himself to consider it last evening, but since he intended to ask Elizabeth to be his wife, he could not keep such a secret from her.

Elizabeth must rightfully be furious with me. Their next meeting would go better if they were both of a calm, decided temper. She was a sensible woman, and by the time he returned with Bingley, she would not avoid him.

Darcy set his horse at a gallop to catch up to his friend. Bingley would be placated by a humble apology and a few kind words about Miss Bennet, but what of Elizabeth? He had all but declared himself last night. Now he would be obliged to wait, and before he confessed his love, he had to speak of George Wickham and Georgiana to her and apologise for his losing his temper.

The liberty that his anger and imagination had dared him to disparage her intelligence and doubt her affection for him—could she ever forgive it?

Thursday, November 28

LYDIA AND KITTY WERE WILD TO GO INTO MERYTON TO ENQUIRE IF Mr Wickham had returned. Elizabeth had no interest in joining them, but given that the alternative was to remain at Longbourn and suffer her mother's petulance and her cousin's resentment, she agreed. She did not blame Mr Wickham for her quarrel with Darcy, but neither did she relish the reminder that his presence would necessarily evoke.

Mr Wickham joined them on their entering the town and attended them to their aunt's, where his regret at missing Mr Bingley's ball was talked over. He paid Elizabeth no attention in Meryton, but as he and another officer walked the Bennet girls back to Longbourn, he slowed his pace so they fell behind the others.

"Miss Elizabeth, please assure me that you suffered no ill effects from your being caught in the rain. It did not affect your dancing, I hope."

"I have always been blessed with excellent health."

"I presume you enjoyed your dance with a gentleman from Derbyshire."

"I have agreeable reflections of the ball, thank you." Her true opinion was better left unsaid.

Mr Wickham lowered his voice. "I also meant to enquire if Mr Darcy called at Longbourn after the ball."

Elizabeth's stomach fell to her feet. "I do not have the pleasure of understanding you."

"Forgive me if I offended you. I thought it would be the sort of custom that would appeal to a formal man such as Mr Darcy."

"Mr Darcy showed me no particular notice." Her hand twisted Darcy's handkerchief as she remembered their near-kiss.

"Yes, I have said too much. An eager call by any gentleman upon a lady may lead to unwarranted speculation."

Elizabeth felt her chest tighten, but did not allow her true feelings show. "I am certain Mr Darcy would not act in a manner that might in any way reflect poorly on his reputation."

"Mr Darcy would do nothing to appear to disgrace his family. Familial pride is a powerful motive for his being prudent and to act with caution and propriety."

"Yes." She remembered their conversation in the breakfast room when Darcy spoke of his father's last words. However fleeting it was, the sadness in Darcy's eyes was undeniable. "I have no doubt of his feelings on that point."

They walked a little further in silence before Mr Wickham added, "You have an intimate relationship with that gentleman, do you not?"

Elizabeth stopped walking and looked sharply at her companion. "You have lately been in London. Tell me, has delicacy gone out of fashion?"

"Forgive me if I appear forward or indelicate. I wished to discern if you were on such terms with Mr Darcy that would have allowed you to speak well of me to him. My enthusiasm for mending the breach has caused me to go beyond what is considered appropriate discourse with a young lady. On this point, I shall remain silent."

Elizabeth wished Mr Wickham had chosen another one of her sisters to walk alongside. "I did speak of your honourable intentions to Mr Darcy. Whether any good may come of it, I could not say." *No good from it came to me.*

"I wish nature had made such hearts as yours more common."

As much as she enjoyed speaking about Darcy, she could not say she enjoyed Mr Wickham's company. While she was gratified that both Mr Wickham and Charlotte saw that Darcy held her in esteem, it would not do to have their speculations or her desires become public knowledge. She must appear indifferent, but all the while her imagination passed over wild flights of fancy in which Darcy threw open the parlour door and, on discovering her alone, confessed his fervent love and admiration.

Since she had to appear like her usual self, she feigned interest in Mr Wickham's conversation. At home, she went along with her sisters to introduce Mr Wickham to her father and mother. He was immediately welcomed, declared by her parents to be a likable, pleasant fellow, and he spent fifteen minutes charming all who spoke with him.

Chapter 19

Friday, November 29

Tomorrow they would leave for Hertfordshire, and Darcy intended to call at Longbourn before the day was out. If he was profuse enough in his sincere apologies, if Elizabeth believed him when he spoke of the strength of his regard, he hoped both he and Bingley would be married early in the new year.

"You do not mind that I dine out this evening?" Bingley looked up from his breakfast. "In fact, I expect to be occupied for the day."

"You may come and go as you please," Darcy replied. "I beg you will consider yourself as much at home here as you did in your father's house. I expect to pass our remaining time in London with my sister."

Breakfast was soon over, and Darcy consulted the clock on the mantle; it was not yet ten o'clock. If his sister was still eating breakfast, it was of little importance to him. *I need not stand on ceremony with Georgiana.* It was less than a mile to Upper Wimpole Street, and when Darcy arrived, it was quarter past the hour.

The servant who opened the door at his sister's home led Darcy into the breakfast room where Georgiana and Mrs Annseley were seated together. His sister ran around the table and threw herself into his arms. Although she was a tall, full-figured young woman, Georgiana's enthusiastic hug reminded Darcy of the younger girl who played with dolls, made artificial flowers, and nursed dormice. Darcy hugged her tightly; there was no other person in the world who embraced him with such heartfelt regard.

"Fitzwilliam! I did not expect you until later!"

"I saw no reason to put off calling on you."

Georgiana pulled her arms from his waist. She held her grin for a moment, and then it slipped away. She walked towards her chair, but remained standing, biting her lip.

"Should I not have done that in front of you, Mrs Annesley? Ought I to have shaken hands and invited Fitzwilliam, Mr Darcy, to sit? But he *is* my brother, or does that not matter? Did I act wrongly?" Her eyes beseeched her companion to help her.

The older woman smiled. "If Mr Darcy sees nothing wrong in your pleasure to see him, then no one else could speak against a display of genuine affection."

Georgiana exhaled in relief. Darcy expected his sister would now remember him to Mrs Annesley and they might all be seated, but she stood with clasped hands and seemed to be focused on breathing in and out. *Why is she in such a tremble?*

After both he and Mrs Annesley looked expectantly at Georgiana, Darcy said, "I hope I have the pleasure of seeing you well, Mrs Annesley. I trust you will forgive me for calling so early and, if you are not finished, you will allow me to join you?"

Georgiana's head snapped up. "Oh, forgive me! I must invite you to join us. I shall call back the servant; no, I can bring you a plate. Is it right for *me* to bring him a plate, Mrs Annesley? *Would* you care to join us, Fitzwilliam? Yes, you said you would, but would you care to eat?"

Darcy replied that he would be happy to join them while they finished and, no, he was not hungry. He was torn between amusement at her earnest desire to act properly and compassion as she struggled with the simple task of inviting her brother to breakfast.

Mrs Annesley led by example and asked him about his journey

and remarked about the weather. Darcy remembered to act kindly to those outside his own circle and asked after her family. Throughout their conversation, Georgiana's fingers shook so much that her fork clattered against her plate. He shared a quick, cautious look with his sister's companion, who could only shrug her shoulders in answer to his silent question. Mrs Annesley then suggested to Miss Darcy that her brother might like to retire to her more comfortable sitting room.

Darcy noticed that his sister had refurbished her private room since he had last visited; he expressed his admiration of her taste.

"Do you like it? Mrs Annesley said the room ought to reflect my own likes. It is simple, but I like the floral-papered walls. I enjoyed selecting the furniture and colours and fabrics. It kept me busy all through the autumn. I cannot believe it is nearly time to return to Pemberley for Christmas."

At the close of this speech, Georgiana became self-conscious and closed her lips. Darcy thought giving his sister a project, even something as trivial as refurnishing a room, was a wise idea. Not only was it practice in decision-making and managing her expenses, but it gave Georgiana something to think on other than the events at Ramsgate.

"It is a pretty room, elegant and light."

"I am happy you approve. Is there anything I can get for you?" She gestured to the bell, but Darcy shook his head. "I hope I am not deficient in what is due to my guests, but I have not yet learned all I ought to do and say."

"Your desire to act well and your kind manners will make up for any small matter that you might not yet know and, as you get more used to company, I am confident you will find it easier. You are getting on well, then, with Mrs Annesley?" The companion had come with excellent references, but they had been deceived before.

"Yes, I admire her. She is well-informed and patient. I have already learned so much from her. She is a model of proper behaviour."

His sister's countenance faltered. She breathed rapidly and brought a hand to her chest. She was dreadfully white as she sank back into her chair. Darcy rushed to her side, kneeling next to her and taking her hand. This was not the first peculiar episode he had witnessed, but it tore at his heart every time.

"Georgiana, you look extremely ill! Shall I call your maid?"

This produced a frantic shake of her head as tears seeped out of her tightly closed eyes. This agony continued as Darcy sat in useless suspense while his sister clutched his hand. Her gasps for air subsided into normal, steady breaths, but she was still distressed. It was several minutes before she was able to speak.

"Is this why you called earlier than expected? I swear to you, she has done nothing improper! I have not been left alone with anyone. I do not entertain anyone unaccompanied, let alone a gentleman! Please believe me!"

"Georgiana, I do not understand you." He gently brushed back the sweat-drenched hair on her forehead, trying to hide his own distress.

"You will be able to trust me again, I promise. I know you do not trust me to do what is proper, but you can trust Mrs Annesley. It is not at all like the last time!"

Why does she think I find her to be untrustworthy? He gathered his sister into his arms and she wept into his shoulder, muttering to herself, "Not like the last time." He stroked her hair while his mind raced over what to heaven she was upset about.

Then it struck him: the last time he had called on her unexpectedly, at Ramsgate, he had learnt she had planned to elope with that wretched excuse for a man.

"Dearest, do you think I called earlier than expected because I do not trust you? That I expected you to be recklessly carrying on with some man?"

Behind the wet handkerchief she clutched against her face, Darcy saw her nod.

"I came because I was eager to see you! Georgiana, look at me." She flinched, but she uncovered her eyes. "You know you acted wrongly in agreeing to an elopement, but you admitted the whole to me, and I forgave you long ago. You could never have known that he was using you to revenge himself upon me, that he and Mrs

Younge saw your fortune as a prize to which they were entitled. Your innocence was abused, and I know you have learnt to be more aware of the dangers of the world."

"Do you not find me lacking in morality?" she whispered.

The poor girl was still so fragile. Darcy tipped her chin up to force her to meet his eyes. "I see no lapse in your morality, and I challenge anyone to find your goodness lacking in any way. You must know how precious you are to me."

Her face was still red and swollen from crying, but her breathing had slowed and she did not appear as though she was about to cry anew. Darcy would do anything to see his sister happy once more. He thought it best to distract her before she went to pieces again.

"How shall I entertain you today, my dear? I am at your disposal."

"You need not indulge me."

Darcy did not wish to push her. Still, he silently agreed with Mrs Annesley that occupation was better than her fretting in self-doubt.

"I shall send for my carriage to pick us up at twelve o'clock, and then your brother is going to make a great fuss over you and spend his money in any frivolous manner of your choosing."

This provoked a smile. "That does not at all sound like a day you would enjoy."

"Nonsense. I can think of no better way to spend a day with my sister than on Bond Street, Piccadilly, and the Mall." *And if we encounter anyone of our acquaintance, I can keep our conversations brief and extricate ourselves easily.*

Georgiana's giggle encouraged him, and he continued in the same style. "We shall first go to Harding, Howell, and Co. in Pall Mall, for I am certain there must be some new muslin you have had your eye on. No? Is there a smart bonnet you have long admired that you must have? Do you prefer we make a visit to Finsbury Square?"

"I think you hope to visit Lackington's bookshop there. If that is the case, I have no objection to accompanying you."

He saw she was putting forth an effort to be agreeable. "No, unless there is a book you want, we need not go. Shall I take you to Birchall's or some other music seller?"

This produced a sincere smile. Georgiana went to tidy her appearance and to inform Mrs Annesley of their plans. She had his reserve, but combined with her shyness, it made her appear cool when, in fact, she was an affectionate girl who was eager to please, eager to be loved. Darcy sighed. Wickham had an easy conquest.

Saturday, November 30

When Elizabeth awoke Saturday, it was with the hopefulness that today she might hear news of Mr Bingley's return. While she, of course, wished the culmination of Mr Bingley's attentions towards Jane might end with the promises that would be so agreeable to her sister, Elizabeth thought on the occasion with more selfish hopes.

The family lingered over their breakfast for the first time in a week. The intimacy of their own family party, with their relaxed silences and familiar conversations, left everyone at ease. Mr Collins had begun his return journey too early in the morning, and the ceremony of leave-taking had been performed the night before.

"Mamma," asked Kitty, "why do you suppose Mr Collins seemed eager to return to Longbourn after Lizzy refused him?"

"How can you be so stupid? He intends on paying his addresses to one of you younger girls, since Lizzy has set her expectations so high she will end up an old maid like Miss Lucas. Mary might be prevailed upon to accept him."

Mary unfurled herself from over her book. "Although Mr Collins is by no means as clever as I, if encouraged to read and improve himself by such an example as mine, he might someday become an agreeable companion."

"Those are the fitting words a young lover ought to profess," remarked her father. "Mary, should you be so fortunate as to receive and accept Mr Collins's addresses, I wish you the joy of a long life with the man, for it will take you that long for your endeavour to find success."

Charlotte Lucas called after breakfast, and she drew Elizabeth into a private conference. "Yesterday, Mr Collins made me an offer of marriage, and we are engaged."

"Engaged to Mr Collins! My dear Charlotte, impossible!" Elizabeth shuddered to think how much a woman must have to dissemble and do violence to her sense of delicacy in order to be the proper wife of Mr Collins.

"Do you think it incredible Mr Collins should be able to procure any woman's good opinion because he was not so happy as to succeed with you?"

"Of course not!" Elizabeth felt startled and shocked, and the idea of her dearest friend married to such a man filled her alarm. *How could Charlotte have made such an untoward choice?* Still, she recollected herself and grasped her friend's hands. "I am very gratified to hear of your engagement! I wish you happiness with Mr Collins." Although she smiled, in her heart she felt it was an unsuitable match.

"I see what you are feeling," replied Charlotte. "You must be surprised as so lately Mr Collins was wishing to marry you."

Elizabeth felt the strangeness of Mr Collins's making two offers of marriage within three days was nothing in comparison to his being *accepted*, but she held her tongue.

"I am not romantic, you know; I never was," Charlotte continued. "I ask only a comfortable home; and considering Mr Collins's character, connexions, and situation in life, I am convinced my chance of happiness with him is fair."

"Undoubtedly."

Charlotte did not stay longer, and Elizabeth was left to reflect on what she had heard. It was a steep price to pay in order to be preserved from want. Elizabeth was about to proceed along this familiar disapproving path when she checked herself. *Is this the sort of friend I wish to be?*

Simply because *she* would find being the wife of Mr Collins to be ... *unpleasant* was the mildest term Elizabeth could apply, her friend would not be miserable. Although she suspected his regard for Charlotte was imaginary, she might make him happy. Charlotte would have a comfortable home, and it may prove to be a good match for her.

I will do my best to be happy for Charlotte. If she did not want to become scornful like her father, if she wanted to stop passing harsh judgments unfairly, she ought to show her closest friend greater kindness.

Elizabeth doubted she was authorised to mention what she had learnt of the engagement and so joined the ladies of her family in their usual comforts and lively conversations. It was not long before the door was thrown open for Miss Bingley and the Hursts. Mrs Hurst said nothing while Miss Bingley addressed only Jane. Mr Hurst took up a newspaper and looked at no one.

"Jane, I have come to take leave of you," said Miss Bingley in a voice lacking in warmth. "We intend to follow my brother to town."

Jane's expression displayed her genuine disappointment. "The suddenness of your removal surprises me. Do you leave now, Caroline? When do you intend to return?"

"We shall dine at Mr Hurst's home in Grosvenor Street tonight, and we have no intention of coming back again. Many of my acquaintances are already in town for the winter, and I long to partake in more varied society."

"I regret you are leaving, and so suddenly. I shall miss you more than I can express, but of course you know that, as I am certain you must feel the same."

"I do not pretend to regret anything I shall leave in Hertfordshire except your society, my dearest Jane."

It was clear to Elizabeth that Miss Bingley had no affection for her sister, but Jane appeared to take her alleged friend at her word.

"When does your brother return to Netherfield?" asked Mrs Bennet.

"I do not know his plans, ma'am. He sends you his compliments. However, when Charles gets to town, he is often in no hurry to leave it again."

"We shall miss having the society of such fine ladies as yourselves, but it is not to be supposed your absence from Netherfield prevents Mr Bingley's being there." Miss Bingley made her no answer.

The Hursts had joined Miss Bingley in calling at Longbourn, but not Darcy. Even Mr Hurst had come into the house. She hated giving Miss Bingley any satisfaction, but Elizabeth put aside her pride. "Does Mr Darcy remain at Netherfield to await your brother?"

Miss Bingley's eyes widened. "Mr Darcy left with Charles on Wednesday to help my brother with his business. He is a good friend to our family. Besides, Mr Darcy was not at all fond of—let us say he was impatient to return to town."

"London does have its amusements, but as the owner of such a fine estate as you have described Pemberley to be, I am certain Mr Darcy holds a fondness for the country. We shall all look forward to seeing Mr Darcy and Mr Bingley when they return."

Miss Bingley gave her a cold glare; she then turned to address Jane in a quieter voice so only Elizabeth could overhear. "Mr Darcy was eager to call on his sister. To confess the truth, we are scarcely less eager to meet her again. I do not think Georgiana Darcy has her equal for beauty, elegance, and accomplishments, and the affection she inspires in Louisa and myself is heightened from the hope we entertain of her being hereafter our sister."

The delight on Miss Bingley's face was insufferable; but fortunately for the sake of Elizabeth's own good manners, Sir William Lucas then entered. *He must be here to announce Charlotte's engagement.* Elizabeth cringed in anticipation. *That Miss Bingley would be witness to the disrespectful exclamations that would follow this announcement!*

With compliments to them all, and much self-congratulation on the prospect of a connexion between the two houses, Sir William unfolded the matter to an audience not merely doubting, but incredulous.

"No! No, you are mistaken, Sir William! It cannot be. You must be mistaken!" protested Mrs Bennet.

"Good Lord! Sir William, how can you tell such a story?" Lydia cried. "Don't you know Mr Collins wants to marry Lizzy?"

Miss Bingley could not keep her countenance, and she shared an expressive smile with Mrs Hurst.

"Yes, Mr Collins asked Lizzy to marry him not three days ago! You must be mistaken!" continued Mrs Bennet.

Sir William's good breeding carried him through it all, and

though he begged leave to be positive as to the truth of his information, he listened to all their impertinence with courtesy.

"I beg you would believe Sir William, Mamma," Elizabeth said, loudly enough to gain the room's attention. "I have prior knowledge of his account from Charlotte herself. She told me her happy news this morning."

Elizabeth then offered her hand to Sir William. She was joined by Jane, and they both made all the appropriate remarks on the happiness that might be expected from the match, the excellent character of Mr Collins, and the convenient distance of Hunsford from London.

A servant then entered with a summons for Miss Bingley and the Hursts. The visitors took their leave with no more cordiality than Miss Bingley's handshake with only Jane. Sir William Lucas, with more compliments and smiles than were necessary, soon followed.

Mrs Bennet could now give vent to all her feelings. Her ranting was insensible, but the premise was that Elizabeth was the cause of all their trouble. Her shrieks of dismay brought her husband from his library.

"It is regrettable you are put out by this news," he replied when Jane was able to explain. "I own that I am gratified."

"How can you say such a thing? If only my thankless daughter had accepted Mr Collins! I will never, ever forgive that artful Charlotte Lucas!"

"It is agreeable news, my dear, because I have discovered that Charlotte Lucas, whom I had been used to think tolerably sensible, is as foolish as you are, but far more foolish than Lizzy."

Elizabeth sighed quietly and left her quarrelling parents to seek out Jane. Elizabeth had observed Jane's countenance change when Miss Bingley mentioned Georgiana Darcy.

"Are you disappointed by the Netherfield party's sudden removal?"

"It is a shame they will not return this winter. I have every hope we shall remain close friends, and I intend to lessen the pain of separation by corresponding with Caroline."

"Then the delightful intercourse you have known as friends will be renewed with greater satisfaction as sisters." Jane did not answer. "You cannot fear that Mr Bingley will be detained in London by his sisters?"

"No, 'tis not his sisters' wish for his company in town that worries me." A few tears fell from her eyes. "What of Georgiana Darcy?"

Elizabeth put her arms around her. "Miss Bingley sees her brother is in love with you, but wants him to marry Miss Darcy. She follows him to town in the hope of keeping him there, and tries to persuade you that he does not care about you."

Jane shook her head and did not speak.

"No one who has seen you together can doubt his affection. Miss Bingley, I am sure, cannot. Could she have seen half as much love in Mr Darcy for herself, she would have ordered her wedding clothes." *I saw that much love in Darcy for me prior to our disagreement at the ball.*

Elizabeth collected herself and continued. "We are not rich enough or grand enough for Miss Bingley, and she is anxious to get Miss Darcy for her brother from the notion that when there has been *one* intermarriage, she may have less trouble in achieving a second."

"I cannot accept that Caroline wishes to deceive me."

"But you also accept that Mr Bingley is fond of you. You cannot have it both ways. Either Mr Bingley is an indifferent lover, or his sister is a liar."

Jane shook her head again. Her arguments, though likely true, were not helping to ease her sister's sorrow. Jane was too hurt from the idea of thinking ill of anybody. "I understand from Mr Darcy that Miss Darcy is a shy girl of fifteen, and, despite her accomplishments and wealth, I do not believe Mr Bingley holds her in particular regard."

"I do not know if I dare to continue to hope."

"Of course you can! Check these tears; they will exhaust you. Let us go out; the cool air will do you good. We will have the shrubbery to ourselves and will be all the better for air and exercise."

Jane agreed, and Elizabeth continued to be cheerful and of use to her sister. All the while she tried to strengthen her own mind against the fear that, should Mr Bingley remain in London, Darcy too might never return.

Chapter 20

Saturday, November 30

Darcy was preparing to change into clothing suitable for the ride to Hertfordshire when Bingley tapped on his door.

"An express has come from my sister."

A sickening feeling settled into Darcy's stomach as he imagined the dreadful events that might have befallen those who remained at Netherfield or, closer to his heart, a young woman in the village of Longbourn. Fire, illness, injury, and death all crossed his mind before he was able to ask Bingley what the letter contained.

"My sisters have shut up the house and are on their way to London. They do not intend to return to Netherfield this winter and estimate they will be at Grosvenor Street by two o'clock. Caroline intends to wait on me as soon as she arrives and begs me not to leave until she calls."

Darcy's alarm gave way to annoyance. "It is nearly one o'clock! If we wait to speak with your sister, we will not have time to ride to Netherfield before the light fades."

"I cannot ignore such a directive as this. It must be important for Caroline to go to such trouble. We will alter our plans and return first thing Monday morning."

"Bingley, I called for the horses. Our plans have been laid, and I want to depart."

"I daresay you enjoy having your own way!" Bingley laughed, but Darcy glowered. "Why are you so desirous to begin our journey? It is not such an inconvenience to remain in town until Monday."

Darcy did not speak his first thought aloud: that nearly as often as he breathed, he thought about Elizabeth Bennet. Despite their quarrel at the ball, Darcy wanted to beg her forgiveness and secure her joyful presence in his life sooner rather than later. Yearning to feel Elizabeth's arms around him was not an appropriate answer to Bingley's question. "I might ask you the same. Is there not a lady in Hertfordshire who you are wishing to see?"

"That is beyond a doubt. But we can easily depart on Monday instead of today. The end result, I hope, will be the same."

That Bingley could speak so composedly about deferring an event to which Darcy had looked forward with impatient desire made Darcy grind his teeth. He was spared trying to make a civil reply by the sound of the house-bell.

Bingley, surprised, pulled out his watch. "They cannot have arrived so soon."

"It is my sister. She wished to bid me goodbye."

"What a kind girl! You must be proud of Miss Darcy. I have not seen her since the spring."

Georgiana was alone in the drawing room and offered her hand to her brother. Darcy suspected had Bingley been absent, she would have greeted him more affectionately. Bingley held out his hand; she could not refuse to give him hers. Darcy was relieved his sister was able to speak without shaking.

"I am pleased I have the opportunity to speak with you, Miss Darcy. It has been above five months since I saw you last."

"I, I am pleased to see you are well."

"Is your companion not with you?"

"My footman rode with—that is, Mrs Annesley said I could come alone. It is not far and, since he is my brother …" Georgiana looked at the floor.

"You quite mistake me!" Bingley gave a disarming laugh. "I only wished to make her acquaintance."

Darcy watched his sister and closest friend. Bingley spoke animatedly and kindly, while his sister ventured a yes or no when needed. Georgiana was a shy young woman, but also acted as though she had something to fear in every person and place. Either she was afraid of everybody or ashamed of herself, and her quiet, though anxious manner could be thought inexplicably strange. In every conversation, Georgiana struggled to subdue her agitation, and it was painful for him not to know how to help her.

"Did you not wish to leave by now, Fitzwilliam?"

"Our plans are not as fixed as I had thought them to be. Bingley's sisters left Hertfordshire this morning and are on their way to town. He will speak with them before we return to Netherfield, and we now intend to leave Monday morning." He gave Bingley a significant look.

"Yes, yes! It shall be as you say." Bingley gave an impatient wave, then returned his attention to Georgiana, who shrunk under his notice. "If you are willing to wait but an hour, you will be sure to see my sisters, for they intend to call here the moment they arrive. I know they will be glad to see you and hear how you passed your summer."

Georgiana's eyes flew to Darcy's. She breathed quickly, but she gained courage when Darcy laid a gentle arm across her shoulders. "I am not certain that, that I am at liberty to linger…Mrs Annesley will expect me, and …" She looked at her brother.

"Georgiana has other appointments today, and she wishes to remain punctual."

"Of course. 'Tis a family trait, Miss Darcy. I do not fault you for it."

"Yes, I prefer to be in very good time," Georgiana spoke to the floor, but when Darcy squeezed her shoulder, she raised her eyes. "Please remember me to your sisters."

"When Georgiana receives Miss Bingley's card, you may be assured she will call," Darcy added.

"Since I have now an hour or so at my leisure, I shall go to Bond Street. I cannot sit idle when I was expecting so soon to be on my way. You need not fear I shall force you to come with me. Miss Darcy, may I escort you back to Wimpole Street? I would not wish to detain you from your morning's appointments, and it would be my pleasure to see you home."

The Darcy siblings shared a look; he would have preferred to remain with his sister, but their deception forced her to depart. Georgiana looked as though she might be afflicted with panic again at being left with Bingley for five minutes. It could improve her confidence to know he trusted her to be alone with his friend. Darcy gave her shoulder a small squeeze and smiled. "May my friend accompany you? He will talk and laugh the entire carriage ride, and he shall not allow you to speak a word."

Bingley laughed and agreed, and Georgiana gave a relieved smile at not being expected to speak. She still looked disappointed to be going.

"My dear, since I am to remain in town another day, will you entertain me tomorrow? Perhaps you might play some of the new music you purchased."

Her sincere smile made his sister appear handsome. "Yes, I would like that!"

"I expect we will leave early Monday. But I shall be up again by the end of a fortnight." He hoped his Christmas plans at Pemberley would be contracted as he prepared for his impending wedding, but there was no need to speak of it to Georgiana yet.

"Whatever suits you best will satisfy me."

Bingley and Georgiana then departed, and Darcy was left in his own house with nothing to do but imagine what it would be like to finally kiss Elizabeth.

It was five o'clock, three hours past her time, when Miss Bingley deigned to call at Darcy's home. Bingley had grown tired of waiting and went out again, promising to return in time for dinner. Darcy had little occupation for these idle hours, and his temper suffered for it.

Miss Bingley entered alone, and the triumph in her eyes upon being left in the sole company of Mr Darcy did not improve his mood. *His* emotion on seeing her was less enthusiastic. One glance at Miss Bingley made Darcy realise that she had not just alighted from her carriage after a three-hour journey. Even to his untrained eye, he determined she must have changed her clothes and rearranged her hair.

"Mr Darcy, it is kind of you to receive me in my brother's absence. I told Louisa there was no reason for her to join me to call on Charles. She was so satisfied to return to her own home that I could not ask her to venture out again." Despite the draught in the hall, Darcy left the door open as he led Miss Bingley to a chair.

Darcy wanted to ask, "What can have made you so late?" but he could not speak rudely to a lady and a guest. He was out of temper enough that he did not feel guilty when he made a show of checking the time. "Bingley was surprised to receive your note."

"I cannot imagine why. I longed to return to town with its superior society, and after all, none of us have any reason to remain in the country."

"Is that the truth in the present case? I was under the impression Bingley had specific reason to return."

Miss Bingley laughed. It was a hollow, brittle sound that lacked all the warmth of Elizabeth's laughter. "You divert me. He is often in and out of love. Charles has no serious design on Jane Bennet."

Darcy rose to warm his hands before the fire. "I believe your brother was in earnest. Please allow me to recommend that you resign yourself and be happy that your friend will in all likelihood become your sister."

"Jane Bennet is a sweet creature, but she has no accomplishments or connexions. The best thing I could say about her is that if she did wed my brother, she would be so compliant that Charles may always have his own way. It would be a shame were Charles to throw himself away on that Jane Bennet! You cannot tell me a girl like her is the sort of wife you are desirous of having?"

The way Miss Bingley's eyes lingered on him made Darcy ill at ease as he settled back into his chair. "No, and I am well able to decide such matters for myself."

Whatever his guest felt upon hearing this pronouncement, Miss Bingley now seemed to think enough had been said on that subject, for she stayed silent.

"Did you have occasion to call at Longbourn? I hope you left all of our friends in Hertfordshire well." If he could not be in Elizabeth's presence, due to the interference of this woman, it would lessen his irritation if he could hear of her.

"Irrespective of my brother throwing himself away on Jane, I do not mean ever to like the Bennets! Is a woman of mean understanding and uncertain temper to be Charles's mother? And the shocking impropriety of the younger girls' pursuit to anyone in a scarlet coat will be a perpetual embarrassment. They are all common and vulgar!"

However little Darcy might have liked such comments about the family he hoped to marry into, he contented himself with coolly replying that he did not feel that the eldest two Bennet daughters were deserving of her censure. "I will be certain to pass on your wishes for their good health when I return to Netherfield."

"You cannot mean to return with Charles? For you to join him in Hertfordshire would be to sanction his intentions towards Jane Bennet."

Darcy bowed.

Miss Bingley then said, "We did call at Longbourn to take leave. Eliza Bennet looked very ill this morning. I never saw any beauty in her. At least Jane is a handsome girl. But not Eliza. Those eyes, which have sometimes been called fine, have a sharp, shrewish look that I do not like. She did not impress you in the beginning, I remember."

"Yes, but *that* was only when I first knew her; I now consider her as one of the handsomest women of my acquaintance."

Miss Bingley marched towards the fire and held out her hands. She stood there for, what seemed to Darcy, a longer time than necessary to warm them. She then sat, fixing him with a pointed stare.

"I do not believe I have told you all the news from Hertfordshire."

Darcy had no interest in her gossip, but since it would spare him the necessity of thinking of something civil to say, he gestured she might continue.

"Mr Collins made an offer of marriage to Eliza Bennet."

This did not surprise him, but he was startled that Caroline Bingley learned of the refusal and she would then spread that news. He said nothing, in the hope she would drop this inappropriate communication. "Did you not hear me? Mr Collins is an engaged man. Mrs Bennet told us that he made Miss Eliza an offer of marriage three days ago."

Elizabeth would not have accepted her cousin. Darcy kept his features neutral when he asked Miss Bingley to repeat herself with more clarity.

"Mr Darcy, I shall fear that you are being inattentive! Mr Collins asked his cousin Eliza to be his wife. Mrs Bennet was animated in regard to the entire situation."

The heat from the fireplace felt uncomfortable, and Darcy, although seated several feet away, got up to pace. "Miss Bingley, am I to now understand Mr Collins proposed to Miss Elizabeth Bennet and she *accepted* him?"

Darcy waited an eternity for Miss Bingley to answer. "Mr Collins proposed to Eliza Bennet, and he is now engaged." Her brittle laugh assaulted his ears again. "You amuse me, sir! Is that not what I have been telling you?"

Darcy tried to speak, but his mouth had gone dry. He crossed the room to pour himself a glass of wine. "What precisely did Miss Elizabeth say when you called at Longbourn this morning?"

"I hardly remember anything in particular."

"What did she say in regard to Mr Collins?"

"Eliza Bennet said all the appropriate statements on the happiness that might be expected from the match, the excellent character of Mr Collins, and the convenient distance of Hunsford from London. She did not express the warmest professions of a lover, but her words are nonetheless true."

Darcy finished the contents of his glass and sank back into his chair. *Elizabeth accepted Mr Collins?*

"It is deplorable that Miss Eliza, for all her talk about mutual love and esteem, accepted him from the desire of having her own establishment."

Throughout his life, Darcy had avoided occasions of exhibition. It was one of the many lessons his father had imparted to him. *"Of course you have your feelings, son, but never exhibit them to the world. A gentleman hears of the death of his pointer or the loss of an estate with entire calmness when others are present."* He had to remain composed.

"*If* it is true, do you know how, how soon will Miss Elizabeth gain that establishment?"

"I could not say. Do you recall at Netherfield, she professed she might as well sell herself to slavery at once as marry a man she disliked? Is it not amazing what changes a proposal can work?"

She broke out into a shrill laugh that put Darcy to his wit's end. He could not, would not allow his feelings to be put on display for Miss Bingley. He rose, begged her pardon for leaving her alone while she awaited her brother, and made up some errand that needed his attention. Miss Bingley did not detain him, saying that since her brother was so often late, she would do better to return home and await him there.

Darcy concealed his anxiety from Miss Bingley, but when he reached his own apartments, he allowed himself to consider all he had learned. *Elizabeth accepted her cousin's proposals? That foolish, insensible, obsequious man would be her husband?* The thought of this final separation between him and Elizabeth, to think of her as the wife of another man, was intolerable. It seemed to squeeze the blood out of his heart.

How could she have resigned her self-respect? What sort of parental interference was induced to persuade her to lower her standards to accept Mr Collins? Darcy ceased his pacing long enough to fill his tumbler and, after taking a long swallow, resumed his wearing away of the carpet. The brandy did nothing at all to dull his grief. The stab of a knife could not inflict a worse pain than he now suffered.

Did she not suspect how much I love her?

After another brandy, Darcy wondered if it did not take much persuasion. *Did she think I would not return? Did she think that, after her defence of Mr Wickham, I would not have her?*

Darcy brought the decanter back to his chair and collapsed into it. He poured himself another glass with unsteady hands and dropped the heavy crystal with a resounding thud on to the side table, sloshing the liquid.

An engagement is a solemn and binding agreement; there is nothing I can do. Elizabeth would be another man's wife. It was gall and wormwood to Darcy's mind to imagine that lovely, witty, accomplished woman sunk to be the wife of a ridiculous man she could not respect.

Darcy was bitterly disappointed, more than ever before in his life. How might things have been different had he not left with Bingley? It came like a thunderclap on him, and the rest of his evening passed in a haze of refilling his brandy tumbler and being haunted by the memory of a fine pair of dark, beautiful eyes.

Sunday, December 1

Mr Wickham and other officers met the Bennets on the way home from church. They made themselves courteous to Mrs Bennet and were invited to tea. Elizabeth soon found herself alongside Mr Wickham. She refrained from shrugging her shoulders at another tête-à-tête, but strove to be polite to her family's newest acquaintance.

"I see Mr Collins is no longer in residence. Does Longbourn now seem to be a quieter place?"

"Mr Collins will not neglect us long, for my cousin now has a nearer connexion to Lucas Lodge. I believe he intends to wait on us in less than a fortnight." Elizabeth laughed as she remembered. "My father begged him to stay in Kent and not to risk offending Lady Catherine by coming to us again. Alas, Mr Collins could not be persuaded."

Her companion looked questioningly at her, and Elizabeth explained, "Mr Collins has been granted a living by Lady Catherine de Bourgh. He is extraordinarily deferential to his patroness."

Mr Wickham's attention was caught, and after a moment, he asked Elizabeth in a low voice how intimately acquainted her family was with the de Bourghs.

"I hardly know how Mr Collins was first introduced to her notice, but he has not known her long."

"Lady Catherine de Bourgh and Lady Anne Darcy were sisters; consequently, she is aunt to the present Mr Darcy."

"I had not known their precise connexion, only that Lady Catherine was his relation."

"I have not seen Lady Catherine for years, but I remember her. I regret to say, I never liked her. Her manners were insolent, and she has a dictatorial manner. She has the reputation of being sensible and clever, but I believe she derives her abilities from her rank and fortune."

"Mr Collins speaks highly of both Lady Catherine and her daughter; perhaps his gratitude misled him." Elizabeth suspected the woman was conceited and arrogant, but since it was still possible she would be introduced to Lady Catherine as the wife of her nephew, she would do well to be circumspect.

"You are an astute judge of character." After a pause while Elizabeth hoped this assessment was true, he then added, "Her daughter, Miss de Bourgh, will have a very large fortune."

"I understand from Mr Collins that she is of a sickly constitution."

Mr Wickham shook his head. "No, Miss de Bourgh has a healthy complexion and a remarkably pretty figure. Most would say with her good features and sweet smile, Miss de Bourgh is a striking woman. Mr Collins must be mistaken on this point."

If he believed I would accept his proposals, then Mr Collins could easily have misunderstood the nature of his patroness's daughter.

Mr Wickham continued, "She is a charming woman, never cross, at least in the few times we were ever thrown together. Miss de Bourgh is the heiress of Rosings and has extensive property. It is believed she and her cousin will unite the two estates."

"This would be a son of Lord Fitzwilliam, or does Lady Catherine have other siblings?"

"Forgive me for not speaking clearly. It is believed the present Mr Darcy will wed Miss de Bourgh and unite Rosings and Pemberley."

She first felt astonishment, and it would have been as painful as it was strong, had not an immediate disbelief of the assertion attended it. "You must be mistaken!"

"You forget that I passed my youth alongside the Darcy family and have had ample opportunity to observe their behaviour and hear their opinions. Why should not Mr Darcy, a man of impeccable connexions, splendid property, and noble kindred, marry his wealthy, pretty, well-connected cousin? I should think that to marry anyone less than Miss de Bourgh would be disgraceful to his notions of dignity and familial responsibility."

"Simply because his nearest relations desire the union, it does not follow that Mr Darcy will marry Miss de Bourgh to oblige them." She attempted to keep her tone from becoming defensive, but doubted her success.

"Knowing as I do of Mr Darcy's family pride, I beg leave to disagree with you. Not to disgrace his family or lose influence is a powerful motive for him to marry his rich, nobly bred cousin. He no doubt considers it a way to honour the memory of his departed mother and father."

Elizabeth was transported back to Longbourn's breakfast room where she recalled Darcy's words as they spoke of their families. "*I do think that it is natural to want to do right by one's parents.*"

"He is loyal to his family, but it does not follow that Mr Darcy is"—she struggled with the word—"engaged to Miss de Bourgh."

"I always thought of it as a tacit arrangement, a union wished for by all the family, not excepting Miss de Bourgh as well as Mr Darcy. What could be more natural for two cousins of nearly the same age? They are destined for each other, and *who* could divide them?"

"I cannot think of anyone." *How could Mr Wickham suspect,*

because of a friendship and a dance, that I had hoped to become Mrs Darcy? She added, "Does Mr Darcy admire Miss de Bourgh?"

"I have no right to give my opinion," said Mr Wickham, "as to his being in love with her."

"You have known him for a long time and could be a fair judge."

"As for his wish of forwarding the match, I am certain he has it at heart. However, I do not think he is in love. When he weds Miss de Bourgh, it will be entirely for wealth and connexion."

Elizabeth's hand was clenching Darcy's handkerchief so tightly that her nails began to wear a hole. Mr Wickham looked at her, then glanced at the clouds and continued, "And to marry for money, I think the wickedest thing in existence."

At length, forcing herself to speak, she said with a calmness of manner which she hoped concealed her disbelief, "Mr Darcy will marry for money?"

"This may open your eyes to a shade in Mr Darcy's character; such things are too common with men such as he. When one lives in the world, a man of his consequence marrying for money and connexions is too common to strike one as it ought. He, I am sure, takes it as a matter of course."

A silence stretched until the house was in sight. "When can we expect Mr Darcy and Mr Bingley to return?" he asked.

Of course! When Darcy comes back with Mr Bingley, it will prove all of Mr Wickham's conjectures to be wrong. "Mr Bingley said he expected his business would keep him in town three or four days. I do not pretend to know Mr Darcy's plans."

"I can never talk of Mr Darcy without being grieved to the soul by a thousand tender recollections." Mr Wickham attempted to engage her on other subjects, but her answers were so unenthusiastic that he could not advance in any, finally saying, "I see your mother has been left to walk alone. May I leave you while I pay her my compliments?"

Later, after she lay on the bed and dried her eyes with Darcy's handkerchief, she felt better. The anxiety of not knowing the state of her relationship with Darcy was clouding her reasoning. Mr Wickham's claim that Darcy would wed his cousin, a striking woman with splendid property, purely for the sake of her fortune and connexions, had shocked her to the core. His absence, and their manner of parting, was why she was affected.

Darcy's return tomorrow with Mr Bingley will put the matter to rest.

Chapter 21

Monday, December 2

Some believed that to drink at least a bottle of wine a day was the proper way for a gentleman to pass through the world. Darcy, however, was a temperate man.

Consequently, the whole of Sunday had been spent suffering the effects of too much drink. He passed a terrible night after he learned Elizabeth was to marry her cousin, and was still so out of sorts he had to send his servant to deliver a message of apology to his sister for cancelling their meeting. He spent the day with such an aching head and heavy heart that he did not leave his own apartments until Monday.

"I am glad you are no longer ill," Bingley said at breakfast. "Your valet seemed concerned whenever I asked after you."

"I am well, thank you." It was better to tell this falsehood rather than explain he spent the previous day recovering from a night of drinking.

"Your man said you did not intend to return with me to Netherfield. I hope you have changed your mind now that you are well."

"Now that I am settled here, I am not eager to leave. Also, you do not need your bachelor friend in the way while you court Miss Bennet."

"Too true!" Bingley smiled. "But you must return to be my groomsman, provided the lady accepts me."

Darcy made some indeterminate sound, deciding it would be easier to refuse this office by letter rather than discuss it now. To stand at the altar alongside Bingley if Elizabeth was a mere six feet away would be intolerable.

Soon Bingley was ready to leave, and Darcy accompanied him to the door.

"You are welcome at Netherfield at any time. You have always accepted me into your home as though it were my own, and I am impatient to return the favour."

"I shall wait until I receive an invitation from the new Mrs Bingley." The match would throw him into the way of the future Mrs Bingley's sister, and he would avoid a visit until Elizabeth left as Mrs Collins. It was painful to even reflect of his loss of Elizabeth; to speak of her engagement with Bingley would be intolerable. He did not think he could yet hide his distress so soon after having learnt that she was promised to marry someone else.

"You need not stand on ceremony with me, and I am certain Miss Bennet would agree. I shall pass along your compliments to all our friends in the neighbourhood."

Darcy managed a tight smile, but he did offer an earnest shake of the hand to Bingley as he left. He threw himself into a chair to think on his own regrets.

It seems so out of character for Elizabeth to be persuaded to accept her cousin, even if she did not love me. Could Miss Bingley have been mistaken? Could I allow myself to hope Elizabeth is not engaged?

This was not a rational hope, but love and reason did not go hand in hand. Miss Bingley was not a reliable witness to anything in connexion to the Bennets. But he could not believe that an otherwise respectable lady would commit such a moral lapse as to lie to him outright. The repercussions for Miss Bingley, for the truth would eventually come out, would be socially disastrous. *But she might have been in error.*

No proper gentleman persisted in a suit when the object of his admiration was engaged. *If Elizabeth is promised to another, I must avoid causing her any uneasiness in seeing me. A continuance of my attentions would be an insult to her wishes and her solemn promise to marry another man.* If Elizabeth was engaged to Mr Collins, they were bound in a state of approximation to marriage, and Darcy's arrival on her doorstep would insult her and her family.

When Bingley was engaged, it would be enough, at a time when the expectation of one wedding made everybody eager for another, to ask if any of his betrothed's sisters were also soon to be married. *I shall wait until Bingley writes to announce his engagement to Miss Bennet.* It would force Darcy to wait in wretched suspense for a week or so, but it was a small price to pay to know for certain if Miss Bingley had been correct.

If Elizabeth was not engaged, he would return to Hertfordshire and explain it all: Mr Wickham's treachery, the affair at Ramsgate, Miss Bingley's misinformation. She would be angry at his absence but, he hoped, not willing to throw away their relationship because of it. Darcy clung to the hope that Miss Bingley was wrong.

"I wish my mother would be more reasonable when she speaks of Mr Bingley's return," Jane said.

"She ought not to speak about his love for you, but you cannot disagree with her expectations?" Concern for her sister gave Elizabeth an object on which to concentrate, rather than wondering if Mr Bingley would bring Darcy.

"Let me first see how Mr Bingley behaves when we see him again."

"At his own ball, he offended two or three young ladies by not asking them to dance, and I spoke to him twice myself without receiving an answer. Is not general incivility the very essence of love?"

"You are trying to divert me with your nonsense."

"It is not nonsense. Now all you need do is become even more beautiful so as to make Mr Bingley incapable of doing anything other than falling at your feet the moment he sees you."

It was fortunate that Jane's beauty needed no such improvements because hours later Mrs Bennet ran down the stairs shrieking, "Mr Bingley is come! I saw him from my dressing room window. And on the day of his return!"

Elizabeth went to the window and saw that Mr Bingley was alone.

Elizabeth's security sank; she choked back the sob that threatened to escape from her throat. Jane was too intent on staring at the door to take notice. Elizabeth raised the handkerchief she clutched in her hand, but quickly shoved it into her sleeve when she discerned the F.D. embroidered in the corner.

When Mr Bingley came in, he was occupied again by Mrs Bennet's overbearing attentions.

"It is a long time, Mr Bingley, since you went away."

"'Tis less than a week!" Lydia rolled her eyes.

"I always intended on soon returning and, in fact, would have returned on Saturday if I had had my own way."

"Miss Lucas is to be married to Mr Collins since you were away. It is hard to think that Charlotte Lucas should be mistress of this house. I did not anticipate their match; we all thought Lizzy would have him, and I do wish I had the comfort of a daughter married."

Although Elizabeth was made to feel uncomfortable, Mr Bingley gave no indication he wished to be elsewhere. The half hour was chatted away, and by the end of it, Mr Bingley enthusiastically agreed to join their evening party tomorrow.

Tuesday, December 3

ELIZABETH WAS WRITING AN OVERDUE LETTER TO HER AUNT Gardiner. It was shorter than her relation deserved, but her heart was not in it. Mr Bingley had remained with them tonight, and although his cheerfulness rendered him an agreeable addition, Elizabeth could not yet look at him without thinking of Darcy. To make matters worse, to call Darcy's absence a loss was a presumption for which she had not words strong enough to satisfy her own humility.

Dare I ask Mr Bingley if Darcy wishes to forward a match between Pemberley and Rosings? Or if Darcy has any intention of returning to Netherfield before Christmas? She would ask him now; the uncertainty and wishful thinking were taking a toll on her equanimity.

But on returning to the drawing room, she perceived her sister and Mr Bingley standing together, as if engaged in earnest conversation. Elizabeth was on the point of going away when Mr Bingley whispered a few words to her sister and ran out of the room.

Jane then embraced her with a countenance of joy. "I am the happiest creature in the world! Why is not everybody as happy!"

Elizabeth congratulated her sister with sincere delight. "Did I not say he was in love with you? I have no doubt you will be happy with Mr Bingley!"

"I must go to my mother," she cried. "He is gone to my father already. Lizzy, how shall I bear so much happiness!"

And how shall I bear so much melancholy? Elizabeth allowed herself this one indulgence into self-pity before smiling at the ease with which Jane and Bingley had come together. If any woman deserved to be married to an amiable, handsome young man who sincerely loved her, it was Jane.

She was soon joined by Bingley, whose conference with her father had been short and to the purpose. He came up to her and claimed the good wishes and affection of a sister.

"I am so pleased, Mr Bingley! I can think of no finer man than you to make my sister happy. I have always wanted a brother, and I am delighted you and I shall have a nearer relationship."

They shook hands with great cordiality. "Since you are to be my sister, you must call me Charles!"

"My family calls me Lizzy, and I shall expect such familiarity from you, too."

This was not the moment to enquire if Mr Darcy was likely to marry his cousin, and until her sister came down, she had to listen to all he had to say of his own happiness.

Friday, December 6

Neither proper spelling nor punctuation was featured in any letter from Bingley, but between the blots and barely legible words, Darcy was confident Bingley was engaged to Jane Bennet. Now he could congratulate Bingley and ask if one of the other Miss Bennets would also soon be married. One wedding begets another, as the proverb goes.

Elizabeth would not marry such a detestable man as Mr Collins only to please her parents. Miss Bingley must have been in error!

Darcy was so engrossed by writing that he did not hear the bell and was taken by surprise when he was told his sister was in the drawing room. He entered with a quick step and a ready smile, but he faltered when he saw his sister's drooping shoulders. Her red eyes and the wet handkerchief crumpled in her hands suggested she had just composed herself after a fit of tears.

"Good morning." She kissed his cheek. "I hope you are well."

Darcy recognised her false cheer; he led her to a chair and asked her to confess what the matter was.

"I have had a letter from Lady Catherine. You can guess the contents."

"Given that there is nothing beyond the reach of her ladyship's curiosity, the possible topics are limitless."

Georgiana handed him a letter. His attention was soon caught by the phrases that likely upset her:

> *I will be seriously displeased should you refuse to join in the evening parties. You are nearly sixteen, and although you are full young to be in much company, I advise you strenuously to apply yourself to joining the conversation and play the pianoforte whenever you are asked. Miss Darcy, the daughter of Mr Darcy of Pemberley and Lady Anne, must not shirk her responsibilities nor act with impropriety.*

The rest demonstrated that the minutest concerns were not beneath Lady Catherine's notice and closed with her ladyship's pronouncements on what weather she determined they were to have a fortnight from now. To a temper delicate and nervous like Georgiana's, Lady Catherine's advice was soul-crushing.

"I do not wish to have her scold me and disapprove of me. Pemberley will be a torment if she is always pressing me to speak and demanding me to be on display!" Another burst of tears erupted.

While Darcy could concede that Lady Catherine might be intimidating, both in stature and demeanour, his sister's fits of anxiety could not continue. "Well," he said, in a tone he tried to prevent from becoming impatient, "well, my dear, dry up your tears. There is not use in them; they can do no good."

She took a few gasping breaths to collect herself. Darcy handed her his handkerchief, one she had embroidered with his initials.

"You need not worry about Lady Catherine expecting much talk from you; you know she has a tendency to crowd others out of the conversation." This earned him a nod. "Besides, she shall have all of her nephews at Pemberley upon whom she may endow her advice. Anne will never trouble you, let alone speak, and Milton will see you as a child. As for the colonel and me, you are perfectly at ease with us."

"I am disappointed Lady Milton will not be at Pemberley. Why would Lord Milton join us when his wife is soon expecting?"

Because he wed his cousin out of obligation and cannot be bothered with her any more than she must produce his heir. Leaving his family behind would make it easier for Milton to see Lady Hancock, his mistress, who would certainly be installed at some estate neighbouring Pemberley while Milton was in residence.

"Milton need not explain his motives to us." Darcy's sympathies were roused by her sadness. "You cannot be so overcome by a trifle." His fear that there was more to her near-elopement than he knew pulled at his heart.

"Not everyone is blessed with your self-control."

Darcy's eyes widened, and Georgiana rushed to apologise. "I spoke out of turn. You are right, you always are!"

"I am not always right, Georgiana. In fact, I am sensible of having done wrong."

"Do you refer to your letter from Netherfield?"

Darcy stared at his sister in confusion. He had been thinking of Ramsgate, of trusting Mrs Younge, of losing his temper when Georgiana confessed her planned elopement with Mr Wickham, of his pitiable attempts at consoling his broken-hearted sister.

"You wrote how you insulted one of Mr Bingley's houseguests. I could not believe you would ever act in a spiteful manner."

The letter Elizabeth read and that Consequence game! It felt like a lifetime ago.

Darcy stood, tugged absently at his waistcoat, and paced. "I acted in a manner unbefitting a gentleman. I had left behind one page of that letter to you, and when she returned it to me, having read it, I feared that Miss Bennet might expose you. She did not take kindly to my presumption against her character. As a result, during the course of an evening's game, we both were cruel to one another. That was after a ball at which I told Bingley, with the full knowledge that Miss Bennet could hear me, that I did not find her tolerably pretty enough to dance with."

"No, you would not—"

"I have been a selfish, prideful man," he interrupted her. "Miss Bennet had many reasons to disapprove of my behaviour. I tell you this in the hope that you might be spared my mistakes. Simply because you are a Darcy, you are not entitled to think poorly of nor act meanly towards those who lack your rank or your wealth. I challenge you to consider your own values and actions and decide what manner of woman you wish to be."

His sister's manner became very agitated, and she struggled for speech. "Does… does she—does this woman *know*?"

Darcy sighed and slowly sat down next to her. "The letter mentioned no identifying details, no full names, but she discerned that Miss Darcy suffered in some vague way through no fault of her own. She never asked me what happened; she only expressed concern for your happiness."

"I do not wish for anyone to know of my shame." Georgiana's voice was barely audible.

"I trust her, and I am grateful for her. She showed me that I had fallen away from the good principles I had been taught. Miss

Bennet has a great deal of warmth and liveliness. I hope I have the opportunity to introduce you to her."

Georgiana agreed to meet anyone he wished to make known to her, and then excused herself to tend to her appearance. Not for the first time did Darcy wish that Miss Bingley had been mistaken about Elizabeth Bennet and Mr Collins. Elizabeth would be good for both him and for Georgiana.

Monday, December 9

"We always spend our income, Bingley," Mrs Bennet continued, "but Mr Bennet has, in order to give our dear child enough for respectable wedding clothes, sold out one hundred pounds of money for the purpose." Jane winced, and Bingley's attempts to help made matters worse.

"I hope you should not give yourselves trouble about Jane's—"

"That is not the trouble! The trouble is it is out of question to suppose she could wear as Mrs Bingley anything made for her in the country as Miss Bennet! She ought to go to the shops in London and—"

Jane made a pleading expression to her sister, and Elizabeth asked Bingley if he would accompany her on a walk. The six weeks between Bingley's declaration and the departure of Jane from Longbourn would at times, Elizabeth suspected, feel long to the couple.

"Tell me, Miss Elizabeth—I mean, Lizzy," Bingley asked as they walked along the gravel, "are you truly a great walker, or did you find it tiresome to be hearing about wedding clothes? You must have no secrets from your brother."

"I take a good walk every day if the weather permits. In fact, I walk constantly to keep myself from growing fat."

Bingley looked at her askance. "I believe Darcy was correct, Miss—Lizzy: he once said he thought you enjoy professing opinions that are not your own."

Hearing Darcy's name stopped Elizabeth's heart for a moment. "Bingley—"

"You must call me Charles when we are among our own family."

"Charles, I only meant to enquire after Mr Darcy. I hope he is well." *I hope he is coming back.*

"I left him well, thank you. I wished he would return with me, but Darcy would not yield. He chose to remain close to his sister and did not wish to be in the way while I courted yours. He gave me little reason to suppose I will soon see him." Elizabeth held on to her future brother's arm as he unknowingly pierced her heart.

"He will go to Pemberley at Christmastime?"

"Yes, his mother's sister and Darcy's three cousins will be there. He is particularly close to one of his cousins, whose acquaintance I have had the pleasure of making."

Particularly close? Darcy will not return and will soon be in the company of Miss de Bourgh, a woman who Mr Wickham described as handsome and amiable as she is wealthy.

"Charles, would you mind if we returned to the house? My father might be prevailed upon to join you in a game of backgammon if you do not wish to have your opinion solicited in regard to the lace on my sister's gowns." *Maintaining this determined good cheer will exhaust me.*

He agreed, and Elizabeth made her escape to her own room that she might have no concern beyond consideration of her own thoughts. She cried, covering her face with her hands and stifling her sobs lest anyone hear.

She had no claim on Darcy; he had not declared himself. She suspected he once felt the same as she, but after she defended Mr Wickham's reformation, Darcy's resentful nature made it easy for him to cast her aside.

If he was intending to marry Miss de Bourgh, Darcy is blameable in remaining at Netherfield after he first felt my influence over him. I may be a fool for love, but I shall not allow anyone to know how much I suffer the extinction of my dearest hope.

She gazed at her pallid reflection in the glass and attempted a smile. *Pitiful!* Elizabeth pinched her cheeks and tucked stray tendrils back into their pins and smiled again. *Better.* A deep inhalation and another dab at her eyes with the handkerchief, and she smiled again. *That looks more like the lively Elizabeth Bennet everyone expects.*

Thursday, December 12

WINTER IN LONDON IS MISERABLE. HIS SISTER AND HER COMPANION joined Darcy this morning and had arrived with black snow clinging to their coats. The smoke of coals formed a murky atmosphere that was perceivable for miles. When the weather was cloudy and foggy, as it was often in winter, the smoke increased the dingy hue.

The servant had brought in the morning's mail, and there was a letter with Bingley's terrible handwriting. As always, there was a general inattention to stops and a frequent ignorance of grammar. Every line contained a blot. Individual letters and entire verbs were left out and Bingley called his intended bride 'Miss Bennet,' 'Jane,' and 'my angel' all within the same sentence. His future sister was alternately called 'Miss Elizabeth,' 'Miss Lizzy,' and 'Lizzy.'

It was not until the bottom of the second page that Darcy found the paragraph pertinent to him.

> *... You...right one weding may beget...Mrs B laments that Miss Lizzy did not accept when Mr Collins...his declarat... She wishes daughters be settled. However soon Miss L...accepted Mr Collins...and are to m...the new year.*

A rush of bitter pain coursed through Darcy's veins. Miss Bingley was correct, and Bingley confirmed his fears: Elizabeth had refused Mr Collins, but she ultimately accepted him to oblige her parents and secure her family's estate.

She did not love me enough to have faith that I would return. How much time passed before she succumbed to Mr and Mrs Bennet's inducement? Days? Hours? How could she have held any love for me only to accept such a man? Was what she said at Netherfield, about the value of mutual love, a lie?

The absolute necessity of seeming like himself produced an immediate struggle. Darcy pushed away from the table and stood. The ladies looked up at him with surprise.

"We leave for Pemberley today. I want to be at the Hatfield

coaching inn before we lose the light. Shall you be ready to leave by two o'clock?"

Georgiana stared, and Mrs Annesley managed to answer, "We will do all we must to have everything arranged, sir. May I ask, why such haste?"

Darcy cast about for something to say. "The miserable weather prompts me to leave London as soon as possible." He then wrenched open the door and slammed it behind him.

Tuesday, December 17

Mr Collins's return to Hertfordshire yesterday was no longer a matter of intense displeasure to Mrs Bennet. Now that Jane was engaged to Bingley and his four thousand a year, the wound of not having one of her daughters wed to Longbourn's heir was somewhat lessened. Thankfully, Mr Collins spent the chief of every day at Lucas Lodge, and he sometimes returned to Longbourn only in time to make an apology for his absence before the family went to bed.

Tuesday evening, he arrived in time to take supper with the family while Bingley yet remained. Bingley was speaking quietly with Elizabeth and Jane, but Mr Collins interrupted their conversation to enquire after Mr Darcy.

"I assume by now my friend has left for Pemberley."

"I have no doubt he would have been delighted to learn that Lady Catherine speaks with the greatest satisfaction of joining him at Pemberley in a se'nnight's time. She spoke on the subject when I informed her that I had the good fortune to make that gentleman's acquaintance. Her ladyship is certain Mr Darcy's attachment to the family at Rosings is ever increasing."

Mr Collins gave a forced laugh; but no one was paying him attention save for Elizabeth. "Naturally, I made an elegant compliment and an allusion to the natural event that must follow, which was smiled on by both her ladyship and her daughter."

Elizabeth's spirits were sunk anew. Was Lady Catherine the sort of woman to proclaim the attachment between her daughter and nephew if she was not convinced the match would take place? According to both Mr Wickham and Mr Collins, Miss de Bourgh had every recommendation of person and mind as well as fortune.

Once again she felt the crushing weight of disappointment. *It does not matter if he is to marry Anne de Bourgh or any other woman. He has made it clear that he is not going to propose to me.* Darcy had left, and he was not coming back.

Chapter 22

Friday, December 20

Darcy paced along the windows, appreciating both the fine prospect and a calm moment before his family was to occupy his house. He looked on the whole scene—the river, the trees scattered near its banks, and the winding of the valley—and tried to feel all the delight he usually felt while at Pemberley.

It was not that Darcy did not wish to host his Fitzwilliam family. He was struggling with how to reconcile himself with the cheerfulness that the season generally brought and his regret, grieving over what was and wishing for what could never be.

He shut his eyes in disgust. How could he hold Elizabeth Bennet as a paradigm when she sacrificed her self-respect to marry Mr Collins?

I hate that I still love her.

A servant told him one of the expected carriages had passed the lodge. By the time he arrived in the drawing room to await his guests, his sister and her companion were there. He shared a glance with Mrs Annesley, who nodded in reassurance as they heard a sharp voice from the hall.

Lady Catherine entered with her usual self-important air. She was a tall, large woman with strongly marked features who, when she smiled—which was not often—reminded Darcy of his mother. This fond recollection lasted so long as his aunt remained silent.

Darcy held out his hand. "Welcome to Pemberley."

She glanced at him, but did not break her stride and continued to Georgiana, who would have taken a step backwards had not Mrs Annesley rested a hand on her arm. Aunt and niece stared at one another for a long moment. "Good afternoon, my dear. Have you nothing to say to your mother's sister?"

"You are very welcome at Pemberley, Lady Catherine." Georgiana took the proffered hand and kissed her aunt's cheek.

Lady Catherine then turned to Darcy. "A guest must pay their respects to the lady of the house before she acknowledges anyone else in the room."

Darcy ground his teeth. "Georgiana is fifteen and is *not* my hostess. As I am a bachelor, *I* will host our party. Therefore, my greeting of you first was correct, and Georgiana would have erred had she anticipated me." This elicited raised eyebrows, but Lady Catherine had enough sense to remember whose house she was in. "I trust your journey was satisfactory?" Hearing her criticism of the journey was a necessary part of welcoming Lady Catherine anywhere.

Georgiana gestured towards the chairs by the fire, and Lady Catherine sat with all the regality of a queen on her throne. "We did not leave Milton Hall as early as we ought. The harness did not fit properly and so the horses did not draw evenly. I ought to have overseen them myself, rather than leave the horses to the mercy of an ignorant post boy. No one knows how to properly drive a team better than I. The post boy hurried down hills and galloped when he ought not to. Anne's nerves are consequently weak from being jolted."

Darcy had forgotten Anne in the face of Lady Catherine's indignation, which seemed to take up all available space in the room. He made her a slight bow that she acknowledged with only a blink before she sank into a seat.

His cousin was a pale, sickly woman who looked more like a child than did Georgiana, although she was ten years her senior. Where Lady Catherine was tall and commanding, Anne gave one the impression of being about to fall asleep. Her features, though not homely, were of no consequence; and she spoke only with her companion, Mrs Jenkinson.

Darcy looked at his sister, who was cringing as though she might as soon be struck as be spoken to by her aunt. "Madam, would the ladies care to rest before dinner? If the gentlemen are not much behind you, shall we dine at half past five?"

"I do not at all require rest. I am of a healthy constitution."

"Then I will ring for some—"

Lady Catherine rose. "Anne, perhaps you would like to attend to your toilette?" She looked at Darcy and said, "As you know, Anne takes particular care of her appearance."

Anne's drooping form was swallowed by a voluminous mantle that appeared to have been made for a woman twice her size. Her hair might have been in full curls some days ago, but now lay dishevelled and limp. She turned her unfocused gaze towards her mother and dragged herself to her feet.

"Of course she does." Darcy pulled the bell, and the housekeeper arrived to escort the ladies to their apartments. He could hear the overbearing tone of his aunt's voice and the short conciliating replies of his housekeeper as they ascended the stairs.

His cousins' quarrelling voices rang from the hall long before they entered the drawing room. Charles Fitzwilliam, Viscount Milton, was, as usual, arguing with his younger brother.

"I still say there is nothing so fine as travelling with six horses; 'tis a shame we could only get four."

"Milton, have you never travelled with fewer than six? What a blow to your self-respect to be seen arriving anywhere with only *four* post horses."

"You would have me demean myself, as I have seen you do, and travel in a one-horse chaise?"

"Not at all, *m'lord*; I think a horse and cart fitting for a man such as you."

"And a porter and a wheelbarrow more appropriate for you!"

Darcy groaned inwardly. The viscount and the colonel had always argued as boys, but Darcy had seen a change in their relationship during the last five years. Their bickering had lost the good-natured teasing of brothers fond of one another and had taken on a more cutting tone.

Milton made up for his natural defects by adorning himself in the first style of fashion. He had a reputation as a man of honour, even though he kept a mistress at great expense. Milton was a chattering coxcomb whose vanity had no equal among other gentleman. Darcy suspected that, upon seeing his apartments at Pemberley, the first thing Milton would do was request a second looking glass.

Milton's younger brother, Colonel Fitzwilliam, was dear to Darcy. There was an ease and genuine friendship between them, whereas Darcy doubted Milton would tip his hat if he passed him in the street, had they not been blood relatives. The colonel was thirty, with an intelligent and lively eye. He shared guardianship of Georgiana and was the only other human being, besides the participants, who knew what had happened at Ramsgate.

Milton bestowed on him a full scrape and twisted his head into a bow as he addressed Darcy. The colonel stood behind his brother and rolled his eyes.

"What sort of a starched dandy bows to his own cousin?" Fitzwilliam stepped around his brother to shake Darcy's hand.

"I would not be so gauche to not properly acknowledge my host."

Fitzwilliam ignored him as he went on to greet Georgiana. "My dear, you are looking well. You flatter us all; you look smart for greeting your old relations."

Georgiana glanced at Mrs Annesley and in an anxious voice asked, "Am I dressed too fine for afternoon?"

Fitzwilliam laughed kindly. "The appropriate response is to blush and say, 'thank you, cousin.' Unless of course, it is Milton who says it; then I advise you to turn away in disgust at his forward compliments." He winked.

Milton looked at his brother oddly. "Why would I notice the child's gown? She is not out." After observing Georgiana's downcast expression, he forced a smile before adding, "I am certain she is as appropriately dressed as my own daughters."

Darcy rolled his eyes; Milton's daughters were ages four and one. "Georgiana will turn sixteen in the spring. She may not be full out in company, but she goes on calls and has left the schoolroom behind. You have my leave to notice your own cousin."

"That is hardly proper." Milton was affronted. "She is not out. She is socially invisible, and I would not insult you or her by complimenting her appearance."

Darcy and Fitzwilliam shared a knowing look. Milton's formality, far more reaching than Darcy's sense of decorum, often drained the life from a family party.

Fitzwilliam redirected Georgiana's attention. "I know your companion by reputation, but would you do me the honour of introducing me?" Lord Milton might be heir to the earldom, but it was the colonel who was truly the gentleman. After speaking with Mrs Annesley, he said, "Georgiana, my father sent a gift for you. He found a miniature of your mother when she was not much older than you are now."

Georgiana stammered with great emotion that she should very much like a picture of her mother.

"He said more," Milton added. "You are so forgetful. My father also wished her to know that he suspects her to be as like her mother in delicacy and taste. He said Lady Anne would be proud of the proper young lady Miss Darcy has become."

Georgiana's confidence after Ramsgate was not strong enough to withstand the comparison to a long-dead mother who could have no fault in the eyes of an orphaned girl, and she began to cry. Colonel Fitzwilliam instantly intervened.

"Milton, you have overwhelmed her with your accurate memory." He stepped between them, handed his cousin his handkerchief, and all but pushed her into the arms of Mrs Annesley, who led her away. "Perhaps we might retire until dinner, Darcy?"

Darcy pulled the bell and reflected on his family as the others filed from the room. He loved his family, faults and all. He was certain that, despite their natural personality conflicts, they would be merry and pleasant together. He hoped they would be enough to distract him from all he had left behind in Hertfordshire.

Saturday, December 21

NOW THAT MR COLLINS HAD TAKEN LEAVE OF LONGBOURN, THE Bennets settled into their usual employments and habits. Elizabeth would not shut herself away from her family, or walk for hours in solitude, or lay awake the whole night in meditation on the subject of Darcy. She would admit to herself the sad change in her life now that he was gone, but she would not allow any other person to know her heartache.

"That was the last," Jane said as they left the village after spending the day delivering clothes and blankets. "Next Christmas I shall do this as Mrs Bingley."

"You are not going to make me to call you 'Mrs Bingley,' are you? I hope your eagerness to assume that name will not force those who know you best to address you as such?"

"Of course not. If I could but see you as happy! I could ask for nothing more if you were happily married and settled nearby."

Who would come within the Longbourn circle who could bear a comparison to Fitzwilliam Darcy? A heartbeat later, Elizabeth berated herself. *I could ask for a less resentful man with greater constancy!* "I have little intention of marrying."

"But what of love, Lizzy? Romantic as you are, I cannot believe you would forsake all possibility of love and marriage at the age of twenty. You will not always wish to be at Longbourn. And do you not want children?"

Elizabeth pushed aside all thought of a quiet evening in an elegant home, playing the instrument while Darcy spent more time stroking her hair than turning the pages, with children playing noisy games on the floor.

"I shall be very well off with all the children of a sister I love to care about." Elizabeth nudged Jane's shoulder with her own.

"I accept that for the present and will hold my tongue when you give up the title Miss Bennet. Besides, I think you require a clever man, a reading man, and I can think of no one in this neighbourhood who would suit you."

"The matter is settled, then: I shall remain at home at the ready to amuse your score of offspring."

"I do not wish for you to remain at home. After the wedding, Charles and I plan to proceed, after a few days, to Brighton and take a house there for some weeks. When the novelty of amusement there is over, we shall go to London before we return here. Say you will agree to join us!"

Elizabeth smiled with genuine delight. "I will! I know it is usual for a bride to invite a sister on her wedding tour, but I confess your request surprises me."

Jane blushed and shook her head. "It will be a private time, but I still want you there. All the well, for we shall have a bustle of activity after we all return to Netherfield."

"You cannot mean that you wish me to remain with you and your husband indefinitely?"

"Of course I do. Charles understands that I want a female companion with me, especially when his friends make their visits in form after we settle here. All of his friends are unknown to me, except for Mr Darcy. I would like to have you with me when I must meet and entertain them."

Elizabeth's stomach dropped to the ground. "I daresay once you are mistress of your own home, you will not need your sister to remain at your elbow."

"Charles has been a guest of many of his friends and is eager to return the favour now that he has a home and will have a wife. Mr Darcy, for example; I know Charles is eager for him to be among the first to stay, and other friends will also visit for weeks at a time. I want you there with me, Lizzy, someone I love and trust."

She knew someday she would be thrown together with Darcy, but it was too soon for Elizabeth's courage.

"I shall go to Brighton with you, and as for the rest, let us come to a decision another time." Elizabeth was vexed for feeling the need to keep her distance, but until she was certain she could meet

Darcy with indifference, she thought it best they not reside in the same house.

They entered the breakfast room as Bingley was arriving, and all were in time to hear her mother speaking to her aunt Philips.

"I can hardly believe it myself!" said Mrs Bennet. "Four thousand a year! Jane will be the envy of every old friend in Hertfordshire, with a carriage at her command, a new name on her visiting cards, and a brilliant exhibition of hoop rings on her fingers!"

Bingley and Jane spent some time in quiet conversation, ignoring vulgarity such as this, but Bingley soon stood before her, saying, "Lizzy, walk with me to the drawing room? I wish to speak to you about a gift for Jane."

Mrs Bennet and Mrs Philips shrieked with delight while calculating how many jewels the new Mrs Bingley would likely receive. Elizabeth was ashamed to have Bingley's value as a son be credited as relating only to his yearly income.

"I hope the feelings that Jane inspires in your heart have not been shaken by my mother and aunt's remarks," Elizabeth stated when they were alone. "Now, you must know that Jane's favourite colour is green, and although she will protest it until the end of days, I know she would love a jewelled diadem."

"Any suggestions you have for a gift will be welcome, but I misled you. I do not seek your advice, but would rather speak to you about something close to Jane's heart. You must know how much Jane wants to have you live with us after we are married."

"Charles, I thank you for your kind offer, and I would like to join you in Brighton, but I am afraid joining your household on a permanent basis would not make me happy."

"I suspected you had some particular reservation against remaining with us. I am aware that after what has passed between you both, it would ill suit the feelings of either to remain long in the same house."

Elizabeth gasped. *I was so circumspect!* She could not imagine Darcy speaking about their private matters.

"Do not be distressed, I beg you! I do not at all hold your reservations against you. You need not fear to speak plainly with me."

"I, I hardly know what to say."

"More than anything does Jane wish to have you with us, and I want her to be happy, and I have no reason to think that the three of us would not get on"—Bingley raised his eyes to look the question, and Elizabeth nodded—"so I promise that Caroline will never be a permanent member of my household."

"Miss Bingley?"

"You need not prevaricate to spare my feelings; I am not blind! I know Caroline was not as welcoming to you as I would have liked. Do not ask me to account for her coldness towards you; I do not comprehend it, nor can I excuse it. I cannot promise she will never visit, but what I can reassure you of is that she will not reside with us."

Elizabeth now saw with perfect clarity what Bingley thought what was the cause of her reluctance: not frequent encounters with Darcy, but the fear of living under the same roof as Miss Bingley.

"You must know how much Jane and I wish for you to reside with us, and I will do all I can to ensure you are happy in our home. We cannot avoid my sister indefinitely, but you, Lizzy, are the sister I most wish to have in my home and to keep company with my wife."

He offered her an earnest smile. How could she refuse such generosity and sincere consideration? Elizabeth found herself obliged to consent to an arrangement she otherwise would have tried to avoid.

Chapter 23

Monday, December 23

Elizabeth walked to Lucas Lodge to spend the day with Charlotte; however, she found the Lucas household awash in wedding arrangements, as the day of Charlotte's wedding was now set for the ninth of January. She quickly made her excuses for a walk in the cold morning air.

While on her way home, it began to drizzle. It was not enough to inconvenience her, and she had not gone much further when she, upon hearing herself called, turned around. Several officers had entered the lane from Meryton.

"I hope you do not venture far this morning. I fear you will become wet."

"I am indulging myself in air and exercise, Mr Denny. It does me good."

"Not a walk in the rain, I should imagine," said another officer.

"No, but it did not rain when I set out. I did not aim to become wet."

"Forgive me, but I disagree," said Mr Wickham. "I have

witnessed that Miss Bennet deliberately sets out on rainy days, and never with an umbrella."

Elizabeth laughed at this picture of herself. "You have seen me in the rain without an umbrella, but it does not follow that my unpreparedness means I desire to have wet stockings and a ruined bonnet."

"Then allow me to be of assistance," replied Mr Wickham, and he darted away with so much gallantry to borrow an umbrella for her from a farmer whose cottage was beyond the lane that Elizabeth could not refuse when the officers offered to accompany her home.

She walked with Mr Pratt and Mr Denny, but as they neared the village, Mr Denny fell behind and traded places with Mr Wickham, and together they soon outstripped Mr Pratt.

Mr Wickham seemed inclined to reminisce about his earlier years at Pemberley, and Elizabeth was inclined to hear of Darcy so long as she did not have to encounter him.

"Lady Anne had been married ten years and had never expected before. There are those at Pemberley who still talk about the great joy it occasioned. Is it any surprise that Mr Darcy, the long-awaited heir, who was thought highly of before he was even born, would grow up to become a man who thinks too highly of himself?"

"I did not think you would accuse Mr Darcy of improper pride. You had seemed to wish reconciliation."

"Too true," Mr Wickham quickly rejoined. "He would not wear away life in a round of frivolities, without moral aim or intellectual dignity. But he left this neighbourhood on such an impulse, did he not? What a trifling man."

Elizabeth was injured and angry on Darcy's behalf. No other gentleman of her acquaintance took his responsibilities or loyalties more seriously—certainly not Mr Wickham. "Few would call Mr Darcy a trifling young man." She might have spoken further about Darcy's merits had she not remembered that she *had* been trifled with. Thoughts of their familiar encounters and his hasty exit and his likely marriage to Anne de Bourgh were not far from her mind.

"Of course not; just a rich man used to having his own way." Elizabeth made no answer. "You are quick to defend your absent friend. May I be so bold as to suggest you held Mr Darcy in some admiration?"

"I respect Mr Darcy, but that is a different thing from admiration."

"I know you danced at Mr Bingley's ball, but Denny and Pratt tell me you alone were singled out for that privilege."

"Yes, you must imagine everything profligate in the way of dancing and sitting down together." She could not keep the sarcasm from her voice.

"You need not speak of your disappointment; you had hoped to make a great conquest. It would have been an excellent arrangement. He is rich, and you are handsome."

"Mr Wickham! I abhor such indelicate phrases and all they imply. You presume too much."

"I mean no disrespect; I only wish to advise you to beware how you give your heart. Some gentlemen are not worthy of your regard," he added with a pointed look.

An extreme weariness of Mr Wickham's company crept over Elizabeth before they were in sight of the house. Thankfully, the officers did not stay, and less than an hour thereafter, the Bennets welcomed their relations from Gracechurch Street. Mr Gardiner was a sensible, gentlemanlike man, greatly superior to his sisters by nature as well as education. Mrs Gardiner was an amiable, intelligent, elegant woman, and a favourite with her Longbourn nieces.

Bingley called after the Gardiners arrived, and the entire party was forced to listen to Mrs Bennet recount how fortunate Jane was to have caught such a wealthy young man. Bingley bore it all with admirable patience, while everyone else felt mortified until Mr Bennet had been sufficiently amused by their discomposure. He then invited his brother and future son to join him in the library and leave the ladies to their 'folly and gossip.'

After Mrs Gardiner spent an appropriate amount of time lauding Bingley, Mrs Bennet turned her attention to Elizabeth.

"It is hard to think Lizzy might have been Mr Collins's wife had not it been for her own perverseness. The man was in love with her, and she turned him down! Now I shall have to make way for Charlotte Lucas because Lizzy is strange and selfish."

It was the innate respect due to one's mother that prevented Elizabeth from protesting Mr Collins's being in love with her, and the impossibility of her having ever accepted him. *He was not in love with me if he made two proposals of marriage within three days. I could never debase myself and marry such a man.*

"Let us not dwell on that, and instead think about what a blessing it will be to have Jane settled near to you," said Mrs Gardiner. "Now, did I not tell you that long slashed sleeves are still the thing in full dress? Jane will be very fashionable, I promise."

Elizabeth was grateful to her aunt but still decided to go to her own room, and it was there later where Mrs Gardiner found her.

"Beware, my spirits are in no cheerful humour. I will give my opinions, and you may not like to hear them," Elizabeth said as her aunt sat next to her on the bed.

"Lizzy, you know your mother is …" Mrs Gardiner hesitated.

"Tactless? Silly? Unkind?"

"Lizzy!"

"Indulgent towards her younger daughters while refusing to recognise the integrity and talents of her two eldest? No, she recognises Jane's beauty and good nature, so she is just incapable of comprehending *me*. It is insulting that she wished to condemn me to a life with such a man as Mr Collins."

"She worries for your future, as any mother in her situation would."

"Then she ought to practice greater economy and behave with a little more decorum and not deter eligible suitors. And my father ought to have set aside some of his income for the maintenance of his daughters."

Elizabeth lay on the bed, staring at the ceiling. Mrs Gardiner took her hand and gave it a comforting squeeze.

"You must maintain respect for your parents in general, even if they often do not deserve it. I know how hard it can be to be among those who do not understand you, who do not share your intelligence and values."

"I am tired of being a dependent!" Her words burst from an over-charged heart. "I am trapped here with parents who scarcely understand my character. What life is there for me here? If I remain single after the death of my parents, I shall have an annual income of fifty pounds. The best I can hope for is to make my home in one of my happily married sisters' households."

Mrs Gardiner, always a calm and patient counsellor, was not at all taken aback at this outpouring. "You will soon be in Brighton, and Bingley and Jane tell me you are to remain with them upon their return. I think a change of scene, and yet to be still near to Jane, will be helpful to you."

Yes, I shall look forward to living with the joyful couple when they host their friends, first and foremost to be Darcy, who in my nightmares brings his wife, the beautiful and wealthy former Miss de Bourgh. It felt so much better when she was furious with Darcy than when she remembered how heartsick she was at losing him.

Elizabeth said nothing, and her aunt continued. "Perhaps you feel envious. It would be natural. Your best friend and your beloved sister are both to be married. Your relationship with them will change, and you are too intelligent not to acknowledge that. It is no wonder you feel they are moving towards something while you are not."

Charlotte and Jane were indeed moving towards something that Elizabeth could merely imagine. The only thing she was jealous about was that she would never know what it would feel like to have Darcy wrap his arm around her waist and tug her against him. Her aunt was still looking at her, and Elizabeth felt her cheeks grow warm.

"I do not begrudge those in love their happiness." Elizabeth forced herself to smile. "Perhaps my being out of sorts is a sign of repentance at realising all I have given up in refusing Mr Collins!"

"There is my lively Lizzy." Mrs Gardiner smiled and embraced her niece. "As for those in love, I do not believe you will have long to wait to join their numbers. Bingley might have rich single friends to throw in your way!"

Tuesday, December 24

THE PEMBERLEY FAMILY CONVERSED WITH SPIRIT AND FLOW, THE

gentlemen enjoyed their talk of horses and politics, and in the evenings Georgiana performed with only some anxiety while the others played cards. Conversations with Milton were conversations *about* Milton; Fitzwilliam took every opportunity to nettle his brother and speak on how comparatively poor he was; and Lady Catherine, never one to let ignorance stand in her way, gave unsolicited advice on subjects of which she knew nothing. Despite this, the evening parties at Pemberley had thus far been agreeable family affairs.

"I cannot remain longer than the end of January," Colonel Fitzwilliam replied to Georgiana at dinner. "I am obliged to return to my regiment. They do not pay me, you understand, to squire you around London and fend off your beaux."

Georgiana turned scarlet. "If your father's Ireland estate is intended for you, then why must you also serve in the army?"

"He needs employment to distract his mind." This earned Milton a cold stare. "Otherwise my brother would be restlessly miserable."

"My father believed it expedient to give me some employment. As Milton shall participate in public affairs, naturally his younger son shall serve in the army."

"My brother has the right of it," said Lady Catherine. "Although there are moments when we could all wish Fitzwilliam disengaged from every tie of business, you must not, Georgiana, presume to intrude into the affairs of a gentleman."

Darcy heard a stifled sound from Fitzwilliam, and they shared a look. He tried not to laugh at the irony of Lady Catherine advising anyone to refrain from intruding where one is not wanted.

"Yes, your ladyship. I was only hoping for company." Georgiana slumped in her seat.

"If your brother were married, his wife would be your friend, and her company would be all the society you would require." Lady Catherine looked at Anne, but her daughter did not look up from pushing her food around her plate.

Darcy gave his aunt a look that was enough to prohibit Lady Catherine from pursuing a point that none but herself wished to discuss. That did not, however, at all prevent her ladyship from speaking.

"Milton, I have not had a reply to my letter to Mary." Her tone implied this was the viscount's fault. "How does your wife get on?"

Viscount Milton took a large drink from his wine glass. "She was in good health when I left, as you know, since we departed there together."

"We have been at Pemberley four days! I always take care to write to those I left as soon as I am safely arrived. I would have thought since she was so close to her time that she would be at her leisure to write."

Milton took another long swallow. "I could not tell you how my wife spends her leisure time. My father and mother are with her for the Christmas holiday, and until her time comes, that is all I know."

"If the child comes too soon, you return home immediately, won't you?" asked Fitzwilliam.

Milton looked bewildered, but said nothing.

"Of course he would return!" snapped Lady Catherine. "I would advise any father to make his way home as soon as he hears of his child's arrival."

"No, you are mistaken." Milton gestured for the servant to refill his glass. "I have no intention of being discourteous to Darcy or forcing those of you at my disposal to disrupt your plans. All infants are alike, and I have no need to depart Pemberley early to lay my eyes on this one."

Darcy thought this opinion was unfatherly, but Milton's mistress, Lady Hancock, was installed at nearby Harper Hall. Milton would not leave her so soon, even for the sake of promptly seeing his newest child.

"She will hopefully deliver a boy this time," Lady Catherine said. "I hope, on the whole, she has an easy time. When I write to her again, I shall advise her on what she ought to do."

"It is little concern to me how the matter goes, so long as my wife and child survive."

"I am certain that even if she were to have a dreadful time, Mary would bear it like an angel," said Fitzwilliam softly. Darcy was too embarrassed by his cousin's reply to meet his eye. Milton swiftly emptied his wine glass.

Lady Catherine addressed Darcy. "It is Christmastide, and as you are the principal landowner, you ought to entertain more than you do. I have acquaintances in the neighbourhood, and I shall write to them and determine when they are able to join us."

"You are kind, but I will not trouble you to give any invitations." He would not allow Lady Catherine to reign over Pemberley like a queen.

"It is hardly trouble! I am experienced in such matters and will take it upon myself to invite appropriate guests."

"No," he firmly replied, "there is but one woman whom I can allow to invite what guests she pleases, and until Mrs Darcy is in being, I will manage matters myself." It had been nearly two days since he had thought of Elizabeth Bennet, but with the words "Mrs Darcy," he imagined her at Pemberley. He remembered her worthy qualities before he recalled how her strength of character was lacking. *That she would ever agree to be the wife of Mr Collins!*

Darcy's distraction went unnoticed, as his aunt was accustomed to delivering her opinion on every subject in so decisive a manner as proved she was not used to having her judgment controverted.

"Georgiana, your improvement on the harp is sufficient; in some points, it could be said you are at least as proficient as Anne would have been."

Anne's contribution was to raise her unfocused eyes from her plate. Darcy noticed that, even in the darkened room, her pupils were like small pinholes.

"We will withdraw." Lady Catherine rose, not waiting for her niece's reply. "Mrs Jenkinson, I require that you bring Anne's tonic." Her ladyship addressed the others. "Anne's tonic has done wonders for her constitution."

If by tonic, you mean tincture of opium.

Milton bolted from his chair to the sideboard and opened the cupboard underneath as soon as the ladies were gone.

"It is not like you to imbibe so much at dinner," admonished his brother.

"It is better to raise my glass and drink rather than to speak my first thought and risk offending my aunt. I have drunk enough to elevate my spirits, not at all to confuse my intellect."

Darcy felt a pang of guilt for judging Elizabeth by her family when he considered the behaviour of his own.

Milton finished availing himself of the chamber pot and returned to his chair. "She is right on one point, Darcy. You are independent, and you should be married as soon as you could be tempted."

He *had* been tempted, for all the good it did him. "Perhaps were I to fall in love, I would be settled right away."

"There are more important things to consider. An alliance with Anne would be a tremendous match for our families. I do not understand why you have not come to an agreement."

"Is that because one great fortune must seek another?" Fitzwilliam asked his brother coldly.

"Precisely." Milton then turned to Darcy. "Respectable incomes and fortunes, as well as rank and connexions, are what are necessary for a successful match. Anne has splendid property and twenty thousand pounds."

"I am no more interested in speaking with you on this matter than with Lady Catherine," Darcy said with practiced patience.

Milton brought out an overly decorated snuff box. "I chose what was in the best interest of my family and my position and married my cousin."

"The lady, in cases such as these, I suppose, had no choice in the affair?" asked the colonel.

"Choice!" replied Milton in a tone of perplexity. "How do you mean?" He looked back to Darcy. "I grant you Anne is lacking in what typically attracts a man, but what else are you hoping for? You would have the approbation of your family and the acquisition of extensive property for your second son as well as thousands of pounds."

"I hope for a woman who is accomplished, sensible, a woman to be a real companion to me. A clever woman with strength of character, who could be a trustworthy mistress of Pemberley, a woman who would make me happy and to whom I could devote myself to making happy." The colonel raised his eyes in question, but Darcy gave a subtle shake of his head.

"Clever? Clever women are alarming!" Milton shuddered. He flipped open his snuff box with a sweep of his hand, a performance to show off his signet ring and the box.

"How many hours have you been practising that move?" Fitzwilliam scoffed. His brother merely looked his nose down on him with a happy air of real conceit and affected indifference. Darcy thought it best to separate them.

"I know my sister has her heart set on playing Snapdragon. She has likely extinguished the candles and is awaiting our arrival to set the brandy on fire."

Milton groaned. "Are we not too grown up for Christmas gambols?"

"Do not be a killjoy!" cried Fitzwilliam. "You are reluctant because you know I will beat you!"

"Indeed not! I simply wish to retain my dignity."

"If Lady Catherine will play snapdragon and bullet pudding, then so can you!"

Darcy, frustrated with thoughts of Elizabeth and irritated with their bickering, lost his patience. "Would you stop antagonising Milton? And you," he turned to Milton, "when your host suggests an activity, a gentleman agrees. Now, are you ready to cheerfully join the ladies?"

"Yes," mumbled the brothers.

Chapter 24

Wednesday, December 25

The Bennet family was full of good cheer at Christmas, and the conversation during dinner turned upon family topics, to which Bingley was a stranger. Much of the dinnertime passed in a flow of innocent hilarity as Jane's future husband was introduced to all the jokes, stories, and eccentricities of his new family. Their cheerfulness was sincere, and Elizabeth felt happy.

She had lately only *pretended* to be happy; this moment struck her because she had forgotten what it was like to *feel* happy.

The family from Lucas Lodge and some officers were to join them in the evening. Jane was speaking with Elizabeth in the drawing room, but was called away to her mother. Elizabeth then stood by the window looking for Charlotte Lucas, when Bingley tugged her arm and pulled her to the centre of the room.

"Charles! What are you doing?"

"Come here, if you would—no, *here*." Bingley pulled her into place and gave her a chaste kiss. "Happy Christmas, Lizzy!"

Elizabeth followed Bingley's gaze and looked up to see a

kissing bough above her head. Bingley pulled off one of the white berries. "You know no unmarried girl can refuse a kiss if she is underneath the mistletoe."

She shook her head with mock severity. "You do not fool me. How long will it take for Jane to return to speak with me? You are using me to lure my sister under the mistletoe!"

"You have found me out. Please make sure your sister stands *there*."

"You are fortunate that you are marrying into a family eager to oblige you."

"Indeed!" He added, "My sisters are currently the guests of Hurst's brother. I have only ever been the guest of another man's family. I have not had the pleasure of being with my own family at Christmas for a long time."

Elizabeth blinked back tears and offered her hand. "We are very, *very* pleased to have you, Charles."

He cleared his throat and blinked a few times. "My sisters will be in London in January, and they shall attend my wedding."

"What a considerate gesture of sibling affection."

"I know they had their reservations, but they wish me happy." Elizabeth thought there were other things Miss Bingley and Mrs Hurst wished for above his happiness, but she held her tongue. "I shall see them only briefly, for they intend to leave after the ceremony."

"I am sure you will be pleased to have friends there to wish you well."

"I have not had a reply from Darcy, but I presume he will stand up as my groomsman. I shall not be all alone among Jane's friends and neighbours."

Elizabeth offered Bingley no other answer than an assenting smile. Jane then returned to resume their conversation.

"I am sorry, Lizzy, you know how—" Jane was interrupted as Bingley pressed his open lips against hers. Jane's eyes closed while she brought her hands to Bingley's shoulders. There was a dreamy intimacy to their kiss, and Elizabeth suspected it was not the first time they kissed in such a way.

They finally parted, and Bingley plucked another berry from the bough, while Jane turned pink even though no one else noticed their embrace.

"I was telling Lizzy how those who love me best will attend our wedding. My sisters will come, and I expect Darcy will be my groomsman."

"Is it not wonderful that Caroline and Louisa will come?" Elizabeth only smiled at this. "And of course to have Mr Darcy there would mean so much to Charles." Elizabeth let her smile fall, and Jane frowned. "I remember you saying, after we left Netherfield, that you had a favourable opinion of Mr Darcy?"

Elizabeth prevaricated, until Jane said, "Lizzy, now that I consider it, you and Mr Darcy have a great deal in common and could be good friends."

"Indeed not!" To lessen the sting of her vehemence, for Bingley's sake, she added, "I suppose we have points in common. Both of our Christian names contain the letter z."

The Lucases arrived, as did the officers, and little groups formed and everybody grew comfortable. The younger children were engaged in their own high revel, while Mary purchased praise by playing lively airs at the request of her younger sisters who, with some of the Lucases and the officers, joined in dancing. Some of the older generation played a round game, and all were boisterous, noisy, and happy.

Likely due to a general indulgence in wine and punch, the Scottish and Irish reels evolved into a game among the dancers. Whenever a lady passed under the mistletoe, the gentleman nearest to her leaned towards her to steal a kiss before the lively steps separated them. Most of these playful liberties resulted in lightly grazed cheeks or the gentleman tripping off balance when the dance forced the young lady to leap out of his reach.

After two hours of dancing and tilting her face out of the way of her Christmas admirers, Elizabeth observed Mary at the instrument. *We always assume that Mary would rather play than dance.* Elizabeth left to offer her services.

"I am not tired," Mary answered, but not without a glance towards the dancers.

"I am certain you are not, but I am, and if I dance another reel, I will end up walking rather than dancing. You would be doing me a service if you take my place and allow me to sit."

Only then did Mary agree to exchange places. Elizabeth had the pleasure of watching her often-neglected sister dance with a continual course of smiles.

As she was beginning her second spirited air, Mr Wickham joined her at the instrument. She refrained from rolling her eyes at being singled out again. Had she not been performing, she would have crossed the room to stand with a group so she would not have to suffer another tête-à-tête.

"Do you not dance, Mr Wickham?"

"Most readily if you will dance with me."

"Me! Oh, no! I am finished for the evening."

Mr Wickham drew up a chair and placed it by hers. "Then I will sit by you while you entertain us." He fell into his chair with an awkward thud.

Mr Wickham seemed to have trouble maintaining his balance in his chair while he swayed to the melody of her song. Elizabeth saw his flushed skin and attempted to stifle her laugh at his intoxicated state, but he asked her what she found amusing.

"Only the joyous, jolly party."

"Yes, one must be holly—I mean, jolly at Christmas."

"You ought not to be allowed more wine if you are going to misspeak."

"Be that as it may, Christmas is a jolly time. I enjoy the greenery and gaieties of the season." His aqueous eyes looked towards the dancers. Lydia and Kitty pouted their lips and eyed the gentlemen provocatively, her mother was clapping and watching the dancers, and her father had his back turned to the entire proceedings.

Elizabeth attempted to make light of their imprudence. "I hope, since it is Christmas, the ladies are not shocked by the advances of your fellow officers."

Mr Wickham rested his arm across the instrument to keep his balance. He now blocked her view of the most of the room. His gaze was intently focused, and Elizabeth supposed he was attempting to concentrate through the haze of inebriety. "Why would the ladies be shocked at a little inoffensive kissing under the mistletoe? They ought not to be fastidious about a privilege by which they are the greatest gainers."

"You hold a high opinion on the gentlemen's talents."

Mr Wickham laughed too loudly and breathed whisky. "You misunderstand me. If a lady does not receive a mistletoe kiss before the greenery is taken down, she will not marry in the year eleven."

"Next year is eighteen hundred and *twelve*." She must have her mother bring in the coffee a little sooner.

"Yes, twelve. What did I say?" He teetered in his seat. "It would be ungentlemanly of me not to do all I can to ensure these ladies have the good luck required to marry."

"You are shocking, Mr Wickham, but since it is Christmas and high merrymaking is expected, I will forgive you."

"You"—this word was enunciated loudly—"you are lovely." Elizabeth completed her song. "Although there is no greenery above us, I still hope that you manage to marry next year." Before Elizabeth could think on this, Mr Wickham bent towards her, wrapped his arm around her neck, trapping her head in the crook of his elbow, and pressed his mouth against hers. It was dreadful. He kissed her crudely, forcibly thrusting his tongue into her mouth. As soon as this shocking invasion began, it was over, but not before alarm and anger rippled down her spine. Mr Wickham pulled away, his florid face smug with satisfaction, and Elizabeth spluttered in silent indignation.

"Lizzy! Mr Wickham!" Lydia ran up to the instrument. "We are to play buffy gruffy! You must come!" Mr Wickham managed to stand upright and, with a ready smile, allowed himself to be led away. Elizabeth was frozen in place.

Did no one see? Elizabeth looked at all the people who had the right to chaperone her: her father and uncle were engaged in conversation with Colonel Forster and Sir William Lucas; Mrs Bennet was directing the officers to arrange the chairs in a circle for the next game; Mrs Gardiner was out of the room; and Charles, though not yet her brother, was engrossed by Jane.

The room was crowded, loud, and full of adults and children rapidly and constantly moving about. It seemed no one had noticed

Mr Wickham's terrible overture. Elizabeth crossed the room towards the trays bending under the weight of food to pour a glass of wine. She had an appalling taste in her mouth.

A little kissing under the bough or games with kisses as forfeits were nothing to shy away from. But Mr Wickham's drunken, unwelcome advance, without even the pretext of mistletoe or game, was beyond the pale. Elizabeth drank a long mouthful. It helped, but did nothing to remove the memory of having Mr Wickham's tongue alongside hers inside her mouth.

The noise and the press of all the others soon became too much for Elizabeth. She left the room, chancing upon her aunt in the corridor.

"Are you well, Lizzy?" Mrs Gardiner's face was creased with worry. "What is it?"

"Nothing, I assure you."

"Lizzy, I know your looks too well. Is it a headache?"

Elizabeth did not deny it. Her aunt allowed her to pass with the promise of checking on her before she retired for the evening.

She felt encroached upon by Mr Wickham, and she also felt embarrassed for him. It was horrible, inconsiderate, and vulgar, and not at all in keeping with the spirit of Christmas revels. Surely he would be ashamed of himself as soon as his wits were returned to him. She was certain he held no genuine attachment for her.

I gain nothing by speaking of it and becoming the subject of curious gossip. She would do well to keep the incident to herself and draw back from her acquaintance with Mr Wickham.

Darcy had said Mr Wickham was destitute of principle and prone to every vice that could be common to youth. Mr Wickham professed that he had long seen the error of his ways, and Elizabeth had taken him at his word. But his actions this evening demonstrated he was not as reformed as he had claimed to be.

Friday, December 27

"THREE FRAMES WERE DESTROYED. THOSE RESPONSIBLE MUST BE punished."

"And what of the textile workers who find themselves out of work when they are replaced by these machines?"

Darcy did not often keep his opinions to himself, but since Milton and Fitzwilliam's petty arguments were never truly about the subject at hand, he judged it best to remain silent.

"They destroyed the property of an honourable gentleman. An act ought to be passed making machine-breaking a capital offense."

"An act of parliament will not crush those who resist mechanicalizing. You are a fool to think otherwise! The livelihood of those workers is being threatened."

"Labourers who destroy a gentleman's property hold back progress. Have you taken leave of your senses? They are vandals and must be stopped!"

"They are resisting oppression! How do you not see that?"

"Upon my word!" barked Lady Catherine. "I insist you end such a quarrelsome conversation. Anne's nerves cannot tolerate such a disturbance."

Darcy was, for once, grateful for his aunt's interruption, even though Anne gave no indication of having heard the conversation, let alone be insulted by it. She had likely recently had another dose of her 'tonic.' Thankfully, Milton and Fitzwilliam did not wish to argue with Lady Catherine more than they wished to argue amongst themselves, and the subject was dropped.

Darcy's housekeeper entered the breakfast room, and he subtly tilted his head towards his sister. *It might improve her assurance to have more experience managing a large household with guests.* Mrs Reynolds bowed in acknowledgement and went to Georgiana. They spoke in hushed tones.

Lady Catherine, as usual, noticed. "If you wish me to talk to Mrs Reynolds or to inspect—"

"I have not the least wish for it, your ladyship." It was much easier to suffer Lady Catherine at Pemberley than at Rosings. Here, Darcy was master of his own home and could keep Lady Catherine and her unwanted advice at a distance.

Darcy looked through his letters and stopped at one whose handwriting was unfamiliar to him; it was spidery and frail.

Mrs Finch and her guest Lady Hancock request the pleasure of Mr Darcy's company, and all the gentlemen of his party, to remain at her lodge at Harper Hall to shoot on Tuesday 31st inst. through Monday 6th proximo.

I remain, &etc,
Louise Finch

Darcy sighed at his cousin's machination. Milton had arranged for Lady Alexandra Hancock, his latest mistress, to be the widow Mrs Finch's guest because she lived near to Pemberley. The invitation was a measure for Milton to spend more time with his mistress.

"Milton, Mrs Finch asks us to remain at her lodge to shoot pheasant. I was only a bowing acquaintance of the late Mr Finch."

"Perhaps there has been no one to shoot her birds since Mr Finch died. I hope you accept the invitation so we might be of service to his widow."

Milton could be a man of easy civility with those of his own rank, but Darcy was still amazed that he did not appear embarrassed for his subterfuge.

"Fitzwilliam?" Georgiana asked from the other end of the table. Mrs Reynolds had departed, but Darcy motioned for his sister to wait.

"Milton, I hardly know the Finch family," Darcy said. "I doubt we ought to accept."

Milton set aside his cup and stared at Darcy. "The widow has ladies staying with her over Christmas; one of them is Lady Hancock."

'Ladies' is too generous a term.

"Fitzwilliam?" his sister whispered. Once again, Darcy motioned for her to wait.

"Why do you hesitate to visit my friends?"

"Are those friends all of impeccable character?" Consorting with courtesans was a disreputable pursuit, and beneath him.

"Darcy!" Milton bristled.

"Fitzwilliam," Georgiana called a little louder.

"One moment," Darcy answered, his eyes still on Milton.

"Darcy, I wish to go shooting." "Shooting" was a convenient euphemism. "Many of your neighbours may also be in attendance. It would not speak well of you to be the only local landowner absent."

"Fitzwilliam?"

"They are not the company I typically keep."

"Are you suggesting my friends are not suitable?"

"Fitzwilliam?"

"What is that you are saying? What is it you are talking of?" Lady Catherine called from the other end of the table.

"The gentlemen have been invited to spend several days shooting at a neighbouring estate, your ladyship," the colonel answered.

"I am willing to manage affairs in your absence, Darcy. Georgiana will have the greatest advantage of being able to observe the proper way to manage a household through the example of Anne and myself." Anne closed her eyes, until Mrs Jenkinson prodded her.

"Fitzwilliam!" Georgiana exclaimed.

"Yes!" all three gentlemen cried together. Even Milton, who had for years been known by his courtesy title, replied sharply.

The sudden attention was too great for his sister to tolerate with equanimity. Her eyes widened in alarm, and her mouth hung open. The longer the gentlemen looked expectantly at her, the more she trembled, until she gave a whimper and ran from the room. Mrs Annesley rose and slowly followed.

"What is the trouble with that girl?" Lady Catherine called the others out of their silent perplexity.

"A gentleman has not the ability to comprehend the minds and hearts of young ladies," Colonel Fitzwilliam answered. "Perhaps she was distracted by what the housekeeper told her and could not wait to set it right."

"I cannot agree with you. Georgiana's behaviour has been peculiar."

"How do you mean?" Darcy thought his sister had behaved well since they returned to Pemberley.

"She acts as though the rooms are too large for her to move in with ease. It is as though she creeps about in constant terror of something or other. I shall speak with her at once; she is acting in a way that does not do credit to the Darcy name."

Darcy shared a glance with Fitzwilliam. If Lady Catherine told her she was a discredit to her family, Georgiana would never recover from Ramsgate.

"Georgiana is inexperienced in the art of conversation. Her lack of confidence has caused her to behave in a manner that you, as a woman adept in conversation, find odd. I wish I knew how to best advise her."

That was laid on with a trowel, but her ladyship sat up straighter. "That girl must learn to speak up; she is always the last to make her way in conversation. There is no one whose manners are more admired than my own, and I will soon have her conversation on a par with the good breeding expected of Miss Darcy of Pemberley."

"I thank you." Better his aunt focus on the style of his sister's conversation rather than wonder why Georgiana's manner was nervous and strange.

"The girl also must be taught to listen well. To listen well is almost as great an art as to speak well. She must endeavour to seem interested in the conversation of others."

Colonel Fitzwilliam deftly turned a laugh at this irony into a cough. "Darcy, play billiards with me before I bring Georgiana some music?" He clapped his brother on the shoulder and said, "Do not neglect to inform Mary that you are at Harper Hall. You would not wish for your wife's letters to go astray while you are *shooting.*"

Darcy joined his cousin in the billiard room. He struck his cue ball and hit each of the other two balls in succession as Fitzwilliam said, "Georgiana will not enjoy remaining under Lady Catherine's tutelage while we are at Harper."

"I can remain while you and Milton go shooting. It is no punishment for me to avoid a party full of courtesans."

"Georgiana cannot always have one of us near. Besides, how will you explain your remaining behind? It will raise more questions than we are willing to answer. It might be good for her confidence to say that she kept her equanimity with Lady Catherine. Mrs Annesley will not allow her to be oppressed."

"I suppose five days with our aunt will not do her lasting harm." Darcy paused to take his shot. "I would rather my aunt focus on conversation style than discover why Georgiana is now the way she is."

"I think Lady Catherine is not altogether wrong. Georgiana seems afraid to appear before Milton, and our aunt's voice makes her start."

"Lady Catherine has a similar effect on me; I only hide it better."

Fitzwilliam laughed, and then moved to the table to take his turn. "Ramsgate was nearly five months ago, and she still cannot bear to speak to those outside her small circle."

"There is perhaps more to the story than she confessed."

"She would have told us if there was. I was amazed by your account of seeing Wickham in Hertfordshire. You must have wanted to strike him."

Darcy tensed, and sent his own cue ball into the pocket. "We managed to meet with cold politeness, but it was not an event I wish to repeat. Wickham caused me enough damage without having to encounter him again."

"What damage did that dissolute man cause in one meeting?"

Darcy did not answer. He stepped from the table to allow Fitzwilliam to play, but his cousin leaned against the wall and looked at him.

"It had nothing to do with Georgiana. Let the matter rest."

"Oh, no! What damage did he cause you? Did he spin a tale of your wretched neglect? It would not be the first time he was violent in his abuse of you to anyone who would listen."

Darcy gave an angry laugh. "No, from what I suspect, he spoke well of me."

Fitzwilliam took his shot, then raised his eyes, prompting Darcy to continue.

"I was attending a lady into the market town when we encountered him. My reaction to seeing that scoundrel was out of character, and she could not help but observe it. I felt the need to explain myself. This young lady was... a friend, so I made her aware of the faults of Wickham's character."

Fitzwilliam stepped forward with wide eyes. "You did not tell this woman about Ramsgate?"

"Of course not!"

"Then I fail to see what injury Wickham caused to you."

"He employed his usual happy manners and later befriended this lady. He did not deny his misconduct, but claimed that he had for many years regretted the folly of his youth. She believed he was no longer a self-interested wastrel."

"It is of course a lie, but I do not understand the problem."

"He told Miss Bennet that he wished to earn my forgiveness and, I presume, begged her to intercede with me on his behalf. She was determined to believe in his goodness."

Fitzwilliam nodded. "But you did not tell the lady that his claim was false since not three months before, he attempted to revenge himself upon you by eloping with your sister."

Darcy pressed his billiard cue into the floor and leant his weight against it, not looking at his cousin. "I was angry at her for supporting him. She wanted to believe her judgment was sound and he was repentant. I, of course, could not tolerate to hear her speak highly of him and refused to yield. She accused me of being resentful, I accused her of lacking in discernment, and we have not spoken since."

"'Tis opportune that you confess your history with Wickham to one specific woman, and he thereafter set out to befriend her in order for her to become his advocate."

"We were alone together that day; she was on my arm. And she called me Darcy in his hearing." He paused before continuing. "Miss Bennet may have spoken of me to Wickham with some slight... admiration."

"You were *particular* with this woman? I have never known you to allow a woman outside of your family to call you by your surname alone. And when do you go anywhere in public in the company of only one unmarried lady?"

"I have already realised Wickham wished to injure me by turning us against one another. May we leave off this subject?"

"No, I am fascinated. I think I may barricade the door and find myself a chair! Your comment after dinner Tuesday night is seen in a new light."

"What do you mean?"

"You said one of the reasons—and I grant you, there are many—that you did not wish to marry Anne was that you preferred a pretty, clever, sensible, accomplished woman."

"Any gentleman might wish for the same. I am not fastidious."

The colonel gave a snort of derision. "Of course. A little beauty, a few smiles, and you would have any woman between fifteen and thirty who complimented Pemberley."

Darcy rolled his eyes. "I thought we were speaking of Wickham?"

"We were speaking of Georgiana, which led us to Wickham, and I am now to find that man has led us to a pretty and accomplished woman to 'whom you could devote yourself to making happy.'" Fitzwilliam's eyes were alight in amusement.

Darcy held his composure. "The lady and I are no longer on intimate terms, and you ought not to speak of her in that way."

"He is a deceitful, manipulative scoundrel; the greater blame must fall to him. Do you hold this Miss Bennet's misguided acquaintance with Mr Wickham against her?"

"No!" He had trouble keeping his voice even, and the emotions he had held under regulation threatened to break through. "My own father held the highest opinion of Mr Wickham. I had a tolerably powerful feeling towards Miss Bennet, and once my temper was under control, I pardoned her kindness to him."

"You and this Miss Bennet took a liking to one another?"

"Yes."

"You formed a particular attachment to one another?"

"Yes."

"Fell in love?"

"Yes!" Darcy yelled and tossed his cue on the table, raking his hand through his hair.

"Then what irreparable damage has been done?"

"I left!" he shouted. "She had every reason to expect my proposal, *and I left*." Fitzwilliam stared in amazed silence. "I was not master of myself after our quarrel and decided to go up to town with Bingley. She and I both have unyielding dispositions, but after I was calm, I resolved to return and explain everything. I was prepared to tell her about Ramsgate. I was going to beg her to forgive me for not laying everything before her at the time, then ask her to be my wife.

"But I left." His throat burned, and he had to blink his eyes. *My sorrow is all of my own doing*. All of his anger towards her for accepting Mr Collins was gone, turned now towards himself. "I let my temper rule my judgment, and it cost me my future happiness. From her perspective, I left in a fit of pique without a word, and she, believing me inconstant, yielded to her family's persuasion and is to wed her cousin after the new year."

"Good God! Is it certain?"

"I have heard it in person from Bingley's sister and by letter from Bingley himself. Bingley is marrying Miss Bennet's elder sister."

"I am sorry. I have nothing to say to bring you comfort. It is no creed of mine, as you must be aware, that such disappointments kill anybody."

Darcy was no longer certain whose turn it was, but nodded and approached the table. He could not admit aloud that he felt his sufferings to be severe.

"Perhaps your time at Harper Hall will not be ill-spent."

"How do you mean?"

"Whoever of Milton's mistress's intimates who are unattached are always in her company—and some who are attached, come to think of it. There will be ladies at Harper who are eager to be under the protection of a gentleman worth over ten thousand a year."

"You cannot compare the respectable woman whom I expected to make Mrs Darcy against some courtesan."

"The two are not mutually exclusive."

"Every courtesan is the same, and although I have been enticed, I have never met one on whom I could abide to waste both my time and my money."

"You have never found *one* to capture your attention?"

"They claim to be accomplished, but they are indolent; they

claim to be witty, but are ignorant of anything beyond society gossip; they profess their affection, but their object all the while is to captivate some other man of better fortune."

"You are missing the most important reason for having a mistress at your disposal."

Darcy could not help but laugh. "You think I am immune to sexual attraction?"

"I think you are fastidious and lonesome."

He felt the hit directly in his heart. "If that be true, then Lady Hancock's friends will not bring me any lasting comfort."

"I am not talking about *lasting* comfort. But a temporary comfort would help you forget the lady from Hertfordshire."

"If I want a distraction, I shall go shooting. Or riding. Or read a book."

Fitzwilliam returned his attention to the billiard table. "I will only add that I think you should go to Harper with an open mind. Enjoying the amorous attentions of another woman will remind you that second attachments are expected."

Darcy then took a clean shot, hitting his cousin's ball into the pocket. "Then why do not you maintain one?"

"Too expensive. I cannot afford the annuity a mistress would claim on top of the other gifts. That is Milton's privilege so long as Mary, innocent heart that she is, never learns the truth. No, instead I see an excellent lady in King's Place off Pall Mall."

Darcy raised his eyebrow. "Is it always the same lady whenever you go?"

"Of course not. But whoever she is, she is always excellent." Fitzwilliam flashed a roguish smile.

Darcy doubted that indulging in a woman like that would rid him of the memory of Elizabeth with her hands on his chest, her eyes closed as she waited for him to kiss her.

A servant entered saying that Milton wished to speak with his brother. The colonel laid his cue aside and walked to the door, but he stopped and exclaimed that he had forgotten to give Georgiana the sheet music, and Darcy volunteered for the task.

"I should speak with her now and warn her about Lady Catherine's upcoming conversation lessons. Is the music in your dressing room?"

He said the music was in the cabinet, and Darcy went to his cousin's apartments. There was an old-fashioned black cabinet, and the key was in the door. He looked through the larger drawers in search of the music. He opened and shut them, until his attention was caught by a miniature.

It was a half-length portrait of the honourable Mary Dundas, before she became Lady Milton. She was never a great beauty, but with her open countenance and fashionably short curls, she was not a woman anyone would call plain. Darcy looked around, fearing he had entered the wrong brother's room.

But no; there was the cravat pin Darcy had given Fitzwilliam at Christmas. And there were not enough looking glasses for this room to belong to Milton.

Pausing to feel a moment's pity for the cousin he loved as a brother and to reflect on his own disappointed hopes, he placed the miniature back in its drawer. Darcy found the sheet music and went to present it to his sister.

Chapter 25

Darcy gave his sister the Pleyel sonata from Colonel Fitzwilliam, and before she could do more than promise to thank him, he sat beside her and said bluntly, "I have come to persuade you not to hide in the music room while I am shooting at Harper Hall next week."

Georgiana turned pink. "I will not avoid my family."

"I fear you will not stir farther from this room than to the head of the great staircase till you are satisfied Lady Catherine has left the house."

"My reserve is not unnatural. At times, you are not so different, you know," his sister said with a smile.

"Georgiana, *you* speak only when you cannot help it."

Her smile faltered. "I am shy."

Darcy attempted not to allow his frustration to show. "Do you remember when I suggested you consider what sort of woman you wish to be? You are of an age where your disposition and character are being formed. You have a quick comprehension as well as good sense. I wish you were not so afraid to give your opinion. Your one misstep at Ramsgate does not undo all that is worthy in your character."

Large tears rolled from her eyes. "I shall never be lively."

"I do not expect you to be lively!" Georgiana flinched, and he tried again. "I wish for you not to isolate yourself and to demonstrate an interest in the world around you." It broke his heart to see his sister perpetually dispirited. "Even I, who am reserved among strangers, would not remain as withdrawn as you. Will you not tell me why you refuse to engage with your own family?"

"I do not know what is wrong with me." She dashed the tears away with the back of her hand. "I am not accustomed to anyone other than you taking interest in me, and the one time that I believed someone cared, I was mistaken."

Darcy drew her into his embrace, and as he stroked his sister's hair, he cursed the existence of George Wickham. Georgiana, inexperienced and ashamed, was so fearful of betraying the truth of her imprudence that she withdrew from everyone.

"Do you not think that if you retreat from those who love you that you will become lonely?"

A long silence stretched out. "I am already lonely. What does it matter if I am shy and silent?"

"Are you without friends? For shame! This house is full of people who love you. You have a kind companion, friends in town, a brother who—"

"I am not ungrateful!" Georgiana cried anew. "On this point, I shall be silent."

Darcy sighed and stood to pace. "No, you must have no reserves from me. Speak your mind." *Asking her now to tell me more about what happened at Ramsgate might destroy her spirits.* "You said you have felt lonesome…"

"I have many lonely hours," she whispered, "but I shall endeavour to behave in a manner that is a credit to the Darcy name."

"I am not your father to whom you ought to defer. I may be your guardian, but I am also your brother who wishes for your happiness."

"I suppose I feel this way because I have been without a mother or a sister. Pemberley ceased to be my home when my father died, but when you removed me from school, I was even *more* alone."

Darcy stared at his sister, unsure of what to say. Georgiana quickly added, "You are very affectionate! And we are a great deal together; as much as you can, I know."

"But a mother or a sister would have been always present?" Georgiana might not have been so willing to align herself with Wickham had she not been lonely.

"Yes, someone to love me completely and unreservedly, who might be more often with me."

How often had he had the same longing thoughts about Elizabeth? She would never love him completely and unreservedly, would never be his dearest companion or the closest friend his sister needed. It was not something to recover from lightly, and worse yet, his own temper was primarily to blame. She had likely been prevailed upon by parental authority to marry Mr Collins, and he could not fault Elizabeth for that when he never made her any promises or declarations. He should have trusted her more.

He had lost her through his own mistakes, and there was nothing he could do. No good could come from his yearning for a woman who was engaged to another man. He would never forget her face if he did not put in the effort. Some action or progress had to be made for him to gain any ground in recovering from his disappointment. Perhaps Fitzwilliam was right that a diversion with the courtesans at Harper Hall might do him good.

"Are you angry, Fitzwilliam?"

"No, only lost in my own lonely thoughts."

"I cannot believe that a gentleman of the world with a wide acquaintance could ever feel solitary or friendless."

To confess all in his heart to a sister who looked up to him as a father went against his nature. "You are not strange for feeling lonesome. It is all the more reason for you to engage with those here who love you." He pushed aside his own disappointments. "Are you ready to entertain Lady Catherine?" He winked, and she smiled. "I have confidence in you."

"What shall I do with her for a week?" Georgiana's voice held a mixture of amusement and trepidation.

"Ask her for her advice."

"What?" She looked incredulous.

"Solicit her opinion before she thrusts it upon you. Furnish her with a topic, and you need only listen. Remember that people take more interest in their own affairs than in anything else. Lady Catherine will find you agreeable and sensible and well informed, which of course you are. Just reply 'yes, your ladyship' and instead follow Mrs Annesley's advice." It could be good for Georgiana's confidence to remain at Pemberley on her own.

Georgiana laughed, lessening the small pang of disappointment he felt in knowing of her constant sadness. He watched the shortlived amusement fade from her eyes. She was never confident like him but she was, in general, a content, good-natured young lady. He hoped he would soon see her happy again.

"I hope you enjoy the music your cousin brought. When we return, you can entertain us with a concert." He walked towards the door before he remembered something and turned back. "At breakfast, after Mrs Reynolds left, was there something you wished to tell me?"

"All the laudanum is gone from the stillroom. Three phials of Kendal Genuine Black Drop are missing. So is the syrup of poppies, and even a Godfrey's Cordial phial is gone, yet no one is ill. Mrs Reynolds wished to know if she ought to question the servants, but I wanted to consult you first."

Darcy knew where the phials had gone. "I need not question the servants; I do not suspect them."

"But who—"

"Say no more about it. It is not worth putting everyone involved into an awkward situation."

Still bewildered, his sister nodded and he left.

Anne, or Mrs Jenkinson on behalf of Anne. His cousin must have already depleted whatever supplies they had brought with them from Kent. He had long suspected Anne felt sick when she did *not* take her 'tonic.' Her perpetually constricted pupils and her dull, lethargic disposition could be explained in no other way. But was her habit worse than the intolerable distress she would suffer were she to stop? Darcy was again humbled to recognise there were problems he could not solve.

Saturday, December 28

"DO YOU NOT THINK JANE WOULD LOOK FINE IN A PURPLE PELISSE lined in yellow, Mr Bennet?"

Mr Bennet made her no answer. Mrs Bennet looked at Bingley and said, "He does not hear me; he never does sometimes. Do you not think Jane requires another pelisse, Bingley?"

Jane's betrothed had been composing a letter, and by this long into his courtship, he had learned to agree if possible or otherwise say that whatever his angel wanted was enough to satisfy him.

"Forgive me, I am writing to Darcy; in his letter, he implied he would not be my groomsman, but that cannot be true. Whatever Jane desires will be pleasing. Will not Lizzy also have new clothes to go to Brighton?"

Elizabeth, hidden from her mother's gaze, glared at Bingley, who gave her a wink and returned to his letter.

"Mr Bennet! You must advance some money for Lizzy! She might have refused to marry Mr Collins, but it shall not be said I sent my daughter away from home without new clothes. Do you think seven yards shall be too much for a new gown, Lizzy? You are almost of a height with Lydia, but not so full and stout. We shall get you a pretty-coloured muslin."

It was not that Elizabeth had anything to say against new clothes. What she did *not* enjoy was suffering her mother's attention while she suggested styles Elizabeth did not like and insisted on ornamentation that Elizabeth would later unpick. Mrs Bennet was proceeding to all the particulars of calico, muslin, and cambric, when Mr Bennet suggested his wife make haste into Meryton and make her purchases at once.

"I am certain you need not bring Lizzy with you," he continued. "You shall manage it all well on your own."

Mrs Gardiner offered to join her, and Elizabeth suspected she did so to offer restraint and promote Elizabeth's preferences. The younger girls were not about to stay at home when they might get some pretty ribbon or silk stockings for themselves at their mother's expense.

"Let it not be said that I do nothing for you, Lizzy," Mr Bennet told her when all the ladies, save she and Jane, were gone. "I just saved you from three hours of listening to your mother prattle about finery. That goes for you as well, Jane."

"You are all politeness, Papa," Elizabeth said drily. "Since you were acting solely for our sakes, perhaps you might like to join them to ensure that they purchase what we need? I can tell them you wish to go along." She began to rise.

"Gardiner!" Mr Bennet called to his wife's brother on the other side of the room. "Let us go for a ride." He threw his newspaper aside and rose. "Bingley, I assume you prefer to join us old men rather than remain alone indoors with these two pretty young ladies."

Bingley passed uneasy glances between his betrothed and Mr Bennet. His preference for one battled against the desire to defer to the other. Elizabeth bit her lip to refrain from laughing. After unleashing her mother's attention on to *her*, she was not about to help him.

"Sir, I would like Bingley to remain, if it pleases you."

"Indeed. To be separated from your young man for an afternoon would be the unhappiness of your life."

The three who remained entered into the comfortable familiarity that Elizabeth hoped portended well for their tour of Brighton.

"Will your promenade clothing will be ready by Wednesday, the fifteenth of January?" Elizabeth teased Jane, who feared not all would be complete before her wedding day.

"They will be, unless my mother insists on my having more."

"Whatever is incomplete can be sent along after us, and the Brighton shops will have all that is fresh and elegant," Bingley said.

"Where shall we be staying, Charles dear?"

"Marine Parade, close to the ocean and perfect for taking the air. You shall need that purple pelisse, my angel. Lizzy will wish to walk every day regardless of the weather."

"I once walked through a little bit of mud to tend to you, and now I have a reputation as an imprudent walker!"

"That was hardly the first time you walked when you ought not to have," Jane said with a smile.

"If this is the thanks I am to receive, I shall no longer offer my services at your sickbed, and you will be obliged to remain ill longer than you ought. My reputation cannot afford another walk in inclement weather."

"Why do you think I insisted on having you join our household? You shall have no farther to walk than down the corridor to be my angel's nursemaid!"

"And here I thought I was invited to intervene when the two of you quarrel."

"No, Lizzy! We are desirous of your company."

Elizabeth knew her sister's gentle heart could not handle much playful teasing. "I expect yours to be a happy match; on both sides, you have good principles and good tempers, and I will not be needed to mediate a quarrel."

The door was thrown open, and several officers entered, including Mr Wickham. Elizabeth had not been in his company since Christmas, and she had not been keen for their next meeting. It would be awkward for him if he remembered his drunken advance, and it would be awkward for her if he did not remember and spoke to her as agreeably as he had once been known to do.

It would do neither of us credit if his indiscretion became common knowledge, but he does deserve to be set down! She was uncomfortable in Mr Wickham's company, but how could she act with a friend of her family's other than with civility?

More than once did Mr Wickham attempt to draw her into conversation, but she politely dissuaded him. Elizabeth saw no indication that anyone other than herself wished the call to end. When a half hour passed, Mr Wickham gave an expressive look towards Mr Denny, and he and his fellow officers rose.

"Perhaps, Miss Bennet, you, Mr Bingley, and your sister may like to take a turn with us before we make our way back?" Mr Wickham asked with his typical cheerful manners.

"I can assure the ladies the weather is fair, despite the brisk wind," added Mr Denny.

Jane glanced at Bingley, who said, "Miss Bennet and I are not hearty enough, but I have never known Miss Elizabeth to turn down a walk. I comprehend my future sister well enough to say that she always enjoys walking out."

How I hate the laws of politeness! How could she insult Bingley's knowledge of her character and insult her guests by refusing to join the officers? At least she would be not be alone with Mr Wickham.

But once they were along the gravel walk, Mr Denny and the two other officers departed for Meryton, and Mr Wickham remained with the avowed purpose of escorting her back to the house. As they left, Elizabeth gave Mr Wickham a frosty glare.

"You have no doubt discerned our little pretence, but I could find no other way of speaking privately with you."

"That is the least of your offences."

"Miss Bennet, please!" He reached for her arm. She drew back, and her grave looks showed how little she desired his company. "You must allow me to apologise."

Elizabeth stopped walking, and he took this as leave to continue. "I throw myself upon your mercy. I have little memory of what nonsense I spoke at Christmas, but the following morning, I well remembered the despicable way I imposed upon you." Mr Wickham shook his head. "I am mortified, and I can say nothing to excuse my behaviour. I may explain it by speaking of the evening's high spirits, too much wine, and the enjoyment of your company, but nothing can justify my kissing you."

"I am at a loss to explain how any amount of merriment and drunkenness could even begin to make you believe that your behaviour was welcome. You have entirely mistaken my amity towards you. Believe me, I am far—very far—from gratified in being the object of such attentions." She shuddered again at the memory of his tongue inside her own mouth.

"You need not fear that those attentions indicate any intentions beyond friendship or that they will ever be repeated."

"I should hope not!"

"I would be grieved if we could not someday meet again as friends."

"Let us speak no more on the matter. I can meet you with politeness for the sake of our mutual friends, although you must understand how uncomfortable I may be in your presence for the near future."

"You are so good! I should never have doubted that you would treat me better than I deserve." He bowed, and insisted on escorting her the rest of the way. "From your sister's conversation, I am to understand that you are all to travel to Brighton?"

It was difficult for her not to converse with him; he had an easy civility that was welcoming. "The plan is to take a house there for some weeks."

"Are you fond of watering places?"

"I have not had the pleasure."

"I love nothing more than to visit a watering place. I have been to Brighton, but more often at Scarborough and Weymouth, and last summer I was at Ramsgate for several weeks. I expect that for you, it will be the company of your dear sister that will afford you the greatest pleasure."

"Yes, indeed." Mr Wickham could be pleasing and gentleman-like, and he gave away not one indication that he was like the man who had insulted her at Christmas. *Which is the true Mr Wickham?*

"And you shall take up residence at Netherfield? May I enquire as to how you shall tolerate it when the Bingleys entertain their friends?" He looked at her pointedly. "I presume the friends of the happy couple will make their wedding visits not long after they return."

Elizabeth looked at him sharply, but Mr Wickham did not look away. *Was there anything to gain from prevaricating?*

"I will meet all of the Bingleys' friends with equanimity," she began cautiously, "although there are some whose company I prefer less than others."

Mr Wickham looked at her expressively. "I know you have a particular gentleman on your mind. Had I not imposed upon you, I would insist that you talk to me. As we stand now, I will only say I am sorry for your disappointment."

Her wretchedness had been acute in being obliged to hide her broken heart and contain her teeming anger at being abandoned by Darcy. Perhaps if she acknowledged it, she could move past her anger and disappointed hopes. Mr Wickham suspected her attachment, and it would not pain her more to speak of what he already knew. To confess the truth aloud—for once—rather than brooding over her sorrows in silence might help her forget Darcy.

"Thank you. Although we both know about my former relationship with our absent friend, I beg you not to speak of—"

"Miss Bennet, you wound me! Has my behaviour led to you to believe I would confess to others your attachment to Mr Darcy? You may be assured of my secrecy. I wished to offer my support since he will eventually return."

"That is a kind sentiment, but I do not think you, or anyone, can help. Time and distance are all that are required."

"Nonsense! I can offer my silent companionship when the fateful visit comes. You do not know when, precisely, Mr Darcy is to visit his friend? Perhaps by then I shall be restored to your good graces and you will receive me at Netherfield. I will sit by your side while Mr Darcy visits the Bingleys, near enough to you to count the stitches of your work. I need not say a word, but at the least you will have a friend in the room who is in sympathy with you."

"I think your presence will bring more displeasure to Mr Darcy than it will bring comfort to me."

"Perhaps Mr Darcy's displeasure itself will bring you comfort?"

"You are too cruel. And no one could contrive that meeting. Who knows when and where that first meeting shall occur?"

He smiled widely. "I am not cruel. As much as I would enjoy seeing the expression on Mr Darcy's face were he to see me sitting near to you, perhaps you can speak about me to him, to remind yourself that you do not suffer alone?"

"I think it is a punishment for him to hear your name. If I dare introduce you into the conversation, I shall refer to you as Mr W."

Elizabeth had begun to speak the letter 'w' when she was struck by the memory of seeing the letters *Mr W* printed on a page. The familiarity of it prodded against her mind with such force that she stopped walking to think about it.

"Are you well?"

She recalled reading about the character of a Mr W, perhaps in a novel?

"Miss Bennet?"

Elizabeth closed her eyes and recalled the writing table in Netherfield's library, a page with sharp, even lines.

I saw little reason to enlighten you of Mr W's character, as never in all my considerations did I believe that he would follow you to R.

She gave a sharp intake of breath and felt lightheaded. Her mouth slackened, and her gaze went blurry.

"Miss Bennet, forgive me to say, but you look dreadfully ill."

She was suffering from such terrible shock she could not find her voice. Despite her fur-lined cloak, she shivered.

"You look cold. Let us return to the house."

"R is for Ramsgate." Her words came out in a harsh whisper. "You said you were at Ramsgate last summer."

Realisations and memories assaulted her mind one after another.

'*You are but fifteen years old and must not allow what happened at R to continue to plague you.*'

'*... last summer I was at Ramsgate for several weeks.*'

Miss Darcy suffers from low spirits.

Darcy was worried both for his sister's happiness and her reputation.

'*His engaging manners hid vicious propensities that could not be known by you.*'

He hoped his sister would soon put an unpleasant episode behind her.

'*I might hope that you, and your intimates, will be informed enough of his true character as to make it impossible for any young woman of character to confide in him. Or to love him.*'

'*I implore you: be cautious of Mr Wickham.*'

"You are unwell." Mr Wickham laid a hand on her arm.

Elizabeth tore her arm away, backing up with quick steps and raising a hand as though to strike him. "Do not touch me!" Her skin felt clammy and cold, despite the sweat that had broken out across her body.

Mr Wickham raised his hands in surrender, anxiety clear across his features. "Shall I escort you back to the house? Or may I bring your sister to you?"

"What have you done?"

"I do not understand you. Please, come with me back to the house. I fear you are not well."

"You have *not* for many years now regretted your trespasses against the Darcys."

"I have not the pleasure of understanding you."

"You have *lied* to me from the beginning!" The shocking insight made her feel a sickening, whirling sensation and she thought she might faint.

Mr Wickham's concerned expression darkened. "Miss Bennet, you have mistake—"

"Did you follow Miss Darcy to Ramsgate?" He said nothing. "Can you deny that you have done it?"

"I did renew my acquaintance with Miss Darcy at Ramsgate, but I do not understand why you are distressed. I fear some grave misunderstanding—"

He moved closer, but Elizabeth cried "Stop!" and took another step away. "What cold-hearted, manipulative being are you? What happened at Ramsgate?"

Mr Wickham's expression lost its supplicating entreaty, and he was now looking on her coldly. "If Mr Darcy did not see fit to speak of it, then I shall not illuminate it for you."

"You do not deny that you wronged Miss Darcy in some way?"

Mr Wickham was silent. A more terrifying realisation washed over her. "Why did you beg me to recommend you to Mr Darcy? Did you suspect he would hate me for it?" This was too scandalous to comprehend. "You and I had just met. Why did you wish to injure me?"

"It was not my purpose to hurt *you!*" Mr Wickham snapped at her.

"You realised Mr Darcy admired me? You suspected our mutual admiration from that first meeting in Meryton?" Another thought struck her. "Why did you kiss me?"

"Because I was very drunk, and I suspect that Mr Darcy has not had the pleasure."

She shut her eyes as a shudder of revulsion passed through her. Elizabeth thought of the eager way she had spoken about Darcy, how Mr Wickham had always been pleased to introduce him into the conversation. "You hold such animosity towards Mr Darcy that you… I have been so trusting… You insinuated yourself into my good opinion to inflict pain on Mr Darcy!"

She turned on her heel and ran to the house. She approached the door out of breath, with tears pricking at her eyes. Her fingers were shaking as she attempted to take hold of the handle. She swallowed a few times as she fumbled with it, and Mr Wickham caught up to her.

"Miss Bennet, you ought not speak before others of things about which you know nothing." His tone was menacing.

"What did you do at Ramsgate? What did you intend when you followed Miss Darcy there?"

Mr Wickham gave her an ugly smirk. "Her temperament was warm and easily worked upon. I succeeded as far as I wished."

Elizabeth felt the bile rising into her throat as she finally wrenched open the door. She left it open as she went into the vestibule and nearly ran against the butler. She called out as she ran up the stairs to her own apartments, "I am no longer at home to Mr Wickham!"

Most bitterly did Elizabeth cry. Her folly and susceptibility were all exposed to Darcy, and he must despise her forever. She had allowed herself to be taken in by Mr Wickham because she had too much pride in her own judgment. Darcy left her, not because he was fickle or because she defended a man whom Darcy could not respect, or even because he did not love her; he left because, despite his warnings, she had championed the scoundrel who may have ruined his sister.

Chapter 26

After fleeing Mr Wickham, Elizabeth lay on her bed, vexed beyond what could be expressed. Never before had she felt so agitated, mortified, and grieved. Time did not compose her. As Elizabeth reflected on Mr Wickham's duplicity, her gullibility, and her culpability in driving away Darcy, she felt it more. She could barely form the words to tell the housemaid who came in to tend the fire that she was ill; later, she had pretended to be asleep when Jane came in to dress for dinner. When Jane returned to tend to her, tears were running down Elizabeth's cheeks.

"How is your head—Lizzy! Are you crying? What is the matter!"

"He tried to give me caution. I wish I had attended to it, but I thought I could judge better for myself."

"Lizzy, what happened?"

"Blind, I have been absolutely blind!" Elizabeth sobbed into her hands. "Mr Wickham is not reformed. It was all a lie. Everything Mr Darcy claimed that was reprehensible in Mr Wickham's character is still true. He is the same immoral, selfish, deceitful man that

Mr Darcy knew. All of his claims of penitence and reformation were false."

"No! How can you be certain?"

"He pursued Georgiana Darcy to Ramsgate last summer. She is a shy, fifteen-year-old girl. Neither he nor Mr Darcy confessed the particulars, but I think he seduced her."

"Lizzy! How can you make such a claim?"

"I had the first hint from that letter of Mr Darcy's I saw at Netherfield. It must be why he was anxious when he realised I read it. What I read was that a man of disreputable character, a Mr W, followed Miss Darcy to R. Today, Mr Wickham admitted to me that he had been at Ramsgate last summer and that he had met Miss Darcy there."

Jane's expression faltered. "Perhaps they engaged in a flirtation that came to nothing? Or Miss Darcy fancied his admiration meant more than it did?"

"I do not know how far his seduction went, but I must suppose her fortune and the chance to revenge himself upon Mr Darcy influenced him. Mr Wickham gloated that he succeeded with her as far as he wished." Elizabeth shuddered at the memory of his self-satisfied smile.

"I...what a terrible—it must be true, but I had no notion..." Jane could hardly speak a word. "I do not know when I have been more shocked!"

"There is more." Elizabeth reached for a handkerchief to dry her eyes. "Mr Wickham's desire for revenge has other manifestations. He wished me to become his advocate so that... He wanted to hurt Mr Darcy by driving us apart!"

"What do you mean?"

Elizabeth twisted her handkerchief. "My acquaintance with Mr Darcy was not insignificant. We formed a friendship, and Mr Wickham, knowing Mr Darcy's manners so well, perceived his regard for me. On later occasions, my interest in Mr Darcy was expressed so warmly that the scoundrel realised he could injure Mr Darcy by making *me* become his advocate. Mr Wickham knew my defence of his character would be insupportable to Mr Darcy."

"That is despicable," Jane gasped. "It would be difficult for any gentleman to forgive a friendship with the man who harmed his sister. It is fortunate that your affections were not further entangled."

Elizabeth began to cry again.

"Oh, no!" Jane cried. "You formed an attachment?"

"I fell in love with Mr Darcy! And he loved me, too. The foundations were laid while we stayed at Netherfield. I had every reason to expect him to make me an offer of marriage."

Jane's eyes expressed astonishment that her lips could not utter.

"You are shocked, I see. Yes, I have been circumspect." Having a mother inclined to criticise and gossip, and a father inclined to tease, Elizabeth had learnt the value of discretion. "Believe me when I say we loved each other and that, had we not quarrelled at the ball, he would have asked me to marry him. But I defended Mr Wickham. I told Darcy to forgive him and renew their acquaintance. Our discussion became heated, and I accused Darcy of being resentful … And the man may have ruined his sister …" Elizabeth devolved into sobs again.

Jane wrapped her arms around her as she continued, and Elizabeth knew she saw the embroidered initials F.D. on the handkerchief she clutched against her face. "That is why he left, I know it is. Darcy warned me about Mr Wickham, but I was determined to discern his character myself. I was such a fool!"

"You could not have suspected such wickedness existed in one man."

She allowed Jane to direct her to bed, and the last thing Elizabeth recalled before falling asleep was her sister stroking her hair.

Sunday, December 29

ELIZABETH WOKE THE NEXT MORNING TO THE SAME CONSCIOUSNESS of misery in which she closed her eyes. She heard two hushed voices from the dressing room that adjoined the bedroom she shared with Jane. Elizabeth discerned what was said: Mrs Gardiner had heard Elizabeth sobbing during the night, and Jane, without mentioning Darcy's name, explained Mr Wickham's deception.

"Poor Lizzy!" Mrs Gardiner exclaimed. "Mr Wickham has acted despicably." Her aunt must have realised she had raised her voice, because her next words were softer. "But that does not explain …"

There were indeterminate mutterings and Elizabeth heard "… attachment that Mr Wickham sought to dissolve … Lizzy championed Mr Wickham, and Bingley's friend could not forgive … young lady under his protection was fifteen."

"Oh good heavens!" Mrs Gardiner exclaimed, raising her voice again. The rest of the discussion focused on her aunt offering to bring Elizabeth to London until Jane's wedding to avoid meeting Mr Wickham before they left for Brighton. Elizabeth moved about the room with more noise than was necessary, and as she suspected, the voices were silenced.

She was pained again by the realisation of how much her defence of Mr Wickham must have wounded and offended the man she loved. Had she only trusted his word more. Had he only explained more to her.

Elizabeth considered how often Mr Wickham had sought her out and how far his seduction of Miss Darcy went, and with a rising fear and increasing fury, she wondered if Mr Wickham would have attempted the same with her. She would never have consented to an assignation, but after his behaviour at Christmas, he may have forced himself upon her.

I have to convince my parents of Mr Wickham's worthlessness before I go to London. She could not tolerate spending another moment in his company and showing him civility, and there was no telling what he might do or say to her or any of her sisters. She did not wish to describe her previous attachment to Darcy, and she dared not reveal what she suspected about Miss Darcy and Mr Wickham, but she had to try.

"Lizzy, you are once again amongst the living." Mr Bennet beckoned for her to come in. "I thought your headache was a contrivance to spare yourself the sight of the happy lovers. Have they become too cloying for your affection for them both to overcome?"

"I was sincerely out of sorts."

"I understand you are going to London until Jane's wedding. Your mother is in favour of the scheme because she wants you to procure more fripperies, but it makes little sense for you to go to town for only a fortnight."

"I believe a change of scene will do me good."

Mr Bennet turned back to his book. Elizabeth refrained from heaving an exasperated sigh. "Have you no curiosity as to why I wish to leave Longbourn?"

"The wedding planning is so tiresome as to drive you from home?"

"No, the only thing that I wish to absent myself from is parties with the militia officers."

Mr Bennet's lips quirked upward. "Have you been crossed in love? You need not run to London if your man has jilted you. There are eight companies here, so four-and-twenty officers are yours for the taking."

"I have no lovers in the militia, and am now of the opinion that the welcome they receive at Longbourn may be undeserved. Mr Wickham in particular has demonstrated behaviour I find worrisome."

"Mr Wickham must have been a sad flirt and cared little for the havoc he might be making in your affections."

"You are wilfully misunderstanding my meaning! Who are these officers that we admit into our home? We do not know anything about their character."

Mr Bennet cast a longing look at his book. "You would have me refuse to allow the officers in the house because I know nothing of their reputations?"

"Yes, I would. I know it cannot be helped to meet them elsewhere, but I do not believe their company is a welcomed addition at Longbourn."

"Imagine how unvaried will your life be without the presence of the officers. Be not alarmed if one changeable officer has gone on to make love to another girl. May I recommend you aim higher and try for one of the five captains?"

"Papa, I am not speaking about romantic entanglements! I have reason to suppose Mr Wickham is not a trustworthy man."

Mr Bennet laughed. "Poor little Lizzy! If one of those officers jilted you, there is always the hope that Bingley will be able to find a man for you."

"Will you not consider the possibility that these officers are not suitable acquaintances for your daughters? At the least, we ought to be properly chaperoned when in their presence."

Mr Bennet picked up his book. "I will not waste my time sitting in the room while you and your sisters smile and flirt. And I would have no peace at Longbourn if I forbade your mother and sisters from entertaining the officers. You are too clever for them by half, and whoever this officer is, he is not worth your tears."

Elizabeth left her father disappointed and sorry, but not surprised at the outcome of her interview.

The remainder of the day was spent visiting Lucas Lodge to take leave of Charlotte, who would be married while she was in town. She was pressed by her friend to visit her in March, and Elizabeth promised to go to Hunsford. She did desire to see Charlotte happily settled; and more to her purpose, the idea of being in London, then Brighton and then Kent—thereby avoiding both Mr Wickham and Mr Darcy—was the first good news Elizabeth had in a long while.

Later Sunday evening, Elizabeth and Jane were confined together in her mother's apartments while Mrs Bennet laid out the commissions she desired Elizabeth to execute in town.

"And Colonel Forster may give another ball; Lydia and Kitty will need another pair of gloves each."

Elizabeth thought this the best opening she was to receive. "Do you not think we mix too freely with the militia officers?"

"How can you not have satisfaction in the society of a militia officers?"

"I am not opposed to showing the officers civility, but we know nothing about them. These officers can pretend to be men of character when they may have dubious reputations."

"You are the first to mix in the neighbourhood and be agreeable."

"So long as they exude fine manners, we do not question their past. Mr Wickham, for example, is now an officer by title, and his true self is covered by his red coat."

"Oh, Mr Wickham! So charming and handsome!"

Jane and Elizabeth shared a pained look. "I wonder if we ought not to allow the officers at Longbourn," Elizabeth said.

Mrs Bennet stared at her second daughter. "There is nothing wrong with the company of the officers. I remember the time when I liked a red coat myself. It is well and good for you to refuse any offer of marriage to come your way, but you will not ruin the prospects of your sisters."

Elizabeth was about to throw up her hands when Jane added, "But Mamma, only Colonel Forster, the lieutenant-colonel, and the major may have an income enough to marry. The officers' ranks are related to the value of the property owned by them or their families."

"Yes!" Elizabeth cried, eager to have found a way to reach her mother. "The rest of the officers may be poor! Many, like Mr Wickham, are serving in the place of a landowner for a paltry sum."

"I know the value of a good income as well as anybody, but even if the officers cannot afford to marry my girls, there is no reason they should not enliven our parties."

"It would be a shame if they formed an attachment that could not be acted upon," Jane mused. "You would not wish for any of your daughters to make an imprudent match by fixing on an officer without fortune."

Elizabeth added, "Can you imagine your daughters marrying on a narrower income than she had been used to look forward to, and forced on a strict line of economy?"

Mrs Bennet threw herself into her chair. "If the officers must marry with attention to money, then I suppose they would not be interested in my girls. But that is no reason to lose their company."

Jane shrugged her shoulders in defeat, but Elizabeth tried again. "I have learned that one of the officers is not what he appears to be."

Mrs Bennet's enthusiasm for salacious news made her lean forward. "Who?"

"Mr Wickham. Bingley's friend, Mr Darcy, told me about his proclivities and misdeeds, and although I did not believe him at first, I now know them to be true."

"Oh, when has proud Mr Darcy had anything good to say about anyone?"

"My dear Bingley is in agreement with Mr Darcy; Bingley knows Mr Wickham is a man of questionable morals."

Elizabeth knew Bingley did not know half the truth about Mr Wickham and the Darcys, but the mention of Bingley's name was enough to give Mrs Bennet pause. "Well, I am certain Bingley must be right, but I cannot imagine a pleasant man as Mr Wickham doing anything very wrong."

"Miss Bingley considered not inviting Mr Wickham to the ball, but Bingley saw no way to properly avoid it."

"I cannot believe Mr Wickham is so corrupt that he ought not to be welcomed at Longbourn."

"He is false and as deceitful as he is insinuating!" Elizabeth cried.

"Good heavens! What are you talking of?"

She dared not confess her loss of Mr Darcy's affections nor could she hint at Mr Wickham's seduction of Miss Darcy. The former would cause her mother to rant over her losing a man worth ten thousand a year, and the latter was too confidential to speak of before a woman who loved to spread news. Elizabeth had but one remaining option.

"Mamma, Mr Wickham kissed me on Christmas night." If it kept that wretched man from Longbourn, Elizabeth would sacrifice her privacy. "I did nothing to encourage him, but he nonetheless stole a kiss."

Mrs Bennet laughed. "You girls were dancing under the mistletoe! A harmless kissing game is no reason to forbid the man from Longbourn."

"I was seated at the instrument."

Mrs Bennet's smile slipped, and Jane covered her mouth with her hand. "Well, a small kiss is not serious. A bit of high revel—"

"He put his tongue in my mouth!" Her mother was stunned into silence. "Bingley's friend warned us about his character, yet because of his red coat, Mr Wickham is free to mingle among us. I know from both Mr Darcy *and* Mr Wickham that he wasted the three thousand pounds Mr Darcy gave him in lieu of a living Mr Wickham renounced, yet he is welcomed to flirt with your daughters when he has no prospects and a reputation for dissipation? He has gentlemanlike manners, but after imbibing too much, he saw nothing wrong with imposing on me in a dreadful way."

"He might admire you and it was a lapse due to—"

"Mr Wickham told me himself he had no design on me. Even if he did admire me, nothing could come of it, and I do not welcome it. He has squandered all that he ever had. He is untrustworthy, he has no prospects, no profession, and no friends to help him."

Jane sat next to Elizabeth and took hold of her hand. "Mamma, Bingley would be appalled to learn Mr Wickham made advances against Lizzy. Given what my dear Bingley knows about Mr Wickham's lack of character, were he to learn that Lizzy was insulted in this way and Mr Wickham was *still* permitted to call at Longbourn, he would be displeased."

This was as close to a threat as Jane could utter, but Elizabeth saw her mother was captivated. "Yes! I would not offend Bingley! And I shall not have it said I allow my daughters to be disrespected in their own home. A little flirting is harmless, but how dreadful! Lizzy, you need never be at home to that scoundrel. In fact, none of my girls will be at home to Mr Wickham or any party of officers that include him. Wait until Lady Lucas learns—"

"Mamma!" Jane exclaimed. "You cannot spread news about this. It must be humiliating for Lizzy to even speak of it!"

"No," Elizabeth replied. "Tell Lady Lucas and my aunt Philips that Mr Darcy told Bingley about Mr Wickham's dissipated past, but we all thought him reputable until he had the effrontery to kiss me, inebriated, and in full view of a crowded room. I can tolerate the neighbourhood knowing the truth if it keeps Mr Wickham away. It is possible someone saw, and if we receive Mr Wickham at Longbourn, then everyone may think there is an attachment between us, or that I welcomed an improper advance."

"Indeed not! My girls need husbands who can provide for them. I will never speak to Mr Wickham again!"

Elizabeth could not believe it; her mother's whole heart was in the subject of breaking with Mr Wickham. It was better to admit to being kissed by Mr Wickham than confess the full truth. Other than Jane's wedding, she would spend the next three months in London, Brighton, or Hunsford. It would not be the first time a young woman was removed from the advances of an unworthy man, and if the neighbourhood whispered about her being the subject of Mr Wickham's unsolicited kiss, it was a small price to pay.

Chapter 27

Monday, December 30
Harper Lodge

After going into the woods and bringing back eight brace between the cousins, Darcy knew they had nothing to occupy them until his neighbours arrived tomorrow. He and his cousins were now indulging in too much port as well as anecdotes of the sort that could not be told before mixed company. The alcohol and the convivial nature of their successful shoot, as well as their relative isolation, led to a more relaxed evening than they had been used to enjoying.

"Now you must tell Darcy what happened," Milton clumsily poured the remains of the bottle into his glass.

Fitzwilliam held his head in his hands as he rested his elbows on the table. He narrowly missed knocking over his own glass. "No, it was awful."

"You cannot mention it and not tell me the story!" cried Darcy. "Speak, or let your brother tell it in his own way."

"Very well, but prepare to be scandalised. I was sitting by a gentleman with whom I was unacquainted in the pit, and I saw two women come into the box opposite. Both were more frightful than imagination can paint or pen can describe. Feeling sociable, I turned to my neighbour and asked, 'Good God, can you tell what ugly bitch that is?'"

Darcy gave a shocked stare. Fitzwilliam pointed to Milton, yelling, "I *told* you he would not be amused by my drunken rudeness!"

"Tell the rest!"

"The gentleman answered, '*Who, sir?*' 'That lady coming into the box.' '*It is my sister.*' 'No, sir!' I cried. I did not intend to offend him, so I tried to repair the damage. 'I mean that shocking monster with her.' '*Oh, sir,*' said the other gentleman, '*that is my wife.*'"

His cousin's laughter, as well as his own, filled the room. Their companionableness reminded Darcy that they would be joined by other gentlemen tomorrow, and he was reluctant to have their familiarity curtailed. He asked Milton when the others would arrive.

"It shall only be the three of us."

"You led me to understand Mrs Finch invited many gentlemen to shoot for the week. You said most of my neighbours would attend."

"That was a lie to get you here so I could see Alix. Also, Mrs Finch departed for Bath. Alix and her friends remain alone at Harper in her stead."

Fitzwilliam and Darcy exchanged a look. "How long do you suppose before Lady Hancock invites the small party from the Lodge to remain at the great house?" Darcy asked drily.

Milton brought another bottle to the table. "There is no reason to remain at the Lodge when we can be accommodated at the great house."

"This is a contrivance. Shall we even bother to take out a gun while we remain?" Fitzwilliam asked.

"Of course. I intend to spend my days out of doors."

"And your nights in your mistress' bed?"

"If you practiced greater economy, you might be able to afford your own exclusive convenience. Although you ought to instead find yourself a wife."

Darcy feared the brothers' long-simmering tension was now about to boil over, but he underestimated Fitzwilliam's self-possession. His cousin refilled his own glass. "It is not *I* who have the greatest need."

Darcy, perhaps for having had a third glass, did not at first realise his cousin was referring to him. "Lady Hancock and her friends can offer nothing that I need."

"Come now! You have been crossed in love, and it has been too long since you had a woman."

"Darcy? In love?" Milton stared. "I do not believe it."

"Is it so difficult to believe that I have a heart?"

"That a sensible man like you would yield to it? Yes, that is alarming."

"His heart is not what needs attention," muttered the colonel, who then made an obscene gesture.

Darcy winced. "You become vulgar after you have had too much port."

"I have not yet begun to be vulgar. But, for your delicate sensibilities, I will be mild. Since Milton has the exclusive rights to Lady Hancock, I recommend that we foster your attachment with one of the others." Fitzwilliam turned to his brother. "What fair ladies does Lady Hancock have in attendance?"

"Alix's youngest sister, Miss Violet Ewell, and her friend Miss Fisher."

"Do you think either would suit for Darcy?"

"I am still in the room!" exclaimed Darcy.

"Vi is not one who will be praised for her looks, but she is at least ten years younger than her sister; I do not think she is eighteen. Alix tells me she hopes of marrying her next protector."

"That will not do for Darcy. A temporary relationship will suit him."

"Yes, such a woman may do well for a mistress, but not as a wife. Brood mares and hacks are different things. Besides, Violet Ewell is a simpleton, according to Alix."

"Darcy will prefer to have some conversation with whoever he takes to bed. A talented but stupid woman will never do for him. He is so impatient of imbecility."

The brothers rolled their eyes. Darcy bristled in indignation. "Yes, my standards are high indeed!"

"What of the other woman?"

"I am not acquainted with Miss Fisher beyond her reputation. She is not beautiful, but Alix speaks of her as a saucy girl with blue eyes and black hair. She changes lovers often, as easily as she changes her shoes; she is very sought after."

"Perfect!" Colonel Fitzwilliam clapped his hands and grinned at Darcy. "Milton and I shall do all that we can to promote your intimacy with Miss Fisher, and after a night or three or five with her, you will forget the lady from Hertfordshire."

Darcy narrowed his eyes. "I am not interested."

"Why not?" Milton took a pinch from his snuff box. "It could do well for your reputation to be an object of envy by having that coveted woman as your mistress."

"You are speaking of your own concerns rather than mine."

Fitzwilliam took Darcy's glass, refilled it, and pushed it back in front of him. "Miss Fisher is the sort to charm you out of your troubles for a week in return for some pecuniary advantage."

Darcy was aware that his disinclination for mistresses, brothels, courtesans, and adulterous affairs placed him in the minority of gentlemen. "Why have you taken this task to heart?"

"How could I not? After all you told me about the woman in Hertfordshire, you could use a damned good piece."

"What woman?" asked Milton, his voice slurring with inebriety.

"Darcy fell in love while staying with his friend Bingley. He was prepared to marry some country girl, but it fell apart, and it is up to us"—Fitzwilliam gestured between himself and his brother with his glass, splashing wine on to the table—"to see that he has no more lonely nights on her account."

"In love? Why?" Milton set aside his glass. "I would have thought that was beneath your dignity. Was she handsome? Submissive?"

"Intelligent and compassionate. Of lively and sensible talk between us, there could be no end. She was not a difficult person to love." Darcy took another drink, and the words flowed off his tongue. "A lovely, indescribable charm. Not classically beautiful; a light figure, small waist, shapely legs whose outline you could easily detect as she crossed over a stile."

"An awkward country girl without style, elegance, and beauty?" Milton was incredulous. "You *do* need a damned fine piece, and as soon as you can find one willing."

"What of her family?" Fitzwilliam asked. "You never mentioned this woman's connexions."

Darcy drained his glass and dropped it to the table. "Mother's family is in trade. Father is a gentleman with two thousand a year. A respectable family in general, although the mother and younger sisters are …" Darcy trailed away. "There is no dowry for her or her four sisters."

Fitzwilliam and Milton snickered. Darcy was caught off-guard: the brothers were getting on so well. Darcy's muddled mind was beginning to think they might be working in concert against him when Fitzwilliam asked, "And she had nothing to recommend her?"

"I hope I may count myself able to set a value on character, and not merely on rank and fortune."

"She believed Mr Wickham's lies, and days after you left, she pledged herself to her cousin. Perhaps her character is not all that you thought it was?"

All of the air was pressed from Darcy's lungs, and his stomach churned when he thought of the despair Elizabeth would suffer as Mrs Collins because he did not confide in her when he ought to have, because he lost his temper and left.

Milton emptied his own glass. "Thin as a reed, with neither bosom nor bottom? No fortune and connexions to trade? What a narrow escape!"

"Yes, think of it as an escape! You ought to seduce this Miss Fisher, or rather let her seduce you. We shall treat you! What shall Miss Fisher cost for the week?"

"Mistresses are damned expensive. I can scarcely manage between Mary's pin money and Alix's annuity, and that does not count all the gifts that find their way into their hands." Fitzwilliam stared at his brother, who realised he had not answered the question. "Alix was known to charge one hundred guineas for a few hours' dalliance."

What started from the bantering of drunken gentlemen was now becoming too real for Darcy. "You may keep your fashionable impures to yourselves."

"You need not be alarmed; I make use of armour; it is quite effective."

Darcy stared at Milton, his mouth gaping open as he now considered another reason not to engage a mistress.

"Milton, you frightened him. After Darcy has a chance to admire Miss Fisher, we shall have an easier time convincing him."

Milton downed his glass and stood up on unsteady legs. He leant a hand on his chair-back to steady himself while he checked his reflection in the mirror, then went to bed.

Darcy now spoke more freely than he could while Milton remained. "What the hell is the matter with you? When have I ever been known to consort with courtesans?"

The colonel dragged a hand across his bleary eyes. "Why are you against it? It is not as though you are married and promised to forsake all others. Does it offend your romantic delicacy?"

"I am not a romantic."

"Of course you are!"

"I am not."

"Yes, you are, and have always been!"

"How can you claim I am a romantic when it was only after I met *her* that I considered marriage, let alone a marriage of affection rather than one of affluence and power?"

"Because you are not as damned clever and aware of your own character as you think you are! Because I *know* you. Of course Miss Fisher is not going to console you if you loved Miss Bennet enough to marry her. But it will help remind you that you will be happy with another."

Fitzwilliam moved towards the door. When he heard the handle turn, Darcy asked, while still staring at his empty glass, "Did it help you?"

He heard his cousin sigh and rest his head against the door. A long silence stretched between them, and Darcy regretted giving voice to that which, by unspoken agreement, was never to be discussed.

"The first few times, I thought of Mary, but it served its purpose." A little louder, he said, "And you shall have an easier time of it since you will never see this Miss Bennet again."

"Her sister is to marry Bingley! And the lady's betrothed has been granted a living by none other than Lady Catherine!"

"You know, I think the charm of a few nights with a woman might go a long way in driving away your sorrow. And I suspect that it has been months, if not years, since you have had your—Do not glare at me! I shall say no more." He left Darcy alone.

Darcy had never before wanted for a mistress to command his purse, or his time, or his heart, but if Miss Fisher struck his fancy, then possibly Fitzwilliam—who knew something of the subject of the distraction from disappointed hopes—was right.

I have no wife to forsake. If an unattached courtesan could force Elizabeth Bennet from my mind and fill a few lonely nights, do I have anything to lose?

Wednesday, January 1, 1812
Gracechurch Street

ELIZABETH HAD BEEN IN TOWN FOR TWO DAYS, AND IT WAS A RELIEF she no longer had to suffer the fortitude it took to conceal all that she had felt when she realised that she had driven Darcy away by blindly supporting Mr Wickham. Her parents and sisters, save Jane, never knew of her lost attachment; the family at Gracechurch street knew of her regrets, but did not speak of them. They did not even know the gentleman's name.

"I intend to go into *that* part of town on Saturday so you have no excuse not to call on her," Mrs Gardiner said with a sly smile.

Elizabeth had letters that Charles and Jane had begged her to deliver to Miss Bingley. "Can I not place them in the penny-post?"

Mrs Gardiner shook her head. "You can withstand fifteen minutes in the company of the woman who will be your sister."

"Believe me, she will be equally reluctant to receive me. Jane may be deceived about her regard, but Caroline Bingley and I understand each other. She will never be glad to see me."

"It is strange that if she is affecting politeness towards Jane that she would show dislike towards you."

"She had the hopes of attaching herself to… her brother's friend, and her dislike of me originated in jealousy."

"Oh, Lizzy, you must have been grieving for your disappointed hopes long before you realised Mr Wickham's duplicity. For all your liveliness, you are a private girl. You have kept your serenity to such a degree that I wonder if you did love this man or if he was worth your tears."

"I was in love, and with a proper object, I assure you. Do not let Miss Bingley's preference for his fortune speak against him."

"You will not even say his name? I had hoped you would speak freely with me."

"It is not because I have no confidence in you. I am certain that we all will, in the coming years, hear a good deal about the Bingleys and their friends, and I cannot tolerate to have eyes turned on me whenever *his* name is spoken. It will be bad enough I shall *feel* I ought to be looked at whenever he is mentioned. He and Bingley have a steady friendship, and it shall sadden me enough to know that he is to visit or that he is to marry." Elizabeth's voice broke, but she did not cry.

"Since you tell me nothing, I shall suppose him to be terribly ugly, below middling height, and poor due to excessive gaming and drink." Her aunt gave her a smile and winked.

"Mr Bingley's friend is tall and handsome." She gave a pensive sigh. "He has striking eyes, his figure is broad in the shoulders, and he has a fine waist." Elizabeth wished she could forget the bright and breathless way Darcy appeared after a ride. "He has many virtues: he is a responsible landlord, charitable, clever, and he has good sense and good judgment."

"His sense and judgment cannot be perfect; he left you."

"I drove him away. I did not depend on his good sense as I

ought to have, and I instead believed the man who seduced his sister. He is a good man, the best I shall ever know."

"Now, Lizzy, none of that! Time will heal the wound. Another man will have the power of attaching you more, and *he* will be in your eyes the most perfect of men."

Elizabeth thanked her aunt and said all that was grateful and cheerful, and did not believe a word of it.

Chapter 28

Wednesday, January 1, 1812
Harper Hall

"Milton spoke to Lady Hancock, and she to Miss Fisher, and if all parties like what they see, you could be a lucky man. However, Miss Ewell, Lady Hancock's sister, is still in the hopes of securing a proposal from her next protector." Fitzwilliam heaved an exaggerated sigh. "I shall, for your sake, my dear Darcy, distract the ignoramus so *you* may focus on securing the transitory comforts of a lady who does not want to be led to the altar. Let it not be said that I do nothing for my favourite cousin."

Darcy rolled his eyes.

Fitzwilliam whispered to Darcy at the door, "And try harder than you did at dinner. A few smiles would not go amiss."

Darcy entered the drawing room and took in the scene. Three ladies, if they could rightly be termed, were in conversation before a large fire. They were laughing, and their knowing glances told Darcy that the men, or himself alone, had been the subject of their effusions.

Lady Alexandra Hancock—Alix to her intimates—glided to Milton's side. He threw an arm around her waist as she said, "It is intolerable for you to remain in the dining room! You ought not to stay away from me for so long. I insist you sit by me." Darcy could well imagine her stamping her foot.

"As you wish, madam."

Lady Hancock leaned coquettishly towards Milton. "I do wish. And for dragging me away from town to Derbyshire solely for your comfort, I demand recompense. It is a veritable crime for my box at the theatre to be empty. Caro and Vi were the only ones good enough to accompany me here. Do you know how many invitations I declined in order to be here? Imagine, me, away from London at this time of year!"

"As I am the one paying for that box, I shall decide when you may use it. I pay you handsomely for the privilege, Alix, of having you at my beck and call."

"You *should* be generous to me! I am very much in demand," she pouted, her eyes blazing. "I should be sorry to be put in the position of having to tell your wife that I have taken her place in your bed. The little darling would be devastated."

"Would a trip to the jewellers' be in order when I am next in town?"

Her angry eyes turned flirtatious again. "A fair beauty such as myself is well suited for emeralds. Besides, you know"—she dragged her fingernails across his chest and looked into his eyes—"how much I am worth it."

Darcy observed her coquetry and bribery, and Milton's ready acceptance, with shame. Her reputation was part of the reason Milton maintained her. She had been briefly married to one of her protectors who left her little after he died other than the title that promoted her from Miss Ewell to Lady Hancock. She pulled Milton to the sofa and angled herself so she was in Milton's line of sight.

She is a woman accustomed to spending her days shining at the centre of her own narcissistic solar system. Lady Hancock was short, well made, but rouged a good deal more than necessary. Her vermilion lips were curled into a smile as she employed her arts in captivating Milton and indulging his vanity.

Darcy walked to the table where Violet Ewell, Lady Hancock's sister, was pouring tea. One could not praise her looks or her intelligence. She was two years older than Georgiana, but looked younger by far.

Miss Ewell poured him a cup and assumed his taking up the sugar tongs was an invitation to further discourse. "We have had cold, disagreeable weather, have we not?"

They had spoken of the weather at length while they sat together at dinner. "I agree it is a cold night."

"Is it snowing fast? Do you believe it shall continue?" She looked out the nearest window.

Darcy looked; they could both observe that very few flakes were falling and the clouds were parting. "I do not, madam. It gives me every appearance of its being soon over."

"But Alix insisted the gentlemen stay here. Was it not because of the snow? Did we speak of the weather at dinner? I cannot remember." She was sincerely confused. "I enjoyed the roast loin of pork."

Darcy bowed and took his cup to the other side of the room; he found Miss Ewell exasperating. Darcy suspected the reason she had success as a courtesan was because her talents in maintaining a protector's interest lay in a different arena than conversation.

"Darcy!" Colonel Fitzwilliam called from where he sat near the third lady. "You must prevail upon Miss Fisher to entertain you." Darcy was so horrified at his cousin's forwardness he stopped in his path. "Miss Fisher sings and plays very well."

Caro Fisher was Lady Hancock's friend who had, by general consensus, been appointed his object. She had blue eyes that scrutinised him and an overly voluptuous chest. Her features were not regular, her looks too emphatic for prettiness.

"Oh, no! Do not let Caro be troubled to exhibit," Lady Hancock exclaimed. "What a dead bore! I thought we were to play cards."

"You just fear it will strike these gentlemen that I play well and that you do not," she addressed this to Lady Hancock, but held Darcy's eye with a knowing smile. "I do not think it a trouble in the least."

Fitzwilliam was staring at him, but Darcy could not comprehend him. The colonel coughed and said, "Miss Fisher, the instrument is unlocked, and Darcy is prepared to be charmed."

Miss Fisher rose. "Perhaps a song or two; I was never vain of music." When she passed Darcy on her way to the instrument, she brushed a hand along his arm and let her gaze linger over him. Some baser instinct overtook Darcy, and he watched her hips sway as she walked. Remembering himself, he turned away and found Fitzwilliam standing by him.

"Her conduct towards me is proceeding from the most audacious and unprincipled coquetry," he said in a low voice.

"That is the *point*!" Fitzwilliam whispered angrily. "Your refusal to flirt will not endear you to her."

"I do not have a talent for trifling with women."

"How did you interact with Miss Bennet when you first saw her?"

"We were at a ball and I refused to be introduced to her, and knowing she could hear me, I said she was not handsome enough to dance with *me*."

"Right," the word dragged out slowly. "And you presume she loved you a little?"

"I know she did."

The colonel blew out a breath. "That is not likely to work a second time. You must admire Miss Fisher's performance. Tell her how much it moves you."

"I cannot."

"Why? Her performance leaves nothing wanting."

"It is fine in its way, but I cannot say it moves me. Miss Fisher has adequate skill, but she plays with precious little feeling. To say more would be dishonest."

"I am going to give you some advice: Your reserve will come across as arrogance and formality. Complimenting a woman is not beneath your dignity, and if you look at a woman only to notice her faults, Pemberley is going to pass to Georgiana's son."

Fitzwilliam crossed the room to admire Miss Ewell's work, and Darcy was left alone with his thoughts.

Darcy had realised that while in Hertfordshire, and likely elsewhere, he had by a contemptuous manner created dislike. He ought to emulate his father's benevolence and attempt, through greater affability, to become an object of esteem and affection. Of course, seducing a courtesan was not what his father had had in mind.

Darcy stationed himself so as to command a view of Miss Fisher.

"You look severe." Her cold blue eyes fixed on him.

"I have no design of alarming you."

"What manner of design *do* you have on me?"

"You do me no credit by implying that I employ cunning in coming to hear you play."

"No one comes to my side because I play well. I told you, I am not vain of my talents. Not in singing, nor music, nor drawing. My only pride lies in my other *abilities*." She held his gaze a long moment, but Darcy ignored her hint.

"That is a remarkable comment from one who, if I understood what Lady Hancock said at dinner, began her career as an actress."

"Alix was being facetious; I started out selling oranges in the theatre." Miss Fisher raised an eyebrow to assess his reaction, and Darcy tried not to show his disgust at the euphemism. "I have moved to the expensive boxes in the pit, but the skills are all the same. I have only improved with time and experience."

Had this conversation happened at any other time in his life, Darcy would have walked away and spoken neither *of* nor *to* Miss Fisher again. But his desire to purge Elizabeth from his mind forced him to, at least, remain at the instrument.

Darcy took a closer look at her as she finished her song. Her black hair was curled fashionably, and her blue eyes were piercing. He tried to keep his attention on her face, but her two greatest attributes were so prominently displayed he could not long keep his gaze from them.

When she was finished, she said, "Mr Darcy, would you be so good as to tell me why a man with everything in his favour has his cousins pursuing a mistress for him?"

"I do not seek out female company at the risk of raising expectations, nor do I seek female society of your…type."

"You are not the sort of man who usually befriends me, but I still cannot believe a man such as you cannot recommend himself to a woman."

"I am ill qualified to recommend myself to strangers, whether or not they are courtesans."

Miss Fisher stood from the instrument and looked at Darcy until he offered his arm to lead her to a chair. "Then we have something in common: we neither of us perform to strangers. Whereas you are —forgive me to say—too reserved, I am candid to a fault. Come, sit by me, and let us become acquainted."

They joined the others by the fire. Milton was engrossed by Lady Hancock, who made sure that both he and Fitzwilliam were attending to her conversation, while Miss Ewell sat at her needlework and listened.

"Mr Darcy, Milton tells me that you were saved from being leg-shackled to the worst sort of country nobody with no respectable relations and no settled provisions," Lady Hancock addressed him before he had even sat.

Darcy glared at Milton, but he was too busy looking on Lady Hancock to feel the indignation in his gaze. Fitzwilliam addressed her with an easy civility that Darcy envied.

"I think our discussion can run on other topics than matrimony, courtships, and fortunes? There is nothing so disagreeable to a man as gossip and pestering one about being married."

"I would enjoy being married," Miss Ewell said wistfully. "I hope my next protector is a man whose happiness it would be my joy to make forever." She looked sideways at Darcy. Her childlike appearance revolted him.

"Violet, you know nothing of the matter!" said Lady Hancock. "There is no notion I hate more than marriage—I mean marriage in the weak sense of two fools agreeing to unite by some tie of feeling. But an advantageous connexion, such as can be formed in consonance with mutual interest, is not bad, is it, Milton?"

"That is precisely the truth in my own case," replied Milton. *How could a man with any self-respect be gratified by such excessive admiration?* "Sentiment and feeling have no place in a significant union such as marriage."

"Are you telling us your heart was not at all consulted when you agreed to marry Sir Francis Hancock?" Miss Fisher asked her friend.

"Of course not! He gave me a title, and I enlivened his final months. It was a mutually beneficial arrangement, and thankfully, it is something I need not do again. Although I did adore Sir Francis, and I was loyal to him until the end."

She is a vain coquette. Lady Hancock does not have a heart to lose.

"Do you not wish to be married someday, Caro?" Miss Ewell asked.

Miss Fisher laughed, a harsh, unfeeling sound that struck Darcy cold. "No! My mother's marriage proved to me the miseries of a couple punishing each other to the end of their lives, so I will live free from any restraint but that of my own conscience."

"How does your dull wife do?" Alix asked Milton. "I warrant you she is a fine size by this time."

Colonel Fitzwilliam begged leave to retire and was on his feet before his request was granted. Milton waited until his brother left before he replied.

"I have told you not to speak of Lady Milton in coarse terms. She is my *wife*." Lady Hancock relented with an exasperated huff. Darcy rolled his eyes. *If Milton is concerned with the respect due to his wife, he should not forsake his marriage vows.* "My wife is well, and I expect to have news of her and the child within a fortnight."

"Perhaps this one will be your heir, and then future attempts need not be often repeated. I would delight in you spending more time in town. Come, my Lord Milton, the hour grows late, and I insist upon you taking me to bed. I hope my guests will not stand upon ceremony and give me leave to retire with my lover whenever I wish."

Milton held out his hand. "You need not wait a minute more."

Darcy was certain he turned bright red; Miss Ewell was inured to it. She spent several moments lamenting that they were not to have a proper supper, and how she yearned for some minced chicken or an apple tart before she yawned and left.

Miss Fisher poured herself a glass of wine and sat next to Darcy on the sofa. "Might we not see what can be done to elevate our relationship from strangers to friends?"

He doubted she was implying they have some conversation. "Is it not very late?"

"I am fond of good living and late hours."

"I am certain your manner of living is different than mine."

"And yet here you are. I think you and I could be good for one another."

"Forgive me for being blunt, Miss Fisher, but I fail to see what I could do for you that any other man with a heavy purse might not."

A flash of anger darkened her eyes before they returned to their regular placid hue. "I appreciate your honesty. You mistake me for Violet, I think: willing to enter into an arrangement with any single gentleman with the hope he marries her; or Alix, who will sell herself to whatever gentleman will offer her more than her current protector."

"I cannot believe you live the life that you do without any claim to pecuniary advantage from the gentlemen to whom you attach yourself."

"Of course I do. If I had been born a man, then I might have been able to live a more respectable and independent life." She took a long drink from her glass, emptying it. "I am now to understand that you nearly threw yourself away on some country upstart. Your cousins are of the opinion that you need a cure. What a diversion you might be beneath your reserve!" Miss Fisher pushed her glass into Darcy's hand with a pointed look.

Darcy walked to the table to pour a small glass for her, and when he returned to the sofa, he sat as far from Miss Fisher as possible. She smirked, fixed her pale eyes on him, and slid over until her shoulder brushed his arm. The memory of walking along Longbourn's gravel with Elizabeth and tugging her closer to his side came to mind the instant Miss Fisher's sleeve touched his.

The sooner I recover from my disappointment, the better off I will be. Elizabeth would soon be Mrs Collins, and there was no just cause for his pining—or lusting—after another man's wife.

"Why are you willing if I am not your usual sort of patron?"

"You mean other than the money Colonel Fitzwilliam has promised me for every morning I wake up in your bed?"

He only nodded. She finished her wine in a long swallow and laid the glass on the table.

"You pay me no compliments, your opinions seem unbending, and I would not say you are pleasant by any common rule. But I am curious to see that unconquerable passion I suspect you are capable of. You are handsome, and you can afford me. Now, tell me what you think of me."

The flickering candles, her brazen manner, the lateness of the hour, and their seclusion all combined with Darcy's desire to forget Elizabeth Bennet. "Miss Fisher, I think at this time in my life, you might possibly be worth knowing." He twisted a glossy curl between his fingers. It in no way stirred his heart, and he dropped his hand. *What the hell am I doing?*

"No, no surnames! It serves to make me the possession of a man or a family. Call me Caro." She laid a hand on his thigh, scraping her fingernails back and forth. He flinched at the contact.

"Forgive me if I decline, Miss Fisher."

She rose. Darcy habitually began to stand, but she laid a hand on his shoulder and pushed him back to the sofa. She shook her head with mock severity. "I can never take a man to bed who will not address me by my Christian name. How can I expect reciprocity from a man who calls me 'Miss Fisher'? Still, you shall be a grand diversion while I am here."

Darcy, admittedly, was only attending to parts of her speech as Miss Fisher stood in front of him and her *décolleté* was distracting. "Given your history, your scruples surprise me." Inwardly, he was relieved to have been granted this reprieve.

"It serves me well to be eccentric and outspoken. I daresay you admire me for it." She leaned forward and scraped her teeth against his earlobe. "Mark my words, you will be calling me Caro before the week is out," she whispered into his ear. Miss Fisher then left without a backwards glance.

Darcy attempted to gather what remained of his wits. Miss Fisher was, as his mother would have termed her, a worthless hussy. Her conversation, or rather her talk, began and ended with herself and her own concerns. But she was agreeable to distracting him from all that he left behind in Hertfordshire.

Any rational creature would say I owe no loyalty to a woman who is engaged to another man.

Miss Fisher bore no resemblance to the compassionate, respectable woman to whom Darcy had expected to make his proposals. But, if he actually tried, he maybe could envision a shapely woman with black hair and blue eyes in his bed, rather than a light but pleasing figure with dark eyes. Elizabeth might by this time be the wife of another man, and he must do something to forget her; perhaps Miss Fisher could help him.

Chapter 29

Thursday, January 2

The gentlemen went shooting in the morning, but the brothers were too interested in the results of Darcy's evening to pay any mind to the matter at hand. Darcy was content to let them wonder and spoke only about pheasant.

"Oh, shut up! If you will not tell us how Miss Fisher was, I do not want to hear your voice!" Fitzwilliam cried.

It was past midday when they walked back. When they were half a mile from the house, they saw a rider cresting the hill. The horse turned and came towards them, and it did not take them long to realise the rider was Miss Fisher.

"I hope your flirting has improved," Fitzwilliam teased. "Try not to stand in silence this time."

The lady was now near enough to hear. After greetings were exchanged, Darcy said, "It is a pleasure to see a lady with such a good heart for riding."

Miss Fisher's blue eyes flashed, and she gave him a smile. Darcy felt Fitzwilliam's incredulous stare at his gallantry, but all

Fitzwilliam added was "Indeed, I have never seen one sit a horse better. Milton has a hunter in the stables if you are up to a challenge."

"This mare is more than enough for me. I never go faster than a trot in Rotten Row. Shall I walk back with you?"

"Darcy will help you dismount." Fitzwilliam elbowed his spine.

She sprang down with his help. Miss Fisher kept her hands on Darcy's arms and, by scarcely leaning forward, deliberately grazed her breasts against his chest. She eyed him at his sharp intake of breath. He let his eyes wander the length of her body. She was active, fearless, and although she was rather small, she was strongly made.

Darcy swiftly pulled his hands from her waist. Milton and Fitzwilliam exchanged a glance and walked to the house without them. Miss Fisher left her horse with her groom, and she linked her arm around his.

"How shall you address me today, now that we are alone?"

"You are due every courtesy, and I shall continue to call you Miss Fisher."

Miss Fisher made a disapproving sound. "What a shame! As I crested the hill and saw you, I thought you an attractive man with an impressive bearing. I was hoping to see more of you tonight. Or sooner, if you would not like to wait."

Darcy, although becoming slightly more comfortable with trifles, had no flirtatious reply. "It is a rather dark and cold day; I am surprised you decided it a suitable morning for a ride."

She threw him a disapproving look. "Yes, the wind was piercing. I ought not to have ventured out."

After a short pause, Darcy replied, "I am pleased you did."

"That is better. Though I am not ignorant of the fact that our relative isolation makes us more sensible to the charms of each other's society."

"Am I to assume that if there were ten other men in the party, you would not be on my arm?"

She paused to consider. "It would depend on the relative attractiveness and wealth of the other gentlemen. You have a great deal in your favour, although you are not even an Honourable, so much the pity. However, you are well connected, and the Darcy name and fortune is not without its own advantages."

"Yes, I could well afford you anything."

Darcy had said this drily, but Miss Fisher responded with sincerity. "Yes, I expect you could. But those sorts of arrangements do not at all suit me."

"You are not desirous of having an exclusive arrangement as Lady Hancock has?"

"No! I shall not give up hosting parties and entertaining any gentleman who suits my fancy."

"If your affections were—"

"Stop! I beg you please! To think that I could be such a fool as to fall in *love*. Where Alix professes to hold such principles, she only says what Milton wishes to hear, whereas I believe it. It is to my advantage to have as many gentleman friends as I can. I will indulge in any preference anytime the opportunity presents itself, but do not speak to me of love."

"You would never enter into an arrangement with one gentleman at a time?"

"So long as I appear youthful, I will remain single and available to any man who attracts me and who can properly reward me. When I become wealthy enough, perhaps I shall retire to Paris and live out the rest of my days as richly and indulgently as I now do."

"I know little of women's hearts or courtesans' expectations, but I was of the opinion that most wished to marry."

"I thought you were cleverer than that! I have expensive jewels, lavish apartments, and fashionable gowns bestowed upon me for being fascinating and alluring, and I am free to entertain whomever I please. I would not be content to remain at home, in solitude, while my husband enjoyed other entertainments and amusements. I expect none of my lovers to be faithful to me, and I should coquet all the world and take as many lovers as I can rather than belong to one man."

Having a proper discussion with this woman was no simpler than flirting with her. He missed the ease of his conversations with Elizabeth all the more, which did nothing to soothe his temper. "Forgive me; I meant no offence."

"Not at all. It is refreshing for me to encounter a young man such as yourself. You must understand how it is to my detriment to marry or even to consent to enter into an exclusive arrangement. Would *you* forget your rank and station for a woman who brought you no advantages?"

He was silent. Miss Fisher looked at him appraisingly. "Well, the less said on that subject the better. May I call you Darcy?"

"No, Miss Fisher, you may not."

"What a severe man you are!" She pulled her arm from his and clasped hers behind her back. "I cannot accept that an obdurate man such as you was about to marry."

"You ought not to judge a gentleman by his composure."

"I want to see what is beneath that composure." They were now nearing the house, and Miss Fisher held out her hand. "Now, let us shake hands. I am too familiar for your liking, but there is no changing my nature to suit your gravity. I cannot part from an eligible man on disagreeable terms."

When her hand was gripped in his, she stepped close enough to whisper, "No man can secure my sole attentions, but I hope you make better use of your week. This is the only time you are likely to have me all to yourself. My nights have been lonely."

She gave him a significant look before she broke away.

So have mine.

Friday, January 3

LAST EVENING HAD BEEN INSUPPORTABLE. THERE HAD BEEN LITTLE leisure given for general chat with Miss Fisher, and none at all for particular discourse. Darcy had not a single opportunity to enter into any semblance of a conversation with her. He often felt her watching him, but she never allowed him to speak to her. Tonight was passing in the same dreadful manner. He was being teased, toyed with for Miss Fisher's amusement.

Why else would she encourage me yesterday but then spurn my attempts to speak with her?

The previous evening, Darcy had been better prepared to move on from flirtation to a rendezvous, but Miss Fisher coyly kept him at a distance. Tonight was the same: every time he moved to speak with her, she repulsed him or drew another person into their conversation. She would smile provocatively, but other than that, he received no encouragement.

Tonight, once again, the party met for the sake of drinking and laughing together and playing any noisy game. He was forced to contend with Miss Fisher's trifling with him, Miss Ewell's insipidity, and Lady Hancock's heartless talk. Not even the game amused him. The others were laughing at nothings and had drunk more than even they were usually known to.

What am I doing here?

"Mr Darcy, you are inclined to be silent," said Lady Hancock after she dealt. "What think you of my merry parties?"

Darcy had found the evening tiresome and lost his patience. "I would have to say that our table is not one of prime intellectual state and dignity."

Lady Hancock pursed her lips. She was a woman used to being complimented and indulged at every turn. "I always supposed that a visitor is bound to conform to the habits of the house."

"Of course, madam. However, it does one well to remember that the truest hospitality is that which places the visitor most at his ease and affords him the greatest opportunity for enjoyment."

Milton scowled at him; Darcy wondered how many jewels it would cost Milton to placate Lady Hancock this time.

"Invitations to my parties are very sought after, are they not, Milton? My champagne suppers after the opera are always full of company. To be seen at *my* home in Dorset Square means as much as to be seen at White's or at the Argyll Rooms," she said with an air that Darcy knew meant he was supposed to be impressed.

"My dear Alix, Darcy meant no insult." Milton glared at Darcy until he bowed his head in apology. "His manner of amusements is different from ours. London and its society could never compete, in his mind, to time spent at Pemberley. Do you need new Mechlin lace?" Milton stroked her arm, as though she were a lapdog that had become distressed by a clap of thunder.

"Yes! It can be used to trim my new gown; I ought to have another carriage gown. You may also buy me the satin to make it."

Throughout this and for the rest of the evening, Miss Fisher's only contribution was to nudge Darcy's leg higher and higher with her foot under the table while ignoring his conversation.

Darcy did not speak or raise his eyes from his cards until an hour later, when he heard Miss Fisher exhale sharply. "I declare I am ready for bed."

He knew those words were for him. He remained in silence until the game was over and everyone but Miss Fisher retired. When they were alone, she poured two glasses of wine and held one out to him. He observed that she had already drunk twice as much as he had and set his own glass aside.

"I am not certain I ought to remain with you. You put my friend out of spirits." Miss Fisher had an impish smile.

"I intended no disrespect to my hostess."

"Come now, say what you mean."

"Lady Hancock is remarkably good-tempered so long as she has her own way."

She laughed; it was a severe sound. "And spirited when she is out of humour! Alix's downfall is believing that she has any value beyond her knowledge of the arts of love."

"I presume she resorts to extortion against those who do not keep their promise to provide for her after their relationship ends?"

"Alix settles for trifles while her protector shares her bed, then demands recompense for her silence when it is all at an end. Most gentlemen do not care to have their former mistress tell all, but there are some willing to pay her to keep silent. I make use of a man's money and his attentions for as long as possible because I do not fool myself into believing I have any power after a man has put his boots back on."

"You, of course, are not in so precarious a situation as the extravagant Lady Hancock or simple Miss Ewell?"

"Quite right! I have no pretensions, except the expectation that I shall always live in the style I do now, even after my beauty and youth have faded. My choices separate me from respectable women, but I am free to love for myself."

Darcy wondered if Miss Fisher was able to speak at length about anything other than herself.

Miss Fisher emptied her glass and set it aside as she stood. Darcy did not rise to acknowledge her. She rested one hand on his shoulder and with the other stroked his hair. "I doubt you remained behind in order to talk."

He scarcely remembered the last time he had felt the soft curves of a woman's body. *Will I even recall what to do?* He had expected the next woman he would take to bed, for the rest of his life, would be Elizabeth, but now he would never feel the warmth of Elizabeth's body against his. He was so weary of feeling lonely. Elizabeth Bennet was lost to him forever, and it was his own fault.

He sighed, and she dropped her hands. "As much as I enjoy your conversation, I shall retire now, Mr Darcy."

"Stay, Caro."

There was no mistaking the triumph in her cool eyes. "Is it any consequence to you if I stay?"

"Yes, I should be glad if you remained with me tonight."

"Then I shall see you in your chamber in half an hour."

DARCY WALKED IN AGITATION ACROSS HIS ROOM. IF HE WAS TO rally again, if he was to purge Elizabeth from his mind and his heart, then he had best let Miss Fisher do what she was proficient at and enjoy it—even if he found nothing admirable about her other than her willingness. *I have to forget Elizabeth.*

He reached to consult his watch, only to remember that he had torn off half of his clothes upon entering his chamber. The fob had fallen somewhere on to the floor and was now lost in the carpet. He paced, wondering if she would come and wondering if he wanted her to.

He started when Miss Fisher entered, with her jet-black hair down and wearing a green dressing gown. His first thought was a wish for her to turn around and leave. He exhaled a shaky breath and tried to give the impression that he was as self-assured as he had been used to feeling.

"I was not certain you would come, given how you enjoy trifling with me."

"It was an unsuccessful manoeuvre on my part. I retreated, but you did not advance."

"I cannot comprehend you."

"Cannot you? I wanted to see what lay beneath your reserve. I thought I would amuse myself by forcing you to pursue me. You were going to throw yourself away because of your irrepressible desire for some country nobody, and I wanted a hint of that fervour directed towards me. I need to be entertained, but my game was a failure. I will make it up to you."

Darcy wondered if she could construct two consecutive sentences that did not use the word "I." Over the course of this speech, Miss Fisher had advanced into the room and stood in front of him. Her nearness compelled him to take a step in retreat, but the back of his legs reached the bed, and with a firm hand, Miss Fisher pressed against his chest until he sat.

"You are too generous, but—"

"No, I am not; I expect our evening to ultimately be to our mutual benefit."

She loosened the tie around her waist and let her dressing gown fall. He had presumed she would be *déshabillé*, but was taken aback to see she was entirely naked save for her slippers.

He made a pointed and, in his mind, valiant effort to keep his attention on her face. Her blue eyes were clear, bright, and without a shred of passion shining from them. The wish again passed through him that she would change her mind and go.

Miss Fisher put her arms around his neck. Darcy knew he ought to pull her against his body and bring his mouth to hers, but he looked into her blue eyes and felt nothing. *Am I the sort of man who uses a woman, no matter how willing, in this way?*

His pressing doubts grew stronger, but how would sending her away help him forget Elizabeth?

"Your cousins are concerned for you." His mind spun at the change in topic. "They told me you are an exacting man, and I shall have you know that I am proficient at what I do." She then knelt in front of him and slowly dragged her fingernails up his thighs.

"Good God," he breathed, closing his eyes. His heart hammered against his ribs.

Darcy wanted to indulge in the dull ache of desire that had been present since Elizabeth stayed at Netherfield, but wondered how many other men had paid Miss Fisher for the same privilege. *Elizabeth will never be alone with me like this.* His eyes still closed, he felt her touch the buttons on his breeches.

"Do you want me to take these off?"

Darcy's hands clenched the bed clothes. "Yes, Elizabeth!"

Her hands withdrew, and Darcy blinked open his eyes. She stood bare before him; her eyes were icy and pitiless. He did not know why she did it, but he was relieved she stepped away. Annoyance at the situation had replaced lust, and reality and his principles resumed their proper place in his mind. *This is not who I am.*

"Miss Fisher, we ought not to go through—"

"So you do recall my name! Who is Elizabeth?"

Recognition of his unintentional slight dawned and gave way to shame. "I—I can say nothing to defend myself."

"I shall not be a friend to a man who cannot remember my name!" she shrieked.

"I do know your name…" Darcy, as he always did when under tension, felt compelled to pace, but the enraged, unrobed courtesan stood directly before him.

"But you wish that I was her, this Elizabeth? I am an exceedingly desired courtesan; my *conversation* is coveted by men of rank. To be *seen* with me will raise a man's status. I will be the mere instrument of pleasure to no man!"

"I had no intention of insulting you while I availed myself… You are nothing like her." As soon as he said this, he knew it would not help.

"If you are not entirely mine for the time that I am in your bed, then I shall certainly not be yours!" She drew her dressing gown around her, flung open the door, and was gone.

Darcy felt all the justice of her anger. How had he allowed things to progress as far as they did? *What has gone wrong with my life?*

He pressed his fingers against his temples, a headache throbbing in his skull. Although he was ashamed he had said Elizabeth's name, he was more ashamed at having been drawn in by Miss Fisher at all. He was disgusted with himself for what he had almost allowed to happen.

His chamber was now deserted and was once again occupied by only his lonely, pensive self.

DARCY AWOKE ON SATURDAY MORNING WITH THE SAME SHAME HE had faced the night before. It was raining, but Darcy ordered his horse as early as possible. He was anxious to avoid Miss Fisher and return to Pemberley. He could not defend his conduct, and he had no reason to believe she would conceal his insult from the others. It was best that he contrive a reason to draw him back to Pemberley to save the shreds that remained of his dignity.

I should never have come here.

He hurried to leave without encountering another person, but his hopes were dashed when Fitzwilliam rapped on the door and entered without being invited in.

"Am I to understand that you are leaving?"

"Yes."

His cousin widened his eyes and raised his hands in an open gesture of enquiry. Darcy ignored him and scanned the floor for his missing watch fob.

"Why?"

"Here it is." He bent to pick it up. After securing it, Darcy collected his correspondence to pack it when his cousin snatched it from his hands. Darcy reached to take it back, but Fitzwilliam stepped away and held it behind him.

"You are *leaving*? It is just dawn, and it is pouring. What to heaven are you thinking?"

"The dinner with my tenants is set for Tuesday, and I am needed."

"You are needed at Pemberley to plan a dinner with beef and plum pudding and as much liquor as can be had so your tenants pay their rent? Between Georgiana, Mrs Reynolds, and, let us not forget,

Lady Catherine, Pemberley may plan a respectable dinner without you departing early from your friends."

"I must pay my servants their wages, and I have not yet gone over the accounts."

"We both know you are lying."

"You may believe what you wish, but I am needed at home." Darcy suddenly stretched his arm around his cousin to seize back his letters. Fitzwilliam bounded away and put them in his other hand.

"We were to remain until Monday."

"You and Milton must remain and keep his carriage. I shall leave as soon as my horse is readied."

"You shall take your death of cold."

"Thank you, mother. Now may I have my letters?" Darcy darted forward to take them by surprise, but Fitzwilliam blocked him with the chair. "Damn it, I have had enough of your games!"

His cousin kept the chair between them as Darcy attempted to circle around. "And I have had enough of your evasion!"

Darcy gave an exasperated sigh. "I had a disagreement with Miss Fisher, and it would be in the best interest of both of us if I depart."

"No, you always do this. You storm off when you are angry or feel injured. No one else will tell you, but you have an unyielding temper. So consider your thoughts in whatever way you must, and when you are in a sounder mind, you can decide what is best to be done to reconcile with Miss Fisher."

Darcy gave a bitter laugh. "You may be right about my nature, but the damage is irreparable."

"You are too cross now to speak with Miss Fisher, but if you remain, you may repair the damage when you are calmer."

"I forgot her name!"

To his credit, the only hint of amusement Fitzwilliam portrayed was a brief twitch at one corner of his mouth. "That is not so bad. Your lady is named Caro."

"I did not *forget* her name… so much as call her by a different one."

His cousin swore. "You called out another woman's name while you were with one of society's most sought-after courtesans? Not the Hertfordshire woman?" Darcy nodded, and Colonel Fitzwilliam brought a hand to his forehead with another quiet curse. "It is not hopeless if you want another evening with her. She will not be pleased to let this story get abroad. We—"

"I was tempted, but—" Darcy clenched his jaw and looked away. "Fitzwilliam, I do not want her. I should not have come."

After a long moment, he tossed him his letters. "You are right; it would be mortifying for you to stay. We must go. Delay but an hour, and I—"

"No, you need not leave with me. You had better stay and enjoy the ladies' company until Monday."

"Of course I am leaving with you."

"You need not sacrifice two more days shooting and evenings with the ladies for my sake. I know how fond you are of good company."

"I am wounded that you think so little of me. How could I remain knowing you cannot stay under the same roof?"

"Milton will not be unendurable company. You can shoot with—"

"Milton can hang! Where do you think my loyalties lie?" Fitzwilliam's countenance expressed a mixture of umbrage and disappointment.

"I know," Darcy said wearily. "Forgive me; I do know where your loyalties lie." The bond between them was stronger than blood. "You are my most faithful friend, and I hope you know that there is nothing that *I* would not do for *you*. But it would be better for my mortified pride if you continued on at Harper and supported my claim that estate business called me home."

"Miss Fisher will tell about your..."—he cleared his throat—"error. They will not believe your story about a tenants' dinner."

"Their complaints and censure, which politeness will restrain in front of me, may burst forth after I am away. What they gossip about in private need not alarm me."

"I daresay it *will* distress you. The thought of it embarrasses you, but you will not be here to see it, and that is what matters."

"I have made an imprudent, horrible mistake. Employing this

courtesan, willing as she was, as a distraction from loneliness and regret ... it is not who I am."

"Go home, and I will talk at length on how Pemberley's tenant dinner could not be put on without your personal involvement."

Darcy gave his cousin a warm handshake in parting, hoping to express all the gratitude and fraternity he felt with only the firm grasp of his hand.

Chapter 30

Saturday, January 4
London

"I can ask the servant to take them in."

"No."

"It is not too late to put them in the post. In four hours, they shall make their way back here anyway."

"Jane's letter might, but I can see from here that Bingley's would not." *Charles's handwriting is terrible!*

"It is a proper attention that you pay a visit and deliver the letters," Mrs Gardiner gently admonished. "I will be back with the carriage in quarter of an hour."

Elizabeth was shown into a drawing room. Mrs Hurst was not at home, but Miss Bingley received her with a frown. Although Elizabeth knew they could find their greatest safety in silence, she was seized by the desire to be as cheerful and engaging as Miss Bingley was aloof and resentful.

"My dear Miss Bingley, I hope you can forgive me for not calling sooner. Neither Jane nor my mother could be spared, so I have come to London in their stead. Also, I am sure you know Charles is reluctant to be parted from Jane."

"Indeed. I presume you have a letter from my brother?"

"I have letters from him and from your future sister. The Bennet girls are pleased to be gaining a brother. I hope the joy you feel on the occasion is comparable."

Miss Bingley ignored her overtures. "I trust your friends in Hertfordshire are well."

"Yes, very well, I thank you." Elizabeth proceeded in the way Jane would behave. "I trust London agrees with your sister and Mr Hurst." Miss Bingley bowed. "Your brother is eagerly awaiting his wedding, and my friend Charlotte Lucas shall be wed next week."

"It is a shame you did not secure Mr Collins for yourself; it would have been a credit to your family to have two daughters married. Your mother had many things to say on that subject."

"I understand you are to attend the wedding! We should be glad to have you stay at Longbourn, since Netherfield will have a new mistress, and I am certain you would not wish to be in Jane's way."

Elizabeth bit the inside of her cheek to keep from laughing at Miss Bingley's shocked expression. "We are to stay at Netherfield and will return to town immediately after the ceremony."

"You are quite right. I see no reason to stay since Charles and Jane shall depart for Brighton after a few days."

They sat in silence several moments before her hostess said, "I presume you will attend Jane to the church to see her hand bestowed upon my brother. Has my brother said who will stand as his groomsman?"

She wants to know if Mr Darcy will be there. How it must gall her to ask me! "Charles asked Mr Darcy, but I do not know his answer." Mr Darcy would not wish to be near to her, nor near to where Mr Wickham would be, no matter how steady his friendship with Charles.

"Of course Mr Darcy would accept! You do not understand his character as well as I. He and Charles are close friends, and the distance to be travelled can be of no consequence for a man such as he. Mr Darcy may soon enter into that honourable estate himself.

One wedding tends to beget another, they say." Her words were made in the menacing tone of a warning.

"I have heard it from several quarters that Mr Darcy is expected to marry his cousin, Anne de Bourgh." Miss Bingley blanched. "Mr Collins has a living granted by Lady Catherine de Bourgh, and he has spoken of their union. One of the militia officers, whose father was steward to the late Mr Darcy, also said Mr Darcy was to marry Miss de Bourgh. And Charles mentioned that Mr Darcy was particularly close to her."

"It is only *wished* that he marry his cousin; he may choose elsewhere. When he does, I hope you are not disappointed when Mr Darcy never again shows you the partiality he showed you in the autumn."

"I imagine Mr Darcy's recent visit with Miss de Bourgh has led him to find in his cousin's society all that he wants in a wife, a lady with superior connexions untainted by trade."

"You ought to look upon Mr Darcy's former attentions towards you as something extraordinary, almost undeserved." Miss Bingley had abandoned all pretence of civility.

"I am satisfied with the acquaintance. But you, my dear Miss Bingley! You must be mortified at the thought of his marrying Miss de Bourgh when you unashamedly courted him, even though it was plain how little he liked your attentions. Only think of how much time and effort you wasted on a man who never admired you! I hope time heals your wounds."

Miss Bingley's triumphant look slipped away; she was so incensed she could not speak. *That was scarcely more dignified than a brawl in the garden where we tear and scratch at each other's hair and skirts.* There was an exquisite pleasure in subduing such an insolent girl, but Elizabeth did her best to keep her jubilant spirit from showing in her expression.

A glance at her watch showed that fourteen minutes had passed, and Elizabeth stood before the servant opened the door to announce the carriage. All was over.

Mrs Gardiner enquired as to the nature of the call. "It was evident Miss Bingley had no pleasure in it. After I presented the letters, all we did was sit and gape at one another as dull as two cats."

Monday, January 6
Pemberley

THERE WAS NOTHING SO GLADDENING, SO CONSOLING TO DARCY AS being *home*. Pemberley was more than its picturesque grounds and its spacious apartments. It was not merely a handsome stone building with beautiful prospects. Evidence of the long and continuous wealth and power of the Darcy family was ever-present, but more important to its master was its being a place of serenity and happiness.

Darcy stood outside the music room, watching his sister's nimble fingers fly over the instrument. It was the piano sonata Fitzwilliam had presented to her less than a week ago.

"She is an accomplished girl," a voice interrupted Darcy's thoughts. Fitzwilliam was standing behind him; it was clear he had just alighted from Milton's carriage.

The 'how d'ye do's were quiet on each side. They listened to Georgiana for a few moments before the colonel asked, "How did she get on with her ladyship?"

"Mrs Annesley said she had never before seen a girl literally play or sing all day long, and she had to force Georgiana to join the ladies. However, she said Georgiana rose to the occasion and engaged her aunt in conversation more than she was known to do. How useful *your* parting advice was is best left unexamined."

"There is nothing to be said against both of her guardians advising her."

"I suggested Georgiana provide Lady Catherine the topic on which to give advice. I am now to learn that you told her to 'just let the old bat play quadrille as much as she likes.'"

Fitzwilliam laughed so loudly that they were obliged to step away from the music room. "Both of our pieces of advice were sound!" They made their way towards Fitzwilliam's apartments. "Shall I tell you how you were spoken of at Harper?"

"No."

"It was not as injurious to you as I imagined it would be."

"I need not hear about it."

"You need not be anxious that the story will get abroad. Of course, Miss Fisher hates you."

"Miss Fisher has an unceasing attention to her own self-interest, and I need not hear another word about it." He was unsure whether the shame of calling out Elizabeth's name was greater than the shame of being prepared to use a courtesan at all; regardless, it was not his finest moment. *It was perhaps my worst moment.*

"I think you need to find a wife and be done with it. Anne is single," Fitzwilliam added with a mischievous smile.

"Ought I to do my duty and marry Anne?"

"What? No! You would gain not only such a wife but such a mother-in-law. Lady Catherine would always be with you at Pemberley, advising, managing, noticing, and judging."

"Marrying Anne is what I have been told to do all of my life, that I owe it to my family to unite our fortunes."

"Anne is destitute of sensibility or affection for anything that cannot be poured from a bottle."

"Perhaps by living at Pemberley rather than Rosings, she may, over time, become less reliant on her tonics."

"You cannot believe that!" Fitzwilliam walked to his own apartments and, upon opening the door, gestured Darcy inside. "Look me in the eye and tell me you believe that marrying Anne would make any difference in her habits."

Darcy could not forget the missing laudanum. "No, I have no hope for her." To deprive her of opium would lead to Anne's excruciating suffering, as well as cause such depression of spirits that would as likely end in a miserable death as not.

"Why would you even consider marrying Anne?"

"Elizabeth Bennet is marrying another man, yet I am under the influence of an attraction that overmasters me. Maybe by marrying, by adhering to the vows I would make before man and God, I could detach her from my mind and from my heart."

Fitzwilliam shook his head. "You will be more miserable with Anne that you will be without this Bennet girl, you know that."

"Then what shall I do?"

"You are the romantic—do anything but marry without affection." A glance at his cousin's face was enough for Darcy to realise he was considering his own affairs.

"Did you—did you never tell Mary …" Fitzwilliam clenched his jaw and exhaled. Darcy made a slight bow and murmured, "Forgive me."

"Mary was intended for Milton," Fitzwilliam said before Darcy could leave, "ever since they were in their cradles. *Our* feelings were not about to get in the way of an alliance approved of, and promoted by, our family."

"You never made your proposals?"

"She wished to keep me from an absolute declaration, as it would have led to a painful conclusion of our present acquaintance. You know her tranquil temperament. Mary was told to wed Milton or she would be thrown off forever. How could a woman of her nature oppose such an injunction? She could not take a stand against parental authority, not even for us."

"How do you tolerate the disappointment?"

"I have the pleasure of seeing her content with her home and children. Although Milton has no affection for her, he does not treat her unkindly. It is his inconstancy, his indifference, to such a lovely creature that I cannot tolerate."

Colonel Fitzwilliam then begged for privacy, and Darcy knew the subject would not be raised between them again. Darcy lamented the sad fate of the new Mrs Collins. He was no longer angry at her for submitting to her parents' demands that she marry the heir to her home, only distressed by the truth that, unlike Fitzwilliam, it was impossible for his lost love to be happy in her lot.

Wednesday, January 8

"While to listen well is as important as to speak well, Georgiana, it is not enough to simply listen. You must endeavour to seem interested in the conversation of others."

Darcy gave his sister a wink in sympathy from across the breakfast table. The letters were brought in, and among them was one for Lady Catherine, which brought a reprieve from her advice. Darcy looked through his own letters and saw another from Bingley. *I need to explicitly deny Bingley's request to be his groomsman.* Although Bingley's handwriting was atrocious, Darcy was able to read that the date of his wedding to Jane Bennet was the fifteenth of January.

"It is ill timed that I cannot be at Rosings this week," Lady Catherine said. "The reverend of my parish is to be wed tomorrow, and they are departing for Hunsford from the church door. The new Mrs Collins shall be in her new home a week before I will be able to advise her on how to set up her establishment."

Darcy pushed his plate away. The foreknowledge of the unfortunate event did not make the acceptance of the unhappy truth more tolerable.

"I remember you saying that you had done a great deal to the house before the current incumbent moved into it," Georgiana said.

Of all the times Darcy had wished his sister would take up the conversation, this was not the one to prolong.

"I personally approved of the alterations he made. Naturally, I suggested several of my own; the closets needed my particular attention. As I have overseen the improvement of his dwelling, there will be nothing his new bride will find wanting."

Darcy brought his letter closer to his eyes, trying to use the sheets to shield himself from Lady Catherine's words.

"Are you acquainted with the young lady?"

"She is not known to me, but I advised Mr Collins on how to choose. I have been assured that Miss Lucas is an active, useful sort of gentlewoman."

"Miss Bennet," Darcy corrected.

"I beg your pardon?"

Darcy set down his letter to see his aunt scrutinising him with her usual haughty air. "The name of the family at Longbourn, which is entailed to Mr Collins, is Bennet, not Lucas."

"I know very well who my clergyman is to marry, and it is *not* one of the Miss Bennets. I understand there are many, and all of them out before the eldest is married, a shocking thing." Her ladyship shook her head.

Darcy was unable to reckon how his aunt, who—for all her pride and officiousness—was not an unintelligent person, could be so mistaken. "Mr Collins is to marry Miss Elizabeth Bennet, the second daughter of the Longbourn family."

"I am surprised that, simply because you met Mr Collins while you resided in the same neighbourhood, you believe your knowledge to be equal to mine! Mr Collins had *intended* to choose one of his cousins, but they were all brought up too high for his liking, and tomorrow he is marrying a sensible woman named Charlotte Lucas. Her father has been knighted."

Darcy was overcome by a sickening sensation of falling, a dizzying feeling as though being on a ship that had tilted sharply to one side. "Mr Collins is marrying Miss Lucas? That cannot be true."

"Let this be a lesson to you, Georgiana, that one ought not to speak on subjects about which one knows nothing."

"Mr Collins is marrying Miss *Lucas*?"

"Did I not just say it was so? I am excessively attentive to all matters that concern me."

"Miss Lucas? Not Miss Bennet, but Miss Lucas? Say it again, madam. Is Mr Collins to wed Charlotte Lucas or Elizabeth Bennet?"

"What is the matter with you? You have heard me say more than once that Mr Collins shall marry Miss Lucas."

Darcy stood and marched around the table. "Show me the letter." He held out his hand.

"I shall do no such thing!"

"Show me the letter!"

"Your behaviour is alarming, and I am ashamed of you!"

"Lady Catherine, I *insist*—"

"Darcy, did you not say that you had to review your week's accounts?" Colonel Fitzwilliam interjected. "Please, do not let us detain you a moment."

Darcy tore his gaze from the paper his aunt held in her hands and glanced at those around the table. The others were staring at him in mute astonishment.

Recollecting himself, he bowed and nearly ran through Pemberley's corridors until he reached his study. He tore through his correspondence, looking for the letter he had received from Bingley while he was still in London. "Damn it, where is it?" Darcy was still searching when Fitzwilliam burst into the room.

"What the hell was—"

"Here it is! Fitzwilliam, read this. It is from Bingley. Read it." He thrust the sheets into his cousin's hand.

"There is no reason for me to read another man's—"

"Read it *now*!"

Fitzwilliam squinted at the paper and held it further from his eyes, then closer. "Is this even English? I cannot read this."

"Read it, here, the bottom of the second page." Darcy stabbed the sheet with his finger. "What does it say?"

Fitzwilliam brought it closer to the light. Darcy watched him mouth the words in an attempt to discern them. "He writes something about one wedding begetting another, although he misspelled wedding. 'Miss Lizzy did not …' I cannot read it, something about Mr Collins. 'Missus …' presumably that reads 'Bennet'? 'Mrs Bennet wishes her daughters to be settled.' Then *someone* accepted Mr Collins, and they are to … do *something* in the new year, maybe 'marry' although it looks like he wrote 'many.'"

"Who!" Darcy shouted. "Who accepted Mr Collins?"

Fitzwilliam stared at the page, shaking his head. "Darcy, there are so many inkblots. It might say Lucas, but to be honest, to me, it looks like smear of ink."

Darcy fell into a chair. His heart was pounding so quickly that he actually raised a hand to his chest as though he could slow it by applying pressure. Despite the fire in the grate, he felt cold and his breathing came in rapid, shallow bursts.

"Throughout his letter, Bingley referred to Elizabeth Bennet as Lizzy, Miss Lizzy, or Miss Elizabeth." Darcy shook his head. "I thought Bingley wrote that Miss Lizzy accepted Mr Collins."

"Good God! Your lady refused her cousin, and he is to marry another?"

Darcy's quickened pulse was a tangible response to his great distress. "I left in anger but had every intention of returning with Bingley." A wave of nausea washed over him, and he held his head in his hands. "She refused that fool and must have expected me to return, that after we had reconciled, I would make my proposal. But a gentleman should retire from the field, especially since she chose another man to oblige her family. An engagement is a binding, legal agreement... She must now think that, after we quarrelled about Mr Wickham, I could not love her! What shall I do?"

"You are asking me? I counselled you to find a mistress, and that ended in disaster."

Darcy looked up. "I have nothing to deserve the name of hope, do I?" *Elizabeth might never forgive me for leaving, for presuming that she compromised her integrity and agreed to marry Mr Collins.*

"Hope? You are *bewitched*." He spoke the word as though it tasted foul in his mouth. "I cannot imagine that this Miss Bennet is worth this torment."

The tormenting idea Darcy could not get rid of was that Elizabeth would justly hate the sight of him. But to go through the rest of his life not knowing if she could ever love him would torment him more.

Darcy rose and rang the bell with a forceful pull. When the servant entered, Darcy told him, "I need a messenger to take a letter to Netherfield as soon as one can be found. Book his passage to Meryton in Hertfordshire, and I want him there before the end of the day tomorrow. Order my carriage and tell my man to prepare; we are leaving for Hertfordshire now."

Fitzwilliam waited until the servant left before he exclaimed, "Do you not see how hopeless the business is? She must hate you."

"I am not returning for Miss Bennet, but I do have much to apologise for. My purpose is to expose Wickham. I could not prevent Georgiana's suffering, but Miss Bennet's sisters and friends will be more fortunate. I will also tell Miss Bennet about Ramsgate. It was my mistaken pride that prevented me from trusting her fully before. She still believes Wickham to be a reformed friend deserving of her compassion."

"You would tell Miss Bennet about Ramsgate now? It would be

one thing if she was your wife, but—forgive me to say something that will pain you—you are less than nothing to her now."

"I owe Miss Bennet my apology for not telling her the whole truth. I thought I could not risk exposing Georgiana, but Wickham's claims of reformation make it necessary for me to refute him before another young lady is importuned."

"You are going to travel *three days* to tell a small neighbourhood of people who mean nothing to you that one of the officers quartered nearby is a scoundrel? I am scandalised. And what is the servant on the mail coach delivering?"

During these speeches, Darcy had sat at the desk, writing a short letter without his usual deliberation. He blotted the single sheet and, after folding and sealing it, set it aside for the servant.

"Bingley is getting married on the fifteenth, and he asked me to stand as his groomsman. I must send an express so he knows I will be there after all, or he may enlist another friend."

Fitzwilliam rolled his eyes. "You would witness Bingley's wedding after all the trouble his poor handwriting caused you? You are on a fool's errand, and you have my pity, but if it helps you to put the matter behind you, so be it." Darcy was lost in thought, but could feel his cousin peering into his face. "I say, whatever is the matter?"

Darcy did not answer; he was remembering the evening Caroline Bingley called at his home.

"*Miss Bingley, am I to now understand that Mr Collins has proposed to Miss Elizabeth Bennet and she* accepted *him?*"

"*Mr Collins proposed to Eliza Bennet, and he is now engaged. You amuse me, sir! Is that not what I have been telling you?*"

Darcy recalled her words with increasing fury. *Oh, she is an iniquitous, cunning woman.* Miss Bingley's deceit was unforgivable.

"Nothing," Darcy replied. "I just realised that I shall have another matter to set to rights when I arrive in Hertfordshire."

Chapter 31

Friday, January 10
Gracechurch Street

*E*lizabeth read the letter from her mother with relief. Elizabeth's fortnight in town had brought her some peace from the affair with Mr Wickham, and the end of the letter made the idea of her homecoming tomorrow more agreeable:

> ...Mr Wickham and none of the officers have been here since. It shall be up to our dear Bingley to throw my girls in the way of worthier, richer men. No officer is ever to enter my house again! I shall tell all who listen what a wicked...

It was of course unlikely that *no* officers had come to the house, but at the least, she could be assured she would not encounter Mr Wickham before Jane and Charles married on Wednesday and she left with them for Brighton.

Saturday, January 11

THE WEATHER AND ROAD CONDITIONS HAD BEEN SO MUCH IN Darcy's favour that he had decided to press on to his townhouse rather than remain overnight at an inn. It was an easy distance, and he gratified himself by sleeping in his own home rather than a comfortless inn crowded with billeted soldiers.

However, Darcy rued his self-indulgence the following morning. There had been a frost overnight, and the muddy roads had frozen into hard, dangerous tracks. His carriage rumbled along the icy roads, lurching dangerously as the wheels slid into the ruts.

Darcy suspected they had less than ten miles until they reached Netherfield when his coachman stopped. Had the cold wind not been lashing against his landau, Darcy would have been more inclined to see for himself what had happened. Several minutes passed before his coachman came to the door.

"There is a carriage ahead that has come unto an accident, sir."

"Was anyone injured?"

"I don't know who remains inside, sir, but the gentleman appears to have sprained his ankle."

"Is his carriage in our way?"

"No, but I shall have to walk the horses around."

Darcy looked out the side glass, but did not see a dwelling within an easy distance. "We cannot leave them on the side of the roadway in this wind. They shall be obliged to wait for hours for another carriage if their man is forced to walk for help. I can transport their party to Meryton, so long as there are no more than three of them."

"Very good. Shall I speak for you, sir?"

"No, I will speak to them myself." Darcy alighted and walked towards the coach, which was at a forty-five-degree angle to the road and whose horses had been untethered and were now in a field. As Darcy got closer, he saw the front of the carriage was bent too low and the box was lurched unnaturally forward.

It was the vehicle of a family man rather than a bachelor. Its owner was leaning against the fence and looking at the carriage, discussing with his man what was best to be done. He appeared to be ten years older than Darcy and carried himself with the air of a gentleman, and his clothes and manner spoke the same.

Not a rich man, but a man of means; he has a manservant and keeps a carriage. Easily two thousand a year, perhaps three?

As Darcy bowed, he noticed the man appraise him and his own carriage and servants in the same manner.

"Forgive me for stopping your progress, sir." The stranger gave a genial smile as he touched his hat. "I think there is room for your team to pass."

"Are any of you injured?"

"Neither of the rest of my party feels more than shaken and bruised. It is I who suffered the greatest injury. I leapt down with the energy of a younger man and sprained my ankle when I slipped on the ice. If you relate this story to others, perhaps you would be so good as to say I injured myself in the course of saving my wife from being tossed about in the carriage."

Darcy was unsure what to say to this playful request, and merely bowed. He walked to the front of the carriage and bent to look underneath. "I think the spring of the box has broken, and the axle is cracked."

"The whole roadway was one mass of depressions, causing the wheels to fly about in all directions. When the axle cracked, the horses bolted, though they are a docile pair and only went a short distance. My groomsman was able to rein them in and cut them loose."

"You are fortunate, otherwise I think the horses may have kicked the coach apart." Darcy shuddered at the thought of a pair of frightened horses tethered to a carriage, furiously kicking and killing the occupants trapped inside.

"I had hoped to hire a carriage rather than risk mine, but my wife preferred the familiarity of her own. Although, if I remind her that I *told her* we ought to have followed my plan, more than my ankle would be hurting."

Darcy smiled. The man's manners were not fashionable, but they were engaging. "I do not have equal knowledge of what would make a wife happy, but I suspect you are correct to err on the side of caution. May I ask how many are in your party?" Darcy thought their coach seated six, but he would only have space to seat three more.

"Two others, my wife and my niece. I know they ought not to remain in the carriage with the axle broken, but this cold wind is too much for them to endure."

He could easily tolerate an hour in the carriage with an amiable gentleman, his wife, and a child. He may not enjoy the company of strangers, but he was not about to allow a lady and a little girl to freeze by the roadside. "Please allow me to be of assistance to you. It is in my power to take you as far as Meryton."

The customary refusal ensued, followed by a second request to be of use, followed by a second civil refusal, and finally a third request that was gratefully accepted.

"I am obliged to you." The man attempted to bow, but remembered his ankle and instead touched his hat. "Would you permit me to add one of our trunks to your carriage? The remainder can wait, but my wife will look on me in silent disapproval if she does not have a gown for dinner."

Darcy glanced at the rear of the coach. "I am travelling alone; you are welcome to load everything. I have no doubt of there being room." The other man limped forward, stifling a grimace. Darcy held up a hand to stop him. "Please allow me to oversee everything while you tell your party of our plans."

"To whom is he speaking?"

"I cannot hear their conversation over this wind. We are turned at such an angle from the road that I cannot see either of them." Mrs Gardiner craned her neck as she leaned against the side glass.

"I hope the gentleman can take John to the next coaching inn." Elizabeth huddled beneath a rug. "We cannot expect him to walk eight miles in this wind to hire another carriage."

Mr Gardiner then appeared at the door. "Mary, Lizzy, we have had good luck! A gentleman has come upon us and has agreed to take us all to Meryton."

"Who is he, Edward?"

"We spoke of the carriage, not one another. His landau is one of the finest I have seen. He offered to take all of us to Meryton. We can send a message to my brother and have him send his coach to meet us."

"You have no doubts as to this man being a gentleman?"

"His dress, his servants, and his carriage all speak to his affluence. I would not be surprised if he was coming from his house in town. He seems a polite young man, and a generous one to offer to help a stranger. He is a little stately in his air, but it is not unbecoming. I shall ask his name at once and introduce you."

Mrs Gardiner glanced at Elizabeth, who shrugged in agreement. Far better to sit across from a gentleman stranger and arrive in Meryton in an hour than sit along the road in a broken carriage while the wind sliced through them.

Mr Gardiner assisted the ladies out of the coach as best he could with his sprained ankle. Servants were in the process of loading their trunks. Mr Gardiner hobbled towards the landau to speak to the gentleman while Elizabeth and her aunt used the broken coach to block as much of the wind as possible.

"Mary!" Mr Gardiner called, and the ladies walked towards the front of the landau just as its owner came around the side after overseeing the storage of their trunks. "I have learned the name of our preserver. May I present—"

"Mr Darcy!"

"Miss Bennet?"

He was obviously struck and confused by the sight of her. She took in a quick breath, while his eyes widened and his mouth hung open. He stared at her in undisguised amazement.

"You are acquainted with this gentleman, Lizzy?" Mr Gardiner smiled, but Elizabeth said nothing, for she was suffering the blinding, bewildering effects of strong surprise. "Mary, may I present our preserver, Mr Darcy? Mr Darcy, my wife, Mrs Gardiner—and I see that you are acquainted with my niece, Miss Elizabeth Bennet."

Mrs Gardiner curtseyed, and after a long moment, Darcy managed to raise his hand to his hat, all the while staring at Elizabeth, who then took an interest in the ruts in the road.

Mr Gardiner suggested they remove the ladies from the wind.

With this gentle reminder, Darcy spoke, if not in terms of perfect composure, at least in perfect civility.

"It is my pleasure to make your acquaintance, Mrs Gardiner. I am delighted to see you again, Miss Bennet." She felt his gaze piercing into her, but nothing could induce her to raise her eyes. "I am certain you are all desirous of getting out of this wind. Mrs Gardiner, may I?"

I do not know how to act with him! Her conflicting desires pulled against one another: one wishing the frozen ground would open up to swallow her, and the other wishing Darcy would return her embrace were she to throw herself into his arms.

Once inside, he entered into conversation with her aunt and uncle with ease. She was surprised at his friendliness with two people he had never before seen.

"You are a friend to Jane's betrothed? What a coincidence to find ourselves travelling the same road at the same time! We met Bingley at Christmas and found him to be a pleasant young man," said Mr Gardiner.

"We have had a steady friendship these three years. I am honoured that he thought so highly of our attachment to ask me to be his groomsman. He is fortunate in his choice of a wife; Miss Bennet will be a credit to him and make him very happy."

"Jane is a sweet girl, and I am certain of their doing well together. I presume you were in town if you were able to come down to Meryton?"

"No, I was at my home in Derbyshire until Wednesday."

"That is a long journey for the sake of a wedding. You are a loyal friend. My wife is from Derbyshire. What was the name of the village your friends are from, my dear?"

"Lambton." Darcy's eyes lit up with interest. "I am familiar with Pemberley and its reputation, Mr Darcy. It is a lovely estate, though I have only seen it from a distance."

The next fifteen minutes were passed with Darcy giving her aunt fresh intelligence of the area. Elizabeth longed to know in what manner he thought of her and whether, in defiance of her misplaced faith in Mr Wickham, she was still dear to him. *What an irrational wish.* The only suitable thing to say to him was to apologise for not trusting his judgment regarding Mr Wickham, but it could not be done before her aunt and uncle.

Elizabeth was looking out the side glass when she heard the deep timbre of his voice say her name. His countenance was as she had remembered it: noble, handsome, and with expressive eyes that at this moment were boring into her with such intensity that she could not look away.

"I was recently informed Charlotte Lucas is now married."

"Yes," she replied, not pleased with the rough sound of her own voice. "Yes, she married my cousin, Mr Collins, last Thursday."

"I believe Mrs Collins will find her new home to be a comfortable house. Lady Catherine was telling me only on Wednesday that a great deal had been done to it when Mr Collins first came to Hunsford." Elizabeth made no answer. "I had ample opportunity to speak with the former Miss Lucas when I last dined at Longbourn. She is a sensible woman."

Mrs Gardiner was now eyeing Darcy appraisingly. Elizabeth did not reply to him until her aunt touched her arm. "My friend has an excellent understanding, and though at first I was not certain her marrying Mr Collins was the wisest thing she ever did, it is a good match, and I hope she will be happy."

"Were you recently in this neighbourhood, Mr Darcy?" asked Mrs Gardiner. "You mentioned that you dined at Longbourn, but we were with my sister and brother over Christmas and did not have the pleasure of then making your acquaintance."

"I spent two months with Bingley in the autumn. The last time I was at Longbourn was on the twenty-first of November. I—I left the neighbourhood shortly thereafter."

Her aunt could be in no doubt that it was Darcy who was the friend of Bingley's she had fallen in love with, then driven away.

Chapter 32

Sunday, January 12

Darcy rode up the lawn to Longbourn at a gallop, in one swift motion dismounted and tossed the reins to the servant, and strode to the door. *What is right to be done cannot be done too soon.* Darcy tugged on the house-bell with a forceful pull. He asked to see Mr Bennet on a matter of business.

Darcy's determined stride stopped short when he saw Mr Gardiner in the room. He sat with a newspaper, his injured foot elevated on a stool. After greeting Mr Bennet, he addressed the invalid.

"I hope you are well on your way to recovery."

"I am not a desperate case," he replied cheerfully. "The apothecary assures me I will be up and about within a week, although I will have to lean on my wife for support if I wish to go farther than a few steps."

"Have you not a cane?"

"I did not bring my walking stick to Meryton, and my brother does not hold to such... how did you call them?"

"Such *tonnish* affectations, is what I said," muttered Mr Bennet, who did not look up from his folio.

"In that case, I shall be happy to loan you mine."

"I shall not put you to any further trouble. I am already indebted to you, sir."

"I must insist on being of further use to you." Over the course of yesterday's carriage ride, Darcy had come to think well of Mr Gardiner and his easy manners. He had had ample time to converse with Mr and Mrs Gardiner since Elizabeth scarcely opened her lips.

No doubt my appearance took her as much by surprise as hers did to me. Once he was master of himself, he had wished to confess all, but the presence of her aunt and uncle, of course, made that impossible. He would make the most of the next half hour in which he could command her attention, so long as he could speak with her alone.

But first I must deal with Wickham.

Darcy still stood, for he had not yet been invited to sit. He was unsure whether this was an intentional slight or due to Mr Bennet's inability to focus on anything other than the printed word.

"Mr Bennet, I must speak with you on a matter of business."

Mr Bennet looked up, surprised, and set aside his spectacles and invited him to sit. "I presumed you called to make your personal inquiries to Gardiner. What else brings you to Longbourn?"

I wish to throw myself upon the mercy of your second daughter. "It is not in my nature to speak of news and scandal. However, in the present case, I would be doing your family a disservice—a further disservice—by remaining silent. One of the militia officers, Mr Wickham, is not a man to be trusted."

Mr Bennet's shoulders fell, but he remained silent. "I have been acquainted with Mr Wickham for my entire life, and his worthlessness ought to have been made known by me when I was here in the autumn. I am here to remedy that evil and confess our history in order to safeguard your family."

"Upon my soul! I do not wish to hear a word about Mr Wickham!"

Darcy had expected to battle disbelief, not regard. "Forgive me for paining you, but it is my duty to confess what I know of Mr Wickham's true nature."

"What have you to say?"

"If you desire corroboration, I will arrange it, but he has a history of leaving considerable gaming debts wherever he goes. But more appalling than that is his history of intrigue and seduction. Although he may claim to be a changed man, he is not a man that any young woman ought to confide in."

"Gossip is Mrs Bennet's pursuit, not mine, but I think you shall find that this bit of old news will not even be of interest to her."

Darcy stared for a long moment. "Do you mean to tell me that Mr Wickham's worthlessness is *already* well known?"

"There was a commotion over nothing more than an unwanted advance, and Lizzy is none the worse for it. It is of no concern now since Mr Wickham does not come to Longbourn. If you wish to speak further on the subject, please call on my wife." Mr Bennet returned his spectacles to his nose and took up his book.

The only words Darcy could attend to were 'unwanted advance' and 'Lizzy'. They repeated in his mind, his stomach churning at the thought of that man laying a single gloved finger on Elizabeth Bennet. He barely suppressed the transports of rage that threatened to burst forth. If he gripped the chair arm any harder, it would break.

Darcy turned to Mr Gardiner. "What happened to Miss Elizabeth?"

"I understand the issue is resolved. It was not as dire as the neighbourhood gossips might wish it to be. Your kindly meant advice is not necessary as my sister has forbidden him from entering the house."

Darcy loosened his grasp on the chair arm slightly. His heart was still pounding angrily in his chest. "Is that true of the rest of the neighbourhood? Mr Wickham would not think twice of importuning a gentleman's daughter. If she were wealthy, he might wish to marry her, but …"

"I understand your meaning, and I thank you for your wish to do what is right by our family. May I ask, do you have another motive in wishing to preserve our family, and Lizzy, from such an unworthy acquaintance?" Mr Gardiner was more discerning than his brother-in-law.

"I could not allow Mr Wickham to insinuate himself into your family. It was the right thing to be done, and I ought to have spoken to Mr Bennet and the other gentlemen the day I met Mr Wickham in Meryton."

"I think Lizzy overreacted, but should you like to know more, you may now call on Mrs Bennet." Mr Bennet peered at him from over the top of his spectacles.

His dismissal could not be any clearer had Mr Bennet physically pushed him from the room.

Darcy found a servant in the vestibule, and he was admitted into the drawing room. Mrs Bennet was with her two youngest daughters; he repressed the desire to ask after Elizabeth. *What had his silence allowed Wickham to do?*

"Our dear Bingley did not join you today?" was the first thing Mrs Bennet said after they were seated. "He has been a daily visitor at Longbourn unless when some barbarous neighbour invites him to dinner."

At least she invited me to sit. "Bingley is dining out tonight, madam, but I know he intends to call tomorrow with his sisters after they arrive."

"It will make Jane so happy to see her friends again! Miss Bingley in particular has affection for my Jane. She is an elegant, gracious lady."

"She is a singular woman." He had become a victim of Caroline Bingley's cold-hearted ambition. She would be dealt with soon enough.

"Bingley was pleased to receive your express that you would be his groomsman," Mrs Bennet went on. "He was here at supper when your rider arrived Thursday night. I told him when his sisters arrive, they must join us for dinner that very night. You may come as well. Bingley scarcely needs an invitation, of course; he often comes before breakfast and remains until after supper."

If Darcy did not take charge, they would be speaking of Bingley for the entire fifteen minutes. "I came to tell your husband of the dissolute character of one the militia officers, but Mr Bennet informed me that Mr Wickham—"

"That dreadful Mr Wickham!"

"May I ask what happened to turn the general opinion against him?"

"Lizzy said you always knew him to be dreadful, but even you will be shocked to hear what he has done."

"It was not so bad!" Miss Lydia exclaimed. "'Tis a pity not to see the officers at Longbourn. Mr Wickham was an agreeable flirt."

"He is the wickedest man in the world, without a guinea to his name! Your brother Bingley will not tolerate the officers coming here after what Mr Wickham did, so you had best wait for him to put you into the path of his single friends."

"I want you girls to get good husbands, I can't think! Not a husband like one of those penniless officers! If only Lizzy had taken Mr Collins."

"I do not think there would be any fun in that," said Miss Lydia. "But Lizzy will be an old maid soon."

"If she had agreed to have Mr Collins, maybe Mr Wickham would not have—"

"You can hang, Kitty! Lizzy is not to blame for that man's behaviour."

Darcy could scarcely believe the turn of events that required him to solicit Mrs Bennet to share gossip with him. "Madam, will not you tell me what Mr Wickham has done?"

"He had the audacity to kiss Lizzy, although he was drunk, but that is no excuse."

"Mr Wickham kissed her?"

"Yes! It was not a game's forfeit or a mistletoe kiss. She was seated at the instrument, and he insulted her before everyone at our Christmas party! I did not see it myself, but Lizzy said it was terrible."

Darcy was torn between feeling tremendous relief that a kiss was all that had happened and tumultuous anger that Wickham had touched Elizabeth at all.

Mrs Bennet went on, perhaps enthused by having his complete attention. "Lizzy tried to keep the affair to herself, but she could not stand the sight of him, and once I knew the truth, I could not allow that man into our home. Besides, Bingley would not allow his sisters to be importuned by that scoundrel! Mr Bennet had little to say, but he trusts my judgment on these matters."

What a sad state of affairs that Mr Bennet has no interest in those who mix with his daughters.

"I came to tell Mr Bennet what I knew of his character, but I now see that my interference was not needed."

"I had always distrusted the appearance of his goodness."

Darcy found this difficult to believe. "I hope Miss Elizabeth will not often have to suffer his presence while the militia is in Meryton."

Miss Lydia cackled. "None of us shall see him again!"

The door then opened, and Miss Bennet and Elizabeth entered. They had been engaged in some amusing discussion and did not know their mother had company. Miss Bennet's smile fell, and Elizabeth's laughter faded as Darcy stood.

"Girls, I was telling Mr Darcy about that horrid Mr Wickham!"

Elizabeth closed her eyes and turned pink, and Miss Bennet led her to a chair, saying, "Mr Darcy is already familiar with how unworthy Mr Wickham is."

"He knew nothing of Mr Wickham's kissing Lizzy against her will!" Mrs Bennet turned to Darcy. "I know you told Bingley and Lizzy about Mr Wickham's past, but we all thought him reputable until he dared to kiss Lizzy in full view of a crowded room! He put his tongue in her mouth. What an outrage!"

Darcy watched Elizabeth clench her jaw and exhale loudly through her nose. She had a fair complexion that hinted at every emotion; he suspected she was holding back tears. Darcy felt a crushing sense of guilt at her misery. Yes, he had told her to be cautious of Wickham, but if he had told her about Ramsgate, she never would have believed that Wickham was reformed. *She was assaulted in her own home because I did not tell her the full truth!* He excused himself from Mrs Bennet and stood before Elizabeth.

"I am sorry for not making you fully acquainted with Mr Wickham's real character, Miss Elizabeth. I wish anything could be either said or done on my part to undo the distress he caused you."

She swallowed audibly. "There is no need for you to apologise. It is my fault for not taking you at your word."

"You are not at all to blame! At least he is not welcomed here or in the homes of your friends, and when the winter is over, the militia will be quartered elsewhere." He longed to say more, but Elizabeth gave no indication of wishing to engage with him. *What more could I expect from her after what I have done?*

"Mr Wickham is gone!" Miss Lydia laughed.

Darcy turned towards the younger girls, but they were engrossed in redecorating the bonnet. Mrs Bennet directed their efforts, and Elizabeth kept her head down while she picked at the threads of the handkerchief she clutched in her hands. He looked to Miss Bennet, who understood his questioning gaze.

"The other families soon knew about Mr Wickham's inappropriate advance and how Lizzy was sent to town. The other officers realised that whenever Mr Wickham was one of their party, they were not admitted in our homes. Within a week, he was cut from all respectable society."

A man such as Wickham, so lacking in inward reflection, and one so eager for gaming and women, could not be satisfied with seclusion. "Mr Wickham will not be content to reside in this area if he is isolated."

Miss Bennet asked for Kitty to bring her the newspaper that she was using to lay her flowers on, and then handed it to him. "Mr Wickham is no longer in the area at all." Darcy read a long list of names and remarks about those who left the militia regiment. At the bottom of the page he read:

DESERTED FROM THE ___TH REGIMENT OF THE __ MILITIA
WICKHAM, GEORGE LIEUTENANT. Age 26, standing 5ft 10in, grey eyes, light hair and fair complexion. Supposed in London

"Mr Wickham has deserted!" Darcy cried in surprise.

"What a joke!" Miss Lydia called. "Mr Denny says that Mr Wickham did not have money enough for a journey half so far as London. After what he did to Lizzy, he had no friends to help him.

Colonel Forster says that anyone deserting from his militia would find himself tried by a court martial and flogged!"

Mrs Bennet addressed Darcy. "So you see, we know what a wicked man he is. Your information was not needed."

Mrs Bennet dispatched Mr Wickham and preserved her family. Will wonders never cease?

Darcy spared a glance at Elizabeth, who did not look at him. She gave him no encouragement.

I am not needed here at all.

Although the hour was late, Elizabeth's mind was full of Darcy. She had expected to have months to recover from her disappointment before she was likely to see him again. At the least, she assumed she would know ahead of time about his visit to the Bingleys, whenever it came. But she was not even calm in his presence, let alone recovered enough to speak with him or think intelligently. As soon as she realised it was Darcy standing in the roadway, she was immediately struck by the same pang of loss, the same jolt of attraction, and the same love for him she had been feeling for months.

He came only to support his friend and preserve her family from an unworthy acquaintance. *But how does he feel as to our meeting?* When they sat across from one another in his carriage, when she was finally brave enough to look into his face, Darcy had looked at her with such a woeful countenance. It was not at all the same way his dark eyes had admired her at the Netherfield ball—before she had foolishly mentioned Mr Wickham. Six weeks passed since the ball, and Darcy was still in her mind—but nothing in his manner in the carriage or when he called the next day showed that he had any remaining affection for her.

Jane entered and interrupted her melancholic thoughts.

"Why do you look disheartened?" Jane asked. "Were you not pleased to learn that you shall never see Mr Wickham again? We had suspected he was gone, but it was not until Colonel Forster issued the deserters list that we were certain; otherwise I would have written to you."

"If I do see him again, I can turn him in and have twenty shillings for my troubles."

"I am sorry that I had not the opportunity to write and tell you to expect Mr Darcy. His letter arrived late on Thursday."

"It was a shock to see him on the side of the road, but now that the first real meeting is over, I feel almost easy."

"He seemed concerned for you. Do you think he may still be in love with you?"

"No, we shall henceforth meet as common acquaintances." Elizabeth strove to be cheerful. "Besides, our dissimilarity is so strong that we would never have been happy together."

"You have moral and literary tastes in common. You have both warm hearts and benevolent feelings. He is the only man of our acquaintance who has cleverness enough for you."

Darcy had given her no reason to believe that he still cared for her, and so Elizabeth concentrated on their differences. "No, our manners are too unlike except we are both quick to anger. I have a propensity to talk, and he has a propensity to be silent. It is for the best it came to nothing."

"There is a difference in your tempers, I allow; you are lively, he is serious, but so much the better because—"

"I defended the man who seduced his sister, after he warned me to avoid him! He may forgive me, but I saw no sign that he may still love me." Elizabeth changed the subject. "I have not stayed up to talk about my disappointed hopes…"

"I was instructed not to tell my sisters."

"Of course she would tell you that. Now what did my mother say?"

Jane sighed. "I do not think I learned anything."

"Our mother had nothing to say that you did not already know? Either she is the most ignorant married woman in England, or you have spent too much time alone with Charles."

"Lizzy!"

"She must have had some knowledge to impart before your wedding."

"My mother spent most of the time talking about what Charles would do."

Elizabeth scoffed. "You could have learned more by sitting beside Mrs Goulding and Mrs Long after they have drunk too much sherry."

"She said I ought not to judge it after the first or even second time. But when I asked her what *I* ought to do, she laughed and said, 'You won't have to do anything!' What is that supposed to mean?"

"Maybe it is one of those things that you will have to figure out for yourselves?"

"That sounds awful."

Elizabeth thought the process of discovery sounded marvellous. Her heart beat faster at the memory of only nearly kissing Darcy in Longbourn's breakfast room. The thought of his low voice saying her name before he was about to kiss her made a shiver run across her skin. Not that she had any reason to hope that he would love her after the way she had trusted Mr Wickham.

She realised that Jane was still looking at her and wanting advice. "You ought to speak to my aunt then."

"Not yet."

"You are getting married on Wednesday! It will do you little good to consult with her after!"

Jane nodded and left again; Elizabeth threw herself backwards to land on her pillows and stare at the ceiling. Jane and Bingley loved one another and were the kindest people she knew. She had no doubt they would grasp it before long.

Any thoughts of what it might feel like to have Darcy stretched out full-length upon her, their clothes discarded and his bare skin against hers, were useless.

Monday, January 13

"I HAVE HAD SUCH GOOD LUCK IN GETTING JANE OFF MY HANDS, and if I don't get one of my other girls married before the end of this year, it shall not be my fault." Mrs Bennet spared a glance at Elizabeth before returning to Miss Bingley. "I am certain your brother will speak a good word for my girls to all the young men he knows."

Elizabeth and Jane blushed at their mother's vulgarity. Tonight there was a party to gather the families before the wedding. Mr Gardiner wished to recuperate in his own home now that his carriage had been repaired, and he and his wife were concerned that the likelihood of snow would keep them at Longbourn longer than they wished if they did not leave right after the wedding. The Hursts and Miss Bingley also cited their fear of snow coming on, but Elizabeth knew they had other motives for departing as soon as possible. Although not a member of the soon-to-be-formed family, Darcy was included as well.

Desiring that not all of Darcy's precious feelings towards her were lost forever, Elizabeth hoped to re-establish an acquaintance with him. At length, the gentlemen returned to the drawing room, and last to enter were Darcy and Mr Gardiner. Her uncle was leaning on the walking stick that Darcy had lent him, and he matched their pace in order to continue their conversation. She was about to approach him, but her mother demanded that she, and not Mary, open the instrument.

While she played, Elizabeth followed Darcy with her eyes and envied everyone to whom he spoke. Her two songs were complete, and she begged Miss Bingley to indulge the group and succeed her. As Elizabeth walked towards the fire, she was stopped by her father.

"Mr Darcy seems more approachable than I remember him before, Lizzy. Not even you can criticise his conduct."

Elizabeth turned to hide a wince. "No, I dare not." Her father laughed and moved away.

Elizabeth was sensible of Darcy having a different manner towards her family, a manner of kindness and civility. *And none of that attention is turned towards me.*

"Miss Elizabeth?"

The object of her thoughts was standing next to her. Everything she wanted to talk with him about was off limits in this crowded room. After he stood by her in silence, he said, "If I am not mistaken, you are in possession of something that is mine."

Her heart leapt to her throat as she thought of the embroidered handkerchief with his initials. She was devastated by how much he must dislike her to demand its return.

"You still have Cowper's *The Winter's Evening*?" He gave a smile that made the commanding Mr Darcy look boyish and charming. It reminded her of her stay at Netherfield in November.

"Oh yes!" She gave a relieved laugh. "Shall I send a servant for it?"

He shook his head. "I mention it so that I might ask, if you do not find blank verse tiresome by now, would you like to read the succeeding volumes?"

"*The Task* is diverting. I could not tire of it."

"Shall I have it brought to you tomorrow?"

Elizabeth was disappointed he did not offer to bring it himself, but since she would be preoccupied with wedding preparations, it was just as well. "Yes, thank you; you are a generous friend."

"Friend?"

"Bingley and my sister are about to be united, and we will often find ourselves in each other's company. Do you not think it sensible for us to be friends?" If she could be secure of his friendship now, perhaps he might forgive her, and then someday love her again.

He looked at her a long moment before saying, "I have no pleasure in the world superior to that of contributing to yours." He bowed and moved away, and they did not speak again.

WHEN THE CARRIAGE RETURNED THEM TO NETHERFIELD, DARCY stormed into his apartments and tugged at his cravat, his fingers pulling uselessly until he gave up in frustration. He walked to the window and pressed his head against the cold glass with a forceful thud. He had hoped when he offered to send Elizabeth the Cowper volume, she would invite him to call.

Friend? How could he be satisfied with only being Elizabeth's friend? *When can I speak privately with her and explain the matter?* It would have to be at the wedding breakfast.

He turned from the window and at last managed to loosen his cravat and unfasten the waistcoat buttons. A better man would be content with her friendship after what his silence had allowed Wickham to do, after he had abandoned her. Darcy kicked off his shoes and sprawled out on his bed, still wearing his shirt and breeches. How could he be content to be her friend when every night he imagined her as his wife?

Illusory sensations flooded him as he visualised Elizabeth undressed before him. He easily imagined drawing her down onto the bed and kissing her, his hands honouring every curve and hollow. Her eyes always looked at him as though they penetrated to the core of his being, and he desperately wanted to see them gazing lustily at him. Darcy's heart rate increased and his invented Elizabeth made a small sound in her throat and her lips clung to his. He could pretend she was impatient with desire, yearning for his touch.

Lust and loneliness drove away the guilt and misunderstandings that stood between his fantasy and the truth of his situation with Elizabeth. When his passion burned out, so did his imagined Elizabeth, the one who still loved him.

Chapter 33

Tuesday, January 14

"What do you mean my brother has gone?" Miss Bingley exchanged a questioning glance with her sister, who entered the room with her. Hurst followed and went directly to the food laid out on the sideboard.

Darcy stifled a cringe at the interruption of his solitude. He had done his best to limit his interactions with Miss Bingley. For his friend's sake, he hoped to end his acquaintance with his sister through a more gradual, natural manner than by confrontation.

"Mr Bingley always departs for Longbourn before breakfast, ma'am."

Miss Bingley's mouth gaped in confusion as she took her seat. She dismissed the servant with a careless wave. "Calling *before* breakfast ... why, Louisa!"

Mrs Hurst shook her head in disapproval. Her husband filled his plate and lumbered to the table without a word.

"Mr Darcy, I cannot imagine you approve of this?"

"Your brother does not need my approval or anyone else's."

"Why must he be scampering to Longbourn at all hours to see Jane? After tomorrow, he will be able to see her as often as he pleases."

"It shows affection for his betrothed."

"Well, yes! I have an affectionate regard for Jane, do I not, Louisa?"

"Yes, you—"

"For my part, I cannot see any reason to stay for the wedding breakfast tomorrow. It is a mark of attention we travelled for the wedding at all."

Darcy flung down his cutlery. He wished for all the world to say what he thought of the scheming, meddlesome woman. No woman of proper feeling would behave the way Miss Bingley had; she was little better than Mr Wickham. Only by remembering that he was required to act in a gentlemanly manner towards his hostess was he able to keep from speaking his mind. He met the ladies' surprised stares with a curt bow and marched from the room.

Darcy went to the library, and had scarcely sat before Miss Bingley entered. He rose out of habit rather than courtesy, but stayed silent.

"You are kind to support my brother. It shows an affection for him, and our entire family, for which I am grateful. It will aid Charles's reputation as he makes Jane Bennet his wife."

"I will return to my book." He turned his back to her.

"Mr Darcy, you seem out of temper. Is it because you once again find yourself among people of such little consequence?" He spun around but stayed silent. "Is there nothing I might do to aid you?"

"Anything you can do?"

"As your friend, I worry for your well-being."

"*Friend?*"

"Of course! I consider the Darcy and Bingley families to be on the most intimate of terms." She laid a hand on his arm. Darcy drew back sharply, and his precarious hold on propriety and its dictates on how a gentleman speaks to a lady came crashing down.

"If, madam, you and I are intimate friends, I wonder why you chose to deceive me!"

"I do not understand you."

"Do you deny that you lied to me about Miss Elizabeth Bennet's engagement to her cousin? I find your artifice insulting and offensive."

Her little sharp eyes went full with comprehension. "It was a blunder. I was misinformed."

"You insult my intelligence. Do not abuse either my patience or my politeness."

Miss Bingley's face turned ashen. "I wished to preserve you from an unworthy alliance, to save you from an imprudent attachment."

"I did not wish to believe that an otherwise respectable lady would intentionally deceive me." Darcy shook his head and paced.

"You were in need of my assistance. You could not have known how disgracefully particular you had been with Eliza—"

He took two quick steps towards her. "You *dare* to presume to know my mind and my heart?"

"It would have been an unsuitable match, and I congratulate myself on preventing you from returning! You might have made a dreadful mistake. I could not preserve my own brother, but there was hope for m—you."

"Did you believe that by keeping me away, I would be more likely to bestow my hand on *you*? That before I learned she refused her cousin, I would find myself as much in love with you?"

"I fail to comprehend this preoccupation with love." She gave him a pitying look. "She has nothing by which to tempt you. I am of a respectable family. I was educated in one of the first private seminaries in town. I associate with people of rank. She has no beauty! I have twenty thousand pounds!" Miss Bingley's manner had begun quite cool, but she gave way to the most violent indignation at realising he would never admire her.

"I would prefer the quiet joy of a private life with a woman whom I love and respect rather than have your twenty thousand pounds and your tainted character. Nothing could compare to the misery of being bound to you and preferring another."

"You will thank me someday for saving you from a dreadful scrape! I granted you time to conquer your infatuation with that poor, impertinent, ill-looking shrew."

Her jealousy had made her desperate. Miss Bingley was petulant, her arms crossed across her chest, her lips pursed.

"Since you have accosted me in private and spoken so frankly, I will speak my mind: I am disgusted by your deceit, and your lack of remorse appalls me. I can scarcely tolerate the sight of you. You are selfish and untrustworthy, and henceforth I shall not know you." Darcy punctuated these last words slowly, and Miss Bingley's hands flew to her mouth. "You will not be received at Pemberley, and I will not admit to your society in town. *Not ever.* I shall suffer your presence while I am at your brother's parties, but this conversation severs all acquaintance between us. If you presume to address me or my sister in society, I will be forced to cut you directly, and then I shall have no choice but to publicly expose your lie and thereby further your humiliation."

Darcy left the library without a backward glance.

Wednesday, January 15

EVERYBODY WAS PUNCTUAL TO THE WEDDING, EVERYBODY IN THEIR best looks, and there was not a long face to be seen, except for the groom's sister. The bride was led to the vestry by the bridegroom, followed by Darcy and Elizabeth, then Mr and Mrs Bennet. Bingley signed the register first, and every subsequent signer must have thought how fortunate it was that the groom's vows were solemnised verbally and not by his illegible handwriting.

The Gardiners, and the Hursts with Miss Bingley, departed from the church door, and Darcy noted how it snowed as the rest of the party went to Longbourn for the wedding breakfast. The snow did not deter most of the villagers from loitering in the churchyard to shout their good wishes and catch a glimpse of the radiantly happy Mrs Bingley.

Although the Gardiners and Bingley's family had departed,

Darcy intended to remain to the last. He hoped to have the opportunity to speak with Elizabeth at the wedding breakfast, but amid so many well-wishers, he could scarcely hear the sound of his own voice, let alone speak privately with the bridesmaid.

"I cannot be satisfied yet, Lady Lucas," Mrs Bennet was saying loudly to her neighbour and, by extension to Darcy, who was seated on the other side of her. "I am anxious to get a good husband for the remainder of my girls. Mr Darcy, do you know how many of Bingley's friends are rich bachelors? I do not know if I hold much hope for Lizzy—so stubborn, though she is pretty—or Mary, for you can see how plain she is, but Kitty and Lydia will make good matches."

"I must let Bingley speak on behalf of his own friends. If he does not now have a friend who is in want of a wife, I daresay the opportunity will soon present itself." Darcy was proud of himself for uttering this with more sincerity than sarcasm.

"Do not you have a sister that you must see well settled, sir?" asked Lady Lucas. "If Mr Darcy knows of any single men of fortune, you cannot expect him to suggest them to *you*, Mrs Bennet."

"Georgiana is not yet sixteen, madam."

"Why, sir! My Lydia will be sixteen this summer, and I see no reason for her not to find a husband as soon as she can. You must escort your sister to one of Bingley's parties, and she and my younger girls can find rich husbands together!"

Darcy supposed this gesture was one of friendliness. "Your plan is a good one, were nothing in question but the desire of soon finding a rich husband. Georgiana will be well married in her own time, so I cede any claim to Bingley's single friends to your daughters."

Mr Bennet was crossing behind the table and stopped to interject. "Yes, Bingley's friends are good enough for our daughters, but not for Mr Darcy's sister. Some men are not rich and noble enough for some wealthy gentlemen's sisters, is that not right?"

Mrs Bennet's foolishness did not try Darcy's patience the way Mr Bennet's mocking did. "One does not need to be titled or wealthy to be appealing to me, and I hope the same might be said of my sister when she is of a proper age to give up the title of Miss Darcy." He bowed to the ladies, gave Mr Bennet a cold look, and then left the table.

He found himself face to face with Elizabeth. He was embarrassed to have her witness how he lost his patience with her father. *She will not welcome one quarter of an hour alone with me now!*

"The wedding went off tolerably well, did it not, Miss Elizabeth?"

"Yes, it was a proper wedding: Jane looked beautiful, and I was duly inferior."

Before Darcy could speak a compliment, Bingley, who was passing near them, interjected, "She is Miss Bennet now!"

"Forgive me, Miss Bennet." She bowed her head and told him it was nothing.

They stood in silence, until Bingley said, "Darcy, I have not asked after your family's stay at Pemberley. All I have spoken about since you arrived is my own wedding; you must think me an indifferent friend! Had you a pleasant time?"

"Yes, thank you. It was a charming visit." *Aside from the quarrelling brothers, an officious aunt, my distressed sister, and a mésalliance with a courtesan that I wish had never happened.*

"How are your Fitzwilliam cousins?"

"Although you have not met him, you have heard me speak my mind about Milton." Darcy rolled his eyes. Elizabeth was attending their conversation, and he added for her benefit, "Lord Milton is the eldest son of my uncle. Every sentence began with 'my friend Lord somebody' or 'when I was invited by Lady someone.'"

Bingley laughed in sympathy. "Yes, I know your other cousin is much more to your liking."

"I cannot deny it," he said with a smile.

Elizabeth suddenly left them. *Why is it that I can be accosted by Miss Bingley in the library and voice all my vitriol, but I cannot speak more than two sentences to Elizabeth?*

ELIZABETH DID NOT KNOW HOW IT WAS TO BE ENDURED IF HIS cousin Miss de Bourgh was to be the wife to whom Darcy looked for all the best blessings of existence. She had doubted Mr Wickham's insistence that they were intended for one another, but her new brother's information, she could not discount. She was vexed and disappointed, but she would learn to match him in his indifference.

The breakfast was now over and the guests almost gone, save for a few neighbours and Darcy. Jane and Charles bid their farewells while Mrs Bennet continued to project weddings among her unmarried daughters. The servants ventured into the vestibule to offer their congratulations as the carriages were ordered. While Elizabeth waited for Jane to part from her father, she moved nearer to the window where Charles and Darcy were examining the weather.

"The weather looks unfavourable, Darcy. Cold, windy, and the snow continues."

"I fear it shall be a dreadful journey."

"I have only three miles to go."

"I was not speaking of *your* journey."

"I forgot, I am sorry."

Mr Bennet glanced out the window on his way to his book room. "This will prove a spirited beginning, Mr Darcy. Something exciting for your coachman and horses to be making their way through a storm of snow."

Elizabeth was mortified. The proper thing for her father to do would be to offer for Darcy to stay at Longbourn until the weather improved.

Charles was a more generous man. "You will not be journeying any farther than Netherfield today!"

"You cannot wish to have houseguests on the day of your wedding."

"You cannot think I would send you to London in this snow. You will scarcely be able to tell where the road is."

"I can find a room at a coaching inn along the post road if the need arises."

"There are soldiers billeted at every inn for miles. You cannot be certain of finding a room before your carriage gets stuck in a drift. You must stay with us."

"I cannot wish to be snowed in at Netherfield."

Darcy dares not spend more time in my company.

Charles told Jane that, given the weather, Darcy would remain with them for the present. If he expected her to readily agree, he must have been surprised when she instead gave a look of alarm to Elizabeth. Elizabeth, in turn, could not help but then look towards Darcy, who observed the sisters' silent communication.

"Bingley, it is now Mrs Bingley's right to invite guests to Netherfield. I shall get home very well. Another hour or two's snow can hardly make the road impassable."

The road is nearly impassable now. Elizabeth did not wish for Jane to choose between honouring her new husband's wishes and placating her. *Besides, I cannot send the man on a twenty-four-mile journey in this weather.*

Darcy offered his hand to Charles to congratulate him and take leave when Elizabeth spoke. "Of course Jane will insist that Mr Darcy stay, Charles!" She was not ready to speak to Darcy directly. "The new Mrs Bingley will not stand for any acquaintance of hers to have their carriage blown over in a common field." Jane looked relieved that she could, with her sister's blessing, invite Darcy to Netherfield.

It had to be the most awkward evening Darcy had ever endured. They ate a small, early dinner and, without separating, went into the drawing room. Throughout the meal, the newlywed couple was full of smiles and fond reflections of the morning. Darcy and Elizabeth agreed with everything the Bingleys said and spoke only to one another as far as the passing of the nearest dishes required. For Darcy's part, the contrast of the happy couple against an irreconcilable pair was painful.

It was clear to him that Bingley wanted to retire, and his bride was either too nervous or too proper a hostess to abandon her guest at so early an hour as six o'clock. She suggested card games suited for four players. She offered to read aloud and asked if anyone wanted music, whilst Bingley commented that the dark evening and eventful morning made it feel so much later than it was.

"I hope everyone made to town," said Mrs Bingley.

"They left scarcely after eleven; I have no doubt of their getting home safely," Elizabeth replied.

"I fear if it continues to snow like this, it will be another two or three days before we can leave for Brighton."

Darcy watched the bridegroom with an emotion somewhere between amusement and pity. Mrs Bingley would not leave her company, and Bingley wanted to retire with his new wife. *It is a hopeless case, and Bingley knows it.* He decided to remove one of the impediments.

"Mrs Bingley, I am unequal to company this evening. As this was always meant to be a family party, I am sure you have been desiring my absence." Mrs Bingley demurred; Darcy saw over her head that Bingley looked hopeful. "I shall be happy to retire early and read in my room."

He bowed and was about to leave when Bingley spoke. "Darcy, it has been a blissful but fatiguing day for me and Mrs Bingley. Jane, do not you agree?" She hardly finished nodding before he continued. "Since you wish to read, Mrs Bingley and I will retire, and you can avail yourself of the lamps and fire here. Miss Bennet is busy at her work and will not argue with you tonight, will you, Lizzy?" he teased.

"As a wedding gift to you, I can promise not to antagonise your guest this evening."

He was now left to face an evening's tête-à-tête with Elizabeth. Ever since he had ordered his carriage at Pemberley, he had wished for time alone with her: to apologise for not properly warning her about Mr Wickham, to beg her forgiveness for leaving in an angry temper, to attempt to explain the misunderstanding that kept him away. He had hoped that, should he be forgiven, whatever tender feeling she once had for him might be rekindled.

But her family dispatched Mr Wickham without assistance from me, and she has shown no sign of our former amity, let alone affection. His silence had allowed her to be cruelly imposed upon by Mr Wickham; he doubted she could forgive that. Although her generous heart would be civil to him for the sake of Bingley, she had too many reasons to hate him.

"You may sit nearer to the light to read."

Darcy moved closer to the fire and sat across from her. She did not raise her eyes, but after so many days of anxiety, Darcy was resolved to speak now that they were alone.

I am no longer in a humour to wait for any opening of hers.

Chapter 34

"Miss Elizabeth," he began.
"Bennet."
"I beg your pardon?"
Elizabeth did not look up from her needle. "We attended my eldest sister's wedding this morning, Mr Darcy. I am no longer Miss Elizabeth, but Miss Bennet."

"I miss your calling me Darcy."

The needle ceased to move, but she did not look up. Her teasing or her anger would be better than her indifference or silence. He had been foolish to wish for more.

"I am exceedingly sorry that I did not do more to make you acquainted with Mr Wickham's real character. I returned to Hertfordshire to redress my errors. Instead, I discovered my advice was not needed. However, I comprehend how greatly my information was wanted in the autumn. I assure you I never suspected that Wickham would take advantage of a woman in the middle of a crowded room."

She finally looked at him. He watched the small movements of her eyes and face. There was no flash of amusement there, no expressive spark. "You are not at all to blame for the event. If anything, you must reproach me for speaking favourably of Mr Wickham after you advised me to be guarded." She touched the handkerchief that sat on her lap next to her work.

"Mr Wickham is a proficient deceiver. He convinced you that he had become a better man than the one I knew him to be, and it is entirely my fault for not telling you then that there was no possible way he could be speaking the truth. I am the only one to blame for"—here he swallowed back his ire and shame—"for his kissing you in such a thoroughly improper way. That you had to flee to town—"

"There is no one but Mr Wickham to blame for his conduct."

"I might have prevented this."

"You are not responsible, and you must not fancy me affected by Mr Wickham's transgression."

"Any woman of credit and feeling would be distressed—"

"I am not distressed by one drunken kiss, just my own stupidity! The neighbourhood would never have known had I not told my mother. Confessing it all was the way to be sure Mr Wickham would no longer welcome at Longbourn without explaining..." A flow of tears fell from her eyes as she trailed off. Darcy reached out to take her hand, but she stood and went for the door.

What did she wish to conceal in order to keep Wickham away from Longbourn? In her haste, Elizabeth's fancywork had fallen to the floor. Darcy bent to retrieve the tambour frame, along with her handkerchief, and was surprised to recognise the latter as his own, with his initials in the corner.

It took him no more than one second to go against every entrenched convention of proper behaviour between a gentleman and a lady. Darcy ran to the door, stood in front of it, and grabbed her hand.

"I am determined at once to know everything."

"I apologise for quitting you so rudely." She pulled her hand away.

"I do not care at all about that! I beg you to tell me about Mr Wickham."

She looked at him a long moment before answering. "You know

he was drunk and kissed me. Several days later, I told my mother about the incident, as well as how you and Bingley knew Mr Wickham to be a dissolute man with no prospects. My mother was so appalled that she forbade him from entering the house. If I had heeded your warning in November, it would not have happened."

"Why did you wait days to confess his misdeed? And if you were not distressed by it, why confess it at all?"

"It was the only way to keep him away from me. It was far better to admit to the scrutiny of being the subject of Mr Wickham's unwelcome attentions than confess the full truth of why he ought not to be trusted." He started at this. "I know about your sister and Mr Wickham."

He struggled for composure, but managed to say, "Did he acknowledge to you what happened?"

"No." She rubbed her eyes with her palms, then dropped her hands as the words tumbled from her mouth. "I remembered the letter you wrote about your sister's low spirits and her unsuspecting the motives of a spiteful man. You wrote of a Mr W and an event at R, and when Mr Wickham mentioned that he had been at Ramsgate last summer, I suspected him of trifling with Miss Darcy. He confessed he had seen your sister at Ramsgate, and his true character was revealed. He did not wish to reconcile with you, he did not regret any of his dissipated youth, and he even confessed that by making me his greatest supporter, it was not his aim to injure me with his lies but *you*."

"You sacrificed your own privacy to protect my sister's?" he whispered. "Had I but told you about Ramsgate from the beginning, shown you the trust you deserved ..." He paced.

"You wished to protect Miss Darcy's reputation and her feelings."

"Her other guardian and I agreed to never tell another human being." He took a deep breath. "Did he ... did he tell you what happened with Georgiana?"

"He claimed that he succeeded with Miss Darcy as far as he wished, but I hardly know what that means or if he only said it to be cruel." She gave him a curious look. "Do you not know what happened?"

Darcy pressed his hand against his eyes as his shoulders fell. She sat on the sofa and gestured for him to take the chair. He fell into it tiredly.

"When I left with Bingley after the ball, after my anger subsided, I had every intention of returning with him and telling you the whole truth so you could fully understand how Wickham had misled you."

Quietly and forcefully, he related the full sordid tale of Ramsgate and the duplicity of Wickham and Mrs Younge.

"I am grieved to hear of his designs on Miss Darcy, but not shocked to hear further proof of Mr Wickham's depravity."

He rested his elbows on his knees and steepled his fingers, leaning his forehead against them. "She was in love with Mr Wickham, as much as a sheltered girl can be, and refused to believe he had abandoned her. Even after he departed Ramsgate, she refused to quit the place. After two days of attempting to reason with her, I had to drag a fifteen-year-old girl, begging and pleading to remain where Mr Wickham might easily find her, into my carriage."

Darcy raised his head and saw Elizabeth had tears in her eyes. "For a fortnight, she refused to leave her room and would not speak; we had to tell the servants and her family she was ill with a fever to explain her isolation, and we hoped if everyone thought her throat was inflamed, she might be forgiven for not speaking. Georgiana expected his letter or call every day. The acuteness of her disappointment was unlike anything I had ever seen."

"That poor girl's wounded feelings! Did she not understand Mr Wickham's chief object was her fortune?"

"That is the peculiar part! She did not doubt me when I told her he wanted her thirty thousand pounds, and yet she told me that if he returned, and if I gave my blessing, she would still have him. It was not until a full month after we returned that she relented and said she would not marry Mr Wickham. But her melancholy state deepened."

Elizabeth winced as though she felt a sickening feeling in the pit of her stomach. Darcy looked at her questioningly. She was about to speak, then shook her head.

Darcy sighed sadly and leaned back in the chair. "You would not suggest a possibility that I have not already considered."

"Did you ask her if—if he—"

"Of course! Before I left to join Bingley here in the autumn, I finally felt I might hear the truth from her. I promised her that she could never lose my good opinion, that if her virtue was lost, it did not mean her future was forfeit, but I did not realise until much later that I did not ask the correct question." In reply to Elizabeth's inquiring frown, he said, "I asked her if Mr Wickham forced himself upon her, and she denied anything of the kind."

"But she may have been a willing participant," Elizabeth whispered.

"I dared not ask her again and risk any setback of her tentative improvement. She often did not speak, she felt as though she could not breathe, and she refused to leave her rooms." After a lengthy pause, Darcy continued, "If he hoped to revenge himself upon me by eloping with my sister, his happiness must yet be complete because however far their dalliance went, my sister's self-confidence is devastated."

"It is possible she is only mortified by her conduct rather than dreadfully ashamed over having given her virtue to Mr Wickham."

Darcy rose to pace. "By mere chance was Georgiana able to escape from the worst of all evils: a connexion, for life, with a corrupt, unprincipled scoundrel who would delight in harming me further by mistreating her."

"And I foolishly believed every word Mr Wickham said."

He nodded distractedly, thinking of Georgiana, and paced the length of the room before he realised Elizabeth was sobbing.

"Good God, what is the matter?"

She looked around her, presumably for the handkerchief Darcy now held out to her. She took it and walked away to face the wall. Darcy watched in wretched suspense as he hesitated between leaving her alone, which is what a gentleman *ought* to do, or taking her in his arms, which was what he *wanted* to do.

"Is there anything I might do for you?"

She shook her head, endeavouring to recover herself. "I am

grateful I have not lost your good opinion to such a degree that it prohibited you from confiding in me such a private matter."

"You are mistaken if you believe that you have lost my good opinion."

"I encouraged you to forgive and support the man who misused your sister! A man you *told me* to be wary of. You have every reason to justly hate me."

"*Hate* you?"

"Yes." Her tears had stopped and her voice was even. "How you must have hated me after that evening."

"I was angry, at first, but my anger soon took a proper direction. I assure you I had not ridden one mile from Netherfield before I intended to come back."

"Then why did you not?" Her eyes flashed, but then dimmed. She blushed and turned away. "Mr Darcy, I spoke out of turn. Would you be so good as to leave me—"

"No, I shall not quit this room until I have had my say!" She looked surprised at his refusal, so much so that she remained silent while he led her to the sofa and sat next to her.

"Do you remember that while we were in my carriage with the Gardiners, I said Lady Catherine spoke of your friend's marriage to Mr Collins?" She nodded. "Until last Wednesday, I was convinced your cousin was marrying not Miss Lucas, but *you*."

She seemed to be looking in his countenance for that explanation that his lips did not afford.

"Why did you believe I would marry Mr Collins?"

"I was told that Mr Collins made you an offer and that he was an engaged man. When I asked specifically what that meant, I was told you accepted him. Given your natural desire to do right by your family, as well as the acrimonious nature of our parting, it was not impossible to me that you would accept him."

Darcy watched her eyes narrow, her shoulders tense, and her fingers open and clench at her sides. When she spoke, he was prepared as much as he could be for the onslaught.

"It was impossible for me to do anything but to refuse him! I would not marry him were beggary the alternative. He is without one good quality to make amends for his having no affection for me. He is solemn, awkward, stupid, ill-mannered, and has no respect for me!" In a lower voice, she asked, "Who told you I was engaged to Mr Collins?"

"It would not be polite of me to open that person to scrutiny." The withering glare he received changed his mind for him. "Miss Bingley."

"And you believed her?" Her tone betrayed her incredulity and her disappointment in him. "You know one sign of partiality from you, and Caroline Bingley would order her wedding clothes! She was in the room when Sir William Lucas announced Charlotte's engagement to Mr Collins."

"I did not believe she would be capable of such outright deceit." He was about to reach for her, intending to lay a comforting hand on her arm, but he realised his touch was still unwanted and stopped. "What person would believe themselves at liberty to tell me such a lie? Or be willing to risk the repercussions to her reputation, her social standing, when her deceit was inevitably revealed?"

"Desperate and jealous people are not wise, be them purse-proud daughters of tradesmen or selfish and corrupt sons of stewards."

"I did earnestly wish it to be false, so much so that after Bingley wrote that he was engaged, I replied to ask if any of Miss Bennet's sisters were also soon to be led to the altar."

"He must have told you that none of Jane's sisters were engaged or had any suitors." Darcy knew her bewilderment and annoyance were justified. Still, he hoped that since her voice had lowered and she spoke calmly, she might be willing to hear him.

"I received a letter from Bingley on the twelfth of December that, as far I could tell, said Mr Collins asked you to marry him, that you refused, that your mother wished for you to accept him, and that within days Mr Collins was accepted by Miss Lizzy, and you would wed after the new year."

"Charles would not have lied to you!"

"He did not misinform me intentionally." He raised a placating hand. "Have you had the great misfortune to read anything written by Bingley?"

Her angry expression relaxed into a knowing one. "I read his handwriting on an envelope with his sister's direction and saw him sign his name on the register this morning. I could scarcely discern a legible letter."

"His letters contain more blots than words, and he still leaves out half of his words. You may read it yourself if you cannot credit how I might have mistaken Bingley's meaning. It was last week, when Lady Catherine told me that Mr Collins was to marry Charlotte Lucas, that I realised he was accepted by Miss *Lucas*, not Miss *Lizzy*. I set off for Hertfordshire within two hours of learning that you were not engaged to your cousin."

She seemed immoveable from absolute surprise. The ache in Darcy's chest became unbearable. Although they sat inches apart, he acutely felt the gulf between them. She stared into the room, refusing to look at him, while he was angled towards her, eager for a sign of her continued attachment.

After twisting his handkerchief around her fingers, Elizabeth tossed it aside. She kept her gaze on her lap when she quietly said, "At first I thought you the most resentful man in the world, but after I realised what Mr Wickham was … I thought you would never forgive me for championing him."

Her ire had lessened, but how could he convince Elizabeth that the powerful affection he held for her had never abated and never would? He desperately wanted to please her, if he only knew what to say. "I was angry, but you never lost my good opinion. Although it is not necessary in the present case, I could forgive you anything. I merely plead that you can be forgiving of me."

"Mr Collins is a conceited, pompous, narrow-minded man. Even if I had not been wishing… I could never have accepted him."

Had she been wishing for his proposals as much as he had been wanting to make them? "I thought you resented me for leaving in anger." Within his own mind, he implored her to turn and look on him. "I thought that you, feeling abandoned by me and hating me for it, had agreed to marry Mr Collins for the sake of his situation and to oblige your mother. You cannot know how the thought of you marrying another man has tortured me."

Elizabeth gave a small sigh of disbelief or surprise, but still she would not look at him. Her silence intensified his sense of loss as well as his anguish that she would never love him.

"Do not send me away." His voice was hoarse with anxiety. "Please do not tell me that I shall never—that I shall never find a way… Please do not tell me that my love for you is in vain."

Darcy bent his head, feeling the profound weight of her silence, when he felt the touch of her fingertips on his hand. He exhaled shakily at her light caress and turned his hand over and carried hers to his lips. He dared to look up when he heard her faint gasp as he pressed a lingering kiss against the back of her hand.

At last she turned her eyes towards his, and Darcy was aware of how her fingers were now lightly curled around his. Her rapt, eager gaze robbed him of his breath and sent his heart pounding in his chest. "I ardently admire and love you, and if you would return a favourable answer to my offer of marriage, you would make me the happiest of men."

He looked and listened to her reply with his whole soul. "I would have given all that I have to dare to *hope* that you still loved me. To marry you would make me the happiest creature in the world!"

Darcy could not have uttered another sentence; his heart was too full. The warm contact of her hand held within his, combined with the delight shining in her lovely, dark eyes, made his pulse quicken. He still cradled her hand in his own, and Darcy now raised the other to trace his thumb along her cheek.

Her complexion glowed, her eyes danced, and she clung to his hand as though afraid he would disappear. Elizabeth's joy tended towards gaiety, and Darcy was delighted by it. The knowledge that Elizabeth would be his wife made Darcy all the more aware of how alone they were. "I ought not to remain long with you. At the least, I fear, your sister would think I was imposing on you."

"Nothing could be farther from the truth!" she cried. "In fact, there is nothing more wonderful than a tête-à-tête with the person one feels is most agreeable in the world."

"You must be the first person, excepting my sister, to say I am the most agreeable person of their acquaintance. I can remember a time when you and I walked outside this house and you called me disagreeable and conceited."

"'Tis the consequence of my being in love with you: I am now full of your merits and blind to your faults."

He could rationalise that Elizabeth would only accept him if she loved him, but to hear the words struck him powerfully. Darcy drew a ragged breath. "Would you say it again?"

"I said I am sensible to all of your merits and—"

"No, before that."

A smile played at the corners of her mouth. "You have grown inattentive to me too soon."

"Humour me in this, and I promise to be entirely engrossed by every speech you utter." Darcy moved closer and raised his other hand to her face.

"I love you."

Her lips were inches from his own, the very air he was breathing heady with expectation. Darcy leaned towards her and allowed his gaze to take in every precious feature. Before he could admire her properly, Elizabeth closed her eyes and quickly and firmly pressed her lips against his and held them there.

Her confident, warm contact made his pulse quicken and when he kissed her more fully, Elizabeth responded. Their lips touched with delicate intimacy. The exquisite sensation of kissing her at last struck him forcibly. *This* was the embrace that he had long ached for.

When he tried to pull back, her lips lingered on his, unwilling to give him up. Elizabeth's eyes were hazy, and she sighed happily. Darcy was marvelling at how quickly they had both moved from abject misery to heartfelt delight when Elizabeth said breathlessly, "I should be angrier with you than I was."

Her light, eager tone did not alarm him. Darcy indulged in a compulsion he had long repressed and twisted a loose tendril of her hair between his fingers. He admired its silky texture before he looked at her questioningly.

"You should have returned even when you believed I was engaged. Your inaction caused me to forgo six weeks of your kisses."

"In such circumstances, a proper gentleman would withdraw to relieve you of any obstacle that his presence may occasion to the furtherance of your obvious wish to oblige your family and marry Mr Collins."

"How unlucky that you should have a reasonable answer to give and that I should be so reasonable as to admit it."

"If I was in error, I am willing to make up for lost time." Darcy took up her hand and turned it over, bringing it to his mouth. He gently grazed his teeth against the inside of her wrist, then softly kissed her smooth skin. He then pressed a lingering kiss on each of her fingertips. Darcy kept his eyes on her face and saw her eyes darken, her mouth part, and her breath come in quick bursts.

The sudden consciousness that she felt desire for him almost undid him, and if he did not leave soon, he might not be able to leave her this evening at all. He stood and pulled Elizabeth up with him.

"It is a rather late hour; I ought to leave you now."

"It cannot be eight o'clock, but I shall let you go as long as you promise to remain tomorrow, regardless of the weather."

"My dearest, loveliest Elizabeth," he said as he placed his fingertips on her back and drew her close enough to press a soft, lingering kiss on her mouth, "now that I know you love me, you cannot imagine that anything in this world would keep me from your side."

Chapter 35

Thursday, January 16

The housemaid's folding back her window shutters at seven o'clock was the sound that roused Elizabeth, and she opened her eyes to see that although a bright morning greeted her, it continued to snow. The weather provided a perfect justification for Darcy to remain at Netherfield for two or three days.

He loves me. He has dearly loved me all this time!

A smile stretched her lips as she remembered how his fingertips had twirled a strand of her hair. She laughed at her own daring for kissing him first. An exquisite flutter of happiness coursed through her when she thought about his words: "You cannot know how the thought of you marrying another man has tortured me."

For how long had she *pretended* to be the cheerful Elizabeth that her friends and family expected her to be? She now both knew and felt herself to be truly happy. The misunderstandings between them, as well as the misunderstandings caused by others' jealousy and malevolence" were all to be put behind them. Happier memories of their reunion would soon replace the unpleasant ones of their separation.

After she dressed, her book, her letters, and her work failed to keep her interest. Elizabeth's disposition was not naturally sedentary, but today she could not employ herself for ten minutes and accomplished nothing until the lady who now waited on her sister entered and said that Mrs Bingley was asking for her.

It would not speak well of Elizabeth's notions of sisterly affections if she immediately told Jane about her good fortune rather than listening to the concerns of her sister. *After sitting a little while with Jane, I will then tell her all.*

"Good morning, Mrs Bingley! You are looking well."

"Good morning. It was strange to wake and know you to be in the same house, but not in the same room as me. It is not at all like at Longbourn, is it?"

"No, but you were not lonely, I expect?"

Jane's cheeks flushed. "I was not lonely."

"Where is the bridegroom?"

"He went out to examine the weather and answer to what degree of difficulty there is in us leaving for Brighton as planned, and of course Mr Darcy will wish to return to town as soon as he is able."

"It is snowing at this moment, and it looks like more snow will fall. Mr Darcy is cautious, and I think we should wait until the roads are in much better condition."

"I suppose you are right. I will dissuade Bingley from venturing tomorrow, but perhaps the day after." Jane looked away, and Elizabeth asked her what was the matter. Reluctantly, Jane finally said, "Lizzy, now I am the mistress of an estate!"

"More importantly, you are now a wife. Yesterday changed a great many things." Elizabeth was about to speak about Darcy, but Jane's expression gave her pause.

"There are more servants here than at Longbourn. *I* have the duty of care towards them, and *I* must learn of their families and concerns, their strengths and weaknesses."

"You are not without experience. You have kept Longbourn in hand whenever my mother was unwell or overcome by nerves."

"I kept the key to the tea and made clothes for the poor." Jane's eyes looked as though they would fill with tears.

Elizabeth squeezed her sister's hand. "I have every confidence in you! You will soon be proficient in all the arts of domestic economy and management, I am sure."

"I look down a page to see how much is spent on sealing wax or how many pounds of mutton are consumed, and my eyes go crossed."

"Mrs Nicholls can purchase provisions and compare prices for your household. That will leave you time to manage the servants—you would not want to be so easy that they cheat you!" Elizabeth smiled when her sister laughed. "You can have no apprehensions over how well you can manage them or care for everyone."

"I am going to meet with Nicholls and Cook soon. I hope to appear before them with sureness in my new position."

"They will not judge you harshly." Elizabeth thought her sister very silly to worry. Jane would never be imprudent or thoughtless in money matters, and it would be unpardonable to her to not act kindly towards her servants. "I think all you need concern yourself with the first month of your marriage is becoming familiar with your new husband."

Jane hugged her and asked her to keep her company until breakfast. As much as she wanted to seek out Darcy, Elizabeth decided the new bride had full claim upon her time and attention. Besides, as she reflected on the matter, Elizabeth wanted time to sit by herself with the idea of being engaged. She was not ready to hear anyone else's thoughts on the subject until she had better arranged her own feelings of overpowering happiness.

"Are you well?" Bingley looked over his shoulder at his friend.

"Yes," Darcy replied between clenched teeth. "Only it is so cold, so very cold."

"You need not have come with me."

"I will not have you go alone since, as you said, it is for my benefit as well as yours that you know the state of the road."

Bingley and Darcy were dressed in fur-lined overcoats and boots and trudged through the snow to ascertain the condition of the lane. Their ankle-length coats were soaked at the bottom. Bingley appeared to relish this winter exercise, and Darcy tried not to allow his being frozen through to pique his temper.

"You must be as eager to return to town as I am to take my bride to Brighton."

"I would rather remain until it is safe to travel."

If they were snowed up at Netherfield for two days or two months, it would not inconvenience him. As they plodded through the snow, Darcy wondered if Elizabeth was awake.

They were now at the end of the sweep and had a view of the lane. There was no need to go any further; the landscape was dismal and covered with snow.

"Shall we attempt to travel a few miles? The horses shall have to walk, I suppose."

"Would you really say it is better to risk stranding your new bride when you could be safe at Netherfield, getting to know each other better? And did you fail to notice that it continues to snow?" Darcy bent and stretched his gloved fingers, but nothing he did warmed them.

Bingley stared at him a long moment. "I am tempted to make a snowball and throw it at your head."

"I am sorry. I am cold, and it is obvious we are not leaving Netherfield today or tomorrow."

They made their way back to the house, trying to step in their footprints as much as possible.

"It is a good thing my sisters departed early to avoid the snow. You might have been snowed up with Caroline."

"Thank heaven for small mercies," Darcy muttered, and they both laughed.

Bingley gave a rueful sigh. "Caroline has not shown Jane the friendliness I might have wished and, until she makes a greater effort, she will not be living with us. Also, I know my wife would prefer to have Lizzy at her side."

"I am sorry the attachment between the new sisters is not what you hoped to see."

"Perhaps Caroline wanted to preside over her brother's home a little while longer."

Perhaps she wished you to marry my sister in the hopes that the nearer connexion between our families would be to her benefit.

"As much as sometimes she vexes me, I do wish Caroline happy. You can understand; you have a younger sister, too."

If Darcy confessed his engagement now, what would follow would be the explanation as to the delay in its formation and the role Caroline Bingley had in that delay. The morning after his friend's wedding was not the time to admit he had broken all ties with Miss Bingley. Besides, his engagement was too precious, too new to yet be spoken of. He wanted more time to enjoy the newfound comfort of knowing that all of his wishes would be realised.

ONCE THE GENTLEMEN DIVESTED THEMSELVES OF THEIR WET clothes and the feeling returned to Darcy's fingers, it was time for breakfast. Bingley filled his plate, sat on the other side of Mrs Bingley, and engaged her in conversation that focused on his admiration for her.

Darcy met Elizabeth's eyes, and the depth of feeling in them briefly rendered him immoveable.

"Good morning, Mr Darcy."

The mere sound of her voice charmed him. The vibrancy in her eyes was all for *him*. "Good morning." He glanced at Mrs Bingley, who did not look at him with any particular interest. He looked at Elizabeth, who shook her head. She inclined her head towards Bingley, and Darcy mouthed the words "not yet."

"I understand you have been out of doors," Elizabeth said to him as he sat. "Will there be difficulty in your getting home?"

"The snow is deep and continues to fall. I will remain here for another two days at least."

"You are welcome to stay, of course, but how distressing to remain when there is absolutely nothing to keep you here. For my part, I was looking forward to leaving for Brighton as soon as possible."

He was being teased, a trial he was more than willing to tolerate, given the woman teasing him had agreed to become his wife. "If not for the fact that it continues to snow, I would leave immediately."

"How unlucky that we are experiencing weather that confines us both at Netherfield."

He gave her a knowing grin. "Bingley and I agree it would not be prudent to leave today or tomorrow. I hope my being fixed here is not an inconvenience to you."

"Well, I would hate to see any harm come to your poor horses. To see them straining away in all this snow on these rough lanes would be distressing. I do feel very much for your horses, Mr Darcy. I think you ought to remain for their sake, if you find it tolerable."

He laughed aloud. "You feel for my *horses*, do you?"

"I do. I am a generous woman, and I could not in good conscience recommend you leave now and risk their health. I hope that, in these days of confinement, you will find yourself comfortable."

He leaned closer and lowered his voice. "Shall I look to *you* first for advice and consideration on my comfort while I remain at Netherfield?" He stopped in his earnestness to look the question; given the blush across her cheeks and the roused expression of her eyes, he had overpowered her emotions.

It was ten seconds before Elizabeth, with a tolerable degree of composure, was able to answer. "I think it best if we leave the happy couple to themselves. If there is anything you have need of, I suggest you speak to me rather than trouble Mrs Bingley."

"You are too generous."

"I only wish to be of use to the bride."

Darcy smiled and in a louder voice asked her what other tasks had been assigned to the bridesmaid.

"Jane will have her cards; it is up to me to direct them."

Mrs Bingley heard her name. "You need not waste your day on that, Lizzy. After I meet with Nicholls, I can write them."

"It is no trouble. Besides, if you had seen Charles's crestfallen face, you would do best to ignore me all together and save your attention for him."

Darcy then asked Bingley if newspapers from town had come with the post.

"The most recent is Tuesday's *Morning Chronicle*. Neither yesterday's papers nor the post has arrived."

"No matter. I will take up a book in the library if Mrs Bingley does not oppose to a fire being lit?" He studiously avoided meeting Elizabeth's expressive gaze.

Mrs Bingley had nothing to say against lighting a fire wherever it was needed. Elizabeth said, "Let us not be frivolous. If Mr Darcy does not mind, I will direct your cards in the library rather than have a fire lit in my own rooms."

"I am willing to share the library with anyone who might wish to use it."

"Do not be too hasty," Bingley called. "I challenge you to a game of billiards first. We shall become restless if we do not have some activity and since I intend to spend the rest of the day with my wife, we ought to play now while she meets with the housekeeper. A few hours and then you can return to your book."

The low, discontented sigh from Elizabeth was his only consolation.

HOW LONG DOES IT TAKE TO PLAY BILLIARDS?

After three cards had their envelopes folded and sealed, Elizabeth opened the door to hear if the gentlemen were still playing. She realised how foolish she was being and returned to her chair near the fire. Two more cards were completed before she returned to the door and strained to hear the sound of ivory against wood or the murmur of the gentlemen's conversation.

This disinclination to sit and employ myself is beneath me. She mended her pen, then stared at the next direction to be written. *I am a rational creature!* She snatched the quill and began again. When this card was finished, the door opened and Darcy strode into the library.

She rushed to encounter him with joyful haste, reaching with outstretched hands, when Darcy made her a proper bow. His formality stopped short her progress. She was suddenly self-conscious and dropped her hands. As he raised his head and saw her nearness and expression, he appeared embarrassed, too. She recovered enough to curtsey at the same moment he stepped towards to take the hands that were no longer reaching towards him. For a long moment, they stared at one another.

"I hope you are well." Elizabeth turned away. "Who is the better billiards player?" She had presumed his affectionate feelings for her would overcome his formality. She felt his hand on her shoulder, gently turning her around.

"I am sorry. I would not have you stand upon ceremony with me." He lifted her hand to his lips and placed a tender kiss on her palm. His eyes of glowing entreaty fixed on her and robbed her of speech. "How did you intend to greet me?"

"I hardly know."

He let go of her hand and gave her a meaningful look. "You were not planning on curtseying. Would you have only offered me your hand?"

She smiled. "You will never know. Perhaps the next time you find me alone, you will be luckier."

"I do not intend to wait, Elizabeth."

If the sound of her given name on his lips was not enough to gladly startle her composure, the fact that Darcy now pulled her against him in an affectionate embrace did. Two strong arms wrapped around her waist and her cheek now rested against his chest, and, by some unconscious motion, her own arms held him in return. He murmured endearments and laid soft kisses on her hair.

"I did." Elizabeth's voice was full of emotion. "I did intend to throw my arms around you and demand a kiss." She tilted her face towards him. "Are you shocked at my forwardness, Darcy?"

"Fitzwilliam, please," he said in a low voice.

She was lightheaded with joy as his dark eyes focused on hers. "Fitzwilliam."

Darcy bent to kiss her slowly and fully on her mouth. His lips were warm and soft; when Elizabeth clasped her hands around his neck and sighed against his mouth, the hesitancy in his overture was lost. The light touch of his lips on hers gave way to something more, and she felt carried away by her own reckless response.

She emerged from the kiss flushed and laughing. "That was preferable to the typical salutations attending your entrance." She hugged him again.

Darcy laughed softly, his breath warm against her neck, but did not yet appear equal to conversation. Elizabeth led him by the hand to the sofa. "You had enough of billiards, have you? I hope for all the time you spent away from me that you emerged the victor."

"I did; I defeated him three times before Bingley conceded."

"Poor Charles has unknowingly kept us apart *again*. Shall you tell him what role his handwriting had in keeping you from returning to Longbourn?"

"I will, and that will be far easier than telling him the role his sister played."

"When I called on Miss Bingley in town, she was eager to speak of the strong connexion between the Darcys and the Bingleys and of how intimately she understood your character. She then implied that you may soon marry, as one wedding sometimes brings about another."

Darcy shook his head in denial, but Elizabeth spoke again. "I then told her of the evidence that supported your understanding with Miss de Bourgh, and how I sympathised with the effort she had wasted on you. It was beneath me, but I confess I took great pleasure in setting her down. I argued the case of you marrying your cousin well."

"I am in no way bound to my cousin, neither by honour nor inclination." Darcy took her hand.

"I know that now." She squeezed his hand. "But when I thought I had driven you away, it was easy to believe since you were lost to me that you might marry her. Bingley mentioned you were attached to her, and both Mr Wickham and Mr Collins suggested that it is the wish of your families that you and Miss de Bourgh marry." Darcy gave her a look, and Elizabeth quickly added, "My judgment was not so bad as to take Mr Wickham and Mr Collins at their word, but with your absence and Bingley's assertions, I did wonder if you would marry your cousin."

"When did Bingley ever say I had a fondness for Anne de Bourgh?"

"He mentioned your mother's family would be at Pemberley and that you were close to one of your cousins. Even yesterday at the wedding breakfast, when you spoke of your dislike of Lord Milton, he emphasised that *another* cousin was much to your liking. Until last night, I feared…" Elizabeth's words trailed off as Darcy laughed.

He kissed her hand with lips that were still smiling. "Bingley will be appalled to learn how he has injured two people he esteems! The cousin that Bingley referred to is thirty years old and a colonel in His Majesty's army."

Elizabeth's jaw fell open. Darcy continued, "My cousin, the honourable Colonel Fitzwilliam, is my dear friend and Georgiana's other guardian, but I have never, ever considered bestowing my hand upon him."

After a laugh, Elizabeth said, "I never supposed you to have any love for Miss Bingley, but knowing how you value duty and familial loyalty, I had visions of you marrying Miss de Bourgh, a woman who could offer you far more in the means of wealth and connexions than I."

"As I had visions of you as Mrs Collins, forced to pledge your love and loyalty to a man I know you could not respect, purely to protect your family from want."

"How fortunate that neither of us were willing to sacrifice every better feeling to worldly advantage and the approval of our families. Speaking of families," Elizabeth continued, "it felt selfish to tell Jane my happy news less than one day after her own marriage. You must agree because you have not told Bingley."

"Yes, and I also do not look forward to explaining his sister's deceit."

"You need not tell him the whole of it. I promise not to allow her to taunt me again if she visits Pemberley."

"That will never happen," Darcy spoke strongly. "She has sunk so low in my esteem that I have already told her that henceforth I shall not know her."

Elizabeth was surprised. "Even with Mr Wickham, you touched your hat when you met in Meryton."

"And if I ever encounter him again, he should be so fortunate as to only suffer my silence."

"Out of consideration for the Bingleys' feelings, we ought to let them enjoy time together before we tell them the entire story. I only wish that there might be just punishment for Mr Wickham's offences."

"He would not care if I cut him, and short of following him through the world and discrediting him wherever he may go, there is little I can do. The most I can hope for is that he is arrested for deserting the militia."

Elizabeth noticed how his expression had turned from pensive to dark. The inability to see Mr Wickham brought to any justice for his many trespasses was distressing. It would be up to her to cheer and sustain her future husband.

"Fitzwilliam?" His smile told her he was still charmed by her use of his Christian name. "I would not have you pursue Mr Wickham wherever he attempts to pass himself off with any credit. You would perpetually be kept from me, and now that I have you near to me again, I am loath to let you go. In fact, I think it best if you come to Brighton with us."

Elizabeth watched his countenance relax. "For me to accompany you, we shall have to first acquaint the Bingleys with the idea that their small circle will become even more intimately connected."

"Another day or two and we will tell them. By then, we should be able to travel the three miles to Longbourn to speak with my father."

"*We*? Do you think that he would refuse me?"

"No, but he gives little attention to what was going forward in his family. He has no knowledge of my heart, and he may question me about my choice."

"What will you say to him?"

Elizabeth pulled her hand from Darcy's and raised it to his cheek. His eyes closed. "I will tell him I am to marry a man who loves me, who will consult me and confide in me. I will tell him that I love you, and that I wish to make you happy, and that nothing will make me happier than spending my life alongside you."

When he opened his dark eyes, she saw the delight emanating

from them. Then he gently kissed her. It was slow, warm, and lingering, and she sank into the heady sensation of him. He then pulled back, exhaling a shaky "I love you" before lightly kissing her again. Elizabeth responded just as lovingly, murmuring his Christian name between kisses. She savoured every touch as uncontrollable joy flooded through her heart.

When Darcy spoke, his voice was low, intimate. "How soon might you make me the happiest of men?" He twirled the strands of hair that hung near her ear, a contented smile playing on his lips.

"I ought to spend time in Brighton with Jane. She is uneasy about her new role as wife and mistress, and I do not want to leave her too soon. You would not be disappointed to wait two months?"

"You alone, who know my heart, can judge my happiness in not waiting a day longer than is necessary. But I cannot fault your goodness in wishing to be of use to your sister."

Elizabeth looked guiltily at the pile on the table. "I have little to show for my efforts thus far. I cannot say that I failed to complete Jane's cards because I passed the entire day in your embrace."

Darcy pulled his hand from her hair. He straightened in his seat and moved away to a more respectful distance. Elizabeth did her best not to laugh at him as she walked towards the table. To her surprise, Darcy joined her.

"You may as well put me to use." He gestured towards the cards.

"I am confident that you write more neatly than Charles, but Jane's friends will be startled to see a gentleman's hand on her cards."

"Then I shall blot and seal them when you are finished." Darcy took a closer look at the tall stack of cards that remained. "If I do not help, you will not be finished before you lose the light."

They fell into a steady rhythm, where Elizabeth wrote the direction and Darcy used the roller blotter and sealed the letter with Jane's new stamp inscribed with a 'B.'

"You have a very elegant hand," Darcy said later as he held the stick of sealing wax over the candle.

Elizabeth looked askance at him and murmured a quiet "thank you."

"I am afraid you do not like your pen. Let me mend it for you. I mend pens remarkably well."

Elizabeth laughed at both him and the memory he evoked; she shook her head.

"How can you contrive to write so even?" He was now laughing, and Elizabeth was charmed by the sound.

"Have you nothing else to do?"

"I am disengaged for the day, and I can think of nothing I would rather do than to sit by you and admire the evenness of your lines."

"Your inexplicable fondness for me makes you blind to the foolishness of that statement."

"My fondness for you is reasonable; it is not at all a blind affection. And for the present, when I have so recently learned that my love for you is reciprocated, I am content to remain where I am and admire you."

"I was certain, so certain, that after my misplaced faith in Mr Wickham, you would hate me."

He shook his head. "I am not without fault. I can hardly bear to think of the grief I caused you."

"And what of the pain I caused you? The recollection of what I said and did is inexpressively painful to me."

"I think it is easier to bear one's own suffering than it is to bear the pain of knowing how much sorrow and heartache one has inflicted on those one loves. We have forgiven one another and now ought to forgive ourselves. I expect in time, every unpleasant circumstance attending to our separation will be forgotten, including our guilt."

"I wondered if you could ever forgive me, and if you did, I doubted you could love me again as I continued to love you."

Darcy kissed her softly on her lips, and then rested his forehead against hers. "My love for you is deathless."

Chapter 36

Friday, January 17

"We won't remain long," Bingley said as he sipped his port.

"I was surprised you wished to separate from the ladies at all."

The gentlemen were seated at the table, the ladies had withdrawn, and Darcy pretended to enjoy a half an hour to themselves. The sight of snow on the ground this morning did further service to those wishing to remain another day at Netherfield. Darcy was well aware, however, that tomorrow there would be no excuse to prevent him from riding to Longbourn to obtain Mr Bennet's consent.

"I hope you have not felt abandoned these last two days. You have not minded spending time with Lizzy?"

"I have nothing to say against how I have passed my time." Bingley might soon notice that he was delighted to be left to pass hours at a time alone with Mrs Bingley's sister.

"Lizzy is in better spirits than she was before she left for London. Mr Wickham acted egregiously! And none could claim that it was Lizzy's fault," Bingley added with a warning expression.

"I cannot imagine a person of sense suggesting it was Miss Bennet's fault. He is entirely to blame for such a violation of decency and honour."

"The idea of Mrs Bennet, who is well known for her love of company, going so far as to prohibit Mr Wickham from Longbourn made a powerful impression as to his culpability. Even if Mr Wickham was drunk, I cannot comprehend why he kissed her."

To spite me. "He is the most unworthy man I have ever known. What did Mr Bennet have to say on the unfortunate affair?"

"He did not blame Lizzy, but a kiss was not enough to take him from his books. *Mrs* Bennet is another subject altogether." Bingley laughed. "Mr Wickham was shunned from decent society within a week! And now that he has deserted the militia, Lizzy will never have to encounter him. Colonel Foster says he shall flog him should he see Mr Wickham again; I hope he does."

"Indeed."

"Since the wedding, Lizzy has seemed more cheerful. It must be because Mr Wickham has fled in disgrace, and she knows she won't meet him again."

"That, undoubtedly, must be the reason."

"Shall we rejoin the ladies?" Darcy rose. "And Darcy? Could you do whatever you can to entertain Lizzy, so Jane will retire early?"

"Lizzy, you will stay by my side tonight? Last night you retired so early that Mr Darcy felt compelled to do the same. The door had scarcely closed behind you before he insisted on going upstairs."

Darcy had, in fact, not gone to bed, but had joined her in her sitting room for another hour where they thoroughly enjoyed the comfort of ease and familiarity that now existed between them. The memory of how their unreserved conversation was often interspersed with affectionate embraces brought a warmth to Elizabeth's cheeks.

"You cannot be reluctant about going to bed with your husband? The first time is behind you; it still cannot be as bad as that, is it?"

Jane turned red. "I am sorry! If you wish to postpone the event, I will remain."

"No, I do not aim to avoid it."

Elizabeth looked at her sister, but Jane gave no further answer. "I do not know what to say to help you. I thought that my aunt—"

"I cannot stand to have you and Mr Darcy ... I do not want either of you to think that you must retire early so Bingley and I ... and what you must think of us should we retire before you!"

Elizabeth could not say that she and Darcy spared no thought to the Bingleys, so eager as they were to be able to spend an hour or two alone. "I assure you no one thinks or says anything improper about you. Can you, in your wildest flight of fancy, imagine Mr Darcy and me discussing, with precise detail, what we think you and Charles—"

"Stop!" Jane laughed, and Elizabeth, unable to keep her countenance, joined her.

When their giggles subsided, Elizabeth added, "You need not stand on ceremony with us, your closest friends."

"We must have some entertainment before I retire with Charles. Will you exhibit on the instrument? Or we can play a game? And I do hate to leave you with Mr Darcy if you do not wish it."

"Mr Darcy and I are more at ease with one another than we were before your wedding. I know you have been preoccupied with your own concerns, as well you should be, but do not worry on that account."

Jane agreed and went to make the tea, leaving Elizabeth to think of Darcy: of their affection, their delight in being together, their hours of happy joking and serious discussion. When the gentlemen came in, Bingley went to his wife while Darcy, with no effort at prevarication, went to Elizabeth. Before Darcy even sat beside her, she asked him the question that had been pressing on her mind.

"What made you shy of me whenever you came to Longbourn before the wedding? Why did you look as if you did not care about me?"

"I felt guilty that my silence allowed Mr Wickham to abuse you. And because you gave me no encouragement."

"I was embarrassed after having misplaced my faith in a man so unworthy as Mr Wickham."

"And I was embarrassed for leaving in anger. I made an error in allowing anything to keep me from you while you still retained the name Bennet."

"You might have talked to me more when you came to dinner or at the wedding breakfast."

"A man who had felt less, might."

"So that was your only hope when you returned: to attend Charles' wedding and preserve us from an unworthy acquaintance?"

"Of course my real purpose was to see *you* and to judge whether I might ever have you love me again. My avowed one was to convince your parents and neighbours of Mr Wickham's worthlessness, and to make the confession to you about Mr Wickham's history with my sister."

"You would protect us all from Mr Wickham, even risk revealing all about your sister when you thought I did not love you? Even after I failed to trust you? You are a dear generous man!" He seemed uncomfortable with her praise, so she teased him. "You would have been our hero. Did you see yourself as the gallant knight, galloping on your noble steed to protect the fair maids of Longbourn?" He began to speak but stopped when his attention was caught by something near to her sleeve.

"What happened to your arm?"

Elizabeth looked at the faded yellow and green bruises. "We were tossed about when my uncle's carriage was damaged last week. I landed roughly against the side."

"You have not worn short sleeves since then."

"You take more notice of ladies' attire than I suspected." She smiled, but Darcy was still staring at her injury. "I thought since they faded, it would be harmless to wear shorter sleeves again."

Darcy reached out with the edge of his index finger and delicately stroked the discoloured skin. She shivered at the intimacy of the contact. The light touch and tender expression on his face did more to stir her heart than some of his more extravagant caresses. "I had no notion you had been hurt in the accident, Elizabeth."

"Did I hear you call her *Miss Elizabeth* again?" Bingley's voice from across the room startled them both, and Darcy withdrew his hand. The back of the sofa obscured it from his friend's view. "You seem determined to demote her from her proper rank."

"I am not offended, Charles. I am still not accustomed to being addressed as *Miss Bennet* when Jane is present."

"You should pay attention to Mrs Bingley rather than oversee how I address Miss Bennet." Darcy glared at his friend.

"It is not even Sunday evening; you should not be so awful an object on a Friday."

"I am not awful; I was making an observation that you are too happily situated to waste your time finding fault with me."

"That is fair!" Bingley laughed. "Few would dare to say that a man such as you has anything of which to complain or be irritable about in any event."

"I have nothing but solitude to complain of, and nothing but a companion to wish for," Darcy whispered and gave her a pointed look. The feeling this statement produced was indescribable, but deeply felt at Elizabeth's heart. Jane was finished with the tea, but Bingley declined, and then asked Darcy if he was at all tired.

Before Darcy could answer, Jane said, "Let us play a game! Lizzy, you would enjoy a diversion, would you not?"

"Very well, but not cards."

She did not wish to force Darcy or Bingley to remain at cards for three hours when both gentlemen wished to be elsewhere. *Jane, in her heart, wishes to be elsewhere, also.* Bingley suggested, with a smile towards his wife, that they play 'I Love My Love with an A.'

Bingley began. "I love my love with an A because she is affectionate, I hate my love with an A because she is artful, I took her to Andover, to the sign of the Angel, I treated her with artichokes, and her name is Anna."

Jane repeated Bingley's piece, then took her turn. "I love my love with a B because he is benevolent, I hate my love with a B because he is boisterous, I took him to Bedford, to the sign of the Bear, I treated him with barley, and his name is Bingley."

Darcy easily recited their words. "I love my love with a C because she is compassionate." Darcy gave Elizabeth an expressive look. "I hate my love with a C because she is capricious, I took her to Cambridge, to the sign of the Cross, I treated her with coffee, and her name is Constance."

"Not *Caroline*?" Bingley teased.

"Certainly not!"

Elizabeth repeated the previous turns before she took her own. "I love my love with a D because he is *devoted*, I hate my love with a D because he is demanding, I took him to Derby, to the sign of the Deer, I treated him with duck, and his name is ..." Elizabeth bit her lip and stared at the man she had promised to marry. "...Daniel."

Jane took her turn, but Elizabeth was watching Darcy shake his head at her in mock disapproval. The game continued with errors from all parties, save for Darcy who, to Elizabeth's annoyance, rattled off every adjective, noun, and name without hesitation. Elizabeth had the pleasure of hearing herself called compassionate, graceful, opinionated, and worthy, if Darcy's looks while he took his turn meant what she presumed they did. After an hour, with much mirth and helpful hints, the game neared its natural conclusion.

"I love my love with an X because...he is...xanthic!" Elizabeth finally cried. "I hate my love with an X because he is...xiphoid, I took him to Xeres, to the sign of the...sign of the..."

"Do you cry forfeit?" asked Darcy.

"No!"

"We could leave off here?" Bingley suggested. "It is rather late..."

"No. To the sign of the..." She threw up her hands in defeat. "I can think of nothing else."

Bingley looked pointedly at Jane, who nodded while blushing. He then wished the party a pleasant evening and led his wife out the door. The moment the door closed, Darcy drew Elizabeth from the table to stand before the fire, still holding on to her hands.

"Xebec," he said.

"I beg your pardon?"

"A xebec is a small, three-masted ship."

Elizabeth rolled her eyes. "Had I known that I may have answered the sign, but even *you* would not have been able to think of a food beginning with X."

"That may be the case, but it was not my turn and *you* are the one who failed to complete her task."

"I take back the generous things I said about you, Fitzwilliam Darcy. You were too caught up in recalling everyone else's blunders to take proper note of why *I* love my love."

"Not at all. You announced I was devoted, handsome, liberal, principled, and trustworthy." Darcy's wide smile told her how pleased he was.

"I should add attentive to your list of good qualities."

He took her hands and raised them to his shoulders, and then brought his hands to her waist. "You failed to answer for the sign, for the food, and for the name of X."

"Why must my forfeits be submitted to you?"

"For every fault he makes, the player must incur a forfeit. You cannot compromise on the rules because the others abandoned the game."

"I see; I must pay my forfeits to you for lack of alternative."

"No, you must pay your forfeits to me because you are fervently anticipating my kisses, and this is the only way that a modest woman can enjoy such good fortune."

She laughed, not dissatisfied in the least. "Fitzwilliam! I am shocked at you!"

"I fail to see why. An old maid such as yourself should not leave the world without having your cheeks kissed by a gentleman's two lips."

"By all means, then, indulge this ancient spinster and grace my withered cheeks with a perfunctory kiss." She made a show of turning her head and pushing out her cheek towards him.

Darcy slowly pressed his lips against the smoothness of her cheek and held them there for a long moment. He then trailed tender kisses along her jaw, and then down her throat as she tilted her head back. An unexpected tremor of pleasure shivered down her back when his lips and tongue lingered on the pulse point at the base of her neck.

"I have wanted to kiss you…here…since you last stayed at Netherfield," he murmured in a low voice. His breath was warm against her skin. Elizabeth's breathing became rapid and she was finding it difficult to speak.

"I hope that was recompense for only *one* of my forfeits." Elizabeth flattened the lapels of his cutaway tailcoat before resting her hands against his chest. She wondered if her heart would ever resume a slower, steady beat. Elizabeth gave him a long, appraising look.

"Is there something wrong about my appearance that draws your notice?"

"I was marvelling at how unfair it is that every inch of you is covered, from your wrists to your neck. A lady's full dress can reveal to the point of provocation, but I am not fortunate in being able to have the same breadth of your skin on display." She leant into him and pressed her lips against his jaw, trailing kisses until the high collar of his waistcoat prevented her further progress.

Elizabeth heard Darcy's sharp intake of breath. He was shocked but, she hoped, not offended.

Her sister need not have been self-conscious: Jane and Bingley were far from Elizabeth's mind.

Darcy kept his hands planted on Elizabeth's waist, only allowing his thumbs to slowly move back and forth. His hands tingled with a desire to touch the soft curves he had been admiring for months. Her hands rested against his chest, scorching him through the fabric. Her nearness, the way she was pressed against him, kissing his jaw, nearly overwhelmed him.

"Fitzwilliam? Have I scandalised you?" Darcy held her in place and brushed a kiss against her forehead; his rapid heartbeat made it difficult to speak.

"I am not shocked," he said in a voice he barely recognised as his own. "Were I a less reserved man, I might burst forth in raptures of admiration and delight."

"You are not alarmed to know I have thought about you in varying stages of undress?"

The intimacy of her tone sent a shiver down his back. "Would you be outraged to learn I have thought the same about you?"

Her lips parted around a shallow breath, and he hurriedly covered them with his own. His mouth moved gently over hers, but the need to taste her welled up inside of him. He ran the tip of his tongue between her lips. Her breath hitched, and she caressed him back, tentatively at first, but in the space of a heartbeat, her tongue swept passionately inside his mouth. It made his heart seize.

He groaned when she put her arms around his neck and pulled him close, her body pressed against his. Darcy was more aware than ever of the shape of her, of every wonderful curve, of her breasts crushed against his chest. He felt her fingers in his hair, her nails slowly scraping against his scalp and driving him mad. Then she arched her hips against him, and wild desire overpowered him.

Darcy brushed his fingertips along the low neckline of her gown and then curved a palm around her breast, sensation and excitement crashing through him. Elizabeth tensed at the evidence of his ardour, but instead of drawing away, she moaned and drew herself even closer. She was wonderfully responsive to his slow, thorough exploration of her breasts. It was a tantalising promise of what their future life would hold.

He wanted more, but Darcy lifted his mouth and pressed his forehead against hers, seeking control. She whimpered in frustration when he stopped, and that did nothing to quell the blaze of desire he was struggling to suppress. In the near silence of the drawing room, he could hear the pounding of both of their heartbeats and feel her whole body tensed with the same barely contained longing as his. Darcy smoothed back strands of Elizabeth's hair that had come free. She held his face in her hands and stroked his cheeks with her fingertips.

"I almost wish you were not so good a man." She kissed him again, but pulled away before tenderness could tumble back into heat.

"You may add that to my list of defects." His voice was hoarse and unrecognisable.

"You have made great strides in being more agreeable in company; you can now work on overcoming your scruples." Her voice lifted with teasing hopefulness.

He smiled. "I, too, look forward to the day when passion might overtake restraint."

Elizabeth's arms encircled his waist and she rested her head against him. "You will come to Brighton?" He nodded and kissed the crown of her head. "I cannot spend a month in Brighton and then another month or two at Longbourn awaiting our wedding. I do not want to wait so long to be wed."

"Neither do I. If you wish to remain a few weeks with your sister, we can marry from Bingley's house in Brighton. Unless you think your parents will disapprove," he added.

Elizabeth was thoughtful for a long moment. "I think once my father is convinced of your worthiness and my affections, his interest in the details will wane. If you remind my mother of your annual income, she will not be disappointed either. A brief visit after the event to show off the new Mrs Darcy will satisfy her."

"Then we will go to Longbourn tomorrow."

"And we will tell the Bingleys in the morning."

DARCY AND ELIZABETH ENTERED THE BREAKFAST ROOM TOGETHER, well after their host and hostess. Although Mr and Mrs Bingley greeted their guests, neither was attentive enough to observe that Darcy's cravat was askew and Elizabeth's hair was loose from its pins on one side.

"Darcy, the coachman says the lane is in a better condition than yesterday. I think we will attempt to make it to London. There is no reason to suppose the roads to be in a worse state as we get closer to town. We should be there not long after dark."

Darcy looked across the table at Elizabeth.

"Charles, I know you and Jane are ready to be on the road to Brighton, but I would like to call at Longbourn," answered Elizabeth.

Bingley looked surprised. "Did you not take leave of them on Wednesday?" He realised the rudeness of his question, apologised, and addressed his wife. "Shall we all take leave of your family?"

"No, you need not come," Elizabeth said. "Only I need to call at Longbourn today."

"We," corrected Darcy.

"What?" Bingley asked.

"Yes. *We* need to call at Longbourn."

"Lizzy?" asked Jane, looking back and forth between Darcy and Elizabeth.

"Miss Bennet and I need to call at Longbourn," said Darcy. "However, I see no reason that she will be unable to leave for Brighton tomorrow."

"Darcy, why are you going to Longbourn?" Bingley looked perplexed.

Darcy continued to stare at Elizabeth, who smiled beautifully at him in return, and reached her hand across the table towards him.

"Lizzy!" shrieked Jane, raising her hands to her face as Darcy took Elizabeth's outstretched hand. "You are not joking, are you?"

"What is happening?" Bingley asked.

The chair legs scraped back against the floor, and the ladies were mingled in embraces of tears and joy. Bingley stared at them in wide-eyed bewilderment, and Darcy watched them in silent satisfaction. Darcy's quiet regard was short-lived when he was forced by his future sister to join in their raptures. They shook hands with great cordiality as Darcy received all the good wishes and affections of a sister. It was not until Elizabeth moved near to him, and he drew out his handkerchief to dry her exultant tears, that Bingley found his voice.

"You and Lizzy? You are engaged?"

"Shall you like to have such a brother?" His voice betrayed his amusement at his friend's confusion.

"Yes, very much! I daresay nothing could give either Jane or myself more delight. I do congratulate you." Bingley rose and held out his hand. He congratulated Elizabeth, who then put her arms around Darcy for an embrace that he did not hesitate to return. Jane burst forth into another round of happy weeping at the affectionate sight.

Bingley stared at the happy couple in puzzlement. "I had no idea."

Chapter 37

Thursday, March 26
Berkeley Square, London

Elizabeth Darcy frowned at the letter that had arrived from Kent. She had read it yesterday privately and was, at first, insulted. A second reading turned her annoyance into bewilderment, and upon this third reading and after a day's reflection, she was sufficiently amused by its absurdity to share its contents with her husband. He would be so indignant that only *her* patience and humour would prevent him from losing his temper.

Elizabeth passed the chamber that had been turned into a music room for Georgiana. Her sister sat at her harp, enraptured by the sound of her own beautiful music. Elizabeth did not tarry; she descended a flight and walked into the library.

Darcy sat writing in his slow and deliberate way. He looked up as she entered and nodded once to indicate he had noticed her. She would receive a warmer welcome when he was finished. She selected Cowper to occupy herself. Not a quarter of an hour had passed before Elizabeth heard Darcy press his seal into the wax.

"What are you reading, dearest?"

"A proud and disagreeable man I once was acquainted with introduced me to Cowper."

"What sort of a wife speaks of other gentlemen before her husband?"

"I had no notion you were a jealous man."

"I have the right to be jealous when I know you are violently in love with that proud and disagreeable man."

Elizabeth grinned and handed him the volume. "I was rereading *The Garden*. My sentiments are like line 41. Does that reassure you?"

"'Domestic happiness, thou only bliss / Of Paradise that has survived the fall!' I am assuaged for the present. Did you come to the library to keep company with me?"

"In part." He looked distracted by what he had been writing; she suspected he was wanted at home. "I thought we might go to Pemberley now rather than in May, if you are willing."

Darcy's shoulders relaxed. "Yes, nothing would please me more than to bring you home, if you feel the new bride has had enough time to be shown to her advantage in town. I shall leave the arrangements in your capable hands. Did you have something to show me?"

She hated to aggravate him after having dispelled some of his gloom. "Lady Catherine"—here Darcy's expectant countenance clouded—"has decided she wishes to re-establish a correspondence with this family."

Darcy stood and held out his hand. "Here," said Elizabeth, keeping her tone light and playful, "her best effort at an olive branch."

Rosings Park, Kent
23 March

When I first learned, madam, of your upstart pretensions in ensnaring my nephew, I supposed you to be lost to every feeling of propriety and delicacy. It is a disgrace that Darcy has fallen victim to the arts and allurements of a woman of inferior birth, entirely without connexions or fortune. From what I have learned of you, I presume you are ignorant and stand in need of someone's advice whose regard for your husband, joined to superior judgment, might authorise her to give it. I am that person, and I challenge you to accept the offer of my notice and of my counsel. Even an artful and selfish girl such as you cannot be unaware of how grateful you ought to be for my condescension. Your alliance will always be a disgrace to Darcy, but since there is no hope of its dissolution, I expect you to accept my attentions and advice. It is only for the sake of my nephew, not for your own, that I will tolerate to be of use to one so underserving as you.

"I warned her, Elizabeth! Her reply to the letter that announced the arrangement of our marriage was so abusive of you that I warned her I would sever all contact unless she apologised. And now, when she is aware I will not tolerate her disrespect, let alone her abusive language towards you, she has the audacity to send you *this*!" Darcy crumpled the letter and dropped it.

"I think Lady Catherine has realised that I will not, despite her hopes, be censured, slighted, and despised by everyone connected with you, save herself."

"That is all the more reason for her to seek reconciliation, not insult you further!" He paced, occasionally raking his hand through his dark hair. "I will not tolerate it."

Elizabeth endeavoured to keep her attention on the subject at hand, rather on her husband's trim waist, broad shoulders, and animated eyes. She smiled at herself for her inattention as Darcy's furious pacing brought him closer.

"You are amused by this insult?" Darcy's expression now was imploring her to make him smile.

Elizabeth held out her hand, and Darcy pulled her into his arms. "I am underserving, our union is a degradation, she has avoided meeting me—and yet this woman cannot repress her desire to give me advice? We must laugh!"

She watched some of Darcy's tension ease while he ran his

hands slowly up and down her hips. "Lady Catherine does love to be of use."

"How shall I handle her letter?"

"It is best used as kindling." Darcy leant in closer and pressed his cheek against hers. His warm breath against her ear thrilled her.

"I agree, but I shall demonstrate to Lady Catherine that among the sins she accuses me of, a negligent correspondent I am not."

"You cannot leave me so soon," he said with a low voice as he brought his mouth to hers. Elizabeth's fingers toyed with the buttons on his waistcoat while she kissed him, but she pulled away.

"We are to ride with the Bingleys at Hyde Park, and I have a letter to write first."

"We need not meet them until three o'clock." He roughly pulled her flush against him.

"Fitzwilliam! It is now after two!"

"We do not need go at all." He pleaded his case by placing lingering kisses along her neck. The hands that had been resting on her hips slid higher.

"If you wish to leave town after Easter, you will not have other chances to show me off to those of rank and fortune."

"You know I do not care at all for that. Besides, it will likely rain. We ought to stay home." His hand now moved between them to one of her breasts. She made a low little noise of contentment before she found her voice.

"Today it is not raining, and you promised Charles. I would hate for there to be any rumour your friendship has faltered now that it is obvious we do not associate with Miss Bingley."

Darcy drew back, and Elizabeth did not laugh at his petulant expression. "*One* circuit around the park."

"They invited us to dine after, and then I promise you"—she pressed a kiss behind his ear, in the place she knew would rouse him—"we need not remain with them in the evening."

His expression managed to convey both the profound attachment he felt towards her and his disappointment in having to delay, demonstrating just how passionate that attachment was.

35 Berkeley Square
26 March

It could be said that you are courteous, madam, to write to me when you have thus far repulsed my husband's attempts to introduce us. However, I am unable to express any sense of obligation for your attention to me. I cannot express how much I enjoy being mistress of my own home, managing affairs to my own satisfaction, and receiving the approbation of my husband and sister. Even as great a proficient in all things as you profess to be, I doubt that you can appreciate the felicity that we now enjoy in our married life, nor the depth of harmony in our lives.

Furthermore, neither my husband nor I can imagine a state of affairs in which any advice of yours can ever be wanted.

I am ever, and to the delight of my husband,
Elizabeth Darcy

THE BINGLEYS AND THE DARCYS DROVE ALONG ROTTEN ROW ON the first dry afternoon in recent memory. The couples spoke animatedly and were so engrossed in one another's company that it was not until the Darcys' driver called their notice that they saw a gentleman on horseback attempting to get their attention.

"Who is the dandy whose collars are so high he cannot turn his head?" Bingley murmured.

"That is my cousin, Lord Milton."

Bingley turned red, and Elizabeth laughed. Before Bingley could stammer an apology, her husband said, "I am not offended; you are not wrong."

Milton approached the barouche-landau and first bowed to Darcy. "Mrs Darcy, it is a pleasure to see you." His tone implied he had no feeling on the matter one way or the other.

"Milton, may I present my friend Mr Bingley, and his wife, who is Mrs Darcy's sister." Milton bestowed upon them a touch of his hat and a careless glance.

"I would like to a moment of your time, if your companions can spare you?"

Bingley offered to escort the ladies on a walk along the footpath. Elizabeth informed them of their plans to leave soon for Derbyshire and asked Charles to tell her about Pemberley. His reminisces filled their conversation for a quarter of an hour until, as they were on their way back, they were approached by a woman Elizabeth did not know.

"Forgive my presumption, but there are times when good breeding must be set aside for the sake of one's curiosity." She was small, with a shapely figure, and wore a blue riding habit that perfectly matched her eyes. Behind her on the bridle path, Elizabeth saw a groom in livery holding the reins to her horse.

"How may I help you, madam?" Bingley asked.

"Perhaps you would be good enough to tell me which of these ladies is Mrs Darcy?" Neither he nor Jane could help but look towards Elizabeth. "So *you* are she. I spoke with Lord Milton—he just left your husband, and he said Mrs Darcy was along the footpath with another couple."

"May I ask how you are acquainted with them?"

"I am Lady Hancock's friend." This information meant little to Charles and Jane, but Darcy had told her of Milton's mistress. "Walk with me, Mrs Darcy? I will not detain you long." Elizabeth dropped Charles's arm and told them to go ahead. The woman drew her to the side of the path. "I have one question to ask you. Is your Christian name Elizabeth?"

"Tell me first how you know Mr Darcy."

"My, you have spirit. If I told you Mr Darcy and I were friends, what would you say?" Her cold stare and inflection of the word *friends* left no doubt in Elizabeth's mind that *lovers* was her intended meaning.

"I would say that marriage is the highest state of friendship two people in love can know."

The woman barked a harsh laugh. "You could not have asserted your claim any stronger had you planted your flag on Mr Darcy's head. I like an assertive woman because I am one. Do you not agree that your husband admires a strong-willed woman?"

"What I can verify is that Mr Darcy admires *me*."

"Is your Christian name Elizabeth, or is it not?"

"It is."

The woman gave her an appraising look, but said nothing.

"I have been gracious in satisfying your impolite curiosity, and now I expect the same: who are you, and how are you acquainted with my husband?" She could not credit the idea that this woman was Darcy's former mistress.

The woman smirked. "I had expected this encounter to be more diverting. I thought you would be an unsophisticated girl who I could reduce to tears with a few vague hints. You are more formidable than I anticipated. I like that, so I shall tell you the truth. I met Mr Darcy in January at a house party with Lord Milton and Lady Hancock. Mr Darcy chose *not* to be my lover, although he was recently crossed in love by a woman named Elizabeth. Does that ease your mind?"

"There is nothing you could say or do that would influence how I view my marriage to Mr Darcy."

"I learnt from Lord Milton that Mr Darcy married, and I had to see for myself if it was to the Elizabeth he was pining for. I wanted to see what sort of a woman had a hold over him and revenge myself upon him a little. I am not accustomed to being denied. You have the privilege, Elizabeth Darcy, of knowing your husband spent his nights thinking of you when he *ought* to have been with me. I hope you will do me the courtesy of not making that information public knowledge."

"I can assure you this is not a conversation I intend to repeat."

"I wish you joy," she said in a mocking voice as she walked away.

Elizabeth rejoined Charles and Jane and did not explain the encounter. When they arrived at the open carriage, Lord Milton was gone and Darcy was standing next to it, waiting for them. Bingley assisted his wife in and followed her, but Elizabeth stopped when Darcy attempted to hand her in.

"Fitzwilliam, what did Lord Milton ask you?" She wondered if his cousin was involved in the courtesan's attempt to speak with her.

Darcy shrugged his shoulders. "He heard that Georgiana told Colonel Fitzwilliam that you are well read. He perceived a danger and wished to caution me. He fears well-read women are argumentative, and he wanted to be sure that my wife would be careful how she presented herself in society."

"How distressing that your wife's mind has been improved by extensive reading."

"Milton is a fool, and next to his wife learning about his mistress, nothing frightens him more than a clever, well-informed woman."

Darcy held out his hand to help her into the carriage. Elizabeth hesitated, and he asked her what was wrong. "Nothing, only—sometimes, I still regret all that kept us apart last winter."

The intensity of emotion shining from his eyes made it impossible for her to look away. She then did something that if Lord Milton learned of it, her argumentative nature would be the least of his concerns. He would be alarmed to hear how Mrs Darcy kissed her husband in Hyde Park, and all Mr Darcy did after was smile.

Chapter 38

April 1812

Darcy found his wife wearing her dressing gown, in her own apartments, after a quarter of an hour of searching.

"You are not often in your dressing room at this time of the day." When he saw her red-rimmed eyes, pale face, and drawn appearance, he cried, "Dearest Elizabeth! Are you ill? What is the matter?"

"There is nothing the matter with me."

"I know you have been crying." He watched her in wretched suspense.

"Georgiana told me about Ramsgate: all of the public meetings and private assignations, all of Mr Wickham's false promises and Mrs Younge's insidious persuasions, everything up until the day you arrived at her door. They manipulated a lonely, shy, affectionate girl for her money, and it sickens me!"

"It must have been a painful confession for her to make and for you to hear." He was surprised by the rough sound of his own voice. "Did she say whether they—did he…?"

"I promised that what she told me would remain between us. What she needed was a friend who comprehended her feelings, someone to tell her everything would be well, and without passing judgment."

Darcy spoke in a voice of forced calmness. "I have a right to know! I comprehend that it would be too much for Georgiana to speak of it to *me,* but I expect you to tell me it all."

"If I thought it in her best interest, I would, but my silence serves her better. It is all in the past, and the remembrance of it brings her anguish."

"Must I remind you of your wedding vows and demand you tell me?"

As soon as the words left his mouth, he regretted the ill-founded scheme to intimidate his wife into telling him what he wanted to know, even in the second before he saw her face change colour.

"By all means, demand that I obey you and break my confidence with Georgiana," she said in a slow, cold tone. "The natural consequences of what follow will be yours alone to suffer."

He began in a different way. "I am grateful to your duty to her—"

"I love her, and I am acting in the way I believe serves her best. She *begged* me not to tell you."

"I am sorry." The fury dissolved from his wife's eyes with his apology. "I would never compel you to do anything that goes against your nature or your conscience."

"I do not keep this from you lightly. If you knew it all, it would affect how you behave towards Georgiana. A sympathetic or knowing glance from you would be too much for her to bear. A disapproving look from you, and she will fall to pieces. She already feels like a failure to you and to the Darcy name."

He walked the room in earnest meditation and admitted aloud, "I cannot at all swear I would not treat her any differently were I to know the particulars of last summer's sad affair."

"She is a girl who is humiliated. To have her surrogate father look on her with pity or revulsion is too much. She is plagued by the past, and both of you need to think about her future."

Darcy heaved a sigh and ran his hands across his eyes. He raised his head and looked at his wife. Elizabeth beckoned him to sit beside her. "I cannot comprehend how talking over the events, even to an approving listener, would be sufficient to raise Georgiana's spirits."

"Georgiana needed kindness and encouragement to improve her spirits, but she could never confess the particulars to *you*. She struggled at first at of talking about it, but, once begun, it was as though a burden was lifted. I think she was relieved to tell someone."

"Do you believe that in confiding in you, Georgiana has made progress in recovering her happiness and equanimity?"

"I am encouraged." She laid her head against his shoulder. "She appeared more at ease and was already less nervous by the time I left her rooms."

Darcy knew he would not even be able to listen calmly to Elizabeth while she related whatever Georgiana confessed. The degree of compassion and delicacy needed to help Georgiana recover from Ramsgate was beyond his ability, but Elizabeth could surely comprehend her young heart and mind.

Darcy looked at his wife and felt most of his tension fall away. *If this is what she says is best for Georgiana, I have every confidence in her.*

"Then you may depend upon my seeking no further. I trust your judgment."

July 1812

June 25, 1812
Brighton

My dear Lizzy,
If you were not so rich, I am sure you would wish you were in Brighton hunting for a husband with me! Darcy is very generous, but I cannot suppose there to be much fun in being married to him.

Darcy looked up from his own letter whilst Elizabeth gave him a stare, hidden from Georgiana's view, that suggested that she found nothing wanting in being married.

You should have seen how Kitty wept with envy when I left with Charles and Jane to go to Brighton! We have been here a fortnight, and there are balls and card parties and gentlemen everywhere! I expected more flirting since the militia is encamped here, but I only see the officers if they call on Jane. I am to walk along the Marine Parade with Captain Carter today. Charles says that Jane must come, too. How strange!

Since writing the above, something so unexpected has occurred! I have news for you, about a person we all hate!

Elizabeth broke off and Darcy shared a knowing look with her. He had managed to parse a letter from Bingley that must have discussed the same topic.

"Georgiana, that is enough of Lydia's nonsense for the present," Elizabeth's voice wavered, but Darcy suspected none but him would notice. "Be thankful you only have a brother, because sisters can be the silliest of correspondents. I have heard it said that your brother writes you charming letters with words of four syllables."

Breakfast was soon over, and Darcy and Elizabeth all but ran to the library to talk once Georgiana went to the music room. They exchanged letters, Elizabeth taking much longer to read Bingley's messy letter than Darcy did to read Lydia's exuberant description of Wickham's capture by his former fellow-officers.

"Good heavens," Elizabeth whispered when she looked up. "What strange luck brought Mr Wickham, Lydia, and the militia together in Brighton this summer. What else did Lydia write? I did not finish reading it."

"She wrote of the general excitement in the regiment upon recovering their deserter and of how amusing it would be for Mr Wickham to be flogged. She suspects that you would be pleased to hear of his capture, and she promises to observe his flogging and report the details to you."

"Did Charles write anything of note after he described Mr Wickham being detained? I do not wish to stare at his inkblots if I need not."

Darcy raked a hand through his hair and walked to the window. "If you remember, Mr Wickham had no money to leave Meryton. Bingley writes that along with desertion, he will also be charged with theft. Mr Wickham stole money from a fellow officer to fund his escape."

Darcy saw his wife was shocked, her hand covering her mouth. "How much did he steal?"

"Ten pounds."

"What will happen to him?"

"For both desertion and stealing property he could be sentenced to death, or transportation for seven years as a felon. Or perhaps for life. Colonel Forster will likely have his opportunity to inflict a few hundred lashes as well."

"I wanted him to be held accountable for his actions, Fitzwilliam, particularly for Georgiana, but not like this. He is an immoral, hateful man, but …"

A few large, wet tears fell from her eyes, and Darcy embraced her. Wickham had wounded his sister's spirits and self-assurance—if not worse—and had caused his wife mortification and heartache. But his stomach twisted at the idea of the companion of his youth, his father's godson, being sentenced to death, or whipped until his back and shoulder bones were laid bare, literally within an inch of his life.

Elizabeth looked up at him. "A man is not put to death for desertion and ten pounds."

For the sake of his wife's benevolent feelings, Darcy bit back the reply that he thought transportation was as certain to cause his death as a sentence of death by the Court.

"The Crown does typically commute the sentence to transportation." Darcy was relieved that his family would never be troubled by him again. "What should we tell my sister?"

"Although she has a superior degree of confidence since the spring, I think we ought to wait until we learn what his sentence will be."

"She has shown great improvement since she spoke with you," Darcy agreed. "I am exceedingly proud of her."

While in general reticent, Georgiana had regained her much of her confidence and happiness over the summer. She no longer flinched when spoken to nor only spoke when absolutely necessary, and would readily enter into conversation with her closest friends, even playing for them if they asked her.

"She has more of that mental strength now, I think," Elizabeth said as she pressed her cheek to his chest.

"Georgiana grows more capable as time goes on. It is not even a full year after Ramsgate, and she has benefited greatly from your friendship and confidence." A feeling of tender affection and gratitude for his wife gripped him. Darcy brushed his lips against the tender skin just below her ear. "I think everyone's spirits have been made right by having you at Pemberley."

Darcy looked into her eyes and saw her devoted attachment for him in her gaze. Elizabeth brought her arms around his neck. "I am grateful for the strength of your confidence in me."

"I could not thank you too much for—"

Elizabeth silenced him with a warm press of her lips. "You need not say such a thing." Her fingers moved from the nape of his neck to slide through his hair.

"I disagree, but whatever difference of opinion may exist between us, we are united in every possible way."

"There could be no two people whose feelings were so in unison."

Chapter 39

December 25, 1812

Garlands of holly and bay were at the entrances to Pemberley and its public rooms and were wrapped around the stair balustrades and columns. Every surface that could support a glossy sprig with red berries sported those emblems of life and gladness.

"I think there is something cheering in the triumph of warmth and verdure over the frosty winter," Elizabeth had said as she decided that the roaring evening fire needed to be built up higher and another stem of ivy added to the mantle.

Darcy knew it was not the greenery that brightened the season, but Pemberley's mistress. Elizabeth was happy herself and disposed to make those around her happy. Everything she did combined to produce joyful feelings throughout the Christmas holiday, and everyone—the servants, the Gardiners, their neighbours—fell under her cheerful influence.

Darcy allowed himself to be taken in by her enthusiasm, and on Christmas evening, he danced, played bullet pudding, and kissed his wife under the kissing bough. His fondest moment of the evening came, however, when he observed the Gardiners' four children engaged in romping games. He happily reflected that if Elizabeth's suspicions were correct, next Christmas their own child would be curiously watching the commotion, though not old enough to crawl over to join.

"Did you see my uncle scrambling for the raisins?" Elizabeth was laughing as she pulled a comb from her hair at the end of the evening.

"Georgiana is a fearless Snapdragon player. She was not going to allow Gardiner to supplant her as champion."

"For all her shyness, she does have that true Darcy spirit. Her competitiveness in games would endear her to the family at Longbourn at Christmas."

"I daresay at Christmas your mother had dinner parties every night, and every evening had a round game of cards, conversation by the fire, a troop of children playing with wooden horses and dolls, and a merry dance. Our evenings at Pemberley have been smaller parties. I would not be surprised if three days in a row pass by where no one comes to call and we do not leave the house."

"What strange ideas you have! I am happy here with the Gardiners and Georgiana, and our neighbours, too. And we shall see Jane and Charles and little Janie in a fortnight when we go down to town."

"Aside from tonight, we have entertained little."

Elizabeth ran her hand through his hair. "You know I prefer the comfort and elegance of our own family party. Besides, Mr Wickham's terrible kiss happened last Christmas. I prefer my Christmas gaieties to be more subdued this year, and every year." She gave a wry smile.

"I have a gift for you," he said, eager to do away with all remembrance of that scoundrel. He retrieved a small box from his dressing room and pressed it into his wife's hand.

"I thought we were to exchange gifts at Epiphany with Charles and Jane and the baby?"

"And we will. However, this arrived yesterday, and I could not wait another day to present it to you."

Elizabeth lifted the lid to see a gold ring. She ran a finger across its delicate surface, then looked at him.

"My uncle, Lord Fitzwilliam, discovered this posy ring at Wentworth House. He writes that his mother's father presented it to his wife on the occasion of their engagement in 1716, and that the ring was passed down to his mother. Since her death, he suspects it sat forgotten in that box."

"That explains why neither your mother nor Lady Catherine inherited it. Why did your uncle send the ring to you, and not to Anne or Georgiana?"

"His opinion was that it befitted a beloved wife. Once I read the inscription, I could not wait to place it on your finger."

Darcy took the ring and tilted it, so the engraving inside was visible. *Vous et aucun autre.*

"You and no other," Elizabeth whispered, with tears shining in her eyes.

Darcy placed the ring on the centre finger of her right hand. "You do not need another symbol of my fidelity and love. Nonetheless, I hope you know that my loving *you* has made me a better man."

He bent his head to hers in a kiss that began in tenderness and flared into a passion. They made their way across the room, leaving a trail of discarded garments. They staggered the last few steps, and Elizabeth, laughingly, leapt onto the bed and gave him a bold look. He immediately stretched out on top of her, resting on his elbows and cupping her breasts with his hands, and she sighed, her eyes closed in bliss. He trailed open-mouthed kisses and sucked the sensitive curve of her neck, his palms fondled her breasts, and he moved with tantalising slowness.

He relished the feeling of her warm body at every place where his bare skin touched hers. She was entirely pressed beneath him, his weight and position pinning her down, and she had to endure every touch and sensation without moving in response. When Darcy shifted his hands to the bed, Elizabeth cried out as his movements were, at last, faster and more powerful against her.

"Good God, I love you," he rasped when she lifted her hips to wrap her legs around him.

Much later, when their breath returned, Darcy cradled Elizabeth against him, smoothing her hair.

"Fitzwilliam? Can you reach the drawer in the table? There is something there."

He was reluctant to move from her side, but he did as his was bid and handed her a small object wrapped in tissue.

"No, it is for you. I was going to wait until the sixth, but I cannot wait to respond in kind."

Darcy unwrapped the tissue to reveal a two-inch lover's eye miniature, set in gold with a loop at the top, to be hung on a fob.

The artist had perfectly captured one of Elizabeth's bright, dark eyes, and it drew him in. Her long, remarkably fine eyelashes framed a brown eye, flecked with gold. None of Elizabeth's expressive fire or intelligence had been suppressed in the rendering in watercolour on ivory. His heart beat fast even at the sight of it.

"I hope you like it. I sat through three renderings before we found an artist that Georgiana said captured my expression."

Darcy looked at Elizabeth in breathless wonder. "Your whole heart smiles through your eyes. They are so bright with intelligence that at times they threaten to distract me from the wit I am attempting to gather from your words." He looked at the miniature again. "Did I tell you one of the first things I admired about you was how uncommonly intelligent your face is rendered by the expression of your eyes?"

"After we married, you told me that you admire my eyes, but I knew you admired them before that."

"I expect you will tell me I ought to have recognised that you are a pretty woman sooner than I did?"

"I already had my say on that subject. What I have not told you is that I overheard you discussing your good opinion of my eyes with Miss Bingley."

Darcy's eyes narrowed in thought. "You mean at an evening at Lucas Lodge?"

"No wonder the woman detested me! No, when you walked with her at Netherfield. I was waiting for Mrs Hurst in an adjacent walk, and I heard Miss Bingley suggest that you could not have your Elizabeth's picture taken because no painter could do justice to her beautiful eyes."

"I remember. I told her I doubted their expression could be captured, but their colour and shape could be copied." He again gazed at the miniature, then back to the inimitable original. "Given your low opinion of me at the time, you must not have been impressed with what you overheard."

"I was not without faults myself. I had too high an opinion of my own discernment. But let us think no longer on that. Had I not overheard you and been flattered, then challenged your conduct, you would not have apologised for your comments at the assembly, and I would not have remained at Netherfield an hour longer than necessary."

"I dare not speculate on what might have become of our comfort had you been unwilling to remain." Painful recollections intruded. *Would I be in this bed with Elizabeth, comprehending how delightful, how talented, beautiful, witty, and generous my wife is?*

"You look fixed by the keenest of all anguish: self-reproach." Elizabeth raised his chin and kissed him firmly on the mouth. "Think only of the past as its remembrance gives you pleasure. At Netherfield, we showed each other our faults and our virtues, the result of which is that I love you with my whole life and strength."

Darcy smiled. "My own happiness is indisputable. I have no greater joy than entwining my lot with yours."

THE END

ACKNOWLEDGMENTS

Thank you to the team at Quills & Quartos. My heartfelt thanks go to Sarah Pesce for being my editor and friend during this three-Smartie bag project. I am grateful to my parents for their encouragement and for allowing me to use their condo as a writer's retreat. I am forever grateful to the supportive community at A Happy Assembly, especially Jim Foster and Katie James. My deepest gratitude goes to my dear husband and son, whose cheerful support and reassurance sustain me through everything.

ABOUT THE AUTHOR

Heather Moll is an avid reader of mysteries and biographies with an MS in information science. She found Jane Austen later than she should have and made up for lost time by devouring all of Austen's novels, letters, and unpublished works, joining JASNA, and spending far too much time researching the Regency era. She is the author of *His Choice of a Wife*. She lives with her husband and son and struggles to balance all of the important things, like whether or not to buy groceries or stay home and write.

Two More Days at Netherfield is Heather's second book. To learn more about Heather and other great historical fiction authors, please visit www.QuillsandQuartos.com

facebook.com/HeatherMollAuthor

twitter.com/HMollAuthor

goodreads.com/heathermoll

ALSO BY HEATHER MOLL

His Choice of a Wife

When a man's honor is at stake, what is he willing to risk for the woman he loves?

After a disastrous marriage proposal and the delivery of an illuminating letter, Fitzwilliam Darcy and Elizabeth Bennet hope never to lay eyes on one another again. When a chance meeting in Hunsford immediately throws them in each other's way, Darcy realizes his behavior needs correcting, and Elizabeth starts to appreciate his redeeming qualities. But is it enough to forgive the past and overcome their prejudices?

Jane and Bingley's possible reconciliation and Lydia's ill-conceived trip to Brighton pose their own challenges for two people struggling to find their way to love. When scandalous news threatens their chance at happiness, will Darcy and Elizabeth's new bond be shattered, or will their growing affection hold steadfast?

Made in the USA
Monee, IL
22 May 2021